EL CHUPACABRA

By Lawrence Fischman

I0618232

Gram's Group, Ltd.
Dallas, Texas
Publisher

El Chupacabra

Copyright © 2015 by Lawrence Fischman

Gram's Group, Ltd. Books may be ordered through booksellers or by contacting:

Gram's Group, Ltd.
18 Royal Way
Dallas, Texas 75229
972/419-8318

ISBN: 978-0-9857232-4-8 ; and ISBN: 978-0-9857232-5-5

Printed in the United States of America

Other books by Lawrence Fischman –
The French Artillery Officer
Requiem for Richard Cory
The Skeleton in the Closet

Gram's Group, Ltd. Rev. Date: 11/2015

In Memoriam
Bernard William Fischman
1947 – 2013

Chapter One

Joshua Loeb put away his toothbrush and snapped his fingers. "That's it!"

"That's what?" Elaine looked up from her make-up mirror and glanced at her husband in the mirror that completely covered the wall behind the his-and-her basins in their bathroom.

"'Callipygous;' the word I've been trying to remember and couldn't."

"And it means?"

"Having a pleasingly-shaped rear end."

Elaine had been sitting on her vanity bench at the knee-hole between the two basins wearing only her panties and bra. She stood up, went to her closet and put on a light robe. "Would you stop ogling my butt and get dressed? We need to be there on time."

Whose butt would you like me to ogle if not yours?"

"You better not be ogling anybody's butt but mine." Elaine blotted her lipstick with a Kleenex so that Josh wouldn't see her smiling. "We're going to a memorial service for a good friend whom we're known for years and all that's on your mind is lascivious thoughts."

"I have lascivious thoughts about you all day every day. It's a wonder that I get any work done." Josh bent down and kissed the nape of Elaine's neck. "Elaine, Sy's dead. If not appreciating your anatomy for a day, or a week or even a month would bring him back, I'd give it serious consideration. But nothing reminds one more of one's own mortality than the death of a contemporary."

"There but for the grace of God…"

"Well, there's that, but what better reminder that you're alive is there than thinking about sex, or better yet having it? In other words, '*erectus ergo sum*.'"

"I can still get it up, therefore I exist? Descartes must be turning in his grave.

"It's not like Sy died of cancer or dropped dead from a heart attack; he died in a car accident. That could happen to anyone at any time."

"All the more reason to get laid every day if you ask me."

"I didn't ask you. Go get dressed."

"Do I have to wear a tie?"

"Wear a tie, Josh; it won't hurt you. I'm sure Sy is wearing one in his casket. And wear a nice suit, not one of your courtroom *shmattes*."

"Are they going to have those little sandwiches after the service?"

"Have you ever been to a Jewish memorial service in Dallas where they didn't have doozies? Don't worry; just to be on the safe side I ordered a tray on Friday and had it delivered this afternoon right after the funeral."

"If there are any left, can we take them home with us? After all, we did pay for them."

Chapter Two

Josh dropped Elaine at the curb in front of the Blonsteins' home. There were no valet car-parkers. Sy would have approved. He would no doubt have vetoed the expense had he been around to do so. Evidently there was a pretty good turnout even though the Cowboys were on *SNF* and had been winning of late despite an inordinate number of turn-overs and a defensive line which from all indications thought that sacking the opponent's quarterback drew a fifteen-yard penalty.

But why not, Josh thought. Free food, free liquor and, all things considered, Sy Blonstein was a good guy, even though he succumbed to frequent outbursts of cerebral flatulence on the subject of the national debt. Josh finally found a parking space five houses down, parked Elaine's SUV and walked back to the Blonstein house. Elaine was waiting at the door along with a young man from the funeral home, dressed in a cheap-looking black suit, who had perfected the art of looking both cheerful and mournful at the same time. He offered Josh a plain, black *yarmulke* which Josh started to decline until Elaine gave him "The Look." Josh gave a small shrug, took the skull-cap and perched it on the back of his head.

The Blonstein house was the standard late-sixties North Dallas ranch-style: yellow Mexican-brick exterior, pitched composition roof, front-entry foyer opening on the left to a ten-by-fifteen formal living room and beyond that a dining room at a right angle to the living room. The living room had a large bay window looking out to the front yard and a "sofa-size" painting of dubious quality hanging behind an off-white sofa against the opposite, interior wall. Behind the living room interior wall was a family room with floor-to-ceiling glass doors looking out to a patio crowded with an elaborate combination barbecue grill and smoker and the usual collection of outdoor furniture. Beyond the patio there was a blandly-landscaped back yard ending in a brick privacy wall separating the back yard from the service alley that ran the length of the block. The kitchen and breakfast area were situated behind the dining room and opened on to the family room. To the right of the entry foyer was a hallway leading to the powder bath, linen closet and the standard four bedrooms.

As Josh and Elaine squeezed themselves into the crowd of mourners packing the den, a young woman, dressed in the female version of the funeral home black suit, was just completing the task of handing out the prayer books for the memorial service. Along with the prayer books, she gave each mourner a sheet of letter-size photocopied paper folded cross-ways in the middle to make a four-page pamphlet. The first page of the pamphlet read "*In Memory of* **SEYMOUR MELVIN BLONSTEIN**" and listed the dates of Sy's birth and death according to the Gregorian and Hebrew calendars. The inside right-hand page listed the names of Sy's deceased parents; his widow, Estelle; their daughters Marlene and Sharon; the daughters' respective husbands; and Sy's and Estelle's grandchildren.

Standing just inside the doorway between the foyer and the den, Josh was to the right of the leather sofa on which Estelle and her daughters were sitting, so he could not see Estelle's face directly. Looking across the room he noticed a slight gap in the phalanx of people standing in front of the glass patio doors that allowed him to look at Estelle's reflection in the glass. She wore no lipstick or make-up, but her hair was nicely done as it always was. Josh wondered whether she'd gone to the hair-dresser after the private, graveside service and before the memorial service guests began arriving. Then, rebuking himself, he decided that one of her daughters had probably done her hair for her.

Apart from her hair, Josh was struck by the way she kept her jaws clenched tightly, that her surgically-redefined nostrils were slightly flared and that she was staring straight ahead. Josh's overall impression was that Estelle either looked grimly determined about something or that she was over-medicated. It was definitely not the look of a woman who'd suddenly lost her mate of forty-plus years. Only when the rabbi, standing in front of the fireplace to Estelle's right, started the first prayer in Hebrew did she turn her head slightly in the rabbi's direction.

Sy and Estelle belonged to the same congregation as Josh and Elaine. Josh could not recall the name of the tall young rabbi, who in his black suit and with his stoop-shouldered posture, elongated neck, fringe of frizzy black hair, beady black eyes and burgundy-colored *yarmulke* reminded Josh of a vulture. But to be honest, other than the head rabbi Josh wasn't sure he could name any of the ever-expanding roster of rabbis comprising the clergy even though he and Elaine had attended the congregation for decades. All Josh knew from his infrequent attendance was that the males had beards and the females, as best he could tell from his preferred seat toward the rear of the sanctuary, did not. One thing they had in common was they all looked far too young to be rabbis.

Alternating between Hebrew and English, with the make-shift congregation reading aloud along with him when prodded to do so, the rabbi plowed through the prayers with celerity, ending with the traditional mourner's *Kaddish*, the prayer for the dead. As soon as everyone said "Amen" he briefly consulted his notes and began his eulogy to "Seymour— 'Sy' to all who knew and loved him—and there are many, many of those as evidenced by this gathering..." The young rabbi was good at his job. It was obvious he had taken good notes in his pre-funeral meeting with Estelle and the rest of the family so that he sounded like he had known Sy for all of Sy's adult life.

He mentioned Sy's Navy service during Vietnam, his pride in being a member of the Cadet Corps at Texas A&M and that he had passed all parts of the CPA exam on the first try. He went on for a bit about how steadfast Sy had been in the face of the most daunting IRS audits and how his clients loved him because he was never judgmental, never asking "How'd you get in this mess in the first place?" (A line that, as intended, elicited a brief outburst of uncomfortable laughter.)

Turning next to Sy the family man, the rabbi recited Sy's virtues as a husband and father: his life-long romance with Estelle, his devotion to Marlene and Sharon and later to their husbands Steven and Todd and finally Sy's delight in his four grandchildren. Then, by way of a peroration, he began telling a lame story about Sy's love of and inaptitude for golf. As the rabbi was winding down Josh could no longer keep from thinking about the fuchsia elephant pacing restlessly in the living room of his mind: the elephant which he'd been trying to ignore since Elaine had called him at the office late Friday morning to tell him that Sy had been killed in a one-car accident late Thursday night. Why had Sy called him Thursday morning to make an appointment to see him on Monday and asked him to recommend a "really-good" white-collar criminal lawyer? Must have been for a client, Josh thought, as he lay the prayer book and *yarmulke* on a small table in the foyer and headed for the dining room and the doozies.

Josh was standing next to the dining room sideboard happily chewing on his third—or maybe his fourth—doozie while Harmon Polikoff, a bariatric surgeon on whose ubiquitous billboards around town he referred to himself as "Dr. Blubberoff," was happily chewing Josh's ear off telling him of his current legal troubles ranging from his ex-wives, to his current wife, to his landlord, to various insurance companies and to the State Medical Licensing Board. Knowing that "Dr. Blubberoff" fired lawyers or was fired as a client by lawyers more often than most men get haircuts, Josh finished his doozie, excused himself and started off in the direction of the small bar which opened into the den. He had almost reached his goal, a nearly-full bottle of Haig & Haig Pinch, when Estelle took him by the arm. "Estelle, I'm so sorry, Sy was…"

"Josh, I need to talk to you. Go ahead and get a drink and join me in Sy's home office. It's the first room on the right down the hall."

Chapter Three

Glancing around the den, Josh noted that Elaine was engrossed in conversation with several of her friends, women who like Elaine were all dedicated volunteers in the myriad of good-works organizations that drew their sustenance from the over-forty Jewish women cohort. Fortifying himself with several fingers of Haig & Haig, and figuring that Elaine's impromptu meeting would outlast whatever Estelle wanted to talk about, Josh did as Estelle had bidden.

Estelle was seated behind Sy's desk in a low-back executive chair staring at the screen of a laptop computer on the desk. When Josh entered the office, she turned off the computer, rose and accepted his consoling hug, a hug which she held a bit too long for Josh's comfort. She removed her silk suit jacket and placed it over the back of her chair. She motioned to Josh to take the guest seat on the opposite side of the desk. As he did she fluffed her hair a little, straightened the cuffs of her white blouse and glanced at her gold Cartier "Panthere" watch. When Josh was seated she leaned forward and, instead of asking about probate of Sy's will as Josh had expected, she slapped her hand on the desk hard enough to cause Josh's drink to slosh precariously. "Josh, Sy was murdered!"

"Estelle, what do you mean 'murdered?' Who? Why would anyone want to murder Sy? He is...was..."

"General Motors, Josh. That's who murdered my husband!"

Josh took a stout swallow of his scotch. "Estelle, why would General Motors want to murder Sy? He wasn't Ralph Nader. Did he find out about some safety issue that GM is trying to cover up?"

"I don't know why, Josh. All I know is that according to the police—Steven and Todd talked to them—Sy jumped a curb and ran straight into a bois d'arc tree at over sixty miles an hour. Even so, he might have lived, but the goddamn airbag didn't open.

"Josh, I want to sue General Motors, the car dealer, and whoever else for ten million dollars—as much as I can get. I want them punished."

"Do the police know why the airbag didn't deploy, Estelle?"

"The detective who talked to Steven and Todd didn't say."

"Did he..."

"She—the detective—is a she. She gave Todd a card; I've got it around here someplace. I'll give it to you before you leave."

"Okay, did she tell them anything else? Like why Sy went off the road going more than sixty miles an hour? The speed limit on Walnut Hill Lane is only thirty-five. I know Sy's a pretty careful driver. How do the police know he was going over sixty miles an hour? Do they have any witnesses?"

"That's all they would tell us. They acted like it's none of our business. The detective told Steven and Todd that the written traffic-accident report would be available on Tuesday or maybe Wednesday and to wait until then."

"Estelle, I definitely think you ought to look into the airbag not inflating. But I wouldn't say that Sy was 'murdered.' From what you say, the police are treating it as an accident; so should you. At best, if there was a factory defect in the airbag, that would make it a negligence or product-liability case. Possibly there could be a gross negligence claim, if you can show that there have been other airbag failures in the same model year as Sy's Buick and that GM knew about them and didn't issue a recall to fix the problem.

"And what if Sy took his car in for service and the mechanic at the shop accidentally did something to it? You should look into that as well before you think about suing General Motors. Do you know where he had it serviced?

"You keep saying '*you* should look into the airbag,' '*you* need to look at the dealer' and 'if *you* can show'.... are you telling me I have to do this without you? You're our lawyer..."

"Of course not, Estelle. I'll do everything I can. But you know I don't handle personal injury or wrongful death cases—which is what this would be. I'll investigate...starting tomorrow. If it turns out there's a claim, I'll get you a lawyer who knows how to handle cases like this to take the case as lead counsel and I'll sit second chair."

"Won't that cost more, two lawyers, I mean?"

"The specialist will take the case on a contingent-fee basis. Sure, that'll be more—a whole lot more—than the zero I'd charge you. But you only pay if you win or settle. There's an old saying, Estelle, 'When you go to a knife fight, take a gun.'

If this were a business versus business lawsuit, I'd be your guy. But if it turns out there is a case, you need somebody who has the knowledge and experience that I don't have. So are we okay with that?"

"Estelle stared at the floor for a while and finally mumbled, "I'm okay with that, Josh. Do what you think best."

"Good decision, Estelle. Now, do you happen to have any idea why Sy was driving at over sixty miles an hour on Walnut Hill Lane at...at...eight o'clock at night? I know Sy worked long hours during tax season, but October fifteenth was over two weeks ago."

"It was closer to eight-thirty. And I have no idea where he was going, or coming from, or why he was working late. He called me a few minutes after six o'clock to tell me he had something he needed to get done and to make him a sandwich when he got home. He's been doing that a lot lately, at least twice a week. I'm only guessing, but maybe it was some kind of report with a November deadline, but I don't know for sure. You know Sy was closed-mouth about his clients and their business.

"All I know is that I made him a sandwich, turkey pastrami, and he never got to eat it." Estelle broke down in tears that lasted for a couple of minutes.

When she regained her composure, Josh asked, "Could we ask his secretary-bookkeeper...what's her name? Margie? Didn't I see her here during the service? I'll go see if she's still here." Josh held up his now-empty glass. "Besides, I think I could stand a refill. Can I get you anything? Coffee? Wine, maybe? Do you want me to get Marlene and Sharon?"

"I think..." Estelle paused for a few seconds and wiped her eyes with a paper napkin. "No, let's leave the girls out of this for a while. There's a bottle of Stoli on the bar. If there's any left bring me some of that on the rocks.

In a few minutes Josh returned with his scotch in one hand, Estelle's vodka in the other and Margie—Marjorie Morrison—trailing behind him, a freshly topped-off glass of red wine in hand. He handed the vodka to Estelle and gestured to Margie that she should take the seat he'd occupied before.

Estelle took a sip of her vodka and stood up. "Thanks, Josh. I'm okay now. Do you want to sit? Here, take my chair; I can stand. All I've been doing since the funeral is sitting."

"No, I'm okay. I…"

"Sit, Josh. I insist." Estelle moved in front of Josh and closed the door. "I think maybe we should have some privacy." Once Josh was seated, she continued. "Margie, Josh…Mr. Loeb…is going to help me find out what happened to Sy. He's got a few questions he wants to ask you."

Margie Morrison was a tall, slender, fiftyish woman dressed in a gray business suit with a calf-length skirt. The suit gave off the faint aroma of cigarette smoke. She had small Cupid-shaped lips painted with a dark-red shade of lipstick. She wore no jewelry except for a watch and tiny diamond ear studs. Her hair was cut medium length and looked like it might have been dyed with Shinola rather than a hair-coloring product. Josh had met her in Sy's office a couple times when he'd brought in his records for Sy to prepare his and Elaine's joint tax returns. From Sy's occasional comments, Josh knew that Margie was on very good terms with both cigarettes and wine glasses. Watching her clutch her wine glass with both hands, Josh was sure she was wanting a cigarette rather badly at the moment.

Josh took a sip of his scotch. "Margie, I know Sy's death has been hard on you. Sy thought of you as a part of his family. I…"

A wait-just-a-minute look from Estelle made Josh decide to get to the point much sooner than he'd wanted to. Recovering, Josh asked, "How long were you with Sy?"

"Over ten years, Mr. Loeb. Sy...Mr. Blonstein...hired me right after my divorce. I was a trained bookkeeper, but I hadn't worked as one for years. When he hired me I could barely balance my checkbook. But Mr. Blonstein took a chance on me and I've been grateful ever since. He was a wonderful employer and a great person." Margie set her glass on the desk and wiped away a couple of tears. The genuine tears seemed to assuage Estelle's snit brought on Josh's "one-of-the-family" comment so she leaned down and gave Margie a brief hug.

Equanimity restored, Josh continued. "Do you have any idea what Sy was working on Thursday? Why he was working so late?"

"No, I'm sorry. I was out of the office from a week-ago Friday through this past Wednesday. I was in Oklahoma City visiting my sister. I usually take a few days off after October Fifteenth. We're pretty worn out from all the last-minute tax returns."

"You said 'we were.' You mean you and Sy?"

"Yes, but this year we had so many returns, Sy...Mr. Blonstein...brought in a couple of temps from one of those accounting temp agencies. He had done that a few times before, but we don't need them every year. And they cost a fortune, sometimes as much or even more than we can charge for doing a return. Also, either Sy...Mrs. Blonstein, do you mind if I call him 'Sy'? After the first few months we were always 'Sy' and 'Margie' in the office."

"No, that's okay, Margie. And please call me 'Estelle.'"

"Thank you, Estelle. Anyway, what I was going to say is that either Sy or I had to check each return line-by-line to be sure they were done right, and that takes almost as long as doing the return in the first place."

"But you did see Sy in the office on Thursday?"

"Yes. He asked me about my trip and asked about my sister—she's diabetic and has had some health problems lately—but we didn't talk much at all the rest of the day. I had a big stack of correspondence to open and deal with. By the time I got through with that and with getting out the bills for the tax-return work, the day was shot. It was after five o'clock, so I asked Sy if it was okay if I called it a day. He said ''bye. See you tomorrow.'" That brought a fresh round of tears from both women. Margie stood and asked if she could get a wine refill and visit the powder room.

"Go ahead, Margie." Estelle looked at her own empty glass. I'll handle the refills. I need to get back to my guests for a while anyway. Josh, do you need another refill?"

"No, thanks, Estelle. I'm good for now. But if there are any doozies left, I've probably got room for one or two."

"Okay. I'll just let Elaine know where you are."

Margie returned first, her clothing and hair reeking of fresh cigarette smoke. Reading Josh's expression she volunteered, "Sorry, I couldn't hold out any longer. There's an exhaust fan in the bathroom, so I stood on the commode and held the cigarette up to the fan. Is it really that bad?"

"Don't worry about it; Estelle's obviously preoccupied just now so I doubt she'll notice. Tell me this: Did Sy keep an appointment book or calendar? He must have kept time records."

"He used a Day-Timer, you know, those little spiral-bound books, one book for each month. Sy kept track of his daily time and his future appointments in his Day-Timer. He also kept track of car mileage, tolls and how much he had to pay for parking when he went to a client's place of business or downtown to the IRS office. Sy would almost always start and end each work day with a visit to a client's office. That way he could take a deduction for the car mileage to and from home. I would go in his personal office once or twice a week, get the Day-Timer off his desk and enter the time in our computer under the client and project number using our billing software. When he was out of the office he always had his Day-Timer with him. I bet it's still in his briefcase in the car unless the police took it."

"I'll be sure to check on that when I talk to the detective. Did Sy have any clients whose place of business is on Walnut Hill Lane? Did he have a lot of Asian clients? I know there are a lot of Asian-owned businesses around Walnut Hill and Harry Hines Boulevard.

"Not many," Margie paused and counted off three fingers. "Just three that I can think of. We do … did … have quite a few Hispanic clients. Sy said that they liked having a Jewish accountant, they thought he knew all the angles."

"Would he have gone to see any of his Asian clients after regular business hours?"

"No, they're all just tax-return clients so we see them only once a year. And that's usually before April fifteenth. We also do their sales tax returns, but they email the information to us for those."

"So you have no idea where Sy was going? Wait a minute. Was he going west or east when the accident...make that the incident...happened?"

"I think I heard one of his sons-in-law say it was east. I..."

"So he'd likely finished with whatever it was and was heading home? And you have no idea where he'd been?"

"I...I…" Tears welled up again in Margie's eyes as she rolled her empty wine glass between her thumb and forefinger. "I...Oh God! Mr. Loeb don't make me talk about this...not in Sy's home...not now. You heard the rabbi say what a wonderful family man Sy was. I won't soil Sy's memory with something I don't know for certain. Estelle will be back any second and…"

Estelle pushed the door open with her behind. She was carrying a serving tray with a fresh round of scotch, vodka and wine along with a stack of doozies and an assortment of sweets cosseted in paper ramekins. Noticing Margie's fresh tears, she set the tray on the desk. "Oh, Margie, you poor dear. Sy really meant a lot to you, didn't he? Let me get you some Kleenex from the powder bath. Here, take some wine. It's a cabernet; it was Sy's favorite." Estelle set the tray on the corner of the desk and went across the hall to get the tissue box.

When she returned, Josh stood. "Estelle, do you mind if Margie and I go outside for a few minutes. Margie's a smoker; she could certainly use a cigarette just now. And I could use a bit of fresh air."

"Of course. There's small deck outside our bedroom with a cafe table and a couple of chairs. Sometimes Sy and I would sit out there and have a drink and Sy would once in a while smoke a cigar. Bring your drinks and I'll bring the tray. Just follow me down the hall. Take all the time you need.

People are starting to leave and I need to be thanking them and saying goodbye. By the way, the Cowboys are losing thirteen-to-nothing late in the second quarter. Someone turned on the TV in the breakfast room. Most of the men are watching the game and the women are chatting."

Estelle led them down the hall to the master bedroom and through a French door onto the small wood-plank deck. She set the tray down as Margie was reaching in her purse for her cigarettes and lighter. "Margie, I'm sorry I don't have an ashtray, but don't worry about it. Just throw the butt in the grass. The yard people come on Wednesday; they can pick up. You all stay as long as you like. Josh, if Elaine gets *spilkes*, I'll tell her what you're doing and keep her entertained until you're through."

After Estelle had gone back inside and closed the door, Margie lit her cigarette and exhaled. "What are *spilkes*, Mr. Loeb?"

"First of all, Margie, call me 'Josh.' Nobody calls me 'Mr. Loeb' except in court. '*Spilkes*' means 'ants in your pants,' 'restless.' I take it Sy didn't use many Yiddish expressions around the office.

"He would occasionally refer to someone, usually an IRS agent, as a *'putz.'* I asked him one time what it meant, but he said it was not for my tender ears and to never call anyone that to his face. I gather from the way Sy used the word that my ex-husband was a *'putz.'*"

"Probably; but then I imagine that most divorced women think their ex-husbands are *putzes*. Be that as it may, Margie, what is it you don't want to tell me? Please don't tell me Sy had a mistress...Sy? Sy Blonstein?"

Margie inhaled deeply on her cigarette and then took a sip of wine. "I don't know if 'mistress' is the right word, but I'm pretty sure there is another woman. I do have some experience with a cheating husband. That's one of the reasons I got rid of mine. "

"Oh, Lord why me? Who is she? Did Estelle know? Is there just the woman, or did Sy have another whole family on the side?"

"I have no idea whether Estelle knows. I think it's just her, the 'girl-friend' I guess you'd call her. I don't know whether she has any kids, but if she does, I'd bet anything that Sy isn't the father. The affair, if it is that, hasn't been going on all that long. Her name, or at least her stage name, is 'Jasmine.' I don't know what her last name is or if 'Jasmine' is even her real name."

"What do you mean 'stage name?'"

"She's an 'exotic' dancer at a 'gentlemen's club' on Harry Hines just south of Walnut Hill."

Josh shook his head in disbelief. "Seymour Blonstein, what were you thinking? How could you let yourself get involved with a topless dancer in a titty bar? To borrow a line from the rabbi, 'How'd you get in this mess in the first place?' Margie, can I have one of your cigarettes?" Margie pushed the pack of Marlboros and her lighter across the table. After a moment's hesitation Josh pushed the pack and lighter back. "No, never mind. My wife would smell it on me the moment we got in the car. I'll just work on the doozies and my scotch."

Margie lit another cigarette off the end of the one she'd been smoking. "About two years ago Sy was an expert witness in some kind of court case. The lawyer who hired him said that Sy had to do all the work himself because he'd be the only one testifying. So I never did learn much about the case. Anyway, he testified in court and apparently made a good impression on the judge. So back in February the judge called him and asked if he'd act as a special master in another case. You know, someone who is appointed by the court to look at books and records and tell the court what's what."

"Yes, I've had a couple of cases where special masters were appointed. I'm familiar with the procedure."

"The case involved some shareholders suing the president of the company for mismanagement and embezzlement. The judge couldn't figure out which side to believe, so he appointed Sy as special master to go over the books and try to figure out which of the two sides was lying the least. The business was a 'gentlemen's club.'"

"Not that I would be familiar with it, but what's the name of the 'gentlemen's club?'"

"Crystal's Palace."

"How do you know that Sy was involved with one of the dancers, one in particular who calls herself 'Jasmine?'"

"I didn't say I *knew*, and I don't know for certain. Obviously I never actually saw them together...*in flagrante delicto*...I think is the term. But there's a lot of what you lawyers call 'circumstantial evidence.'"

"Consisting of?"

"First of all, Sy completed his audit and filed his report near the end of May. He had to appear in court once after that so that the lawyers could ask him questions and argue with his conclusions."

"What were his conclusions?"

"That the CEO was skimming, wasting most of the money he didn't steal and he was forcing the dancers to pay him kickbacks, you know, give him part of their tips."

"What'd the judge do?"

"He removed the CEO and turned the place over to the investors. I think they're still trying to run it themselves. At least I know it's still in business. A friend and I like the hamburgers at Keller's drive-in on Harry Hines. We try to go there once a week or so, so I drive by Crystal's Palace fairly often."

"Did Sy continue doing the books?"

"No, the investors wanted their own accountant. Sy didn't have anything more to do with the business part."

"But I take it Sy was still involved with the other part of the business. As a customer?"

"I think so, but as I said, I don't know for sure."

"Okay, why do you think so?"

"He still is...was...entering the mileage, but not any time, in his Day-Timer. 'CP, thirteen miles.' That's the same notation he'd make when he was working on the court case. I would see the same entry twice a week always on Tuesdays and Thursdays. The last one I saw was Thursday-before-last, before I went on vacation. I didn't get a chance to make the entries for this week when I got back in the office this past Thursday.

"Then there was his leaving the office early sometimes. He'd say he was going to a client's office or place of business."

"But you said that was typical, so he could get the mileage deduction."

"That's right, but what was wrong about it is he didn't always make an entry in his Day-Timer. He didn't put down the client or the mileage. He had never failed to do that before

August. I asked him about it a couple of times when he first started omitting entries. He said to forget it; the time wasn't worth billing."

"Couldn't he have just been going home...to be with Estelle...and maybe he was kind of embarrassed to admit it?"

"I hope that's what it was. But why not just say, 'Margie, I'm knocking off early?' I wouldn't have thought a thing about it."

"Anything else?"

"Sy was using his ATM card to draw out cash from the business account. Two hundred dollars a week. I don't recall him ever doing that as long as I've worked for him. Most of my work is keeping clients' books, but I also keep Sy's practice books. I asked him one time...I think it was in August...about the cash withdrawals. He told me not to worry about it; just charge them to 'client development.' I started to ask him, 'What about receipts?' But I like my job, and as I said, I'm very grateful to Sy. So I decided to mind my own business. It was Sy's money, so he could spend it however he wanted. He prepares his own Schedule C and signs his and Estelle's joint returns; so if there was something improper, it was his problem, not mine."

"This doesn't sound good. Is there more bad news?"

"Two more things: One, Sy was paying rent on a condo. Two months: September and October. Two thousand, four hundred and fifty dollars a month to 'HP Investments, Limited.'

"The other is that there's a picture under the blotter on his desk. Sy with several of the Crystal's Palace dancers. It's signed 'To Sy, from your friend Jasmine.' And she...I mean a woman...called the office once. That was back near the end of June...maybe early July...a few weeks after Sy had submitted his report and was finished testifying. I always answer the phone, it's another part of my job. Sy happened to be out so I asked if I could take a message. She said, 'No, just tell him Jasmine called.' I told Sy and he got all red-faced. She never called the office again as far as I know."

"I assume Sy has...had a cell phone?"

"Sure, but he pays the bill electronically so I don't see the call details."

"Margie, we need to get that photo. I'm executor of Sy's estate. I was planning to ask you to stay on to help wind down Sy's practice, but now I'm begging you: Please stay on. What time do you get to the office tomorrow morning?

Chapter Four

Sy's office was in a mid-rise office building in Preston Center, an eclectic multi-owner commercial area on Preston Road at Northwest Highway. The area, first developed following World War II, was the location of the first suburban Neiman-Marcus store. In the ensuing decades, the area underwent periods of prosperity and occasional stretches of despair. Because of the fragmented ownership, expansion and redevelopment were always haphazard, subject to the whims and varying pocket-depths of the several owners. As a result of this and the 1980s Dallas real estate mania, there were high-rise office towers next to one-story retail strips next to medical/dental offices with restaurants crammed in between. There is no unifying architectural theme except for a utilitarian tackiness that makes the area look like the outdoor set for a grade-D dystopian-themed movie.

When Josh pulled into the parking garage he noticed a police car parked at the curb in front of the building entrance. He found a spot on the visitors' parking floor of the garage and walked down the short flight of concrete steps and through a metal door into the building lobby. He took the elevator to the fourth floor. Sy's offices were around a corner from the elevators and down a hallway past the restrooms and water-fountain. The offices fronting on the elevator lobby were home to a small law firm on one side and a financial consultant on the other, the types of businesses that were willing to pay the higher rents that such proximity commanded.

As soon as he turned the corner of the elevator lobby Josh saw two uniformed police officers standing outside the door to Sy's offices. "Excuse me, Officers, is there a problem?"

"Who are you?" The older of the two officers, a corporal, held up his hand to bar Josh from entering.

"I'm Joshua Loeb, the late Seymour Blonstein's attorney. This is his office as you can see from the name on the door. As soon as the will is probated, I will be the executor of his estate." Josh took out his wallet, showed the corporal his official gold-colored plastic State Bar card and handed him one of his business cards. "What's going on?"

"Do you know a...a..."

The second officer intervened, "Marjorie Morrison?"

"Yes, of course. She's Mr. Blonstein's assistant and office manager. Is she okay?"

"She seems to be, except for being upset." The corporal recovered from his mental lapse. "She called 9-1-1 to report a burglary of these premises. Said she discovered it when she came to work this morning. Real mess inside."

Any idea when it happened?"

"Ms. Morrison said that no one was in the office Friday through Sunday, so it would have happened at any time during those three days.

"You say the proprietor's name is 'Seymour Blonstein' and he's deceased?"

"Yes, he died in an automobile accident Thursday night and the funeral was yesterday."

"Would you mind stepping inside and confirming the woman's identity? We checked her driver's license, but just want to be sure she really is employed here before we put her name in our report."

"Sure, I'd be happy to. I've known Margie for years. I was with her last night at Sy's home for his memorial service. She's worked for Sy for ten years. We agreed to meet here this morning so we can get to work contacting Sy's clients and transferring his files to whomever the clients want them transferred."

The younger officer gave Josh a blank look. "Excuse me, Sir, but who is 'Sy?'"

Josh bit his upper lip for a moment. "Sorry, Officer. 'Sy' is 'Seymour Blonstein' the recently-deceased proprietor of the certified public accounting practice located in these premises."

The corporal stepped aside so that Josh could enter the office. Reaching for the door handle, Josh noticed that there were no indications of forced entry. "It doesn't look like the burglar had to force his way in."

"We noticed that too." The corporal pointed to the electronic key-pad next to the door. "Looks like whoever got in must have had a key-card. Makes you wonder whether it actually was an intruder, especially since there haven't been any reports of other offices in the building that were broken into.

"Do you know whether they keep any cash in the office?"

"I wouldn't think so. They wouldn't have any money belonging to clients and I expect that all of their clients pay by check or credit card."

Hearing the office door open and hearing Josh's voice, Margie came out of Sy's office into the reception area. She ran to Josh and buried her head against his shoulder. "Oh Josh, it's awful. Files all over the place; the computers are missing. Who could have done this?"

After a few comforting pats on the back Josh disengaged himself from Margie and turned to the police officers. "Yes, this is Ms. Morrison, officers, and yes she does work here."

"Okay, thanks for your help. We'll be going now and file our report. A detective from the North Central Division— property crimes are handled by detectives in each geographical division—will get in touch with you in about a week, Ms. Morrison. Please have the inventory of what you think was taken ready for the detective."

"Aren't you going to dust for fingerprints, or take pictures or do any of that other stuff? Do I have to leave this mess for a week or more?"

"That's up to you, ma'am. You can take some pictures with your cell phone if you want to. Neither of us are certified crime-scene technicians so we don't do fingerprints or vacuum for hair or fibers. But even if we could, they probably wouldn't do any good. If this is a burglary, the perpetrator or perpetrators almost certainly wore gloves and even if we did recover some prints it would take weeks to run them through our department database and months to run them through AFIS. That wouldn't happen until we'd eliminated your prints and those of the deceased. And unless the deceased's prints are already in the system, the remains would have to be exhumed. So I don't see any reason for you to wait to start cleaning up if that's what you want to do."

Josh put a comforting arm over Margie's shoulders. "Corporal, from what you say, this isn't going to be DPD's highest-priority matter. But does it really take a week or more to get a detective involved?"

"Ordinarily it wouldn't, Counselor, but right now every detective in Crimes Against Persons is working on the *El Chupacabra* cases. That means that detectives from other divisions, even auto-crimes and narcotics, are having to help work the Crimes Against Persons detectives' other open cases in addition to working their own cases. So that doesn't leave a lot of time for cases like this one."

As soon as the door had closed on the officers, Josh asked, "What about the…"

"The picture is gone, Josh. Of course it's possible that Sy did something with it while I was on vacation, but…"

"But we're not that lucky, are we? Do you think that's what the burglar was after?"

Margie sat down at her desk and took out a cigarette. "Why would someone want to steal the picture after Sy's death? Who would he blackmail with it?"

"What you say makes sense; but why take the picture?" Josh sat down on the couch. "You said your computers are missing? Can you tell if there's anything else?"

"The file room's a mess, files and loose papers scattered all over the floor. Two filing cabinets are tipped over. All the drawers in Sy's desk are open. All his tax code and regulations books and his reference books are on the floor."

"It sounds like whoever did this was looking for something. Do you know if any client files are missing?"

I can't tell until I pick up all the loose papers and put the files back where they belong. Then I'll have to check what's left in the cabinets against the master file list. And I can't do that until I get a new computer. All the practice records—client information, file lists, billing information and probably half the client files—are on the computers.

"But if the computers are gone…"

"Everything is backed up in off-site storage. All the computer files are automatically sent to a local off-site data storage provider. All I need is a computer. I enter our account and the password and I can recover everything."

"Thank goodness for off-site storage. I didn't realize that Sy was so technologically advanced. I wonder whether my office does the same thing."

"Actually, it was my idea; I talked him into it. I…I…goddammit Josh, this is so awful…" Margie stubbed out her cigarette and started sobbing. Josh, not being very good at comforting gestures, just squirmed on the couch until she stopped. She reached in a desk drawer and brought out a handful of Kleenex. "Josh, I'm sorry. It's just so overwhelming: first Sy's death and now this…What in the hell am I supposed to do?"

"Margie, I know you can handle it. Sy had complete confidence in you and so do I. I guess the first thing we need to do is to contact all of the clients so that they can transition their work. If this had to happen, at least it wasn't the first week in April or October.

"But speaking of contacting clients, isn't whoever stole the computers going to have access to the same client information? Social Security numbers, corporation and partnership tax ID numbers?

"Not unless they've got NSA-level hacking skills. I talked Sy into two other things: sixteen-character passwords and encrypting the data. I got him to buy an encryption software program. So I don't think that will be an issue; at least I hope not.

"You're right, Josh; we'll get through this." Margie stubbed out her cigarette and stood. "I need to start cleaning up, then get over to Best Buy and get a new computer. How do I notify the clients?"

"Just get me the list and I'll handle that. I'll send them letters as the attorney for the estate. I don't think we should wait until the will's admitted to probate. Also, if they owe money— and I assume there will be at least a few of those—let me know how much. I might as well ask them to pay up; it'll save having to send another letter.

"I need to get going in a few minutes myself. I'm meeting Estelle at the bank so we can get Sy's will out of the safe-deposit box. But before I leave I've got a couple more questions, one of which I meant to ask you last night but forgot. Do you have any idea why Sy made an appointment to see me in my office this morning?"

"No, I had no idea he did. As I told you last night, I was out of the office for nearly a week, so I didn't have a chance to look at his Day-Timer. He didn't say anything about it to me last Thursday."

"He asked me to recommend a white-collar criminal attorney. Since the Dallas County DA doesn't prosecute white-collar crimes, I assume it has to be federal and that could mean anything from tax-evasion to bankruptcy or securities fraud, RICO or even the Patriot Act. Do you know if any of your clients has any of those kinds of problems?"

"No, Sy never said a word to me about anything like that, at least recently. Since I've worked for Sy we've had probably a dozen or so clients who've been assessed civil fraud penalties by the IRS, and there was one who got indicted for criminal tax fraud, but that's it. And none of those cases happened this year. But I guess it's possible that a new client contacted Sy while I was gone. I'll have to look at his Day-Timer to tell. I don't think Sy knew how to set up a new client and matter in our system."

"I hate to say it, much less even think it, but is it possible he thought that he needed a criminal lawyer for himself? Because of Crystal's Palace and Jasmine?"

"Well it wouldn't be an IRS problem since whatever was going on just started this year and this year's return won't be due until next April. And if it wasn't an IRS problem, I can't imagine what it could be. We don't have any clients that are currently in bankruptcy proceedings. We have a few clients that have government contracts or sub-contracts, but I don't know of any that have been audited or investigated.

"Are you going to tell Estelle about the break-in?"

"I don't know, probably not...not yet anyway. Estelle's not a total airhead. If I tell her she'll start asking a million questions some of which I won't want to answer. I'm not a very good liar, so I'd just as soon keep this between us for the time being. Once we know more, I'll have to tell her something. You know, maybe the break-in isn't related to the...the thing we don't want Estelle to know about. Unless Sy changed his will and left everything he had to Jasmine, or whatever her real name is, I agree with you; I don't see any reason to speak ill of the dead. If she asks why I didn't tell her about the break-in sooner, I can honestly say that she has enough to deal with so I didn't want to upset her with something that isn't important.

"I need to get going, so let me ask you my other question: Who, beside you and Sy have access cards to the building and to the office?"

"Well," Margie sat back down and lighted another Marlboro. "There are probably well over a hundred people that work in the building and they would all have access cards to get into the building outside of normal office hours. You have to use the same card to get in and out of the tenant parking floors in the garage. Then you need either a key for some of the individual tenant offices or a key-card for offices like ours. And I guess the cleaning service must have keys or cards for all of the offices as well. I suppose I could check with the building manager and let you know."

"That's okay; I'll stop in the manager's office on my way out. If you, Sy and the cleaning service, and I assume the building manager, have the only access cards, whoever broke in must have used Sy's cards to get into the building and into your office. I suppose it's possible that it could have been someone in the manager's office or a cleaning service employee. They might have read Sy's obituary in the paper, recognized the name and decided to take advantage of the opportunity. I imagine this wouldn't be the first time that's happened. But when you weigh that scenario against the fact that the burglar was evidently looking for something specific and not just something to steal, it doesn't seem very likely.

"Anyway, I'm out of here. I'm going to be late as it is. Please do one thing for me: Locate the Crystal's Palace file and when you find it call my assistant, Alicia Flores. She'll send a courier to pick it up." Josh took out one of his cards and wrote

Alicia's direct phone number and his own cell number on it. He placed it on the desk. "You'll get along with Alicia. She's been my assistant for even longer than you've been with Sy."

"You got it. I'll do that first thing." Margie came around from behind her desk and held out her hand. Anything else I can do, just ask."

The building manager's office was located on the second floor in the same location as Sy's fourth-floor office. There was no one at the desk in the reception area. Josh could hear a woman talking in the inner office. It didn't sound like anyone was in there with her so she must have been on the telephone. After about ten minutes the one-sided conversation apparently ended. Josh tapped lightly on the office door and was answered with a "Come in."

The voice belonged to a thirty-something woman dressed in a charcoal gray suit over a maroon shirt showing more than a hint of cleavage. She wore several strands of pearls around her neck and a "Realtor" logo pin in the lapel of her jacket. Her blond hair fell a few inches below her ears and curled under at the ends. It looked to Josh like an expensive haircut. She held out a well-manicured hand. "I'm SueEllen Masters. How can I help you? Please have a seat. Were you waiting long? I was on the phone with the main office and couldn't get loose. I'm between receptionists right now. Can I offer you some coffee? And you are?"

Josh took the proffered hand. "I'm Joshua Loeb. I'm the attorney for Sy Blonstein's estate." He handed her a business card. "I'd love some coffee, Ms. Masters, but I'm rather pressed for time so I'll have to take a raincheck. But thanks for offering. I just want to introduce myself and ask you a couple of quick questions, if you have time."

"Of course, Mr. Loeb." She glanced at the card and laid it on her desk. "We, myself, everyone in the building, we were so shocked by Sy's death. He was here on Thursday, and now he's gone; just like that. It's just terrible. I've only been here for a little over a year, but I know Sy was a long-time tenant. He was one of my favorite tenants. Always paid on time, rarely complained. And he was always so sweet to me. He even brought me flowers on Valentine's Day."

Josh thought: Jasmine, SueEllen…how many others? Maybe I didn't know Sy as well as I thought I did.

"Well, his passing surely is a tragedy, for his family, of course, and for his clients and I suppose just about everyone who knew him. I'll be sure and tell Estelle, his widow, the nice things you said. I know your words will be a comfort to her. In fact I'm meeting her shortly and I'm going to be late unless I hurry up and ask you what I came to ask you."

"About Sy's lease?"

"No, we'll deal with that as soon as I file the will for probate. I assume you know that Sy's office was broken into sometime between when he left Thursday night and this morning when his assistant Margie Morrison came to work?"

SueEllen gasped and put her hand to her mouth. "Oh my God! No, I didn't know. I've been on the phone almost the entire time since I got to the office this morning."

"What time was that?"

"Between eight-fifteen and eight-thirty."

"You must have gotten here before Margie. She discovered the break-in as soon as she got in the office and called the police immediately."

"When did it happen? It must have been during business hours. Otherwise the burglar wouldn't have been able to get into the building without setting off the building alarm system."

"That's what I'm trying to figure out. Sy died Thursday night around eight-thirty. His office was closed on Friday so it's possible that it happened during the day on Friday. But I doubt it. First of all, whoever did it would have had to know that the office was closed. Second, the person or persons must have used a key-card to gain entry; there's no indication the door was forced. And third, there would be too great a chance of being seen or interrupted. Is the building open to the public on Saturday or Sunday?"

"No, a tenant would have to meet you at either the front door or the door to the garage and let you in."

"So unless the burglar had a key-card he wouldn't have been able to get in the building without setting off the alarm. I assume you have a security service that monitors the alarm system?"

"Yes, Dal-Worth Security. They also monitor the surveillance cameras and the entry card reader log."

"Then the security company may possibly have a record of who entered the building after hours or over the weekend?"

"If the equipment was working and the records haven't been erased. If you want me to, I'd be glad to check and see what they have.

"Do you have time to call them now? If there's still something to see, would you authorize Dal-Worth to let me have a look?"

"I'll call them right now and tell them to keep everything. But I'll have to get approval from my boss to let you look."

"Sure, I understand. I wouldn't have to ask, but getting the police to make the request will take too long. The officers who responded to Margie's 9-1-1 call said it would be at least a week before a detective would even contact her. As soon as you find out anything could you please call my assistant Alicia Flores? Just call the main number on my card and the receptionist will transfer you to Alicia."

Chapter Five

"Sorry I'm late, Estelle. It took longer than I thought at Sy's office. There's a problem with the computers, but Margie's getting it handled. Then I stopped by the building manager's office just to introduce myself. The manager asked me to pass along her condolences and those of all the other tenants. Apparently everyone in the building knew Sy and thought highly of him."

That brought a handful of Kleenex out of Estelle's purse. "I'm sorry, Josh, I should be over that by now. Marlene, Steven and the kids left to go back to Houston right before I came here. The kids need to be back in school and Marlene and Steven both have work."

"Sharon and Todd live here, don't they?"

"In Plano, and I suppose that's a lot closer than Houston. Still, I'm just beginning to realize how lonely I'm going to be from now on."

Josh noticed that Estelle had already removed her wedding band and wondered how long it would be until Estelle's profile would be posted on J-Date. Although Estelle would not pass for arm candy, except perhaps on the arm of an octogenarian, she was prudent in her use of makeup and dressed well. Neither her body nor her face had as yet succumbed to the ravages of gravity nor, so far as Josh could tell, to the knife of the cosmetic surgeon, except for her years-ago nose job. In fact, Josh mused, I wouldn't be surprised if the J-Date server crashes within minutes after she posts.

"I've already visited with the bank officer. He's ready to take us down to the vault. He says he has to come with us and make an inventory of the contents of the box."

"Yeah, I think it's for federal estate tax purposes. Is that him?" Josh gestured toward a young man walking across the lobby toward them.

"Yes. Arthur Blanding, but he says to just call him 'Art.'"

Art and Josh shook hands and exchanged business cards. The banker led them down a terrazzo stairway to the small lobby in front of the walk-in vault. There an elderly woman had Estelle sign a ledger and produce her driver's license for identification. With those formalities completed the woman opened a stainless steel gate and led them into the vault. They passed by several doors leading to closet-size rooms provided so that customers could examine the contents of their boxes in privacy. She led them along the rows of metal boxes and stopped about midway. She pointed to the numbered box then waited until Estelle had inserted her key before inserting her master key. She removed the box and handed it to Estelle who handed it to Josh.

Art gestured toward the private rooms. "I guess we can all fit in one of the rooms."

Art's guess proved to be optimistic. Art and Estelle were able to squeeze in, leaving Josh standing in the doorway peering over Estelle's shoulder. As Josh held his breath and crossed his fingers about what they would not find, Art opened the box. The first item out of the box was an envelope with the name of Josh's firm in the upper left-hand corner and "Last Will and Testament of Seymour M. Blonstein" typed where an address would usually go. Art handed the envelope to Josh. "Mr. Loeb, you'll need to open the envelope so I can take a look just to be sure that the will is what's inside and there isn't anything else."

Josh handed the envelope to Estelle. "Estelle, you've got fingernails. Could you do the honors?"

Estelle slipped a nail under the corner of the flap and pulled the envelope open. She then handed it back to Josh who extracted the contents which proved to be only the will. Josh flipped to the signature page to confirm that the will was dated several years ago, so there was no chance that the beneficiary had been changed from Estelle to "Jasmine."

Art wrote that down on his inventory list. After that they removed and inventoried a couple of life insurance policies, the deed to Sy and Estelle's home, a deed in Sy's name to an interest in a small strip shopping center, certificates evidencing fractional working interests in oil and gas wells and a velvet bag containing twenty-five pre-1930 silver dollars. The last item to come out of the box was a small key which Art lay on the counter. "Looks like a safe-deposit box key, another one of ours. Mrs. Blonstein, did you know there's another box?"

Estelle shook her head. "No, I had no idea."

"I certainly didn't," Josh added.

"Let me double check." The banker picked up the key and eased around Estelle. "I'll be back in a second."

He returned a couple of minutes later with the elderly vault keeper. "There is another box. Mr. Blonstein rented it just this past July. According to our records he's the sole owner of the box and he's accessed it only twice since renting it. The first time was in July and the second at the beginning of September of this year."

As Josh held his breath Estelle asked, "Can we open that one too?"

"I don't think so," the banker answered. "Since your name is not on the box, we'll have to wait until Mr. Loeb has qualified as executor."

Josh let out his breath. "As soon as we get back upstairs I'll call my office and have my assistant send a courier for the will. We'll file the will for probate this afternoon and I'll ask the court for an emergency order to allow me to get into the box. I don't practice much in the probate court—just an occasional will contest— but I think there's a procedure for opening a box before the will's admitted to probate. That way, by tomorrow morning, assuming the judge is in this afternoon, I'll be able to access the box. The minute I do, Estelle, I'll call you and let you know what's in it. Art, can you hold onto the will until the courier gets here? I'll keep the key and come back in the morning as soon as I've got the court order.

"In the meantime, Estelle, I'll try to contact the detective and make arrangements to pick up Sy's briefcase and inspect the car. I'll also call a friend of mine to go with me to look at the car. He's an expert so he should be able to tell us why the airbag didn't deploy. You're welcome to come with me, but maybe you don't want to."

"You're right, Josh. I don't think I could handle that. Just let me know what you find out. I think I'll go home. There's a ton of food left over from last night. I'll call The Bridge or the Austin Street Shelter and see if they can use it before it spoils."

Chapter Six

"Anything interesting in the safe-deposit box?" Elaine took a sip of her Barolo.

"The chicken cacciatore is great. Is there more?"

"Josh, I know the chicken cacciatore is good; it always is. Or it has been for the last twenty-five years that I've been making it. Maybe the first few times it wasn't great, but that was a long time ago. In any case, that isn't what I asked you. You do remember the question, don't you?"

Josh put down his fork. "Yes, my love, I remember the question. And you know that I don't discuss client business with you or anyone else except clients and others with a need to know."

"Josh, I'm just curious; okay, maybe a little nosy. But whatever's in the box will be a matter of public record as soon as you file the inventory with the court. I'm not asking about anything privileged or confidential. I'm only trying to make conversation. You've been sitting there like a sphinx since we sat down to eat, even worse than usual. You're brooding about something. If you can't tell me, okay. But you don't need any more chicken; I thought you were trying to cut down on your portions."

Opting for the less-risky choice of conversation topics, Josh finished his Barolo. "Nothing interesting in the box. Just the will, some insurance policies and some real estate records. No long-lost Texas & Pacific Land Trust certificate, no deed to a thousand acres in the Pelham Humphries League."

Elaine was well-used to her husband's penchant for obscure references, so she decided to leave those two alone. "How's Estelle? She met you at the bank, didn't she?"

"Still pretty fragile, I'd say. Her daughter——the one who lives in Houston—she and her family left just before Estelle met me at the bank. Estelle was feeling alone. I asked whether her other daughter and her family lived here, and Estelle said 'Yeah, they live in Plano.' The way she said it, it's as though Plano's hundreds of miles away instead of less than twenty minutes up the Toll Road. But she got over it. She's busy disposing of the food left over from last night, making sure it goes to the 'right' organization."

"You didn't. Please tell me you didn't…"

"No, Elaine, I didn't ask for the leftover doozies. The thought crossed my mind, but I kept my mouth shut."

"You sure were closeted a long time with Estelle and that other woman. Isn't she Sy's secretary?"

"Margie's more than a secretary. She doesn't just open the mail and answer the phone. In fact she was Sy's 'Alicia' and then some. I asked her to stay on and help me wind down Sy's practice. Once that's done, I plan to write Margie the best reference letter anyone could ask for."

"And that took over an hour and a half?"

"I didn't realize you were looking at your watch the whole time last night. I'm sorry if you felt deserted. You looked pretty busy to me. Estelle said she needed to talk to me. The way she said it made it clear that 'not now' wasn't an option. What'd you do while I was 'closeted' with Estelle as you put it?"

"I managed to keep occupied. I'm on the steering committee for the 'Project Do Over' fundraiser luncheon in January."

"'Project Do Over?'"

"It's a Temple Sisterhood program providing assistance to paroled female ex-convicts. We try to help them integrate into normal life. One of the main problems is that some of them have never had a 'normal' life. We provide clothing and makeup. We have volunteers that do their hair. We provide transportation to job interviews, practice job interviewing with them and help them put together some kind of resumé. That's often the hardest part. When you drop out of school and have your first child at age fourteen, and before you went to prison the only work you ever did was selling drugs or selling your body, there's not much you can put down under 'education' or 'experience.'"

"What do you do in that case?"

"We help them write an essay about themselves, stress that they are really a good person; that they've learned their lesson and that they're determined not to mess up again."

"Sounds like a good program. Is it long-term, with offices and an executive director?"

"Yeah, I doubt that we'll be running out of clients any time soon. Probably not until men stop buying and selling little girls for fun and profit."

"I don't see that happening real soon, despite the UN and all the other organizations that are trying to put a stop to it. I'll see if I can get my firm to buy a table at the luncheon."

"It's already taken care of. I called Alicia two weeks ago."

"Just for this year, or in perpetuity?"

"We'll take it one year at a time, Josh. I know how your firm works."

"So I suppose you had a productive hour and a half."

"A lot more productive than listening to Harmon Polikoff. Oh! That reminds me; he called here looking for you."

"Oh jeez, just what I need. He called the office too. I spoke with Alicia and she told me he called twice. He must have me on his speed-dial."

"What's he all bent out of shape about now? Which ex-wife is it this time: Myrna or Harriet? Or is it the one he's divorcing now? What's her name? Oh yeah, 'Nurse Toni.' Or is that attorney-client privilege too?"

"Honestly, I have no idea. And he's not a client. He was bending my ear last night, but I wasn't paying much attention. And I have no intention of finding out whether it's Myrna, Harriet or 'Nurse Toni.' Isn't she the one with the great pair of..."

"Boobs. It's okay, Josh, you can say 'boobs' if you want to. I'd bet anything they're aftermarket enhancements. But you wouldn't know that. You're strictly a *tush* man."

"I give up. I will never understand women. A man pays a woman a compliment and she acts like he just pinched her on the butt instead of remarking how shapely it is. Anyway, don't worry about Harmon. You know that he's the poster boy for my favorite motto: 'The practice of law would be wonderful if it wasn't...'"

"...'for clients.' I know Josh, but maybe you ought to stop saying that so often; people may begin to take you seriously.

"And what kind of a compliment is it to say that you find a woman's breasts and hips attractive? I can understand a caveman shopping for a prospective mate would look at those things. He'd want to know whether a woman could bear and nurture children. For all I know amoebas and oysters do the same thing.

"I don't know about amoebas, but oysters are hermaphrodites. They don't have to check out prospective mates. Just think how much trouble a male oyster would have to get a good look at a female? By comparison men have it easy."

"Okay, then make it amoebas and ... and warthogs. Maybe it's just hard-wired in males; a result of that *x* chromosome with one leg broken off."

"Okay. I guess I'm just a simple caveman. Next time, I'll say, 'Elaine, what lovely ears you have!' How about,' Elaine, your elbows drive me absolutely wild?'"

Before the discussion escalated into a fight, Josh changed the subject back to Dr. Blubberoff. "What was Harmon doing there last night anyway? I suppose he must have been a client of Sy's. Or did Estelle have some work done?"

"Not Estelle, Josh. Try Sy. He had gastric sleeve surgery back in August. I had lunch with Estelle a couple of weeks ago and she told me about it after her second glass of wine. She actually encouraged him to have it done. She was worried about his health; said he is...was...way overweight and that he'd been working a lot...working a couple of nights a week...all summer. She said that except during tax season he hadn't worked that much at night in over twenty years."

"Sy had weight-loss surgery? I thought he'd shed some weight when I last saw him. But letting Dr. Blubberoff near you with a sharp instrument? He didn't seem that overweight to me. Why would a guy Sy's age..." As soon as he said it Josh knew he should have stuck with the contents of the safe-deposit box or the virtues of Elaine's chicken cacciatore or even the mate-selection proclivities of amoebas and warthogs.

"Is that what the meeting was about last night?"

"Elaine, I can't tell you what we discussed. But I assure you that the subject of infidelity did not come up during my meeting with Estelle. Estelle just has some concerns about the accident and I promised I'd look into it. That's all she and I discussed."

Elaine decided to let Josh's omission of any details of his discussion with Margie Morrison slide, at least for the time being. "Well, if Sy was fooling around he's lucky Estelle didn't know. I assume his death, horrific as it must have been, was quick and relatively painless. If Sy was having an affair and Estelle found out, I guarantee you his death would have been neither quick nor painless.

"What about the accident?"

"I don't know very much. The police report isn't filed yet, but they did tell her sons-in-law that Sy's airbag didn't deploy. Estelle wants to know why."

"What are you going to do? Hire an accident-reconstruction expert?"

"I thought about that, but I don't think it'll be necessary, at least not yet. As soon as I can get permission from the detective in charge of the case, I'm going to get Louis Prejean to look at the car. If anyone can figure out what happened, Louis can."

"How long will getting permission take?"

"I don't know. I've got a call in to the detective. If she doesn't call back in the morning, I'll try again. If that doesn't work, I have no idea what to do next. I doubt that Louis would be willing to jump over a razor wire-topped chain link fence at the city impound lot to look at the car. Also, I don't think Louis likes dogs and they've probably got one or two of those roaming around as well."

"Why don't you think the detective will call you back? Is she that busy?"

"So I'm told. All the homicide detectives are tied up working the *El Chupacabra* cases. So even the detectives who work other types of cases—burglary, drugs and vehicle crime— are pitching in and working the homicide detectives' other cases. That means they don't have time for run-of-the-mill cases like Sy's death."

"Well I hope they catch that *El Chupacabra* monster soon. It's just awful: tying people down and cutting out their hearts while they're still alive. And then eating the hearts! Didn't they do that in Mexico and Central America in pre-Columbian times?"

"I agree; it's as barbaric as those ISIS fanatics cutting off their captives' heads in Syria and Iraq. From what I read in the paper the other day, the police think *El Chupacabra* may be a lone vigilante or probably a vigilante group. So far all of their victims have been street-level Hispanic and African-American drug dealers, all of whom were grabbed off the streets in South Dallas and Oak Cliff."

"You're not saying…"

"No, of course not. Getting drug dealers off the streets is the job of law enforcement. They devote a lot of time, manpower and tax dollars to doing just that. But I don't suppose they're going to ever make real progress in getting rid of drugs and drug-related crime until people decide to stop using drugs, but that's about as likely as ending child sex-trafficking.

"Even so, that doesn't excuse somebody else taking on the job. You know that at least since law school I've been a devout believer in the Bill of Rights: due process, right-to-counsel, right to a jury trial. And you know how ambivalent I am about capital punishment. I promise you, I'm all in favor of the police taking *El Chupacabra* off the streets."

"What are you going to do about Harmon Polikoff?"

"I'll ask Alicia to call him in the morning; tell him I'm tied up all week on another matter. Ask him what he's calling about and if another attorney in the firm can be of help. He'll probably say no, and that'll be the end of it."

"What if he doesn't say no?"

"Then Alicia will hand him off to somebody else and I'll get credit for the origination. It's a win-win for me."

"Until whoever takes him on as a client comes in your office one day and cuts your heart out."

Chapter Seven

"Thank you, Dr. Polikoff. I'll give him the message." Alicia hung up the phone. "You heard? That's twice this morning."

Josh was standing in front of Alicia's work station. "Sorry. I meant to call you first thing to warn you. Would you mind calling him back? Tell him I'm tied up on another matter all week, which unfortunately may be the truth. Ask him what he's calling about. Say that you'll refer him to another attorney in the firm that handles that type of work and that can give his matter immediate attention. He'll probably say no thanks—or something to that effect, but less tactfully—and that'll be the end of it. If he says that's okay with him, tell me what it's about and I'll see if I can find an associate who needs to bring up his or her billable hours."

"Isn't he the guy who calls himself 'Dr. Blubberoff?' It's a good thing he didn't decide to take up breast reduction surgery. How'd he find you?"

"He cornered me at the memorial service for Sy Blonstein Sunday night."

"Speaking of Sy Blonstein, Mr. Nagle filed the will for probate late yesterday afternoon. We had a copy of the will in the file, so he was able to get the application done along with the application to access the second box even before the courier got here with the original will. As soon as the courier got here with the original Mr. Nagle took everything to the courthouse himself so he could walk it through the clerk's office and get in to see the judge to present the safe-deposit box application.

"I didn't know what to tell Mr. Nagle as to why we needed an emergency application to access the second box since we already had the original will, so he made up some vague mumbo jumbo about assets possibly being wasted. Evidently the judge bought it because a certified copy of the signed order's on your desk."

"Alicia, you're wonderful. The firm doesn't pay you enough."

Alicia smiled, batted her long eyelashes and rubbed her thumb and forefinger together in the universal gesture for money. "I'll remember that when it's time for salary review, especially if I have to deal with Dr. Blubberoff anymore.

"It's been a busy morning, Josh. Have you got time to fill me in on what's going on? I had a phone call from a Detective Turner with the Dallas Police Department and I spoke with a lawyer in Atlanta who represents the people who own the office building where Sy's office is located."

"What'd Detective Turner have to say? Let's deal with that first."

"She actually apologized for not getting back to you yesterday. She said she'd gotten your voicemail about going to look at Mr. Blonstein's 'vehicle.' She said that would be okay, but she'd have to be there with you to make sure that nothing is disturbed. She said she could meet you at three o'clock this afternoon at the impound lot and to call her back as soon as possible to confirm. If she's not answering her phone, just leave a voicemail."

"Great. Would you please call her back and let her know three o'clock is fine? Also ask her if the accident report's been filed and if so could she please bring a copy?

"And what about the lawyer from Atlanta?"

"Actually, he called Mr. Walling before I talked to him. Mr. Walling said the building manager called the owners' managing partner in Atlanta and told them about the break-in and that you'd asked to see the security camera tape, or whatever it is, and the building entry logs. The managing partner called their lawyer in Atlanta," Alicia looked at her steno pad notes, " Helmut Steinhardt, and he looked you up on our firm website. He saw Mr. Walling's name and remembered that they were in law school together at Emory. In fact they were opponents one time in moot court competition. So he called Mr. Walling and Mr. Walling convinced him—I have no idea how—that you are a good guy. Anyway, the end result is that you get access to what you want provided that you give them a letter as executor of the estate that says that the estate isn't going to make a claim against the building ownership, the management company or the security company. In fact, Mr. Steinhardt dictated what he wants and it's also waiting on your desk. He made it sound like the wording of the letter was not negotiable; take it or leave it."

"I hate dealing with lawyers who have all the leverage and are smart enough to know it. But I suppose I'd write the same letter if I were representing the owners. I'll get a cup of coffee and go sign the letter. Do you want anything?"

"No thanks. But Josh, there's one other thing. I've been trying all morning to reach Margie to let her know that the will had been filed, but she's not answering the office phone. I've left a couple of voicemail messages. She left me a voicemail message around ten o'clock last night. She said to tell you she hadn't been able to find the 'Crystal's Palace' file, whatever that is. She left her cell phone number so I tried calling that too. Same thing; went straight to voicemail."

"Well, she's had a rather rough few days. First Sy wraps his car around a bois d'arc tree and then her office gets burglarized and trashed in the process. According to Sy, Ms. Morrison is not a teetotaler. Maybe she did what any reasonable person would do under the circumstances: take refuge in a bottle and then sleep it off. Margie's good people; she'll call you back before too long.

"Can you make a copy of the order for the safe-deposit box? I need to go back to the bank and get into the other safe deposit box before I meet Detective Turner. I'm sure the banker will want a copy of the order. As soon as I sign the hold-harmless letter I need to get hold of Louis Prejean and get him to meet me at the impound lot."

Chapter Eight

As Josh pulled his car into a vacant space in the public-parking area in front of the DPD impound lot administration building he was finishing his cell phone conversation with Alicia. "Margie wasn't at the office. After I got through with the banker I went by Sy's office to see if maybe she was there and just not answering the phone. I stopped by the building manager's office to see if the manager had seen her. The manager, SueEllen...no, Alicia, I'm not making the name up...SueEllen Masters told me that she hadn't seen or heard from Margie either. Margie must have really tied one on.

"Anyway, when you finally do get hold of her, tell her not to worry about the 'Crystal's Palace' file. I found it and one other file in the second safe deposit box. I can maybe guess why Sy kept the Crystal's Palace file in a box that Estelle didn't have access to, but I have no idea about the other file. I looked at it for a minute or two; all it is, as far as I can tell, is tax returns, Sy's work papers and some client documents and records for some apartment complexes. I took both files with me. I'll look at them for a while at home after dinner and bring them in to the office tomorrow morning. Maybe Margie will know something about the apartment file. If not, I'll have another accountant take a look at the file to try and figure out why Sy would want to keep it in a safe deposit box rather than in his office with his other files.

"I don't know; maybe one or both files have something to do with what Sy wanted to see me about. So far as I know adultery isn't a crime, even though it can get you in a world of hurt. But maybe there's more to it than Sy just fooling around. As for the apartments, who knows? Whatever it is, I do know that I need to find out. If there's a problem that didn't die along with Sy, I don't want to get blind-sided and end up with Estelle getting sacked because of it.

"Dr. Blubberoff wouldn't tell you any more than it's urgent and it has to do with Sy's estate? I guess maybe Sy still owed him some money for the gastric sleeve surgery and Dr. Blubberoff's worried about getting paid. Okay, I'll call him. Is there no rest for the weary? Here's Louis; I gotta go. See you tomorrow. Bye."

Josh got out of his car, slipped into his Burberry trench-coat and walked toward the gleaming black tow truck with "Prejean Automotive" and the phone number professionally painted on the door. Louis Prejean got out and held out his hand. "Mr. Josh, good to see you. Been what? At least six weeks? Car must be runnin' pretty good." Louis wore jeans and a brown leather jacket cut like a sport coat. The color of the leather was a shade or two lighter than Louis's skin. He wore full-quill ostrich western boots that matched the color of the jacket. He was bald except for a fringe of frizzy silver hair. He wore gold-rimmed glasses that matched the gold in his front tooth.

"Louis, when are you going to stop calling me 'Mr. Josh?' How long have we been friends?"

"Since August 14, 1989. You know that well as I do, Mr. Josh. And I'll keep calling you 'Mr. Josh' long as the Good Lord lets me stay on this earth. It's just my East Texas upbringing… and the fact you the best lawyer a man ever had as well as one of the best people I know." Louis turned to a young man who had gotten out of the passenger side of the truck cab and now stood diffidently next to Louis. "Mr. Josh, this my nephew DeMontrond Prejean. My little sister's boy. DeMontron' you come shake hands with Mr. Joshua Loeb."

Josh held out his hand which was swallowed by DeMontrond's first-baseman's glove of a hand. DeMontrond stood about six-three. He was wearing jeans like his uncle, but instead of western boots he wore heavy black work boots with thick lug soles. Where the uncle had an incipient beer belly, the nephew was all muscle. He wore a white long-sleeve knit shirt under a Dallas Cowboys replica jersey bearing the number seventy-nine. The jersey looked like it had Eric Williams's shoulder pads still in it. Beneath the jersey's short sleeves the muscles of DeMontrond's arms strained the fabric of the undershirt. How do, Sir? Okay I call you 'Mr. Josh' too?"

"Sure thing, DeMontrond. I'm pleased to meet you. Your uncle and I have been friends for a long time, so I'm glad to meet another member of Louis's and Leticia's family. I've known your cousins all their lives.

"How are Leticia and the kids, Louis?"

"Cassandra likes college, but I think she misses her friends and her mother. I'm not sure she's happy up there in New York City. Maybe it's just 'cause she's never been away from home before."

"And what about Joshua?"

"Doin' just fine down at Rice. He's making good grades and preparing for the law school admission test. If he does well on that, he thinks he may be able to get into UT. He's finally getting some playin' time. The boy plays ahead of him turned an ankle and likely be out the rest of the season. But Leticia, she just as soon it was Joshua turned his ankle and couldn't play. She worried by all that concussion stuff she hears and reads about. Otherwise, Leticia's doin' okay. Arthritis botherin' her some, but we all gettin' older and I 'spect that comes along with it. Lot better than the alternative. Kids both comin' home for Thanksgivin' so Leticia's all excited about that. Hasn't seen Cassie since early August. DeMontrond's momma comin' up for Thanksgivin' so we'll have a pretty full table."

"Elaine's the same way. She's got her brood coming home. She's already baked enough chocolate chip cookies to keep a dozen kindergarten classes happy for a month. Does DeMontrond live with you?"

"Yeah, DeMontron' come to live with us 'bout six weeks ago. He been a guest of the TDC. Jus' finished a three-year jolt out of Harris County. Now he's workin' with me at the shop."

"I don't think they call it the 'Texas Department of Corrections' any more. It's now the Texas Department of Criminal Justice."

"That make it a better place for a black man to be?"

"I seriously doubt it, Louis. DeMontrond, mind if I ask what you went down for?"

"Car theft, Mr. Josh."

"Fool boy stole a Houston Police Department bait car. Caught him 'fore he gone even a mile. Since he know so much about cars, his momma asked me to take him in; see if maybe I can turn that talent into something he can make an honest living at. Fact of the matter, I gotta have somebody to turn the business over to when I'm done crawling' under cars. Joshua, he gonna be a lawyer; Cassie...she gonna be whatever she want to be and I doubt she thinkin' about running a car repair shop. Although with that girl, you can't ever tell what she's thinkin'."

With the feeling just now returning to his hand after having it crushed by DeMontrond's grip, Josh asked, "You grow those muscles in the joint, DeMontrond?"

"Well, Mr. Josh, I played some football in high school. But I blew out my left ACL my last game—State quarterfinals—an' no college wanted to take a chance on me. So yeah, I guess I built up mostly while I was doin' my time."

"How much can you bench press?"

"Least five hundred pounds; that's the most they'll let you do. Don' want nobody gettin' hurt. You know how it is."

"Louis, what have you got DeMontrond doing? Does he hold up the car while you get underneath to work on it?"

"Well, not all the time. Mostly DeMontron' work on electronics. He knows way more 'bout that stuff than I do, or most other folks do for that matter. Self-taught. They got all kinds of repair and service manuals in the library where he done his time. That's why I brought him along. If anyone can figure out why that airbag didn't open, it'll be DeMontron'. Also, I wanted him to meet you. Been tellin' him our history on the way over."

"That's what it is, Louis, history. And ancient history at that. Time to let it be."

"Don' think I can do that, Mr. Josh. Wasn't for you, I'd still be down there in Huntsville waitin' for my first parole hearing."

"Come on, Louis. You were...are...an innocent man. What stories has your Uncle Louis been telling you, DeMontrond?"

"He tol' me the whole thing, Mr. Josh. He be sittin' down at Huntsville doin' seventy-five years for murder. You get appointed by the court an' throwed a writ; get him a new trial based on incompetent counsel. Then when they re-tried him, with you defendin' him, he walked 'cause of self-defense. Then he say how you guaranteed his bank loan so he could start his business. Wish I'd had you as my lawyer."

"Thanks, DeMontrond, but you'd be a lot better off following in your Uncle Louis's footsteps after he was acquitted. You do that, you won't need me or any other lawyer to keep you out of the joint." Josh looked at his watch. "I wonder where the detective is?" It's a quarter to four already. If she'd cancelled I'm sure Alicia would have called me."

As Josh was calling Alicia again, a plain white Crown Victoria drove up and parked in one of the parking places reserved for "official vehicles only." When she emerged from her car Josh noted that Detective Turner was of average height. She wore her dark blond hair pulled back in a ponytail. She was dressed in a navy blazer over a blue oxford shirt and khaki twill pants. Her ensemble fit her well in all the right places. Josh judged her age to be mid-thirties. He had read somewhere that it was bad form to invade a police officer's space so he waited until Detective Turner had closed the distance between them before taking a step toward her and holding out his hand. "Detective Turner? I'm Joshua Loeb."

"Lana Turner, Mr. Loeb." She added perfunctorily, "Sorry I'm late." She held out her hand to briefly grip Josh's and after she withdrew it reached in her shoulder purse and extracted a DPD business card with her name and direct telephone number handwritten in the blanks provided for those purposes. "I thought I was going to have to cancel. There's been another butchered body discovered. It's been all-hands-on-deck since before noon."

"You mean another *El Chupacabra* killing?"

"Well, that's what they called it on the TV local news at noon. But I'm not so sure. The body was found in the same condition as the others…"

"Gutted? Heart cut out and chunks bitten off?"

"That's what I've heard; but this time the victim doesn't fit the pattern. This time the victim's a middle-aged white woman. My own opinion—not that anyone's asking for it—is that it's a copycat case. Some guy gets tired of being married, buries a chef's knife in his wife's chest, removes her heart and then carves out a couple of pieces to make it look like he took a couple of bites. Soon as they ID the victim, they'll pick up the husband and he'll confess in less than an hour."

"I don't know whether to hope you're right or that you're wrong. If you're right, then it may be a one-time thing. Or this may be just the first copycat. On the other hand, if it is the *El Chupacabra* killer, then he's expanded his target market. Either way, it's not a good development."

"Especially for the woman. But whichever it is Mr. Loeb, I don't have a lot of time. I've been assigned to the task force trying to identify the newest victim.

"Who are these gentlemen?"

"These are my automotive experts, Louis Prejean and his nephew DeMontrond Prejean. Louis has been in the auto repair and maintenance business for over twenty years and DeMontrond works for him. DeMontrond's an expert on automotive electronics."

"Gentlemen," Detective Turner nodded briefly at Louis and glanced at DeMontrond as though trying to decide whether her handcuffs would fit if it came to that. "If you all are ready, let's go take a look. Before we go in, I have to ask whether any of you are carrying a weapon."

"Yes, ma'am, I am." Louis stepped forward and reached into the inside breast pocket of his jacket. As he did, Turner stiffened momentarily and then relaxed as Louis extracted his wallet. He removed his concealed handgun carry permit and held it out for Turner to examine.

Detective Turner looked carefully at what Louis had given her and handed the laminated card back to him. "Sir, you'll have to leave your weapon in your vehicle; civilians with weapons not are allowed inside the building or the lot."

Louis did as instructed and when he returned from his truck the three men followed Detective Turner into the administration building. Turner's credentials vaulted them to the head of the long line of disgruntled citizens waiting to bail out their vehicles. No one in the queue looked as though they could afford the parking fine let alone the $175 towing and impound charge. After signing in they followed her to the back of the building and out to an electronically-locked steel gate leading to the lot. Someone inside pressed a button and the lock released with a loud buzz. After they passed through, the gate clanged shut causing DeMontrond to shudder involuntarily. "Louis," Josh stopped for a moment, "You need to be sure to send me a bill for yours and DeMontrond's time."

"I can't be doin' that, Mr. Josh. All the things you done for me. You know I ain't never charged you for my time keepin' that old Jag of yours runnin'."

"Well I appreciate that, Louis, 'specially with parts getting more expensive every time I bring it in. But for this, I really do want you to charge me. I need for you and DeMontrond to be employed as consulting experts; that way, I can keep everything you tell me confidential as work-product."

"Well okay, Mr. Josh, that's what you want." Louis shrugged.

Detective Turner had obtained the number of the space where the Buick had been left by the tow truck. They found it at the rear of the lot along with the carcasses of other wrecked vehicles. The front end of the silver-colored Buick was in the shape of a deep *V*, its baleen-like grill completely invaginated. The impact had sprung open the hood latch and the hood was folded back against the windshield obscuring the interior of the car. As they reached the front they could see chunks of tree bark wedged into the metal. The force of the impact had sheared the engine off its mountings and shoved it back through the firewall so that it was part way into the passenger compartment.

"Must have been goin' pretty fast at the time of impact, Ms. Turner."

"He was, Mr...." She paused for a moment. "...Prejean. Based on the impact depth, our accident reconstruction expert estimates at least sixty miles-an-hour."

First Turner, then Louis followed by Josh edged between the driver's side of the Buick and the vehicle parked next to it. The windshield did not show any indication that Sy had struck his head in the collision. However the steering column was shoved back almost into the driver's seatback. The airbag obviously had not deployed. Pointing with her flashlight, Turner said, "That's probably what killed him. Crushed his chest so he couldn't breathe."

"Does that mean he survived the initial impact? He didn't die immediately?"

"Mr. Loeb, I can't comment on that. You don't impress me as the ambulance-chaser type, but I assume you're here because the deceased's family wants to sue someone. I'm not allowed to get involved in that. You'll have to see what the accident report says and what the autopsy report says."

"There was an autopsy?"

"It's required. I understand it took place on Saturday. The family wanted him buried Friday afternoon before sundown for religious reasons, but the medical examiner couldn't get to it that soon. They did hurry it up as much as they could and got it done Saturday afternoon. But they'll still have to send tissue and fluid samples to the lab. Those lab people have got as much work as they can keep up with and then some. Once the testing's done, the paperwork will get sent to us and we'll know the cause of death and whether alcohol or drugs had anything to do with it or whether he had a heart attack or a stroke or maybe just fell asleep."

"Ma'am, can I get a look inside? I can't tell much just lookin' in the window."

"You'll have to go around the other side; this side got jammed shut in the impact. EMTs had to remove the deceased from between the steering wheel and…

"You, DeMarcus, get out from under the vehicle immediately!"

"His name's 'DeMontrond,' Ma'am."

"I don't care if his name's 'DeMarco Murray' or for that matter 'Tony Romo,' Mr. Prejean. If he messed with anything on this vehicle, I'm going to have to arrest him for interfering with my official duties."

"I didn't touch nothin', Ma'am." DeMontron eased his upper body out from under the front end of the Buick. "Don' need to. Easy to see why the airbag didn't work. The electric wire that goes from the collision sensor in the front bumper to the monitor inside the passenger cabin been pulled loose from the sensor. You can see for yourself; I be glad to show you.

"Whoever done it must have been in a real big hurry or didn't much know what he doin'. There's a bunch of ways to fix it so an airbag won't open without havin' to rip out wiring. Only a fool'd do that."

"Okay, DeMontrond, I guess you'd better show me. You sure you didn't touch anything?"

"No Ma'am. I swear all I did was look. Kept my hands on the ground whole time." He held out his hands, first palms up, then down. "See, don't got no grease or dirt on them."

Josh removed his Burberry and offered it to the detective. "Here, lay this down first so you don't have to worry about your blazer getting ruined."

She accepted the offer spreading the Burberry skin-side down on the ground under the vehicle's front end. She then lay down and scooted her body half-way under. "Is this far enough? DeMontrond, you better come show me what I need to look at."

DeMontrond lay down on the detective's right and slid back so that his head, shoulders and upper arms were under the vehicle. "'Scuse me, Ma'am." He reached up with his left arm and pointed to the wiring harness protruding from the back of the impact sensor. "See how the wire's been pulled loose?"

"Do one of you gentlemen have a smartphone? I ought to get some pictures of this and mine's in my purse. I can use one of your phones, then I can email the pictures to my phone." Louis took out his phone, opened the camera feature and lay the instrument in the detective's outstretched hand. "Thanks. I assume I just have to push the camera icon?"

"That's right. It's set on still pictures. You can change it to video if you want."

DeMontrond wedged his way out from under the car and then walked around to the rear as Turner took several pictures. When she was done she handed the phone back out to Louis. Louis and Josh then pulled on the bottom of Josh's coat until Turner was clear of the bumper. As she got to her feet she picked up Josh's coat, brushed it off with her hand and handed it back to him. "Thank you, Sir Walter." She allowed a brief smile, the first sign of humanity since she'd met them in the parking lot. "Where's DeMontrond?"

"Back here, Ma'am. Somethin' you ought to see."

"What's that, DeMontrond?" Turner led Louis and Josh back to the rear of the Buick.

"Look here." DeMontrond pointed to two curved indentations, each about an inch deep and two inches in diameter in the back end of the trunk above the bumper. "And look at this." He pointed to the left rear quarter-panel just in front of the tail-light assembly. There was a streak of black paint about a foot long and an inch wide. "Driver must have swapped paint with someone not long ago."

"How do you know it was recent?" Turner had her own phone out and was taking pictures of the trunk and quarter-panel.

DeMontrond pointed, being careful not to touch anything. "Car ain't been washed in a while. But there's no dust or road film where the scrape is. Same thing with the dents in the trunk. If you was to ask me, Ma'am, I'd say th' driver of the Buick must have gotten into it with somebody in a truck. Then he be tryin' to outrun him; get away if he could. That's how come the Buick goin' so fast. Truck caught up, bumped the rear end then come around and fender-whipped the Buick. An' that's how the Buick ended up wrapped 'round a tree."

"That's an interesting theory, DeMontrond." Turner put her phone back on her purse. "But it doesn't quite add up. It might, except that it doesn't account for the apparent tampering with the airbag system. Is it possible that the wire got ripped out by the impact?"

"No, Ma'am. They make those wiring harnesses so they can't come loose from an impact. Only way to get one loose is to pull it from behind."

"If you're right, then the only way to account for both events is if they're related."

"You mean someone wanted to kill Sy Blonstein and make it look like an accident?" Josh put his Burberry back on and belted it against the drop in temperature that came with sunset and an increasing North wind.

"That's one possibility, Mr. Loeb. Did Mr. Blonstein have any enemies that would want to see him dead?"

"I can't imagine anyone disliking Sy enough to murder him. I've known him for thirty years. I know his wife and their kids and probably most of his friends and a lot of his clients. Sy was just a hard-working CPA." Recalling the rabbi's words, he added, "Everybody loved Sy."

"Well, I've seen enough to convince me that someone didn't love him. I'll get a tarp thrown over the vehicle and get some technicians out here A-sap. They'll take a sample of the black paint and possibly be able to match it at least to a make of truck. Also, they may be able to figure out what caused the dents in the trunk. In the meantime, Mr. Loeb, in going through the deceased's affairs, if you come across anything I should know about, please get in touch with me immediately."

"I sure will, Detective Turner." Josh hoped his response didn't sound as half-hearted as he felt. "It would be a big help to me if I could have his briefcase. I assume you folks have it. His assistant said he always had it with him."

"I don't know anything about a briefcase. The personal property inventory— it was made by the first officers at the scene—didn't list a briefcase. They found his wallet. It was under the driver's seat when they took the body out. That's how we made the identification. Maybe the briefcase is still in the vehicle. I'll make sure the technicians look for it and let me know right away if they find it."

"Thank you for meeting us here, Detective Turner. I can imagine how busy you must be. Good luck with identifying your 'Jane Doe.' If you'll get us back inside the building, we can find our way out from there."

Outside in the public parking lot the Prejeans walked Josh to his car. Josh shook Louis's hand and cautiously held out his hand to DeMontrond. "DeMontrond, you did some really good work back there. Louis, you should be proud of him."

"Well, I guess in a way I am, Mr. Josh. But then I got to remind myself how come he know so much about cars. Anyway, you tell your missus hello."

"Will do, Louis. Tell Leticia hello from me. Thanks again."

Chapter Nine

"Why would someone want Sy dead?"

"Elaine, I don't know. I just know from what Louis's nephew showed us the airbag didn't deploy because the...the collision sensor was tampered with." Josh gnawed the last shred of meat off his second lamb chop and followed it with a sip of wine. "This shiraz-cabernet blend's pretty good."

"I'm glad you like it; you're the one who bought it. Speaking of buying wine, don't forget that you need to buy the wine for Thanksgiving. I don't want you waiting until Wednesday night like you usually do."

"I promise. When does our daughter get in?"

"Caroline gets in around noon on Wednesday."

"Is she bringing anyone to dinner?"

"She's bringing Bryan."

"The shrink? I thought she broke up with him."

"Well, they're back together and you need to deal with it."

"Elaine, what's there to deal with? The guy never says anything; just sits there like you're a patient and he's psychoanalyzing you. When I try to have a conversation with him I feel like I ought to be lying on a couch. You just like him because he's a doctor. Every Jewish mother's dream: that her daughter should marry a doctor. That's why Harmon Polikoff has no problem finding a new wife when he wants one. I can't imagine what women see in him. For sure it's not his good looks."

"You're probably right: money, prestige…"

"Isn't that why you married me?"

"Yeah. You sure had me fooled. But maybe I'll keep you anyway."

"Anyone else coming besides the shrink?"

"Our son Adam. You remember him, don't you? And his wife Suzanne? And our grandchildren? What are their names? Think, Josh."

"Wait, wait, don't tell me. They're right here on the tip of my tongue. No, sorry; that's a piece of broccolini on the tip of my tongue." Josh removed the offending morsel and put it on his plate.

"I thought about maybe inviting Estelle, but I'm sure she's going to want to be with her family. She always does Thanksgiving."

"Inviting her is probably not a good idea. Besides, Estelle may not be speaking to me by then."

"What are you going to tell her about the airbag?"

"Damned if I know, Elaine. Probably just that the police have taken over the investigation and they'll keep us informed."

"Josh, Estelle may not be the brightest candle on the *menorah*, but do you really think she's going to let it go at just that? She'll know you're lying...or at least not telling her the whole truth. If I were her, I'd fire you and go find myself a lawyer whom I could trust.

"Sy was having an affair and you're covering it up. How long did it take me last night to figure that out? How long do you think it will take Estelle? I know Sy was your friend, but Estelle's your client."

"Maybe Estelle doesn't know me as well as you do. In any case, technically, she's not my client. I don't have a client. I'm executor of Sy's estate, so if anything, I'm my own client. My only fiduciary duty to Estelle is to collect Sy's estate, see that any debts are paid and turn the remainder over to her. I don't have a duty to add to her grief by telling her that her late husband was an adulterer, especially since all I have is hearsay and circumstantial evidence."

"Which I presume you got from the secretary...that Margie. So there are no videos or lewd photos, no love letters?"

"Elaine, I'm not going to tell you what evidence I have. Take my word for it; it's only circumstantial. And I'm not sure I want to even look any further."

"But what if Sy's affair has something to do with his death?"

"I'll tell the detective what I know and leave the investigation to the police."

"And also leave it to them to break the news to Estelle? In the meantime, you're going to have to tell her something about the airbag."

"Your right. I guess I'll just tell her that the wire from the collision sensor to the airbag triggering mechanism was severed—possibly by the impact—and that's why the airbag didn't deploy.

"Do you mind if I don't help with KP duty? I've had a long day and it's not over yet. I've got to read two thick files of Sy's before I go to bed."

"I'll make you a deal, Josh. Do you remember your *memento mori* while we were getting dressed to go to Sy's memorial service Sunday evening? I've been thinking a lot about it ever since then."

"*Memento...mori?*"

"Thoughts about one's life and own mortality." Elaine smiled, pleased that she'd evened the score for "callipygous." She reached across the table and caressed his hand. You are right and the French have got it wrong."

Josh put his free hand on top of Elaine's hand. "I actually got something right? And what is it that the French got wrong?"

"In vernacular French, an orgasm is called a '*petite mort,*' a 'little death.' But I think you're right; it's an affirmation of life. And right now, I'm thinking your life could use a little affirmation. Who knows what'll happen tomorrow? Forget about Sy's files. The deal is: you handle KP while I go 'slip into something comfortable' as the saying goes. When you're done, just whistle. You do know how to whistle, don't you?"

Later, Josh was standing in a corner of a long, narrow fluorescent-lit room in the basement of the "Bureau," the generic-sounding name for a covert Israeli "black-ops" agency. The former chief, Avner Raphael, retired Mossad assassin, now international architectural consultant specializing in the preservation and restoration of landmark buildings, was beginning to brief his old team, reassembled for yet another one-last-mission. This time, their assignment was to take down a drug lord, the grandson of a Nazi war criminal who'd escaped to Paraguay at the end of the war. The drug lord was known to be accumulating a massive fortune and spending it on laying the groundwork for a Fourth Reich and to support quack scholars endeavoring to rewrite the history of the Third.

Avner's beautiful young wife Leah, the great-granddaughter of a *sabra*, was at a large corkboard pinning up aerial photos of the fortress-like compound that served as the drug lord's headquarters deep in the Paraguayan jungle. As described by the author of the book Josh had been reading before falling asleep, Leah was tall, at least five-foot, ten. In her combat boots she was at least six feet tall.

Raphael was just completing his exquisitely-detailed briefing of the team members on their respective assignments for "Operation Condor." There were few questions, and—uncharacteristically in a room full of Israelis—no debate. Avner Raphael was their commander-in-chief. If Raphael said it would go down a certain way, they could be sure it would go down that very way.

Somewhat to his surprise, Josh was to have a key role in the mission. His "legend," to use the Bureau's term for cover-story, is that he is a successful American lawyer with a major gambling monkey on his back and one-too-many women in his life. The extra woman claims to be pregnant and the gambling monkey has him in a fiscal choke-hold.

The deal is that Josh is to act as a mule; he is to deliver a couple million dollars in diamonds in payment for a shipment of high-grade meth to be delivered in Europe. For this service, the neo-Nazi drug lord will cause the extra woman to be "re-located" and out of Josh's life forever. The drug lord will have been persuaded to buy Josh's gambling debt at a deep discount. When Josh makes the second delivery a month later, the gambling debt will also disappear from Josh's life.

Leah has handed Josh a briefcase. It is square-shaped, made of brushed-aluminum with metal reinforcements at each of the eight corners. Leah works the combination and opens the briefcase. With the tip of her little finger she pushes a concealed pressure switch that allows her to pry open the false bottom. The briefcase is fitted with a one-liter cylinder filled with a highly-compressed clear, odorless gas specially developed by the Bureau's scientists. When the release valve is opened the cylinder can fill a room containing up to two thousand cubic meters of volume in less than one point five seconds. Reconnaissance has established that the room where the delivery is to take place is only eighteen hundred cubic meters.

When he meets the drug-lord Josh is to open the briefcase and then press a button in the briefcase handle which will open the gas cylinder release valve. Everyone in the room, including Josh, will be rendered unconscious in a matter of seconds. When everyone's out cold, Avner and the rest of the team will enter the room and complete the mission.

Josh is having difficulty following what Leah is telling him. She is wearing a pair of very short, very tight shorts and her combat boots. Josh can't help staring at her long, tanned legs. Above the shorts, she is wearing only a man's shirt, unbuttoned and tied in a knot beneath her firm, perfect breasts. Leah notices that Josh's attention is wandering. She walks away and comes back a moment later with a hot pastrami sandwich and a Dr. Brown's Cel-Ray.

She sets the sandwich and drink down and smiles invitingly. She takes one of Josh's hands and guides it inside her shirt. Her nipple is hard. She leans toward him, "Oh, Josh, Josh…"

Elaine had fallen asleep a little while ago, the latest Louise Penny "Inspector Gamache" novel spread open across her breasts. When she had stirred, the book fell to the floor waking her. It also woke Josh up. Elaine glanced at the clock on the nightstand next to her. "Josh," she yawned. "It's almost ten o'clock. Do you want to watch the news?"

Josh closed his "Avner Raphael" book, *Operation Condor*, and set it on the nightstand. "I guess so. There was another *El Chupacabra* murder discovered this morning. Detective Turner thinks it's a copycat and not the real thing. I'd like to see if the police have released any more information."

"I heard about it on the six o'clock news right before you got home. They haven't identified the victim, but they did release an artist's sketch. It was a woman, and if I didn't know better I'd almost be willing to swear I've seen her somewhere. Can you get the remote?"

Josh retrieved the remote and turned the set on just as the news program's dramatic introductory theme music was ending and the voice-over announcer intoned "The Channel Ten News at Ten starts...Now!" The male and female anchors were seated at a parody of a Hollywood parody of a news desk somberly looking through the camera into their viewers' bedrooms.

The male anchor led off, "As you probably know by now the killer everyone's calling *El Chupacabra* has apparently struck again. Our news team was first on the scene at around eight forty-five this morning when a man walking his dog on the White Rock Creek jogging and biking trail north of White Rock Lake in East Dallas made a gruesome discovery. The dog, 'Windsor,' a yellow Lab, pulled his owner off the trail into an area of trees and thick underbrush between the paved trail and the creek. The dog, shown here in this Channel Ten exclusive footage with his owner—who asked that he not be identified or his face shown—led his master to the nude, mutilated body of a woman. The man called 9-1-1 on his cell phone and the first-responders arrived in minutes.

"Our reporter and camera crew were the first news organization on the scene, arriving just as the police were blocking off the area with crime scene tape." At this point the director cut to a few seconds of two uniformed officers wrapping yellow plastic tape among several trees. The director then cut back to the anchor who continued, "Our crew did manage to get this exclusive footage of the victim being removed." The director then cut to a few more seconds of a body bag on a gurney being loaded into the back of a Dallas Fire-Rescue ambulance.

The female anchor took up the report. "Sources involved in the investigation tell us there was no identification on the body and police are still trying to establish her identity. Dallas Police detectives and crime-scene personnel have been at the scene since the discovery this morning, staying until it became too dark to make further searching feasible, looking for clues to the victim's identity and any physical evidence that might lead them to the perpetrator of this heinous crime."

Back to the male anchor. "Late this afternoon, authorities released an artist's sketch of the woman which we showed you on our six o'clock broadcast. Since then, indeed within the past hour, the authorities have released an actual post-mortem photograph of the victim's face taken at the Dallas County Medical Examiner's facility. They have asked that we show the photograph on our broadcast in the hope that someone who can identify the woman will come forward. Our station management has agreed to broadcast the photograph because we at Channel Ten believe it is in the public interest. Before we do, however, we must inform you that some viewers may find the image disturbing, so viewer discretion is advised."

"Elaine! I know why you thought you recognized her. It's Margie Morrison, Sy's assistant. I need to call that detective."

Elaine handed Josh the cordless phone which was on her nightstand next to the clock. "I hope Estelle wasn't watching."

Josh got up and retrieved Turner's card from his wallet in his closet. He dialed her number expecting to get her voicemail, but she answered on the second ring. "Auto Crimes, Turner speaking."

"Detective Turner, this is Joshua Loeb. I…"

"I'm sorry, Mr. Loeb, I really don't have time to talk about the Blonstein case right now. I'm going through a foot-high stack of missing persons reports trying to find a match to the victim I told you about when we met this afternoon."

"I'm not calling about the Blonstein case, Ms. Turner. Well, in a way I suppose that I am. Mainly though, I'm calling to tell you that you're right; it is a copycat."

"And you know that because?"

"Because I can identify the victim; her name's Margie…Marjorie Morrison. She was Sy Blonstein's assistant."

"Are you positive?"

"As positive as I can be from the photograph I just saw on the ten o'clock news."

"Would you be willing to meet me at the Dallas County Medical Examiner's office?"

"When?"

"Right now. I'll send a patrol car to pick you up if you like."

"No, that won't be necessary. I'll come in my own car. Just tell me where to go, where to park and where to meet you."

Chapter Ten

Marjorie Morrison wore a black body bag. Josh wore Levis and a faded burnt-orange "UT Law" sweatshirt. He raced his ancient Jaguar down Inwood Road and turned onto the south-bound Stemmons Freeway service road to the Southwestern Institute of Forensic Sciences, which includes the office of the Dallas County Medical Examiner and the county morgue. Detective Turner met him at the vehicle entrance and badged him into a parking place and into the building. Now he stood next to her at the viewing window as the morgue worker unzipped the bag far enough to expose the head and shoulders, enough for Josh to make the identification without having to view the mutilated torso. After confirming Margie's identity and after Detective Turner had reported at length to her boss, Josh allowed himself to be led by Detective Turner to an institutionally-drab breakroom where they sat at a Formica-covered table, their hands wrapped around styrofoam cups of coffee purchased from a vending machine at one dollar per cup.

Josh took a sip of his coffee and grimaced. Noticing his expression, Turner suggested, "Try adding some artificial sweetener and some of that powdered cream. They'll cut the bitterness so that it's almost drinkable. The Crimes Against Persons detectives say that you get used to the coffee after a while; some say they even like it. Story is, that same machine's been here since Lew Sterrett was county judge forty-something years ago."

Setting down his cup, Josh looked around the room. "Well, I doubt many people come here for the ambience or the cuisine. But I don't suppose management gets many complaints from the customers back there." He gestured over his shoulder toward the body storage vault.

"No, probably not." With effort, Turner managed an indulgent smile in response to Josh's attempt at levity. "But let's talk about the late Ms. Morrison and a little more about the late Mr. Blonstein. You say Ms. Morrison worked for Mr. Blonstein for about ten years and that she's divorced?"

"Yes, she told me that Sunday night at the memorial service for Mr. Blonstein. I should add that I've seen her in Sy's office a few times over the years when I've taken my tax records in to Sy so he could prepare the returns for my wife and me."

"You're a lawyer and you have to have someone else do your tax returns? That makes me feel better. I feel so stupid every year."

"I know a lot about accounting and enough tax law to be a menace to myself and others. But I'm a trial lawyer. I wouldn't dream of trying to do anyone's tax return, especially my own. So along with a lot of other folks, I'm going to have to find a new accountant."

"What happens to an accountant's practice when he dies?"

"When the deceased is a sole practitioner like Sy the clients have to be contacted and told that they can pick up any client-provided documents and they should arrange for someone to take over any unfinished work. The estate has to retain what accountants call their 'work-papers' which are documents they themselves generate in the course of an engagement. The estate is obliged to make them available to be examined by the accountant who takes over the work, but the estate keeps them. That's important in case some former client makes a malpractice claim.

"Today, because so much information is kept by electronic storage and retrieval systems, it's a lot easier. I understand you can just pop in a CD, hit a couple of keystrokes and you're done. Marjorie told me that Sy's records were almost all kept on computers with back-up at an off-site storage provider. So but for Marjorie's untimely demise, the job would have been pretty easy."

"Will you be able to go through the records even without Ms. Morrison?"

"I don't know; it may be an issue. Sy had a room full of file cabinets with paper records, so those won't be too big a problem. I gather from what Alicia told me…"

"Alicia, your secretary? The woman I spoke with this morning?"

"Yes. Alicia Flores, my practice assistant."

"She spoke with Ms. Morrison?"

"I don't think so. Yesterday morning I asked Marjorie to locate a file and to call Alicia when she'd found it. When I got to my office this morning Alicia told me that she'd gotten a voicemail message from Marjorie that was recorded at ten o'clock Monday night saying that she hadn't been able to locate the file I asked for. Both Alicia and I have been calling Marjorie all day today, both at Sy's office and on her cell. Neither of us had any luck reaching her. I suppose we now know why."

"When's the last time you saw or spoke with Ms. Morrison?"

"It would have been sometime a little after noon on Monday at Sy's office. I don't recall the exact time, but I was supposed to meet Mrs. Blonstein at the bank at one o'clock to open the safe-deposit box so I could retrieve Sy's will. After I left Sy's office, I stopped off for maybe twenty minutes to speak with the manager of the building. From there I went straight to the bank and got there a few minutes after one."

"At least we know she was alive at ten o'clock Monday night. I'd like to establish a timeline, and that's a place to start. Was it your personal file that you asked Ms. Morrison to locate?"

"No, it was something else, a forensic engagement that Sy had worked on back in the Spring."

"Why is that particular file of interest to you?"

"I'd really rather not say, Ms. Turner."

"Lots of people don't like to tell me things, Mr. Loeb. But they usually end up telling me anyway. If it has anything to do with either Mr. Blonstein's death or Ms. Morrison's I need to know."

"Are you handling both cases?"

"As of now, yes. When I reported your identification, the bosses decided that Ms. Morrison's case probably isn't related to the other so-called *El Chupacabra* cases, but may be related to the Blonstein case, assuming there is one. So they're letting me run with both of them. That's why I was on the phone so long just now; I had to sell them on the idea. Frankly, the cases could be my ticket out of auto crimes where I've been stuck since I made detective. So run with them is exactly what I mean to do."

"'Lana Turner.'" Josh tried another sip of coffee and gave up on it. "'Lana' is an unusual name for a woman your age. It was popular during and after World War II. You know, the actress...mobster boyfriend, Johnny Stompanato... "

"My name's really '*A*lana' and I don't have a boyfriend, much less one that's mobbed-up. An instructor at the police academy started calling me 'Lana' and it stuck. But I don't mind; once in a while it's a good conversation starter."

"Only once in a while?"

"Most of the people I deal with don't know Lana Turner from Tina Turner."

Josh perked up. "Are you a Tina Turner fan? You seem kind of young."

"Sort of. I saw the movie about her life—'What's Love Got to Do With It?'—my senior year in high school. I bought the soundtrack album. I still listen to it occasionally."

"When does it start conversations?"

"If you're asking about my social life, Counselor, it's non-existent. I don't date married men or men who either carry handcuffs or wear them. So if you eliminate married guys, cops and felons, I don't get many chances to meet men I'd want to date."

"How long have you been a detective?"

"Nearly four years. For the last year or so I've been running a bait-car operation. It's a lot better than riding a desk and dealing with the Texas Motor Vehicle Commission people all day. But still it's not exactly the most challenging duty."

"And how long have you been a police officer?"

"Civilian: eight years, four in uniform."

"Civilian?"

"I was in the Army for eight years, all of them in an MP unit after basic training and training in my MOS."

"Iraq? Afghanistan?"

"I did one tour in Afghanistan in a line brigade. That's about as close as the Army would officially let a female MP get to combat.

"Why'd you get out?"

"I loved the Army; I hated the sexual harassment. I made it to W-3, Warrant Officer 3, when I decided not to re-up. My CO threatened to get my enlistment extended, but I had too many stories to tell that the Army didn't want to hear."

"DPD any better about harassment?"

"Physical harassment, yes; discrimination, about the same. But what am I going to do about it? File a lawsuit? With all due respect to your profession, no thanks. Quit? Where do I go from here? Some ticky-tacky suburb where they have one felony a year? So I put on my big girl panties and I deal with it."

"I'm sorry; I didn't mean to take your deposition. It's a bad habit that comes from being a trial lawyer too long. You asked about the files and I told you that the paper ones wouldn't be a big problem. What is going to be problematic is the electronic files. Marjorie told me that they used sixteen-character passwords and that the files are encrypted. I assume she was able to get a new computer yesterday…" Josh looked at his watch, "Or I should say 'day before yesterday.' Unless she wrote down her password and the decryption key and left them where they could be readily found, even if she got a new computer and got it set up before she was abducted and murdered, accessing those files is going to be a challenge."

"DPD's forensic IT department is good; not as good as the Army's but as good as any local PD anywhere. So they may be able to get the files open for you."

"If you are asking me to turn over Sy's files, I'm going to have to say no. They're privileged. Texas Occupation Code, section 901.457."

"I could get a subpoena."

"You can't, but even if you could, a subpoena wouldn't work. The only subpoena you could get would be from a grand jury under Texas Code of Criminal Procedure, section 20.10. I don't practice criminal law, so I had to look that one up on Lexis before I met you this afternoon. You haven't filed a case against anyone yet, so there's no grand jury proceeding pending. Anyway, a subpoena wouldn't work. Under the Occupation Code you need an order signed by a judge. A grand jury subpoena only requires the signature of the prosecutor or the grand jury foreperson; there's no judge involved."

Turner brushed a stray wisp of hair from her forehead. "How about a search warrant, Counselor? A judge signs those."

"True, and from what I'm told by my friends that do practice criminal law, they're easier to get than a discount car wash coupon in the checkout line at the grocery store. But where's your probable cause? Sy's Blonstein's dead and so is Marjorie Morrison. I just confirmed that fact. So they're not suspects. The records belong to me as executor of Sy's estate. Am I a suspect? If so, you'd better read me my rights.

"I have no doubt that you can find a compliant judge who'll sign a search warrant. But I also have no doubt that I will get it quashed so that you'll just have to give everything back to me. Beside not having probable cause, under the statute the warrant would have to identify a particular client and describe specifically what documents are to be seized. Good luck with that. And if the warrant's quashed anything you find—not that there's anything to find—would not be admissible in court. To make matters worse, anything you discovered later that could be tied back to the illegal search would also be inadmissible as 'fruit of the poison tree,' unless you can prove that you would have inevitably discovered it. And good luck with that one too. In short, if you access those records with a subpoena, I think you run the risk that whoever did this will walk.

"Detective Turner...Alana...I don't like getting in your face any more than you like me doing it. But I have a job to do, and just like you, I mean to do it. I have a fiduciary duty and that's important to me. So how about we work together? Sort of like partners." Josh held out his hand.

Alana hesitated a moment and took it. "Okay, partner, where do we go from here?"

"How about home? I was already in bed reading when I happened to turn on the ten o'clock news and saw the photograph. It's been a long day and I'm ready to pack it in. I expect you're about ready too. You're wearing the same outfit you were in this afternoon, so I imagine you haven't had much down-time since this morning. At least I saved you from having to finish going through that foot-high stack of missing persons reports you mentioned."

"True, and I owe you for that at least, not to mention your identifying Ms. Morrison. But before I let you go, I'd like to follow up on something you said. Since you said it to me, I assume it's not privileged."

"What's that?"

"You mentioned Ms. Morrison needing to get a new computer. Why did she need a new computer? If the files were stored electronically, wouldn't she already have one?"

"Actually, Sy's office had at least two, so she told me. But apparently they were stolen by the burglar."

"Burglar? What burglar?"

"You don't know about the burglary of Sy's office? It happened sometime after he died Thursday night and before Monday morning when Marjorie opened up the office. She reported it to the police...called 9-1-1. In fact two officers were there at Sy's office when I arrived. They said they'd turn in a report and that a detective would be back in touch in about a week. They mentioned how hard it is to get anything done on new cases because the *El Chupacabra* case is taking up all the available manpower. I would think that you'd have seen the report since the burglary was of Sy's office and you were working the investigation into Sy's death."

"Dammit! I got the Blonstein assignment Friday afternoon, maybe a hour before I spoke with Mr. Blonstein's sons..."

"Sons-in-law."

"Whatever. I was also working a hit-and run and we're getting close to busting a gang that specializes in stealing third-row seats from high-end SUVs. We're working with the University Park and Highland Park PDs on that one. So I was pretty busy. It's possible that a copy of the burglary incident report was routed to me, but it's more likely that it hasn't been entered into the system yet. Even if it was entered, our new computer system is so screwed up that it either failed to connect the dots or the report's still   hanging around somewhere in cyberspace."

"I can give you the names of the officers that came out, if that would help. They work out of the North Central substation."

"That might help. But if you were there when they were, you know as much as they would, probably more. Let's go find some decent coffee and you can tell me all about it."

Chapter Eleven

Finding a decent cup of coffee in Dallas at one-thirty in the morning, unless you're at home, is about as easy as finding decent steel-platter enchiladas in Portland, Maine. Barbecue at one-thirty in the morning? No problem; just head to Record's in South Dallas. Got to have a two a.m. taco fix? Fuel City's there 24/7. But coffee, that's a challenge.

The dearth of drinkable coffee led the animated Detective Turner and the bleary-eyed Lawyer Loeb to the 24/7 Whataburger on Lemmon near Inwood. Alana ordered a double-meat "Whataburger Junior" with cheese and a side of fries to accompany her coffee. Josh stuck to coffee which wasn't as good as Starbuck's or even Mickey D's, but wasn't too bad, especially compared to the formaldehyde-tainted toxic waste he'd tried at the morgue.

Now that they were "partners" they were "Alana" and "Josh." As they sat at a table sipping their coffee and waiting for Alana's order, she brushed back the same strand of hair that had bothered her earlier. "Josh, before you tell me about the burglary, tell me what you know about Marjorie Morrison. As we sit here, there's nothing to link her death to Seymour Blonstein's—assuming that he didn't die of a heart attack or something—except that she worked for him and his office was apparently burglarized sometime, according to you, after his death.

"What if the deaths are not related? You mentioned that she was divorced. What about the ex-husband?"

"All I know is what I told you. From what Marjorie told me, they divorced about ten years ago. I have no idea what his name is, much less whether he's still around. Your original theory about the case was that it is a domestic violence case made to look like another *El Chupacabra* murder. If I may venture an opinion, I think you're right about the copycat part, but not the domestic violence. Since Marjorie and her ex- have been divorced for more than ten years, that makes it pretty unlikely that the ex-husband had anything to do with it. She didn't mention any kids, so they wouldn't have been fighting over custody or support. And I didn't get the impression it was a 'gold-mine' divorce."

"What's a 'gold-mine' divorce?"

"Where she gets the gold and he gets the shaft. That's what my family-law colleagues call it. She said that after the divorce she needed to go back to work and that her job skills were rusty. Most women who get a substantial property settlement or award from the court don't rush out to go to back to work. If and when they do go back it's usually something more genteel than office work; something like working at Neiman's or selling high-end residential real estate: Park Cities, North Dallas, Collin County."

"Still, I have to eliminate that possibility. Even if we find something definitive linking the two cases, my lieutenant is still going to want to rule the ex- either out or in. A lot of what we do is playing the percentages. Whenever a female dies violently, her past and present persons-of-interest automatically become our persons-of-interest."

"I may be able to help, or at least Alicia will. I'm not sure whether the Dallas County District Clerk's case records going back that far are digitized. If they are, Alicia can go on-line and pull up the records from the divorce case, assuming that it was filed in Dallas. If she can't find it in Dallas County I'll also have her check Collin, Rockwall and Tarrant counties. If Alicia can't do it electronically, I'll either go to the clerk's office myself or send a young associate from my office.

"If we find the divorce case file, it will have enough information—partial driver's license and social security numbers, date of birth, residence at the time of filing—for you to track him down."

"Could we do it now? I've got a laptop in my car and they've got free Wi-Fi here."

"Wish I could, Alana, but it's that kind of stuff that I pay Alicia a very good salary to do. I have no idea how to access trial-court records. I do legal research online and send emails, but that's about it. And I'm not going to call Alicia at two o'clock in the morning. She has a husband and two school-age kids. I watched that TV program '48 Hours' once, so I know that time's of the essence. However, Alicia gets in between eight-fifteen and eight-thirty; it'll have to wait 'till then."

"Order number forty-seven, your order's ready."

"Alana glanced down at her cash register receipt. "That's me. Let me get my food. While I eat you can tell me about the burglary."

As Alana finished her meal, Josh finished telling her what Marjorie had told him about the burglary. Alana patted her lips with her napkin and sipped her coffee refill. "I agree with you that the burglar or burglars were after something and this wasn't just a crime of opportunity, although there is a market for stolen computers. Cyber criminals will buy stolen computers hoping to mine them for data that they can use or re-sell: social security numbers, bank account information, credit card numbers, even email addresses of friends of the victim. They use those to send emails to everybody in the address book asking for money to help bail the sender out of some emergency."

"I've gotten a couple of those. 'Dear Joshua, please send me a thousand dollars. I'm travelling abroad and my wallet and passport were stolen. I'll pay you back as soon as I get home.' I know the messages are fake because they're addressed to 'Dear Josh*ua*.' Nobody I know calls me 'Joshua' except my wife and she calls me 'Joshua' only when she's mad at me. "

"From what you told me about the password and encryption, I don't think there's much risk of cyber criminals. So let's go with the theory that they were after something specific. From the way the file room was trashed, I'd guess it was a file. I'd also guess that they didn't get what they were looking for in the paper files and that's why the computers were taken.

"Earlier, you said that the break-in happened after Mr. Blonstein was killed. What makes you say that?"

"I obviously don't know for sure, but the data point to that."

"The data?"

"There was no indication of forced entry. That means whoever did this had to have access to both Sy's office and to the building itself. If it was after hours or on Saturday or Sunday, it takes an access card to get into the tenant parking and into the building. I confirmed that with the building manager. Sy's office has an electronic lock with a proximity card reader. In other words to get into the building on Saturday or Sunday, and into Sy's office when it's locked…"

"You need a key card to the building and another to the office. So who had cards?"

"According to Marjorie, only she and Sy and the cleaning service had key cards for his office. I assume that the building manager has one also, but if this wasn't a 'crime of opportunity,' as you put it, then we can rule out the building manager and the cleaning crew. Since Marjorie opened the office on Monday, she must have still had her card; that leaves only Sy's unaccounted for."

"Are you saying that someone tampered with Sy's airbag and then ran him off the road just to get his key-card?"

"It's possible. Maybe they took it from his wallet and then threw the wallet on the floor of the car where the officers found it. There'd be no way to tell if the card was in Sy's wallet and someone took it. Did the technicians find the briefcase? Maybe the key-card was in Sy's briefcase."

"I'm not sure they've even been out there yet. I'd better go back myself and have a look. If the briefcase isn't there, then what you're suggesting may be right."

"Alana, you're the detective. But if I may offer another opinion, I think the reason the car wreck was set up was to get the briefcase *and*—more importantly—to assure Sy's permanent silence. They definitely succeeded in silencing Sy, but they didn't find what they wanted in the briefcase and that's why they broke into his office. I think your going back out there is a snipe hunt. The briefcase is gone. Go home and get some sleep. I'll leave Alicia a voicemail right now and call you as soon as she tracks down Marjorie's divorce records. Then you can make your boss happy by scratching the ex-husband off your list."

"Who…"

"Alana, I need to get home so I can lie awake the rest of the night trying to figure out what I'm going to tell Estelle Blonstein. I just hope the Dallas Morning News doesn't decide to publish the photograph of Marjorie on the front page, or if they do, that Estelle isn't an early riser."

Chapter Twelve

Unfortunately, Estelle was an early riser. When he got home, Josh gave a groggy Elaine a recap of his experience and conversation with Detective Turner, omitting only the "Alana" and "Josh" part. He asked Elaine to wake him at seven so he could call Estelle. At six forty-five Estelle called. "...Yes, Estelle, I know. I saw it on the news last night. I called the detective handling Sy's case and met her at the county morgue. I'm the one who identified the body.

"I'm sure the paper didn't have that information because it happened so late.

"Estelle, calm down. I didn't want to call you last night because it was so late by the time I got to the morgue...It's on the other side of Stemmons across from the back of Parkland.

"The police are working on at least two theories...I know because I spent a couple of hours talking with the detective. One, they think that it may have been another *El Chupacabra* killing. It certainly looks that way. The other...no, Estelle, I didn't have to look at her body. They opened the body bag just enough for me to see her face. That was all that was necessary.

"What I started to say is that they're also looking at Margie's ex-husband; or they will as soon as they can locate him. They...No, I don't know his name or where he is or anything about him. I expect that the police will go to her home and maybe they'll find something there...Yes, I know it's been over ten years since they were divorced. But the detective said they always look at the husband or ex-husband.

"...No, I don't know where she lived. In fact, I've got to go to Sy's office...I'll get the building manager...Yes, SueEllen Masters is her name...to let me in...Yes, I'll tell her how much you appreciated what she said. I don't know whether Margie had new key cards made. She said she was going to. I'm sure there's something in the office, maybe a W-2 form, that'll have her home address. If I find it, I'll give it to the detective.

"I've also got to look for the name of her sister so I can...Margie told me that she has a sister who lives in Oklahoma City. Margie said she took a few days off after October Fifteenth and went to visit her sister in Oklahoma City. I'll need to notify her about Margie. If Margie had any other relatives, the sister will let them know.

"...Estelle, I can't imagine that you're in any danger. If it was Margie's ex-husband, why would he want to harm you? If Margie was somehow mixed up in illegal drugs...Yes, I think it's preposterous too. But if it really was *El Chupacabra* why would that have anything to do with you?

"...I'm upset and sick about it too. Even though I only talked to her at any length twice, because Sy thought so highly of her I know Margie was a good person. And whatever she was, she didn't deserve to die like that.

"Let me make a suggestion: If you're worried...Yes, I suppose you have a right to be, go stay with one of your daughters for a few days. I'm sure this will be cleared up that quickly.

"...Oh yes. The car. It...I'm sorry, Estelle. I meant to call you last night but something came up." Elaine elbowed Josh in the ribs and rolled her eyes.

"No, nothing to do with the car or the estate. My experts...Louis Prejean and his nephew...Louis is a long-time, very dear friend who's been in the automotive service business for over twenty years—and his nephew is an expert in automotive electronics—say that the electric wire leading from the collision sensor in the bumper to the control box under the center console that actually deploys the airbag became detached. The police are still investigating the cause, so we won't know anything for a while. The detective said she'd get her technicians out there as soon...it's off West Commerce, just east of Hampton Road...as soon as she can.

"...Estelle, there's no reason for you to go out there. They won't let you near the car without the detective being with you and she's pretty busy right now. She's been assigned Margie's case as well as Sy's and she's also helping with the *El Chupacabra* investigation...No, Sy's and Margie's cases are very important to her; she made that very clear to me last night, and I believe her....Yes, I think she knows what she's doing. She's ex-military and has been in law enforcement for sixteen years.

"By the way, I got into the other safe-deposit box. All that's in it is some of Sy's client files that...No I have no idea why he kept client files in a safe-deposit box at the bank. I'm going to look at them and try to figure that out. If I can't, I'll get some help. But there's nothing personal in there...Estelle, the box is empty now. I've got the files with me so...No, I can't let you see them. Sy couldn't let you see them and as Sy's executor I'm bound by the same confidentiality rules as he was.

"Okay, Estelle. Try not to worry. If you go to one of your daughters let me know. I'll let you know what's going on as soon as I know anything. 'Bye."

"'Something came up.' Josh Loeb, you are awful."

Josh handed the phone back to Elaine and rolled over next to her. "Well, it did, and it might just be happening again. Now that we're both awake..."

Chapter Thirteen

"Good afternoon, sleepy-head. You must have been up pretty late."

Josh glanced at his watch. "I guess five after twelve does make it afternoon. It was after three o'clock before I finally got to bed and a late-night visit to the morgue is not very conducive to falling asleep. Then Estelle called before seven; she saw the picture in the paper so I had to spend half an hour scraping her off the ceiling. She's afraid *El Chupacabra* will be after her next."

"Do you…"

"Alicia, *El Chupacabra* isn't after Estelle."

"That is kind of silly, isn't it?"

"Well, Estelle didn't think it's silly; so I suggested that she go stay with one of her daughters for a few days. Maybe that'll at least buy me some time to figure out what to do about Sy's little dalliance with the topless...excuse me...exotic dancer."

"Did you tell Detective Turner about the 'dalliance' as you call it?"

"What should I call it?"

"Why not call it what it is…was: He was cheating on his wife with a woman…I assume that at least she's over twenty-one, who makes money wiggling her naked tits and ass at a room full of strange men. If my Leo set foot in one of those places and I found out, if he's lucky, he'd be sleeping in his equipment trailer for a year, maybe longer."

"I take your point: You don't think much of men who habituate titty bars or men who run around on their wives. I shouldn't have snapped at you. I apologize. This whole mess has got me in a really lousy mood, but I shouldn't have taken it out on you."

"And I should not have snarled back; I'm sorry too. Okay? So back to my question: Did you tell the detective?"

"No, and unless there's a connection to Sy's death, I don't intend to. If I do tell her the first thing she'll do is question Estelle: 'When did you learn your husband was having an affair? Made you pretty mad, didn't it? You followed him to Crystal's Palace and tampered with the airbag system. Then you waited until he left, followed him and then ran him off the road. Can you prove where you were between six p.m. and midnight the night your husband was murdered, Mrs. Blonstein? At home? Alone? That doesn't look good for you, Mrs. Blonstein. May we examine your vehicle, Mrs. Blonstein? You have a right to refuse, but we'll just get a search warrant.

"'Or did you just hire someone to do it for you? How much did you pay him? You know we can subpoena your bank records and we'll find out anyway. You need to get out ahead of this, Mrs. Blonstein. Tell us who you hired and maybe we can work with the DA on a plea bargain. You know that murder-for-hire is a capital offense, don't you? The punishment is either life without parole or the death penalty. And I'm sure you know that women do get executed in Texas.

"'How much life insurance did your husband have, Mrs. Blonstein? You're now a rich widow, aren't you? Do you play tennis, Mrs. Blonstein? Golf? Your hair looks really nice, Mrs. Blonstein. Is it your hairdresser?

"'Did Marjorie Morrison find out what you'd done? Did you have her killed too? That one will get you the needle for sure. Give it up as to your husband's murder and maybe we can cut you some slack on Marjorie Morrison. Suppose the guy you hired found out that Ms. Morrison knew too much so he did her on his own? That works for us; how about you?'"

"Josh, stop! You've almost got me believing it. Do you..."

"No. There's no way Estelle had anything to do with Sy's death. I'm just thinking out loud about what would happen if I told Alana...Detective Turner...about 'Jasmine' and Crystal's Palace. Why put Estelle through that if I don't have to."

"Alana? I thought it was 'Lana.' Sounds like you and she are now BFF."

"It's a long story. I wouldn't necessarily say 'BFF,' but at least she sort of trusts me for the moment. I didn't give her much of a choice. Did you find anything on Marjorie's divorce?"

"I did, and you're very welcome. I went to the District Clerk's online records. They're kept in numerical order by year. Do you have any idea how many family law cases are filed in

Dallas County every year? Tens of thousands. No wonder family-law lawyers make big bucks."

"I used to handle some 'domestic relations' work—that's what it was called back then—before you came into my life. Trust me, Alicia, the brain damage isn't worth the extra bucks. I take it you were successful?"

"I searched the family law data base under 'In the Matter of the Marriage of Marjorie Morrison and what's-his-name.' I started with eleven years ago and found nothing. Then I went to ten years ago; still *nada*. I was going to try nine years then I figured she said ten years ago, so I'll focus on ten years ago. I started with the first filing in January and kept scrolling through each day's filings looking for any case with the name 'Marjorie' in the caption. It's a good thing 'Marjorie' is not that common a name. If it was 'Mary' or 'Maria,' I'd still be looking. Finally, in mid-March, I found it. 'Morrison' is her maiden name. The case was filed under her married name: 'In the matter of the Marriage of Marjorie M. Carver and Orville Karl—"Karl" spelled with a "*K*"—Carver.' Apparently she asked to have her maiden name restored in the divorce petition or had it changed later."

"O.K., carve her?"

"Not funny, Josh."

"Objection sustained. I withdraw the comment, Your Honor. Did you get a copy of the pleadings so I can give Detective Turner an address or driver's license number?"

"No, the files that old aren't stored electronically. You have to order copies made in the Clerk's office. As soon as I had a case number I called a courier service and put in a rush order. They should be here pretty soon with the file, depending on how far in the weeds the Clerk's office is.

"In the meantime, I did an Internet search on Orville Karl Carver and found some stuff that ought to get Detective Turner breathing hard. Seems old Orville has a bit of a drinking problem."

"Maybe Margie caught it from him, or vice versa."

"Well, I don't know about her, but Orville had one DWI conviction and a couple of earlier public intoxication convictions—probably pleaded down from DWIs—to go along with a misdemeanor assault conviction. All the cases were in Dallas. He also had a family violence charge in Dallas County, but it got dismissed. Probably Ms. Morrison declined to testify. I understand that happens a lot."

"Then Detective Turner will be able to find him in the DPD data base. Would you give her a call and let her know the good news?"

"Isn't she your new best friend?"

"Yeah, but I don't want to put a strain on our brand-new friendship by dissembling about Sy. I managed to duck the discussion last night. If she asks for me, tell her I'm with a client."

"Josh, you know I don't..."

"Well, it's almost true. The client is Joshua Loeb, Independent Executor of the Estate of Seymour M. Blonstein, Deceased. I'm going to be looking at the files I retrieved yesterday from the second safe-deposit box."

"Well, you need to read them quickly; Dr. Blubberoff will be here at three. I'm sorry; I couldn't put him off any longer. Are you going to fire me?"

Chapter Fourteen

The story of Crystal's Palace, as gleaned from Sy Blonstein's file, was not a happy one. The file was divided into two parts: the papers filed in court and Sy's working file which included his work-papers, some forms and documents and a correspondence sub-file. In order to get the broad picture first, Josh started with the court papers.

In their petition initiating the lawsuit, the investor-plaintiffs alleged that the promoter of the enterprise, the defendant Andy Biggers, had persuaded nearly thirty friends and friends-of-friends to invest between ten and twenty-five thousand dollars each in what he promised them would be a "high-class, sophisticated venue where the luminaries of the

Dallas business, entertainment and professional sports worlds would gather nightly."

According to the plaintiffs' petition, Crystal's Palace was to take over the lease of a failing gentlemen's club that had defaulted in the payment of rent and as a result was about to be evicted by the landlord. In addition to promises of a quick payback of their investment and substantial returns for the foreseeable future, each investor was offered a seat on the management committee responsible for hiring new dancers and waitresses. They also received a special membership card that waived the normal cover charge and provided access, at no additional charge, on a space-available basis, to the VIP room where the investor would be able to mix and mingle with Dallas's most well-known celebrities.

Biggers had, the plaintiffs conceded, delivered somewhat on the non-cash perks: the lap-dance interviews of prospective dancers being the most popular. However, no one admitted to having mixed or mingled with any celebrities, unless a couple of guys who'd spent about five minutes on the Cowboys' practice squad, a notorious drug-dealer and a high-end pimp counted as "celebrities."

Biggers had, according to Sy's report, actually spent some of the investors' funds on restocking the totally-depleted liquor inventory. He had a new sound system installed and had upgraded the stage lighting. He had also replaced the decrepit banquette seating areas. And a substantial amount was spent fixing a malodorous sewer leak in the dancers' dressing room. But after these documented expenditures, amounting to a bit under one hundred thousand dollars, the financial records of where the investors' capital had gone became less than transparent.

Indeed, according to Sy's formal report to the court, there were some possibly legitimate legal fees and other expenses involved in obtaining the landlord's agreement to reinstate the lease and in obtaining new cabaret and liquor licenses and the payment bonds that go with them. However these were negligible compared to the high five-figure "consultant" and "expeditor" fees for which Sy was able to find invoices which stated only that they were "for services rendered." However, according to Sy's report, he had been unable to locate even a scintilla of evidence of any work-product.

Sy's report related that he'd been unable to obtain any information about the companies that received the unexplained fees. Sy had contacted the Texas Secretary of State's office and obtained copies of the certificates of formation for the two limited-liability companies that had received the fees. These were off-the-shelf, fill-in-the-blanks forms, copies of which were included in the appendix to Sy's report. The only useful information in the certificates was the name of the sole organizer: the same attorney who had prepared the documentation for the private securities-offering memorandum used to raise the funds from the investors. Not surprisingly, that attorney also represented Biggers in the litigation.

A hearing transcript showed that the attorney had "respectfully declined," on the basis of attorney-client privilege, to identify the owners of the companies. The judge had initially bought the argument but then reversed himself when the plaintiffs' lawyer produced case-law holding that the identity of an attorney's client is not privileged and that even if it was, the crime-fraud exception overrode the privilege.

Once she disclosed that Andy Biggers was the sole owner of the companies and was the "consultant" and the "expeditor," Biggers was toast. The judge immediately entered a temporary restraining order, later converted to a temporary injunction, prohibiting Biggers from using Crystal's Palace funds for any personal expenses, including payment of his attorney's fees. At the investors' request, a temporary manager was hired to replace Biggers with directions to report all revenues and expenses to Sy on a daily basis.

Once the money spigot was turned off, the attorney closed her faux-crocodile briefcase and did not appear again except for the hearing on her motion to withdraw as counsel for Biggers. After that hearing, Biggers had talked the judge into a couple of short continuances to allow him to obtain new counsel. But with his access to the cash register cut off and Sy watching the money, Biggers had no luck in finding a new lawyer. He had tried representing himself, demonstrating, in Josh's opinion, a better-than-average "guardhouse" lawyer's knowledge of law and procedure. On reading them, Josh thought that some of Biggers's motions might actually have had some merit.

But despite Biggers's most creative efforts, ultimately the judge granted the plaintiffs all the relief they had requested and in his bench ruling suggested that the plaintiffs refer the matter to the district attorney for such action as that official might see fit to take against Mr. Biggers.

Having gotten the big picture, Josh decided to take a short break before his meeting with Harmon Polikoff. Josh lay down on the couch in his office and promptly fell asleep.

"Josh...Josh, rise and shine." Alicia stood in the doorway of Josh's office. "Dr. Blub...Dr. Polikoff is here. I reserved Conference Room Four. Do you want to use it or meet in your office?"

Josh blinked a couple times and sat up. "Conference room's probably best. If we're in the conference room I can always get up and leave when I've had enough. Would you call Office Services and have them bring a carafe of coffee?"

"Already done. Do you want me to sit in and take notes?"

"What I really want is for you to meet with him instead of me. You're the one who made the appointment. But I guess I have to be the lucky one. Anyway, I owe you for finding Orville." Josh made it to his feet, straightened his tie and put on his suit jacket. "Might as well have done with it. Do you mind escorting him to the conference room? I'm going to hit the men's room then I'll be right there. Conference Room Four?"

"Josh, before you start your meeting, there's a few other things: First, you had a call from Marisol Obregon-Robertson..."

"The City Councilwoman?"

"I presume so. How many 'Marisol Obregon-Robertsons' are there in Dallas? However, she didn't say that she was calling on City business."

"Didn't she have an op-ed piece in the paper the other day? She was on her soapbox complaining that the chief of police wasn't doing enough to apprehend *El Chupacabra.*'But mostly, if I remember rightly, she blasted the police for devoting too many resources to petty crimes in North Dallas and not enough resources to drug crimes in her district. According to her, that's why vigilantes like *El Chupacabra* have to take the law into their own hands."

"A lot of people agree with her."

"What does she want? Wait, wait, don't tell me: money. What do politicians ever want besides money? Why pick on me? I'm not even in her district. Isn't she term-limited anyway? Or is she planning to run for something else?"

"Actually, she didn't say anything about money or running for office. She's calling about the Blonstein Estate. She said she represents a client of Mr. Blonstein's."

"Now that you mention it, I remember that in addition to being a political force-of-nature she also practices law. Doesn't she have an office somewhere in West Dallas?"

"I've seen several of her billboards in Oak Cliff and West Dallas. I wonder if she uses the same ad agency as Dr. Blubberoff?"

"She say whether her client's fixing to sue the estate for malpractice?"

"She didn't say what it's about. Do you want me to call and ask?"

"No, let's give her the benefit of a doubt. I'll call her back when I'm done with Dr. Polikoff, assuming that time arrives before Thanksgiving. In the meantime, why don't you check her website and also see if anyone here has ever dealt with her and lived to tell about it.

"Alicia, do you remember "The Old Man and the Sea" by Ernest Hemingway? I feel like that old fisherman...I can't remember his name off the top of my head."

"Santiago."

"Right, 'Santiago.' Anyway, he catches this giant marlin, but it's too big to fit in his boat. So he lashes it to the gunwale. But by the time he gets it back to port, the sharks have eaten it down to the skeleton. Well, the only difference between me and that old fisherman is that I didn't go fishing for Sy

Blonstein's estate; it just sort of jumped in my boat. What worries me is that it's about to knock me out of the boat and leave me to deal with the sharks on my own. What other sharks do you have swimming around?"

"SueEllen Masters called. She got the office lock changed and has a new card for you. She told me that several clients of Sy's have come by her office. Some had heard about Margie on TV or on the radio and others had not. Either way, they told her they need to get their files. She told them she couldn't open the office and that they needed to contact you. She gave them your phone number."

"That's what I get for giving people my card."

"I've had eight calls so far, five of them from Mr. Blonstein's clients. I said we're working as fast as we can to get things sorted out and that we'd get back to them as soon as possible. All five were pretty nice about it, but they also made it clear: They want their files."

"Who were the other three?"

Alicia consulted her steno pad: "A Mr. Angus Oakley; a Dr. Rajitraman Singh; and a Mr. Victor Ortega. The first two each said they were calling about 'Crystal's Palace' but wouldn't tell me any more than that.

"Victor Ortega said he was returning a call from Mr. Blonstein from last Tuesday. His English isn't the best so we spoke in Spanish. He told me he's been out of town and just got back on Sunday. He said that Mr. Blonstein had called him to ask a question having to do with some invoices for work he did for one of Mr. Blonstein's clients. He wouldn't tell me which client. He said that Mr. Blonstein asked him to send him the original invoices which he did. He wants to know whether we still need the invoices or can he have them back. Apparently he needs them rather badly. He wouldn't say why. He was almost pleading with me to give them back. He even went to Mr. Blonstein's office to pick them up. Apparently SueEllen Masters put a sign on the door directing people to her office. She's the one who gave him your name and phone number. They all want you to call as soon as possible."

"I'll be sure and thank SueEllen."

"I think it was pretty nice of her to do it. It's what I would have done."

"I suppose you're right, as always. In the meantime, what else have you got?"

"Ms. Masters also said that she had to change the access card for the tenant parking and lobby entrances. She sort of hinted that the estate might want to consider paying for that. She said that you could pick up your cards at her office during business hours or," Alicia paused and gave Josh a look that could just as easily have come from Elaine, "she said she usually goes to Houston's after work for a glass of wine and you could meet her there."

"I think I'll take a pass on Houston's and pick up the cards at her office tomorrow. I need to figure out how I'm going to replace Margie. I don't want to use one of those accounting temp agencies, but I don't know what else to do."

"Good decision, about Houston's, Josh. Last thing: Ms. Masters said that she spoke with the security company and they have everything ready for you. She gave me the contact information. Maybe you could meet her there. With a bunch of armed guards around, you ought to be fairly safe."

"I'll think about it. In the meantime, you might as well bring in the clown."

Chapter Fifteen

Harmon Polikoff was on his cell phone when Josh joined him in the conference room. By force of habit, Harmon had shoe-horned his pear-shaped body into the power seat, the one at the head of the table. To further enhance his preeminence, he was still dressed in his surgical scrubs. Josh thought briefly about taking the seat at the other end of the table, but after pouring himself a cup of coffee he took the first side chair to Harmon's left and waited patiently for Harmon to conclude his conversation. From what Harmon was saying, he must have been haranguing one of his lawyers. Without a "goodbye" Harmon pressed the red "end" bar and placed the phone on the table next to a file-folder he had brought with him.

"Fucking moron! Four hundred bucks an hour I pay this *schmuck* and all he can tell me is that I don't have a case for breaking my lease.

"Josh, how are you?" Harmon held out a pudgy hand for Josh to shake. "*Oy!* Poor Sy. Such a terrible *shande*. And just when I made a new man of him. All that money gone to waste."

"Did Sy still owe you money from the surgery? Is that why you're here?"

"No, no. I don't lay a hand on a gastric sleeve patient without getting all of my fee up front. I'm telling you, Josh, this gastric sleeve thing is like owning your own ATM with no credit limit and no bill to pay every month. Let the patient make the claim to his insurance company; I don't have to fool with those insurance *mamsers* for even a minute. The patient wants to make a claim, all I do is write 'see attached' in my part of the form, attach a standard narrative that I keep in a drawer in my desk, sign it and send it in. That's it. If the insurance company decides to pay, they send the money to the patient. If they don't pay, I tell the patient 'go hire a lawyer.' I can steer them to you if you like. I was even able to get rid of one employee because there's less paperwork to deal with. That alone saves me sixty, seventy-five *K* a year."

"No thanks, Harmon, I don't handle that kind of case. I gather that Sy was your accountant?" Josh asked, wondering how a straight-arrow accountant like Sy could put up with a client like Harmon Polikoff.

"For over fifteen years. I can't tell you how many times Sy saved my ass with the IRS and in my first two divorces. Absolutely the best, that Sy."

"Have you found a new accountant already? And you need to get your files from Sy's office? Harmon, if you need them immediately, that's going to be a problem. I assume you know about Margie, Sy's assistant?

Harmon gave Josh a puzzled look. "Josh, be serious. You think I rescheduled a surgery and two post-surgery follow-up appointments to come down here to pick up my files? It was awful, what happened to Margie. I wouldn't wish what happened to her on anyone...well, maybe to my ex-wives or my current one." Harmon held up his hands in a protestation of innocence. "Just kidding, Josh, just kidding.

"But Sy's death and now Margie's...it's like my files have fallen into a black hole. The IRS wants something? Toni's lawyer wants something? 'Fine; go see Josh Loeb. Knock yourself out. My files are tied up in my late accountant's estate and I don't know when they'll be released.' Believe me, Josh, as far as I'm concerned, take all the time with the files that you want, and then some."

As Josh was trying to decide between calling security to forcibly remove Harmon from the building or simply bludgeoning him to death with the coffee carafe, Harmon finally got to the reason for having so inconvenienced himself by coming to Josh's office. "Josh, I'm here about the condo. I was going to talk to you about it Sunday night but you wandered off. You do know about the condo, don't you?"

"I'm not wandering off now, Harmon, so why don't you tell me about it?"

"It's all right here, Josh." Harmon pushed the file folder toward Josh. "Sy told me he wanted to buy a condo, but he didn't want it in his name. I assumed that maybe he was going to divorce Estelle, or more likely, he was afraid she was going to divorce him. He asked me to do it a few months ago as a favor. He did a few favors for me when I was going through my divorces, so I figure I owe him at least one in return.

"He brought it up at his post-surgery follow-up appointment. I think the reason he wanted the surgery is that he knew he was going to be back in circulation and wanted to look his best. I don't ask a patient why he or she wants the procedure. If it's anywhere close to being medically justified and I can do it safely, and if they can pay, I tell them 'hop up on the table and let's get going.'"

"When did you buy it?"

"When he first brought it up, he'd already found the unit. I signed the contract and closed on the deal at the same time. That was in late August.

"Sy made the down-payment on the condo and he's paid the mortgage payments for the last two months and owners' association monthly assessments for the last three months. That's all the payments that have come due. The deal was—or I should say 'is'—that he also pays the property taxes, the insurance and the homeowners' association assessments. The insurance is paid through December and the property taxes aren't due until the end of December. The deed is in the name of 'HP Investments, LLC.' I'm the sole owner of HP Investments, LLC and I personally guaranteed payment of the mortgage.

"Sy told me that because the unit is rental property, I would get a tax deduction for depreciation and that the income and out-of- pocket expenses would be a wash for tax purposes."

"What was Sy supposed to get out of the deal?"

"I guess he was planning on living there if he moved out or if Estelle threw him out. And then, after his divorce was final, I would transfer ownership of HP Investments to him. That way, since there's no new deed to the property to be recorded, the mortgage company would never know there'd been a change of ownership."

"Is anyone living there now?"

"Yeah, some couple: a man and a woman. I've never met them, or for that matter, ever seen the unit. The reason I know there are tenants is that I've gotten four notices from the condo management company claiming that neighbors have complained about loud, late-night parties and lots of liquor bottles in the trash. One time a party guest peed in the elevator. So I had to write a check for the cost of recarpeting the elevator. Sy owes me three hundred bucks, by the way. The last notice I got was almost a week ago, the day Sy died. I called him...that was Thursday, wasn't it? He said okay, he'd take care of it."

"Do you know the tenants' names or anything about them? Do they have a lease?"

"I don't know a thing about them. Sy handled all of that. If there's lease, it would be in the file. Josh, neither Sy nor I figured on him getting himself killed in a car-wreck. I want out of this deal. I'm just about to reach a settlement with Toni. Her divorce lawyer's a real asshole. She finds out about the condo, it'll be a big problem for me and for Sy's estate.

"Toni's no prize either, by the way. What I'm paying her every month in temporary alimony you wouldn't believe. But as much as it is, it's still less than the bills she was running up every month just at Neiman-Marcus. She was great in bed before we were married, but after that, nothing but 'I've got a headache' nearly every goddamn night. I would have sent her to a neurologist, but I was afraid he'd tell me she was anencephalic. Great tits and an ass like a college-freshman cheerleader, but I can find those at any upscale bar in Dallas any night of the week. Takes about thirty minutes, maybe forty-five on a slow night. Come with me some time, you'll see what I'm talking about."

"Just out of curiosity when you go to these bars do you wear scrubs?"

"Of course. They work wonders. If you want to come with me, I'll loan you a set."

"Thanks, Harmon, but I don't think Elaine would be very happy about me going bar-hopping with you."

"I'll even teach you my pickup line."

"Again, Harmon, thanks, but no thanks."

"Josh, it's so easy. I see a woman that looks worth the effort, I walk up to her and I ask her two questions. Takes less than a minute."

Josh's patience was exhausted, but he decided that if he was ever going to get Harmon back to the point of the meeting without pissing him off, he had no choice but to listen to his pickup routine. "Okay, Harmon, I know I'm going to regret it, but what are the questions?"

"I walk up to her and stand there for a few seconds giving her a kind of quizzical look. Then I introduce myself, 'Hi, I'm Harmon. Can I ask you a question?' Now any good-looking woman, she's heard that question a million times before and she knows the only way to get rid of me is to say, 'Okay, ask me one question.' So I ask her the second question."

Despite himself, Josh asked, "What's the second question?"

"When's the last time you has a man's tongue in your vagina?"

"And then she punches you out, knees you in the nuts, or both?"

"Happens sometimes. When it does, I just hobble on down the road. Sometimes she throws a drink in my face. When that happens, I offer to buy her a replacement and we take it from there. If she says 'never' or she can't remember the last time or says it was last week, then I know right away where we're headed."

"Okay, Harmon, I'm impressed. Now can we get back to the matter that brought you here? What do you want to do about the condo?"

"I want you to buy it from me; not you personally, but in Sy's estate. After all, it does belong to him."

Josh kept his poker face on despite his growing panic. "Why don't you just let Toni's lawyer have it? That would solve your problem and mine. I don't think Estelle needs to know that Sy was contemplating a divorce when he died, do you?"

"Giving it to Toni is not an option, Josh. If all of a sudden I tell my lawyer, 'Oh by the way, there's this condo that I own; why don't we offer it to Toni?' My lawyer calls up Toni's lawyer and says, 'Guess what?' And Toni's lawyer, that shyster-cunt, says, 'Okay, we'll take the condo…and your client will keep making the payments… and maybe we better reopen discovery so we can find out what other assets your client forgot to tell us about.' Believe me, Josh, I can't let that happen."

"Great, Harmon. You and I are in a stand-off. You don't want the damn thing and neither do I." Josh had been thumbing through the file. He closed it and leaned close to Harmon's face. "Harmon, there's no legal way for you to make me buy it; there's not a single piece of paper in the file with Sy's name on it. So what's 'Plan B?' What do you propose that we do?"

Harmon did not like Josh invading his space. He rolled his caster-base chair back a foot. "How...how about a fire? I know a guy who for a price—I'll split it with you— can make people disappear, can start a fire..."

Josh slammed his fist down on the closed file folder. "No way, Harmon. No fire. I don't represent you, so unless you tell me—right now—you're just kidding, I'm kicking you out of here and calling the cops. And if Estelle has to find out and if Toni and her lawyer have to find out, so be it."

"Josh, you shouldn't take me seriously. Ha! Ha! Of course I was just kidding. Forget I even said it." Harmon pushed himself back another foot and worked his face into a smile trying to make himself look innocent and contrite at the same time. "Well, I...I...I guess the first thing is I've got to get rid of the tenants. I'm going to go by there and have a chat with them. Tell them Sy's not paying the rent anymore. So unless they have a lease and want to start paying rent, they need to get out, pronto."

"Harmon, I can guess who these people are, or at least who one of them is. Take my word for it: On the list of all-time bad ideas, you paying the tenants a visit ranks right up there with buying your wife a giant-size jar of luxury wrinkle cream for her birthday."

"I don't know what you mean, Josh ...about the wrinkle cream. I try to get rid of my wives before they need wrinkle cream. But okay, either I go or you can go. If you want, tell 'em you're the lawyer for HP Investments."

"Fair enough. Leave the file with me. Once we get rid of the tenants, we can figure out what to do with the unit. In the meantime, can you handle the mortgage payments, the monthly assessments and other expenses, at least until I get some cash in the estate? I'll also get you reimbursed for the carpet. It shouldn't be more than a month or two."

"I guess I'll have to. I'll just have to make sure that the dragon lady—Toni's lawyer—doesn't find out." Harmon took a Montblanc pen out of his pocket and wrote a phone number on the inside of the file folder. Here's my cell number; stay in touch. Josh, are you sure you don't want to become my lawyer?"

"Yes, Harmon, I'm sure. Don't call me; I'll call you."

Chapter Sixteen

After Polikoff left, Josh stayed in the conference room. At least for the time being, Estelle could keep her happy memories intact. As he went page-by-page through the file Polikoff had left with him, he drank another cup of coffee fervently wishing it were scotch. His guess that there was nothing in the file to link Sy to the condo proved to be correct. He was about to get another cup of coffee when Alicia came in.

"How was your meeting?"

"It was a good reminder of why I don't like representing clients whose occupation begin with the letter *P*: pilots, preachers...and physicians. It's a good thing he didn't bring a scalpel with him. If I had gotten hold of it I would have either slit his throat or my wrists."

"That bad?"

"Sit and I'll tell you about it." Josh gave her a recap of the conversation, leaving out Harmon's *modus operandi* for emulating Casanova. "Any ideas about what I should do?"

"Josh, ideas are what you get paid the big bucks for. But if I were you, I'd tell Dr. Blubberoff to enjoy his condo, tenants and all."

"I'm inclined to agree with you, but for once—and probably only once—Harmon Polikoff didn't design the bus you want me to throw him under. As much as I'd like to throw him under that bus, I don't feel right about doing it. Sy made this mess and now it's up to me to figure a way out of it.

"Besides, if I tell him to take a hike, what's to stop him from hiring some jake-leg lawyer to sue me as executor of Sy's estate, even though he can't win. Harmon's got some kind of personality disorder, probably he's a sociopath. He loves litigation, probably as much as he loves poking holes in people with a scalpel. I don't think he cares about winning; he loves the game. If he files suit, I can't keep Estelle from finding out. So it's a lose-lose situation for me no matter what the court does."

"Well, you did buy some time. You'll figure something out; you always do. And speaking of time, I need to leave. My son's class is having a Thanksgiving pageant tonight at seven at the school. I promised to help set up and I need to be sure he doesn't forget half his costume. He's the Indian chief.

"I made an appointment for you with Dal-Worth Security tomorrow morning at ten o'clock. I put the address and a Google Map printout on your desk along with the contact information and phone number.

"I also spoke with Ms. Obregon-Robertson. She called again. She asked if she could see you here tomorrow at one forty-five. She has a City Council committee meeting in the morning, so she'll be downtown anyway. You don't have anything on the calendar and I figured you'd be back from Dal-Worth Security by then.

"I printed out her web page and I talked with the legal assistant who works for Ms. Rogers—the new real estate lawyer downstairs. She responded to my email asking if anyone knew Marisol Obregon-Robertson."

"Do you have time to tell me about her?"

"Just a minute or two. You can read her web page for the 'official' version. I'll just give you the good stuff. She was born in the U.S., but her parents are probably illegals. Grew up poor in Grand Prairie. Won a full-ride scholarship to U.T. Arlington; got another full-ride to Texas Tech Law School. Made law review; was in Phi Delta Phi. Passed the bar; clerked for a federal judge in San Antonio her first year out of law school.

"Got hired by one of the big Houston firms to work in their Dallas office. That's where Ms. Rogers's assistant got to know about her."

"Know 'about' her?"

"She wasn't too friendly with any of the firm's support personnel. She had other more productive ways to spend her time. If you haven't seen her on TV, she's a real hottie. The picture of her on her billboards doesn't do her justice. Apparently every male lawyer in the firm—single or married—was in love with her, and she probably went to bed with every one of them.

"She did end up marrying a junior partner—Robertson—whose family has barrels of oil money. They had one child. The marriage ended when she got caught screwing one of the senior partners on the couch in the partner's office during lunchtime. The senior partner, whose annual billings were declining anyway, decided to take early retirement. Ms. Obregon-Robertson gave up the kid but got a fat divorce settlement to go along with the settlement she got from the law firm. She used the money to open her own firm: 'Marisol Obregon-Robertson & Associates.' *'Abogada de Inmigración y Accidentes.'* She has a couple of offices: one on West Illinois in Oak Cliff and one on Fort Worth Avenue in West Dallas. The web page doesn't list any other lawyers working for her even though her firm name says 'and Associates.' That enough? I really do need to get going."

"If all of that gets made public, especially the part about giving up her child, isn't that going to kill her chances of getting elected to something else?"

"Probably not. A couple of the politically-powerful Hispanic families are big supporters of hers. If it does get out— and I can't imagine that it won't—she'll just say she was raped, but didn't want to sully the good name of her law firm and hurt all the other fine people who work there by going to the police. She'll blink away a tear or two and add that she was also afraid that she wouldn't be believed. She'll say that she gave up her child because she didn't have the resources to go up against her husband's family and all its money. And even though her husband's family hated her from the beginning, she wants what's best for her daughter.

"I understand Robertson's already remarried to an Anglo girl from a 'proper' Highland Park family."

"Someday all that Park Cities inbreeding is going to catch up with them."

"A lot of people who don't have the good fortune to live in the bubble would say that it already has."

"They may be right. In any case, great job Alicia, as always. You should consider a career as a political consultant; you've got a knack for it."

"I would, but *a,* I doubt that I'd like the people I'd have to work with very much, and *b,* what would you do without me?"

"That is something I don't want to even think about. I know the pageant will be great. Take some pictures and tell Leo 'hi.' I'll see you when I see you. I'm out of here too. I want to get home and maybe take a nap before dinner."

Chapter Seventeen

Elaine spooned about ten milligrams of salsa onto a tortilla chip and delicately took a bite. "Harmon Polikoff hasn't called the house all day. Did you do something with or to him?"

Josh was almost through with his first *Carta Blanca* and thinking about ordering a second. "I met with him this afternoon. Alicia got tired of him calling, so she made an appointment for him to come in."

"How was the meeting? Can you talk about it?"

"He..." The waiter appeared with Elaine's *chicken en molé* and Josh's *tacos de carne deshebrada*. Josh held up his empty beer bottle. *"Uno mas cerveza, por favor."*

"Si, Senor. Y uno más mojito por la Señora?"

Elaine still had half of her mojito left. "No, thank you; I'm good."

"Josh, do you really need two beers? Keep going the way you are and you may end up on Dr. Blubberoff's operating table."

Josh spooned what was left of the salsa onto his rice and refried beans. "Elaine, Harmon Polikoff is as crazy as a road lizard. There's no way I'd let him near me with a sharp instrument. He invited me to go on a *canus pudendum* expedition with him. Said he'd loan me a set of scrubs."

"And that's what was so urgent? Is that what he and Sy were doing? Chasing...you know what?"

"Sy may have gotten the idea from Harmon, but I think Sy was doing what he was doing—if in fact he was doing anything—on his own."

"So how was Harmon Polikoff involved?"

The waiter came with Josh's beer and Josh indicated that they could use a refill of the salsa bowl. "Harmon didn't come to see me about Sy fooling around. He and Sy had a real estate investment together. So now Harmon and I are partners, so to speak. He just wants to know what is going to happen to the investment."

Elaine cut off a bite of chicken and swirled it in the *molé* sauce. She chewed for a moment then she put down her knife and fork and folded her hands on the table. "What kind of real estate investment, Josh?"

"It's a condominium unit in one of those high-rises on Northwest Highway just east of Preston Road. What difference does it make?"

"In other words, it's a high-class..." Elaine leaned forward and lowered her voice to a barely-audible whisper, "...f-u-c-k pad, isn't it? Some place where they could take their whores—or 'girlfriends' if you prefer—for a little 'afternoon delight?'"

It took a minute or so for Josh to stop choking on the piece of taco he'd just forked in his mouth. "It's...it's...not a...a...what you just called it. By the way, where'd you pick up that quaint little term?"

"Do you think that all I read is Louise Penny? I'm all grown up, Josh. I assumed that you'd noticed. I read lots of stuff." Elaine drained her mojito and catching their waiter's eye held up her glass indicating she was ready for another. Is it or isn't it?"

"Elaine, my love, I have noticed that you're all grown up, and may I add that you've done so in a most delightful way."

"Josh, quit channeling Maurice Chevalier. I'm not Leslie Caron and it won't work to change the subject. If it isn't a...a...what I just said, what is it?"

"There are tenants living in it. For all I know, it could be just an investment. Maybe Harmon and Sy got a good deal on it so they bought it for an investment and not for any other reason. Sy did have at least one other real estate investment that he owned with other people."

"And of course Estelle knows all about it. Maybe she helped pick out the new carpet and drapes. Color schemes for the bedroom and kitchen?"

"I don't know whether Estelle knows about it. I haven't asked her."

"If she doesn't know, which I'm sure is the case, what are you going to do? Continue to own it with Harmon Polikoff? You going to take Sy's turns?"

"Elaine, in case you haven't noticed, I'm a happily-married man. Didn't we..."

"Josh, probably ninety-nine percent of men who cheat on their wives are 'happily-married.' That doesn't stop them from cheating; all it does is make them feel guilty about it afterwards...sometimes."

"Elaine, I'm hungry. Can we finish eating? Then I'll tell you everything I can...everything that's not privileged or work-product. But you've got to promise me one thing: Let me deal with Estelle. If I can fix the problem without her having to know, isn't that better than her knowing?

"Since you've managed to guess much of it, does the knowledge make you feel better? Elaine, I carry around a couple tons of other people's dirty laundry that I can't talk about. I take no pleasure in it; in fact it's a burden that I wish I didn't have. If I quit practicing law before I die, that burden will be one of the reasons."

Elaine held up her right hand, "Okay, I promise. My lips are sealed." For emphasis she drew her thumb and forefinger across her lips. "*El Chupacabra* couldn't drag it out of me."

After they finished their main courses they both ordered coffee and declined the waiter's seldom-heeded suggestion that they try the sopapillas or the flan. Elaine overrode Josh's request to the waiter that he leave the remaining chips and salsa. In between sips of coffee, Josh gave Elaine a more detailed version of his meeting with Harmon Polikoff concluding with the standoff over what to do.

"Okay, so you bought some time. What happens when the clock runs out?"

"If I'm lucky, Harmon's divorce will get finalized and I'll be able to talk him into keeping the unit."

"What about the tenants? From what Harmon told you, I doubt that the other unit-owners are going to put up with much more. Hadn't you better get rid of them?"

"That's exactly what I plan to do. The last thing I need is for the condo owners' association to sue Harmon for some violation of the condo bylaws or deed restrictions. If that balloon goes up he'll be screwed with his divorce settlement and justifiably pissed-off about it. He'll drag me into the suit just for fun."

"You said that Harmon told you he doesn't know anything about the tenants. Do you believe him? From his description, they sound like his kind of people."

"I think he's telling the truth. But I can't tell you why."

"Josh..."

"It's work-product privilege, Elaine. I really can't tell you anymore."

"Well, be careful, Josh. From what Harmon said, they're not likely to go quietly."

"I will. I promise."

"And what about Sy's files. If the burglars haven't found what they were looking for, are they going to come after you? I mean the fact that you're the executor of Sy's estate is a matter of public record. Doesn't that put you at risk?"

"The thought has been in the back of my mind ever since I saw Margie's picture on TV."

"Are you going to do something about it?"

"What should I do? Hire a bodyguard?"

"It might be a good idea, Josh. Do you want to end up like that Margie?"

"I'll think about it, Elaine. Can we change the subject? Since you mentioned it last night I've been thinking about the wine for Thanksgiving. Is a pinot noir okay? I'm thinking either Willamette Valley or California Central Coast."

"Sounds good to me."

"Are we having anybody for Thanksgiving besides kids, grandkids, and—lest I forget—the shrink? I need to know how many bottles to buy.

"Josh, if you embarrass Caroline…"

"Don't worry, I'll be my gracious, charming self."

"That's what I'm afraid of. I'm thinking about inviting Nate and Rose Mendelovitz. I saw Rose at a luncheon and she told me that she doesn't feel up to traveling and none of their kids can make it here. I hate the thought of them having Thanksgiving dinner in that dreary retirement home."

"Elaine, you're wonderful! I could kiss you. You've just solved a major problem."

"I did?"

"Yes you did. I've been wondering who I can get to go through Sy's files and help me get rid of them. Nate's the perfect guy. He's retired and has to use a walker to get around, but his mind's still as sharp as it ever was. In fact, Nate's one of the smartest people I know. In his day he was one of the best accountants in Dallas. I need to call him first thing tomorrow. Do you have their phone number?"

Chapter Eighteen

Dal-Worth Security was located in a tilt-wall, exposed-aggregate one-story building in what commercial real estate brokers would call a "Class B" office-warehouse area north of Royal Lane, just east of Denton Drive. The property was surrounded by a tall picket-type fence made of black tubular steel. There was a mechanical gate at the entrance to the parking lot and a gatehouse staffed by a young man in an immaculate khaki-tan uniform under a matching quilted nylon jacket with sewn-on badges over the left breast and on the left sleeve. There was an American flag sewn on the right sleeve. Under the open jacket Josh could see a dark-brown Sam Browne belt. The belt was evidently for decoration since the young man was unarmed. He wore his hair in a military-type brush-cut and appeared to be making progress in his recovery from what must have been a fairly severe case of teenage acne.

The gate was set about twenty feet back from the street so that those seeking admission would not have their vehicles halfway out in the street while their credentials were verified. Only then, if all was in order, would the gate be opened. The gate guard carried a clipboard as he approached Josh's car on the driver's side. "Good morning, Sir. How may I help you?"

Josh had lowered his window as the guard got within speaking distance. "I'm Joshua Loeb. I have a ten o'clock appointment with Jason Bragg."

The guard looked at his clipboard. "Yes, Sir. Major Bragg is expecting you. May I see a picture ID?"

Go along to get along, Josh thought as he dug out his driver's license and handed it through the window. "I assume this will suffice."

The guard held the driver's license up close to Josh's face to verify that the expressionless face in the photograph matched the unsmiling face framed by the car window. Then he turned the license over a couple of times examining it closely to be sure it wasn't a fake.

"You're good to go, Sir." He handed Josh's driver's license back. Then he reached inside his jacket and removed a remote control device clipped to the Sam Browne. He pressed the activate button and the gate started to slide open. "Visitor parking is to the left of the main entrance. Have a nice day, Sir."

"Thank you. Same to you." Josh thought about saluting, but settled for pressing the window up-down control switch.

The large parking area took up the front and one side of the building. Parked in the side-lot were several Chevrolet and Dodge four-door sedans sprouting radio antennas and painted dark green with "Dal-Worth Security" over stylized, star-shaped badges painted on the front doors. There were also two full-size General Motors SUVs with the same logo but done up in elaborate camo paint jobs. Taking up the remainder of the parking spaces were several civilian vehicles, including two full-dress Harleys. The lot in front of the building was filled with American-marque cars and SUVs. Definitely a patriotic outfit, Josh thought, as he eased into one of the two designated "Visitor" places that didn't have a handicap-parking sign.

Entrance to the building was through a sally port consisting of a pair of heavy glass doors tinted a dark grey-green. These led to a short, glassed-in vestibule and another set of glass doors. The outer doors were locked. An arrow on the right-hand door pointed to a buzzer. There was a security camera mounted on the wall to the right of the door. Josh pressed the buzzer and in a moment there was a click indicating the outer doors were open. Josh stepped through and as soon as the outer doors had clicked shut, the inner door-lock clicked and he was able to push it open.

The sally port opened to a lobby that must have been designed and furnished by the same people that did FBO waiting-rooms at general-aviation airports. All that was missing were overflowing ashtrays and some old, well-thumbed aviation magazines. The floor was linoleum tile, the walls painted an off-white. One wall was decorated with a reproduction of that ubiquitous poster depicting a living Vietnam vet resting his hand on the polished, black granite Vietnam Memorial in Washington looking into the spectral face of a fallen comrade who was looking back at him with his hand reaching out as though to touch the live veteran. The other wall held an American flag in the standard tri-corner presentation shape enclosed in an oak shadow box with a small brass plaque.

Seating along both walls consisted of five faux-leather, bucket-shaped seats mounted on a steel bar with brushed-aluminum legs at each end of the bar. Very likely, Josh mused, they had been purchased out of the Braniff International Airlines third and final bankruptcy in 1992.

At the back of the lobby there was a reception desk staffed by a young woman who was definitely not a relic from the Braniff bankruptcy. Indeed when Braniff went under for the third time, she was probably just starting pre-kindergarten. She wore a blazer in the same khaki-tan color as the gate-guard's uniform with a Dal-Worth Security logo patch on the left breast-pocket. Under the blazer she wore a crisp white blouse and gold and green striped tie tied in a perfect military knot. Her features and dark black hair marked her Vietnamese heritage. The bronze name-plate resting on the railing atop the front of the desk read "Kathryn An."

She flashed Josh a smile that made him feel like he really was welcome. "Good morning, Mr. Loeb. I hope you didn't have any trouble finding our office."

"Traffic on Royal Lane was pretty bad; probably because of the construction work on LBJ. But other than that, no problem. My assistant printed out a Google Map for me."

"I'll buzz Major Bragg's assistant and let her know you're here. If you like you can have a seat over there." She pointed to the row of boarding-area seats on her left. "I'm sure it'll only be a moment." She had pushed the microphone arm of her telephone head-set up in order to greet Josh. Now she lowered it and pressed a speed-dial number on the telephone console in front of her. "Pam, Mr. Loeb is here for his ten o'clock meeting with Major Bragg. Okay, great! I'll buzz him through."

"Mr. Loeb, Major Bragg is ready for you. If you'll just go through this door," she gestured toward a heavy-looking wooden door over her right shoulder, "Major Bragg's office is at the end of the hall on the left. His assistant, Pam, will meet you and show you in."

Once through the door Josh proceeded down a hallway that ran the length of the building. There were offices on each side, all with their doors closed and nothing to identify what went on inside. The only exception was a break room about midway down the hall on the right side. Josh stopped for a moment in the open doorway. The room was equipped like a kitchen: refrigerator, sink, dishwasher, a coffee-maker and a couple of microwaves on a counter. There was a school lunch-room folding table in the center of the room. Four men in Dal-Worth uniforms were seated at the table in metal folding-chairs drinking coffee and discussing the Cowboys. After pausing for a moment Josh continued down the hall.

Pam was a one-generation-removed version of Kathryn An. She wore an identical blazer above a matching pencil skirt ending several inches above her knees. In her dark-brown heels she was the same height as Josh. "Pamela An, Mr. Loeb." She held out her hand. "I'm Major Bragg's executive assistant. Would you like coffee?"

"Yes, thank you. Black, please."

"Follow me, Mr. Loeb. I'll bring your coffee in a moment." She led Josh into an outer office past an L-shaped secretary's desk and several filing cabinets. She stopped at a set of mahogany-stained doors and knocked lightly. Her knock was answered with a brusque "Come," which was followed by a soft click as the lock disengaged. Ms. An opened the door and ushered Josh into the inner office.

"Major" Bragg was seated in a high-back leather chair behind a large executive desk stained the same color as the doors and the floor-to-ceiling wall-paneling. The desk was clear except for a leather desk pad, a telephone console and a radio receiver-transmitter. A bronze plaque at the front of the desk read "Major Jason Bragg, U.S. Army (Ret.)"

One side wall was taken up with glass display cases. The one in the center contained an M-16 automatic rifle holding a thirty-round clip. To its left, another case displayed a large-scale, pale-green ordnance map with several red-ink circles. On the right of the M-16, the third case held a partially-scorched crimson over Columbia blue NVA battle flag with a gold star in the center and dark-brown stains in several places.

On the wall behind the desk, in addition to an American flag on a stand, there were a about dozen photographs of soldiers in battle dress standing at ease casually holding their weapons. These were interspersed with framed, official-looking citations and a glass case displaying a combat infantry badge, numerous campaign ribbons and several medals, including a Purple Heart and a Bronze Star. If the room was intended to impress, it succeeded.

"Major" Bragg was in his sixties, a somewhat smaller version of "Jack Reacher." He was an inch and change over six feet and carried his two-hundred pounds well. He wore the company-issue blazer, slacks, white shirt and gold and green striped tie. His hair was a mixture of grey and brown, worn in the military brush-cut that he'd probably worn since his Vietnam days. No John Kerry-style long hair for the "Major." As he walked around his desk Josh saw that his cordovan bluchers were perfectly spit-shined and that he walked with a pronounced limp.

"Jason Bragg, Mr. Loeb." He held out his hand. Josh responded, expecting his hand to be crushed by Bragg's grip.

He was pleasantly surprised that Bragg's handshake was only a perfunctory, gentlemanly squeeze.

"Thank you for your cooperation, Major Bragg. I very much appreciate it."

"Please call me 'Jason,' Mr. Loeb. Only my people call me "Major." It helps maintain the chain-of-command around here. And, as the song goes, "Old soldiers never die....""

"I suppose that means that you can take the soldier out of the army, but you can't take the army out of the soldier?"

"Never thought of it quite that way, but that pretty well sums me up. How about you, Mr. Loeb?"

"You mean military service? And by the way, please call me 'Josh.' I did my service in the reserves. I was in a JAG unit so I never got called up."

"As I'm sure you've noticed, I was in 'Nam. Did two tours, both in-country. That's how I got this hitch in my git-along. Second time around, I caught a feces-smeared punji stick in my calf. Medics kept gangrene from setting in, so I didn't lose the entire leg from the knee down. But I did catch a pretty good dose of septicemia. As a result, about all that's left of the calf is scar tissue, but all-in-all I was damn lucky.

"Let's have a seat on the sofa over there." He pointed to a sofa against the wall opposite the display cases. "Pamela's bringing coffee. She's already set up a laptop." He pointed to a computer sitting on a glass-topped wrought-iron coffee table in front of the sofa. "We transferred the footage from the security cameras to a CD and made another CD of the access-card log. We did that as soon as we got the request from our customer. I've looked at the security camera footage and I think there's some parts that may be of use to you as well as to the authorities. Pamela highlighted some of the access-card log entries for you.

"We'll have to wait for Pamela to crank up the computer. Computers and I don't get along all that well. I'm used to giving verbal orders and having them obeyed. I can't get used to pushing buttons and that's all the damn computers understand. I have to keep up with technology; if I didn't I'd be out of business. But I'm also smart enough to hire good people to operate it."

Josh took a seat on the couch and Bragg eased himself down next to him. "How long have you been in the security business? I'm sure I've seen your patrol cars around, and probably seen your people at the security desks in some office buildings. But I suppose I'm like most people: I don't pay attention to your business until I need you."

"I retired from the Army after twenty-five years and started Dal-Worth not long after I got out. We pretty much stick to the commercial side of the business: office buildings, medical facilities and special-event security. Mostly, we leave the residential side to others, although we do provide service to a couple of gated residential communities and a select-few private residences. We don't do any retail store security. Too much liability risk for us. My people detain a suspected shoplifter who turns out to be not a shoplifter and I've got an automatic false-imprisonment lawsuit the next day. Even when they're caught trying to walk out with half the store, they're gonna say my people roughed them up; used excessive force. And although we were just doing our job—and doing it right—I get sued just the same."

"What about insurance?"

"I carry a standard CGL policy, but it doesn't cover 'intentional injury' and that's what most of those claims are. Between the CGL policy, the vehicle policy, the worker's compensation insurance and the health insurance, I work three months out of the year for the insurance companies. And that's not to mention how many months I work for the IRS.

Before Bragg could get started on "Obama Care," Pamela arrived with the coffee service: a French-press containing an aromatic dark roast on a tray with two heavy ceramic mugs. No donuts or cookies. She did a perfect bunny-dip and deftly pushed down the coffee-pot plunger, poured the coffee and brought the computer to life. Replicating Kathryn's smile, she asked, "Is there anything else, Major Bragg?"

"Which button do I push to show the security camera footage?"

"Maybe I'd better do it, Sir." She turned the computer around toward herself and pressed a couple of keys. "Okay, all set." She turned the computer back toward the couch, came around the coffee table and sat down next to Josh. Josh had to remind himself to stare at the computer screen and not Ms. An's legs.

"What you're looking at is the camera at the gate to the reserved tenant parking. We reviewed all the footage from eighteen-hundred hours on Thursday until the following Monday at zero-eight hundred hours. The first of the footage starts at eighteen-hundred hours, twenty minutes on Thursday. You're seeing a gray or silver-colored Buick sedan exiting the tenant parking. We matched the license plate to the tenant, Seymour Blonstein.

"After that there was nothing out of the ordinary the rest of Thursday night, all day Friday, all day Saturday and all day

Sunday until twenty-one hundred hours, twenty minutes. The time between Thursday at eighteen hundred hours twenty minutes and Sunday at twenty-one hundred hours, twenty minutes has been edited out of the CD. If anyone needs it, we still have it archived on our back-up hard-drive.

"Jason, are there cameras in the garage except at the exit from the tenant parking area?"

"There's one at the main ingress-egress point and one on each floor covering the elevator door and the stairs."

"But none that show the actual parking areas?"

"Not at this facility. We recommend them, but it's the customer's call. Our customer, Alpha-Omega Properties—they're out of Atlanta, as I'm sure you know—decided that the cost-benefit analysis didn't work for them."

"The reason I ask is that someone may have tampered with the airbag system on Mr. Blonstein's car. It's possible that if there was tampering, it may have been done while he was at work that day."

"Josh, I'm willing to admit that anything's possible; look at what happened—twice—at the White House. But we've got a good system and we take care of business. We drive the garage twice a day. It takes a card to access the garage elevator above the main level and to access the stairwell from below the secure area. If someone did get in, they'd have to have been pretty quick, pretty lucky or both. If we spot any suspicious activity during a patrol, it gets written up and I personally review those daily. There weren't any reports last Thursday for this facility.

"Pamela, just to be sure let's check the footage from zero-eight hundred last Thursday.

"Yes, Sir. Do you want to see the footage from Sunday night now or wait until we've looked at the earlier footage?"

"I'd just as soon we go ahead with Sunday night, if that's okay with you all."

Pamela had paused the CD when Josh asked his question. She restarted it and the next image was a white pickup truck entering the main garage entrance. The digital clock in the lower right corner of the screen read "21:20:45." The truck was a crew-cab with four doors. There was a large accessory light bar on the roof and a formidable-looking black brush guard covering the grill and wrapping around the headlights. The license plate was partially obscured with mud and therefore unreadable. The truck had jacked-up suspension and oversize, off-road tires.

"Any idea what kind of truck it is?"

Bragg set down his coffee cup. "I make it to be a Ford 'F-250,' 'Super Duty;' two, three years old at most. Must be a couple thousand of 'em in the Metroplex area, maybe more. Without the license plate it's gonna be next to impossible to trace."

The truck backed into a space closest to the short flight of stairs leading to the lobby. Two people got out. The driver was fairly tall and the passenger of average height. They were both dressed in black jumpsuits under quilted, black ski jackets. They wore plain, black gimme caps with elongated bills and their faces were covered by black balaclavas which had nostril holes and narrow eye holes.

The garage camera followed the two truck occupants to the stairs leading to the lobby door. At that point Pamela paused the CD again. "The next view is from the camera mounted in the lobby. But before we go to that, let me slip in the CD for the access-card log." She removed the video CD and inserted another CD.

"This CD is a record of every time an access card is used to enter the lobby outside of business hours. Each card is registered to a particular individual so we can tell which card was used at a particular time. The access-card time record shows that Mr. Blonstein's card was used to access the lobby at 21:21:55; that's one minute, ten seconds after the truck first entered the garage.

"Of course it can't tell us who actually used the card, but we can determine that by matching the time on the lobby access log to the time readout on the lobby camera. Then there's a lag between the lobby-camera readout and the elevator time log of anywhere from a few seconds to a minute or more. If a person has their card in their hand, it's only a few seconds. If they have to open a wallet or fumble around in a purse it takes longer."

"Ms. An, does a card give you access to every floor in the building?"

"No, the card assigned to Mr. Blonstein allows access to only the floor on which his office is located. That's because two tenants occupy entire floors in the building and their offices are open to the elevators.

"Mr. Blonstein's office is located on the fourth floor, so his card could access only that floor?"

"That's correct Mr. Loeb. And the fire stairs doorways can only be opened from each floor hallway. So once you are in the fire stairway, you can't re-enter the hallway; you can only go down to the ground floor.

"I've marked the access that you're interested in." Pamela pointed to the screen. "You see: It's the last entry on the page. Since this page is for last Sunday, there weren't very many people coming in to work. That's typical for a Sunday, especially when the Cowboys are playing. The next-to-last entry was at seventeen-hundred hours, ten minutes. It was someone on the seventh floor."

"Probably not a Cowboys fan." Jason poured himself the last of the coffee.

"Is there any way to tell whether that person was still in the building after nine o'clock?"

"Yes, Mr. Loeb, by viewing the lobby camera video and checking the tenant parking ingress-egress video. I did both, and confirmed that it was a tenant whose vehicle matched the access-card registration. That individual left at nineteen-hundred hours, eleven minutes. So if he—or she—doesn't live too far away, maybe they made it home in time for the kickoff."

Pamela removed the access-card log CD and put the video CD back in. "Now here's the lobby camera video. As you can see, the same two individuals who exited the white vehicle, swiped the Blonstein card inside the elevator at 21:22:20; that's twenty-five seconds after Mr. Blonstein's card was used to enter the lobby from the garage."

"How long were they in the Blonstein office?"

"I can't give you a to-the-second number, Mr. Loeb. We don't monitor access to the individual tenant offices unless they're customers of Dal-Worth Security. Mr. Blonstein was not. The best I can do is give you an estimate based on when the two individuals exited the lobby and the vehicle exited the garage."

"So assuming they didn't try to enter any other offices or stop to use the restroom, the lobby-camera video time read-out should tell us within a few seconds, depending on how long it took the elevator to take them to the lobby, how long they were in the tenant office."

"Yes, Sir. That's correct, Major Bragg. The next view is the lobby camera. It shows them exiting the lobby at 23:53:43. That indicates they were in the Blonstein offices two hours, thirty-one minutes, twenty seconds, less the time it took for the elevator up and then down and to walk from the elevator to the office and back.

"As you can see, the taller individual is carrying two desktop computers, and the shorter one is carrying what appear to be 'Red-Rope' file folders. Then the next view…"

"Ms. An, can you pause it for a moment?" Josh put down his coffee mug and Pamela pushed the stop button. "I assume you know about Marjorie Morrison? Mr. Blonstein's assistant?"

"Marjorie Morrison?" Bragg turned toward Josh. "Isn't she the woman whose picture was in the paper yesterday? There was something on the TV news this morning that the woman had been identified as 'Marjorie Morrison.' They said on the news that she's latest *El Chupacabra* victim. I had no idea she was Mr. Blonstein's assistant."

"Yes she was. She disappeared Monday night. She left my assistant a voicemail message around ten o'clock and that's the last time we know she was alive. The police are treating the case as possibly linked to Seymour Blonstein's death. I say 'possibly' because they don't know whether Mr. Blonstein's death was accidental or a homicide. If it was a homicide, the two killings are almost certainly linked. Marjorie Morrison's death doesn't fit the *El Chupacabra* pattern at all. She's an Anglo woman and certainly had nothing to do with illegal drugs. So it's possible, if she was taken by force from the

Blonstein office Monday night, you may also have some footage that can help with her case as well."

"Pamela, call monitoring right away. Josh, what period of time do you think we should cover?"

"I was there until about twelve-thirty...I mean twelve-hundred hours, thirty minutes and the voicemail she left was at twenty-two hundred hours…"

"Mr. Loeb, if it's okay with Major Bragg, I'll have all of Monday from twelve hundred to twenty-four hundred hours transferred to a CD and backed-up in the hard-drive immediately. I'll also get them to duplicate the access-card reader log. Once we get that, we can narrow down the time frame so maybe we won't have to look at twelve hours' worth of video."

"Good plan, Pamela. Please see to it at once."

"Ms. An, do you have any idea how long it will take? The reason I ask is that I've got a meeting with a VIP," Josh made quotation marks with his fingers, "scheduled for this afternoon at one forty-five. I'd call my assistant and have her re-schedule if necessary, but the person I'm meeting with probably isn't used to other people rescheduling on her, and in any case, from what I understand, she can't be contacted until our meeting."

"It'll take a while, Mr. Loeb. Major Bragg, you don't have anything this afternoon that can't be worked around. Would it be okay if Mr. Loeb returns after his meeting?"

"That's what we'll do then. Josh, first a burglary, then a possible kidnapping. Dammit, not on my watch! Please call when you're on your way back out here; I promise you everything will be ready. And if there's anything else I can do, just give me a call." He reached inside his blazer and handed

Josh a card. "This has my direct line and cell phone numbers on it. Don't hesitate to use either one."

Chapter Nineteen

The meeting at Dal-Worth Security ended leaving Josh with more than enough time to swing by SueEllen Masters's office to pick up the new access cards. He got to her office just as she was leaving for an early lunch so he offered to take her. She suggested a new Italian place in Preston Center a couple of blocks from her office. Today she was wearing a turquoise suit over a sheer white blouse covering what Josh remembered Elaine calling a 'camisole.' When Josh went shopping with Elaine he always managed to wander over to the men's department when she headed for the lingerie department so his knowledge of women's intimate apparel was limited to the basics.

SueEllen's skirt length made Pamela An's look positively matronly. Ms. Masters was about a decade or so past the age for which the ensemble was designed and marketed. But what the heck, Josh thought, if that's the way she wants to promote the "SueEllen Masters" brand, go for it. To go with the suit she had chosen a red leather shoulder bag and matching red leather heels. Pleading the high heels and chilly weather, she persuaded Josh to ride with her in what was probably a dealer-certified, pre-owned Lexus. Josh used his new access card on the garage elevator and handed it to SueEllen to exit the tenant parking. It worked both times.

She drove the two blocks to the restaurant and stopped at the valet-parking stand. The attendant, at first confused by a woman driving and a man in the passenger seat, started to open Josh's door. Realizing his mistake he ran around the front of the Lexus arriving in time to take in the sight of SueEllen exiting the vehicle. It took him a good thirty seconds to remember to hand her the parking claim check and ask for her name to write down on the part of the claim check he retained. He was still staring as she and Josh walked into the restaurant.

As they were seated Josh crossed his fingers hoping that none of Elaine's ladies-who-lunch friends had decided to give the place a try as well.

Things went as Josh had hoped. SueEllen had a martini; Josh stuck to ice tea; the food was better-than-decent; and none of Elaine's friends—at least any that Josh knew—stopped by his table to arch an eyebrow, and say "hello, Josh," nor ask the obvious question: "Who's the floozie?" After riding with SueEllen back to her building and promising to call her if he needed any further assistance, Josh got on the Toll Road and made it downtown to his office with a couple minutes to spare before his meeting with Ms. Obregon-Robertson.

Chapter Twenty

Ms. Obregon-Robertson and Ms. Masters evidently favored the same clothing designer; the only differences were that Ms. Obregon-Robertson's suit was a cinnabar-red and she complimented it with a black shoulder bag and five-inch black heels with red soles that closely matched the color of her suit. The council woman's lustrous black hair was worn a couple of inches below her shoulders in front and in the back came midway between the collar and the bottom of her jacket. Her smooth, faintly-olive skin needed no makeup and she wore none except for lipstick which emphasized her wide, sensuous mouth, full lips and gleaming-white teeth that showed when she smiled as she held out her hand to Josh. The facial portrait was completed by a slightly aquiline nose and large, dark eyes beneath dark, perfectly-threaded eyebrows.

She was accompanied by a purse-boy Hispanic man, probably about age fifty, wearing sharply-creased black jeans and a black shirt with square, mother-of-pearl buttons. The shirt was buttoned at the collar and accessorized with a squash blossom bolo tie. He wore dark-gray snakeskin western boots with riding heels and pointed toes encased in elaborately-wrought silver caps that matched his saucer-size belt buckle. The outfit was completed by a thigh-length black leather jacket and black western-type hat. The jacket had a scalloped yoke across the shoulders and an inverted skirt-like pleat in the back from the waist down. The hat crown had the standard three creases and was surrounded by a band of linked miniature squash blossoms encased in silver. He was about the same size as Jason Bragg, perhaps an inch or so taller. He had a sallow, pitted face accented by a bushy salt-and-pepper moustache and matching long, thick sideburns. In one hand he carried a squared-off, brushed-aluminum briefcase with reinforced corners. Over his other forearm he carried a woman's thigh-length coat in a muted gray and black plaid.

"Thank you for making time to see me on such short notice. I do appreciate it so much." Her grip was masculine, warm and dry: a perfect politician's handshake. Even so, Josh could not help wishing that she'd held his hand a bit longer. "This is Eloy," she turned slightly and smiled at the Hispanic man. "He's my driver and investigator." And no doubt, Josh thought, her bodyguard as well as purse-boy. Eloy favored Josh with a barely-perceptible nod and a long stare from his obsidian-black, expressionless eyes.

They took seats at the conference table, Josh and Alicia on one side and Ms. Obregon-Robertson and Eloy on the other. No need to jockey for the seat at the head of the table; everyone knew who was in charge. "You've met my assistant Alicia Flores. Do you mind if she stays for our meeting? She's a constituent—and admirer—of yours. She's always wanted to meet you."

"Of course, Alicia, please do stay." Alicia gritted her teeth at the patronizing use of her first name, but managed a demure smile all the same. "Since you're in my district, you'll be glad to know that the police are finally getting the message about the so-called *El Chupacabra* killings. I've just come from a meeting of the Council public-safety committee. I'm the chair, as I'm sure you know. I invited the chief of police and the city manager.

"If you read my op-ed article in the Dallas Morning News last week, then you have a pretty good idea of what I said: Stop spending all your resources on gas-station drive-offs and car burglaries in North Dallas. Put some manpower into catching *El Chupacabra*. He's become a folk-legend in my district, in your district, Alicia. The Mariachi bands are singing a song about him: *'La Canción del Chupacabra.'* Some group recorded it and now it's being aired on the Spanish-language radio stations. Little kids are playing *El Chupacabra* games in the parks and on the school playgrounds. One of these days, a kid is going to pick up a real knife and someone's going to get hurt. Or some gang of ten-year-olds is going to try to take down a street drug dealer who is going to pull out his nine mil…"

"I'm sure you're right about getting *El Chupacabra* off the street, and about cracking down on the drug dealers. But from what I understand, the police department's devoting a tremendous amount of resources at least to the *El Chupacabra* problem. I've been told that the *El Chupacabra* cases are all that the Crimes Against Persons detectives are working now. From what I've been told detectives from other divisions have had to pick up the C-A-P detectives' other cases along with working their own regular caseloads."

"You must have been talking with the DPD, Mr. Loeb. That's the same Kool-Aid the chief and the city manager have been trying to get me to drink. I'm not drinking it. I intend to keep up the pressure until I'm sure *El Chupacabra* is locked up and off my streets. The chief has agreed to put more uniforms on the streets in my district and the city manager has agreed to increase the police overtime budget by twenty percent.

"But enough about *El Chupacabra* and DPD incompetence. As I'm sure Alicia's told you, I'm here about the late Mr. Blonstein. You are the executor of his estate?"

Brace yourself, Josh, here it comes. I hope Sy had professional liability insurance and that it provides extended coverage to his estate. "That's correct, although technically my appointment is not official until the will's formally admitted to probate. Right now, I'm just acting as executor with the consent of his widow who is the sole beneficiary under the will. In the unlikely event someone files a will contest, I'll seek appointment by the court as temporary administrator."

"May I ask what you're doing about his files and his clients?"

"It's my intention to contact all the clients and follow their directions about what to do with their files."

"Can you tell me how soon that will be?"

"All I can do at the moment is assure you that I'm doing everything I can to get it done as soon as possible. Unfortunately I can't give you a firm date."

"Why is that, Mr. Loeb?"

"I suppose you're aware that there was another murder—last Monday night—attributed to *El Chupacabra*."

"Yes, of course. But what does that have to do with…"

"The victim was Mr. Blonstein's assistant. Her name was Marjorie Morrison."

"That's terrible. Poor woman. Did she have a husband? A family? Do you know when the funeral will be? I'd like to extend my condolences in person."

"Did you…"

Ms. Obregon-Robertson shook her head and smiled at Josh's obviously fatuous question. "No, I didn't go to any of the other funerals. I don't think it would be a good idea to be seen at a drug dealer's funeral. Besides, I think all of the Hispanic bodies were shipped back to Mexico or other countries for burial. And by coincidence, I was holding constituent meetings in my district when each of the African-American funerals took place."

"Sorry, I should have thought of that. I expect you're going to have to pass up Ms. Morrison's funeral too. So far as I know, her only family is a sister in Oklahoma City and I don't think she's been notified yet. Ms. Morrison had an ex-husband, but he's in the wind as far as anyone knows."

"I can see how the unfortunate woman's death could possibly cause some delay. I wonder how she got mixed up in drug trafficking?"

"The police don't think she was. They think it may have been a copycat murder; that she was killed for some other reason and it was made to look like an *El Chupacabra* killing. I was told they're trying to locate the ex-husband as a possible person-of-interest."

"Then you have been in contact with the police. Who has the case? I've met a lot of them, maybe I know him. If I do, maybe I can make a phone call or two."

"I identified the body; that's how I got involved. The detective who's handling the case is a woman: Alana Turner. Everyone calls her 'Lana.'"

"Sorry, I don't recall her name."

"Probably because homicides are not her stock-in-trade. She works in auto crimes running a bait-car sting operation. Once the department decided it wasn't an *El Chupacabra* case they gave it to her. She had already been assigned the Blonstein case..."

"Why is DPD looking at the Blonstein death? From what I read in the paper, he died in a one-car accident."

"And that's exactly what it was. However they're trying to figure out why the airbag didn't deploy and so am I."

"So there might be a product-liability claim?"

"Right."

"Do you know yet why it didn't deploy?"

"I really can't discuss that; I've got work-product confidentiality issues."

Ms. Obregon-Robertson gave Josh a pouty look. "Certainly, I understand. So let's talk about Mr. Blonstein's files. I have another meeting to get to."

"Fair enough. Well, besides not having anyone that is familiar with the files to help with the transition, Mr. Blonstein's office was burglarized and trashed last Sunday night. Whoever did it stole the computers, so there's no record of who the clients are. All we have to go by is the paper files."

"Will you and Alicia have to do that yourselves?"

"Well, if we do, it'll be Ms. Flores who does the bulk of the work. I haven't worked on any of my own files all week and I've got clients and cases that need attention too. I'm thinking about hiring someone to do the job, but I'll have to get the widow's okay before I go spending her money."

Ms. Obregon-Robertson leaned forward in her chair and switched to her Do you know who you're messing with? look. Eloy grunted in affirmation. "I don't mean to add to your problems, Mr. Loeb, but that's not going to cut it with my client...or with me. I've been listening to 'the dog ate my homework' excuses from the chief of police and city manager all morning and my patience is worn out. Let me be clear: My client needs its file urgently. If you don't hand it over by Monday, I'm going to ask the probate court to issue an injunction ordering you to do your job."

She stood up and Eloy immediately shot to his feet. "Eloy, *vamonos*."

Josh stood. "I understand your position, Ms. Obregon-Robertson. If you don't mind, I have just one question: Would you be so kind as to share with us the name of your client who so desperately needs its file by Monday?"

Ms. Obregon Robertson held out her hand in Eloy's direction and he handed her the briefcase. She fiddled with the four-ring numerical tumbler lock for a moment until the briefcase lock snapped open. She raised the top and extracted a letter which she lay on the table in front of Alicia. "All the information you need is in this demand letter."

Chapter Twenty-One

Alicia and Josh were seated in his office. Josh had folded Ms. Obregon-Robertson's letter into a paper airplane which he gently flew across his desk to Alicia.

Alicia caught the aircraft one-handed. "I wonder what she's got her panties in a wad about. From what you told me about your meeting with Dr. Blubberoff, he was glad to have his files disappear into a black hole for a while."

"Beats the heck out of me. Elaine gave me an idea about who to get to help with the transition. I need to give him a call. If he's willing to do it, I'd like to have him get started tomorrow."

"Maybe if whomever you've got in mind gets started tomorrow, he'll get lucky and find the..." Alicia paused and unfolded the letter-paper airplane... "'Tezcatlipoca, LLC' file.

That way you won't have to deal with her at the courthouse. We've dealt with some pretty obnoxious lawyers over the years, but she's right up there with…"

"I know who you mean. Let's don't put her in that category just yet. You didn't much like her from the git-go, did you?"

"I didn't much care for her calling me 'Alicia,' but she rubbed me the wrong way even before that."

"I must have missed that. What'd she do?"

"It wasn't anything she said or did; it was what she was wearing."

"You mean the short skirt? Apparently 'If you got it, flaunt it' is in season this fall. SueEllen Masters had on the same outfit in a different color and the executive assistant at Dal-Worth Security wore her skirt about that short."

"Not the skirt length, Josh. Although what would you say if I showed up for work in a skirt that short?"

"I'd…"

"Never mind, Josh. I withdraw the question. It was the shoes."

"What about the shoes?"

"They were Christian Louboutins."

"What kind of 'boots?' They didn't look like boots to me."

"Not boots, Josh. 'Louboutin.' That's the name of the designer: Christian L-o-u-b-o-u-t-i-n. He's French."

"And you could tell just by looking at them?"

"The red soles; they're unique. A few years ago he won a lawsuit to keep another designer from using red soles."

"What's the big deal? Shoes are shoes, aren't they?"

"Josh, you wouldn't understand; it's a girl thing. I saw a pair on sale at Neiman's 'Last Call' and tried them on. And for five minutes...until I looked at the sale price...I was the Duchess of Cambridge, Princess Grace..."

"I take it they're expensive?"

"Only eleven to fourteen."

"That doesn't sound expensive. I spent three times that amount on lunch today. If they make a woman feel that good about herself, maybe I ought to get Elaine a pair, heck a couple of pair."

"That's eleven to fourteen hundred dollars a pair, Josh. Even the ones on sale were six hundred. And if I may offer a bit of advice, you probably don't want to surprise Elaine with a pair. All you're likely to accomplish is make her wonder what you did to feel guilty about."

"At eleven hundred a pair, I think I'll take your advice, cynical though it is. Who do you suppose is behind the Tez...whatsits...LLC beard?"

"I expect I'm about to find out. I assume you want me to do a Secretary of State search to find out who it is?"

"If I'm going to be sued, I'd like to know who's suing me. Also see if that name..."

"Tez-cat-li-po-ca," Alicia read it again from the letter.

"...means anything."

"Sounds like it may be Aztec or Mayan; or maybe just made up like 'Haagen Daz.'"

"The guy I need to call to help with the Blonstein files is Nate Mendelovitz. He's a retired CPA. Lives with his wife in an assisted-living facility. I need to call him and find out if he's willing and able. If he is, I want him to get started tomorrow with the files I got from the second safe-deposit box. That means he'll need to come down here. Would you see if there's a visiting-attorney office available and reserve it for him?"

"For how long?"

"Make it a week and we'll see after that. At some point he's going to have to set up shop in Sy's office. He uses a walker to get around, so I'm probably going to have to hire a temp to help him. I'm sure Estelle's going to be thrilled about that expense."

"What are you going to do about the computer files?"

"I don't know. I haven't been back to Sy's office since noon on Monday, so I don't know whether Margie had time to get a replacement computer. If she didn't, we'll have to track down the off-site storage provider. Once we figure out who that is, I'm sure I'll have to get some kind of court order to get them to give me their files."

"If you get the computer files what are you going to do with them?"

"Unless Margie left something behind with the password and decryption key, probably nothing but sit back and wait for the lawsuits to start raining down.

"I need to go back to Sy's office and see if I can find an insurance policy or anything else. If I can't, maybe Estelle knows who handled their insurance."

"I'll pull the info on Tezcatlipoca and reserve an office for Mr. Mendelovitz. Then what?"

"Then I'll see you in the morning. I've got to go back out to Dal-Worth Security. They're looking for any camera footage from Monday night. I asked them to look in case Margie was kidnapped from Sy's office after she left you the voicemail message. Then I'm going to go up to Sy's office to see if I can find the keys to the computer kingdom, a malpractice policy or hopefully both."

Chapter Twenty-Two

"Did the security company recordings show anything that would help with Marjorie Morrison?" Elaine placed Josh's plate of grilled salmon and sautéed green beans with shallots on the table in front of him as he poured their glasses of pinot gris.

"That she was kidnapped from Sy's office right after she called and left Alicia the voicemail message I told you about. The camera footage shows two people forcing her into a truck at twenty-two hundred hours, forty-three minutes. Sorry, the security people use military time and now they've got me doing it. That's ten forty-three p.m. in the real world. The two people are the same two people—one tall, one average height, both unrecognizable—that burgled Sy's office Sunday night and the truck's the same one they used for the burglary."

"Then doesn't that tie her kidnapping and murder to Sy's murder?"

"If you assume that Sy's death was murder as well."

"But from what Louis's nephew…"

"DeMontrond."

"…DeMontrond said, the airbag system has to have been tampered with."

Josh took a tentative sip of his pinot gris. "True; that's his opinion, and he's probably right. But I'm not sure Detective Turner is quite convinced. It's going to take an examination and solid opinion by a DPD technician for her to be satisfied."

"Well at least she's got to be satisfied that the Morrison murder was a copycat and not another *El Chupacabra* killing."

"She's probably inclined to see it that way because it's in her interest to do so."

"Her interest?"

"If it's not an *El Chupacabra* case she gets to keep it; if it is, they'll take it away from her and give it to the *real* detectives: the Crimes-Against-Persons guys."

"And what if she's wrong and it is another *El Chupacabra* killing?"

"I think she's going to go where the evidence takes her. Since she's been working the case, maybe they'll give her a chance to run with the big dogs. That's what she wants anyway. In fact, what she really wants is to be the alpha dog."

"I'm glad you didn't say 'alpha bitch.'"

"Elaine, assholes come in both genders. Detective Turner's not an asshole. She's smart; she works her butt off; and she's honest. She came from a hyper-testosterone environment and she now works in an environment that's surely just as bad. Do you think that 'Mad Men' is just a cable TV series? She has to compete in her job every day against male co-workers and prove herself to male bosses who tolerate women in their domain because the law says they have to. Ask any one of her co-workers or superiors off-the-record and they'd tell you she's a twit, a product of affirmative-action. That's also what the car-thieves she catches every day think. Both groups are wrong.

"If I were inclined to use a gender-based epithet, I would save it for Ms. Obregon-Robertson."

"What'd she do?"

"She wore a pair of Christian Louboutin shoes to her meeting with me."

"I hate her already."

"So did Alicia. She's the one who told me about the shoes."

"I wondered when you said it. I didn't think you knew Christian Louboutin shoes from a pair of Lucchese boots."

"You're right. I would have been inclined to overlook the shoes, but..."

"I'm sure that's what you were doing: Looking above her shoes."

"Come on, Elaine it's been five days. Besides, I didn't tell her to wear a skirt that hardly covered her behind. Haven't we..."

"Exhausted the subject? I don't know, Josh. Have we?"

"Think back just a minute. Whose butt was I 'ogling,' as you put it, that got this whole discussion started?"

"You're right, Josh. Let's let it drop. I'm sorry; It's just that I'm feeling so insecure." Elaine finished her glass of wine and poured them both refills.

"I won't let it drop until you tell me why you're feeling insecure."

"Okay, Josh; if you must know, I don't want to end up like Estelle."

"You mean end up a widow? Your outliving me is almost a statistical certainty. But that doesn't mean you have to 'end up a widow.' As far as I'm concerned, you can bring a date to my funeral."

"Josh, that's gross. Anyway, that's not what I mean. I don't want to find out that you have a condo that I don't know about."

Josh finished his wine. "Elaine, you don't have to worry about a gaggle of strange women—or even one strange woman—showing up at my funeral. I promise, I'm not creating any Sy Blonstein-type mess to leave behind for our lawyer-son Adam to clean up."

"I know you haven't and won't, Josh. I guess I'm just upset for Estelle's sake and at the same time glad it's her and not me. It's the same feeling you have when someone whom you know well dies suddenly, like Sy did."

"'There but for the grace...'"

"Exactly. But you're not Sy and I'm not Estelle." Elaine puckered her lips in a kissing gesture across the small dining table. "So tell me what'd Ms. Obregon-Robertson do to disturb your usually-placid nature?"

"You mean besides threaten to sue me?"

"For what?"

"Failing to turn over her client's file that Sy was working on."

"But..."

"Don't worry about it; I'm not.

"Not worry about your being sued or not worry about whether you'll turn the file over?"

"Take your pick: either one or both. I'm not giving her anything until Nate Mendelovitz has looked at it, or a judge tells me I have to. And I don't think that's going to happen any time soon."

"That reminds me; Nate and Rose are coming for Thanksgiving."

"I know. I talked to him this afternoon. It didn't take much to persuade him to take on the job. He says they ought to re-name the place where he and Rose live 'Purgatory Manor' instead of '*Chai* Manor.' I'm picking him up in the morning and bringing him down to the office. He'll work there for a few days until I can make arrangements for someone to help him with the bulk of the files in Sy's office. I've already made arrangements with Jason Bragg—he's Dal-Worth Security—to provide security for Sy's office while Nate's working there."

"And what about security for Josh? I was serious when I brought it up the other night."

"I took you seriously. I made a deal with Louis. In the morning, before I pick up Nate, I'm going to take my car to Louis and swap it for another car. He's got a Chrysler Three-Hundred that he did a bunch of work on that the owner can't pay for. He made a deal with the owner to knock five hundred bucks off the bill in exchange for which I get to use the car for two weeks. During that time, my car stays in Louis's shop. Louis is also throwing in DeMontrond as my driver. All I have to do is reimburse Louis for the five-hundred bucks and pay DeMontrond's salary. So don't worry; what happened to Sy, if anything, won't happen to me."

"Will DeMontrond be enough? What if someone comes after you with a knife or a gun?"

"Louis and I talked about that too. Louis told me that people tried twice to shank DeMontrond when he was in the joint. The first time because he respectfully, but firmly, declined an invitation to be a black gang-leader's 'bitch.' You don't want to know what that means."

"I can guess."

"Second time, DeMontrond had a disagreement with a skinhead about the use of the bench press. DeMontrond 'though unarmed, survived both encounters without a scratch, which is something that can't be said for either of his attackers.

"DeMontrond can't carry since he's a convicted felon. But Louis can and does carry. He promised that he and DeMontrond are available 24/7 if I need them. Also, Jason Bragg volunteered to help personally. He says that the M-16 mounted on his wall is in combat-ready condition. He says that somehow the Army forgot to disable the full-automatic feature. He is seriously unhappy about the burglary and kidnapping 'on his watch' as he put it.

"So all things considered, I think I've got the personal-security issue handled."

"Joshua Loeb, have you taken leave of your senses? What you've got is a couple of middle-age guys with guns and, from the way you describe him, an 'Incredible Hulk' clone all running around playing cowboys and Indians. This whole thing sounds like the plot of a Robert Parker 'Spenser' novel. How are you going to contact them in an emergency? Do you have the phone number for Henry Cimoli's gym? What's it called?"

"You mean the 'Harbor Health Club?'"

"Right, the 'Harbor Health Club.' Do you know how to contact Easy Rawlins and Mouse if Hawk's busy? Or maybe you ought to just use the Batman signal light."

"Mouse is dead, Elaine. In any case, I thought I'd use my Dick Tracy two-way wrist radio. If that's not working, I'll use my cell phone. I've got them both on speed-dial. Seriously,

I'm not anticipating the 'Gunfight at the OK Corral.' The car and DeMontrond will be all the security I need. Louis says that DeMontrond is as good as any professional stunt-car driver.

"I just dealt Louis and Major Bragg in to make them feel useful. A guy says he's willing to go in harm's way for you, it's bad form to turn him down. I have one place to go tomorrow night that I would like to have Louis along with me; not for protection, but just to keep me company. Other than that…"

"And where would that be? Why not take me? Aren't I good company? Or don't you want to be seen in public with me?"

"Elaine, I…"

"What's the tile of that song: 'Put Your Biscuits in the Oven and Your Buns in the Bed?'"

"Elaine, I'm not going to a state dinner at the White House. If I were, I'd be the luckiest guy in the room to be there with you."

"Josh, no wonder you're such a good lawyer. You can talk anybody out of just about anything."

"Can I talk you out of your…"

"Quit while you're ahead. Go watch 'Thursday Night Football.' I'll clean up."

The game on "Thursday Night Football" turned out to be a clunker. Even the guys in the broadcast booth—who are paid big bucks to make watching grass grow seem interesting—were yawning by midway through the third quarter. By the end of the quarter Josh was asleep on the sofa in the den. Elaine was at her computer trying to narrow down the list of potential feature speakers for the Operation Do Over luncheon.

Chapter Twenty-Three

Nate Mendelovitz folded his aluminum walker against the wall of the office Alicia had arranged for his use. Using the desk to maintain his balance he eased himself into the low-back executive chair. "Miss Flores, I think this chair is maybe a little low do you think we could get it raised up a bit?"

Alicia set the Crystal's Palace and Tezcatlipoca files on the desk. "Yes, Sir. I'll call Office Services and have someone come right away. Is there anything else you need?"

Nate adjusted his horn-rim glasses. "Well, since you ask, a desk lamp would be nice. My eyes aren't what they used to be. And I could use a pad of columnar paper. I brought my pencils with me." Nate reached into the inside breast pocket of his brown tweed sport jacket and extracted a couple of Cross gold-plated mechanical pencils. "Also, if you could find some real coffee, that would be wonderful. The watery *dreck* they give us where I live...I'd rather drink the water left over from washing the dishes."

"I'll tell Office Services to find you a lamp. I'm sure there's an extra one around here somewhere. I think I've seen some columnar paper in the supply room. As for coffee, that's one thing that I know we've got. Mr. Loeb says that you can judge the quality of a law firm by the quality of its coffee. If he's right, we're definitely a quality law firm. What would you like? Regular or decaf? Light-roast or dark-roast? Flavored? We have French vanilla, hazelnut..."

"Such choices. Regular, dark-roast. No cream or sugar. I think I'm going to like this job."

"Mr. Loeb should be with you in a few minutes. He has some phone calls to return and about a jillion emails to look at. He's been working on the Blonstein estate all week so he's way behind on his other cases."

"Tell him to take his time. He briefed me in the car on the way here, so I know enough to get started. Josh's business must be good these days. He's got this huge Chrysler and his own driver to drive him around. Nice young man, the driver; very polite. He opened the door for me and took care of my walker. Much nicer than the woman who drives the van provided by the old-folks' home where I live. She gets lost everywhere she tries to go and she wouldn't get off her *tuchus* to help you if the van caught on fire."

By the time Josh was able to pry his ear away from the telephone, return a few emails, help a junior lawyer with a question on federal-court procedure and go over Alicia's this-can't-wait list, Nate had his chair at the proper height, his lamp in place and a columnar pad at the ready. He had begun reading the Crystal's Palace file and was finishing his second cup of coffee when Josh sat down in one of the guest chairs in front of the desk.

"How's it going, Nate. Do you have everything you need?"

"Yes, your Miss Flores...if I was still in practice I'd steal her from you. And speaking of stealing, that Andy Biggers...such a *gonif*. Believe me, Josh, I've seen many a *gonif* in fifty-plus years of practice. But this Biggers is right up there with the worst of them. Is he in prison?"

"I don't know, but I doubt it."

"And why not, may I ask?"

"The Dallas County District Attorney doesn't prosecute white-collar crime. They don't know how. Once in a while they'll go after someone, but they only do it if a deep-pocket political supporter says 'sic 'em.' Because the Crystal's Palace investors went to civil court, the DA will say 'it's a civil matter' and won't touch it.

"Did you find anything interesting? I'm not trying to rush you; I'm just curious. As I told you in the car, I'm trying to figure out why Sy had these files in a secret safe-deposit box. I haven't told you yet why I'm so concerned. Now that you're officially working for me, I can tell you. But what I'm about to tell you comes under attorney-client privilege."

"Don't worry about that, Josh. At my age, five minutes after you tell me I'll have forgotten all about it."

"Nate, if I believed that we wouldn't be sitting here. I just want to make sure you know that it's privileged."

"Okay, it's privileged. So tell me already."

"Sy called me last Thursday and made an appointment to see me on Monday. Of course he never made it. He wouldn't say what it was about, but he asked me to recommend a good white-collar criminal-defense lawyer."

"And you think he wanted the recommendation for himself and not a client?"

"I think so. Otherwise he would have told me it was for a client and we could have handled it over the phone. Also, why wouldn't he just tell his client 'You've got a problem; you need a criminal lawyer?'"

"But if the Dallas County DA doesn't prosecute white-collar crime..."

"Then it is probably federal. The feds do prosecute white-collar crime and the government almost always wins."

"Well, I'm just getting started. Since you've already given me the gist of the Crystal's Palace file I pretty much skimmed the court-case file. I'll start on Sy's work papers. If there's anything to find, that's where it'll be. What about the Tez...the apartment file?"

"Let's concentrate on Crystal's Palace first. There are some other aspects to Sy's engagement that I don't want to tell you about unless I have to. I found out some other information that's only indirectly related. Other people are involved and I'd like to protect them if I can. Even though the information is protected as work-product, the work-product privilege is not absolute."

"Whatever you think best, Josh. If I don't need to know it, I don't want to know it. Right now, all I want to know is: Where do I find the men's room? I forgot what real coffee does to my bladder."

"Thanks, Nate. I appreciate it. Follow me; I'll show you to the men's room."

After returning Nate to his temporary office Josh called Alana Turner and got her voicemail. He left a message letting her know that he had important new information on the burglary of Sy's office and the abduction-murder of Marjorie Morrison. He then put in an hour or so reviewing his brief for an upcoming appellate argument scheduled for the week after next.

Finding it difficult to concentrate, he took Nate and Alicia to lunch in one of the table-service restaurants in the warren of tunnels and food courts that underlie Downtown Dallas like the catacombs of Rome or the sewers of Paris. The comparisons are less than perfect because there are slightly fewer rats and no ossuaries, nor, except when there is a sewer line break down, is there an underground lake with swirls of foul-smelling mist floating near the water surface. Dug in the 1970s and 1980s, these air-conditioned chambers and connecting tunnels were intended to be the ingenious answer to the Dallas climate from mid-June to mid-October, a span during which the heat rivals that of Baghdad and the humidity makes the Brazilian rainforest—what's left of it—seem arid. The idea was promoted by forward-thinking civic boosters and was endorsed by a celebrated urban planner-visionary. "Underground Dallas" was supposed to rival, if not surpass, "Underground Atlanta." That never happened. When the Texas economy tanked, the tunnels, like played-out gold mines, were abandoned.

The implosion of the Texas real estate market in the mid-1980s led to the demise of the banking business which, along with the "awl bidness," insurance, agricultural commodity-trading and the garment industry, had built Downtown Dallas. Commodities and garment manufacturing were already long gone. Oil was in the doldrums. The real estate-banking implosion was like a neutron bomb: It killed all the people and left the buildings standing empty.

Banks which had added millions of square feet of facilities and filled them with new employees were closing up faster than fake Rolex peddlers on Fifth Avenue in Manhattan when a cop approaches. Law firms that had added hundreds of lawyers and taken multiple floors in new or newly-renovated office buildings, and title companies that had added dozens of closers and hundreds-of-thousands of square feet of expensive office space were all laying off people wholesale and walking away from leases.

The hordes of dubiously-credentialed bank liquidators, lawyers and accountants that came to roost in the vacant high-rise aeries and to feed on the carcasses of the fallen had come and gone, leaving Downtown Dallas looking like a ghost town. Recovery took its time in coming.

Table-talk over lunch was mostly Nate and Josh reminiscing about the glory days of Downtown Dallas restaurants: The Blue Front, Sam & Pete's, Crowder's Brass Rail, Sol's Turf Bar, the Pulley Bone, Louie's, the Oyster House, Jimmy's Chili Rice Emporium, Vincent's, dozens of hole-in-the-wall hamburger, barbecue and chicken-fried steak emporia, the Greek place and even the venerable Wilson's, every one of them gone. Although in the case of Wilson's there were many who did not mourn its passing. Nowadays, unless one belongs to one of the "exclusive" city clubs, going to lunch means get in your car and go somewhere or endure the fast or slow junk food available in "Underground Dallas." As Josh signed the Amex form, he shrugged and said to himself, "What the heck, thirty-years from now people will call this 'The good old days.'"

It was a little past four when Josh, Nate and Alicia met in Josh's office: Alicia to report on Tezcatlipoca, LLC and Nate to report on Crystal's Palace. Josh had already called DeMontrond to pick him and Nate up at the rear entrance to Josh's building.

Nate didn't want Rose to have to endure dinner alone. Life in a senior living facility did not provide much fodder for dinner-table conversation, but dining together was a habit of nearly sixty years and was better than eating alone. There would be time enough for that when the time came. Allowing for rush hour traffic, and the fact that they had to go all the way out to Plano, it would be a tight fit. Louis would be with DeMontrond so they could go straight to their next stop after dropping Nate off.

Alicia, between sips of her diet Coke, led off. "Tezcatlipoca, LLC is a Texas limited liability company." She produced a copy of the articles of organization and handed the documents to Josh across his desk. "The sole member is...guess who...Ms. Marisol Obregon-Robertson. Since that was no surprise I went ahead and did some further digging.

"I went to the Dallas County Appraisal District website and found over a dozen properties with the name 'Tezcatlipoca' in them. They're all apartments: a couple in the Vickery Meadows area, one on Stone Canyon, off Meadow Road west of Central Expressway, one in East Dallas near Greenville Avenue and the rest scattered in Oak Cliff, West Dallas and South Dallas. They're all limited partnerships with Tezcatlipoca as the general partner. Just about all of them have 'Tezcatlipoca' in the name: 'Tezcatlipoca-Cancun, Ltd.,' 'Tezcatlipoca-Merida, Ltd.' and so on. I didn't have time to count the exact number of units, but I bet it's over fifteen hundred." She handed Josh a list with print-outs of the DCAD appraisals and other information attached. "Here's a list. Maybe Mr. Mendelovitz…"

"Please, Miss Flores, call me 'Nate.' It makes me grind my teeth when the staff at the old-folks' home call me by my first name; it's patronizing. They treat everybody like children. But you, you're a professional just like me and just like Josh."

Alicia smiled. "Sure thing, Nate. But from now you have to call me 'Alicia.'

"Deal." Nate held out his hand which Alicia accepted to seal the bargain. "I haven't looked at the Tezcat...give me time, I'll learn the name...file yet. I'll match up what you found with what's in the file as soon as I finish with Crystal's Palace."

"Good work, Alicia." Josh glanced at his watch. "Did you find anything on the word?"

"Ah, the wonders of Wikipedia. Tezcatlipoca is an Aztec god sometimes referred to, among other things, as the 'Lord of the Smoking Mirrors.'"

"'Smok*ing* Mirrors' or 'smoke *and* mirrors?'" Josh thumbed through the package of DCAD papers as though searching for the answer.

"'Smok-*ing*' according to Wikipedia."

"Interesting play on words. Evidently Ms. Obregon-Robertson has a rather sophisticated sense of humor. On that basis I might even be persuaded to forgive her for the shoes."

"And if she follows through on her threat to sue?"

"Then I won't forgive her for the shoes or anything else."

"Do you think Nate ought to look at the Tezcatlipoca file first? I mean if you can give it back to her, why deal with her at the courthouse?"

"Three reasons. In order of importance: one I don't like the way she talked down to you; two, I don't like being bullied; and three, I'd very much like to know why she wants the files so urgently. Is there something she doesn't want me to know about? But in any case, I think Nate and I had best get going. DeMontrond just texted me. He and Louis are downstairs. Nate can tell me what he's found in the Crystal's Palace file in the car."

Chapter Twenty-Four

On Josh's recommendation Nate had been taking his car to Louis for service on a regular basis so Nate and Louis were already acquainted. While DeMontrond was stowing Nate's walker in the trunk of the Chrysler, Louis asked about Nate's car.

"It's still running, or at least it was last Tuesday, which is the last time I drove it. I don't drive so much anymore. I can't drive at night, so about the only driving I do is to go out to lunch once or twice a week or to take Rose to play mahjong or shopping. We have a group we call the 'ROMEO Club.' We go out to lunch so we can sit and *shmooze* and get away from our wives for a while."

"Romeo Club?" Josh and Louis asked simultaneously.

Nate smiled indulgently. "'Retired Old Men Eating Out.' Maybe you'll join us when you retire. Or more likely you'll start your own chapter."

DeMontrond got in the car and started the engine. "We takin' Mr. Nate back to Plano, Mr. Josh?"

"That's the plan, DeMontrond. Nate needs to be home for dinner. Think you can make it in time?"

"Where are you going after you get rid of me? Crystal's Palace? Have a drink or two? Check out the dancers?"

"Good guess, Nate. I wasn't trying to exclude you. I thought you wanted to get back because you don't want Rose to have to eat dinner alone. Besides, this is strictly business. If I didn't think it was absolutely necessary, I assure you Louis and I wouldn't be going either."

"Josh, I'm eighty-one years old and I've never ridden on a motorcycle or been to a topless bar. When I was DeMontrond's age topless bars didn't even exist; you got your vicarious sex from left-hand magazines. If I have a chance now to check one out and I don't do it, when should I go? When I'm ninety-one?"

"What about Rose and dinner?"

"Rose can survive without me for one meal. She'll find some other *yentas* to sit with and she won't even miss me. Give me your cell phone. If I can remember the phone number, I'll call Rose and tell her I have to work late. Isn't that what you're supposed to say when you're going to a topless bar? Also, I didn't have my nap this afternoon so if I don't get to go with you I might just fall asleep in the car on the way back to Plano. Then you'd have to wait until Monday to hear what I found in Sy's work papers."

Josh dug his phone out of his pocket and handed it to Nate. "Okay, Nate, you win. But this excursion is strictly work-product. You can't tell Rose or anyone else, including the

ROMEO Club, about Crystal's Palace. I haven't told Elaine. And Louis and DeMontrond are under the same gag order."

"Josh, this is something you really needed to tell me? I'm going to tell Rose that I went to a topless bar? And five minutes after I did, she's not going to call Elaine and ask why is Josh taking Nate to topless bars? So instead of Thanksgiving at the Loebs' you and I will be eating Thanksgiving dinner at the homeless shelter?

"Don't worry, Josh, by the time I get home I will have completely forgotten about Crystal's Palace. You know, this work-product privilege is a very handy thing to have."

Mindful of the outbound rush hour traffic Louis suggested that DeMontrond take Harry Hines all the way from downtown out to Crystal's Palace. Traffic was heavy but at least it wasn't a parking lot which is what Stemmons Freeway was bound to be at that hour. As they drove Nate removed a folded sheet of columnar paper from the inner pocket of his sport coat. He wiped off his glasses and checked his notes.

"Sy did his usual thorough job. The money trail was harder to make sense of than the rabbi's *Yom Kippur* sermon. There were checks written to cash and to bogus payees. Sy got copies of the cancelled checks. His work papers show over one hundred thousand dollars in checks to cash and bogus payees that were all endorsed with the same illegible signature. Some of the places where the checks were cashed had a driver's license number written on them as well as a fingerprint. I bet if you could trace that number it would belong to Biggers. Besides that, there were bank deposit slips showing cash taken back out of the deposits.

"Sy contacted the major beer and liquor suppliers; they showed him invoices for about twenty-five percent more alcohol than the alcohol sales tax reports indicated was being sold. Some of that could be inventory on hand, but according to Sy's notes there wasn't that much. That told Sy that this Biggers was skimming big time. I agree."

"Did Sy report all that to the court?"

"Some of it, but not all."

"What did he leave out?"

"It looks like about six weeks' worth of the checks to cash and to bogus payees: the last few weeks before the judge cut off Biggers's access to the money. As I said, I found the work papers for over a hundred thousand, but only forty-eight thousand was in Sy's report to the court."

"Is it possible that he didn't have the information when he prepared his report? Maybe he was going to update his report. Then, when the judge threw Biggers out, the update wasn't necessary."

"It's possible, Josh, but according to Sy's file, one of the first things he did was get the investors' lawyer to subpoena copies of the checks from the bank. That was in mid-February. You know it takes at least thirty days to get a bank to respond to a subpoena. The file shows that Sy got the checks about the first of April. He had plenty of time to go through all of them. It would have taken a couple of days at most. It looks to me like Sy...may he rest in peace...either left out the last few weeks on purpose, or he just screwed up."

"If he just screwed up, he wouldn't need a criminal lawyer. You just go to the judge and say 'Your Honor, I made a mistake.'"

"That's exactly what I would have done and what Sy would have done."

"So you think it was deliberate?"

"When you consider the omissions along with what else I found, there's no other way to read it. I'm sorry, Josh. I know Sy was a friend; I considered him a friend as well even though we competed for some clients. But I've got to call it the way I see it."

They had just passed under the Northwest Highway overpass. "I'm glad we're almost there. I think I'm going to need a drink. What else did you find?"

"You know what a '941' is?"

"The quarterly wage and withholding report that an employer has to file with the IRS."

"Right. Sy filed the ones for the last quarter of last year and the first quarter of this year. The last quarter showed salary to Biggers of three thousand dollars and no withholding. That seems way too low. Same thing for a..." Nate consulted his notes...'Jolene Pervis,' fifteen hundred dollars. Again, who works for five hundred bucks a month? Then in the first quarter Biggers is left off completely and Jolene Pervis is recorded as having been paid only three hundred dollars."

"Maybe Biggers didn't take a salary and maybe Jolene Pervis sprained her ankle and couldn't dance."

"These things too are possible Josh, but do you really think that's what happened? There's a letter from the IRS regarding the fourth quarter of last year. It says that the social security number for Biggers doesn't match anything in their records under that name. Also, Sy was making the dancers and waitresses report their tips. Then, when the judge put in a new manager, the new manager kept an attendance roll. Sy's records and the manager's records showed that Jolene Pervis worked at least three nights every week.

"There's also a letter in the file from the investors' lawyer asking Sy to send Biggers a '1099.' That's the form for miscellaneous income you send to someone who is not an employee. You remember back in the late 1980s, early 1990s, the 'note mongers' who bought the defaulted loans from the federal agency that took over all the failed savings and loans? They bought the paper for pennies on the dollar. Then they would threaten to send 1099s to borrowers who defaulted on their loans. They would show the full amount of the debt as income which the borrower would have to pay tax on. They would use the 1099 threat as leverage to get the borrower to turn over all his assets in exchange for a release and no 1099 to the IRS.

"The lawyer wanted Sy to send a 1099 to Biggers for all the money Biggers embezzled. Sy kept dragging his feet and there's another letter from the lawyer threatening to file a motion to get the judge to order Sy to prepare the 1099 or be removed as special master. Right after that is when Sy filed his final report and asked to be discharged. It looks like he prepared the 1099, but there's no indication in the file that it was ever sent."

"So Sy did have himself in a real jackpot. It looks like he did need a criminal lawyer. But what it also tells me is that Biggers had a damn good reason to shut Sy up permanently and make sure that 1099 never got sent."

"Mr. Josh, Mr. Nate, we're here. Mr. Nate, you want me to get you your walker?"

"If you don't mind DeMontrond, could I just lean on your arm?"

Louis leaned around the front passenger headrest. "It'll have to be my arm, Nate. DeMontron' won't be going in with us. He's still on parole. Police catch him inside that place, he be back in the joint 'fore you havin' your breakfast."

There wasn't a line of patrons eagerly awaiting entrance to experience the delights of Crystal's Palace. Perhaps it was too early. There were a few pickup trucks and cars in the parking lot. One of the pickups, a red Dodge Ram "2500," had a two-tier gun rack and a transparent Confederate battle flag in the rear window. A beer distributor truck was just pulling out. When the beer truck had cleared away, DeMontrond drove up as close as he could to the entrance so that Nate would not have so far to walk. When he had discharged his passengers he backed the Chrysler into a parking place on the row closest to the street and directly facing the door.

Holding on to Louis's arm Nate made it to the entrance without too much trouble. Before they went in Louis took out his cell phone and pressed a speed dial number. "You all set, DeMontrond? Want me to bring you out a Dr. Pepper?"

"All set, Uncle Louis. Yeah, a Dr. Pepper would be good. And if they got some pork rinds or pretzels, they'd be good too."

Chapter Twenty-Five

Using his credit card, Josh paid the five-dollar early bird cover charge for all three men and shelled out another twenty bucks apiece to pay for the two-drink minimum. The hostess wore a black, sequined halter-top that strained against the weight of her thirty-six double *D* breasts. She fumbled a bit with Josh's AmEx card but finally got the reader to accept it. When she came out from behind her podium she was wearing cowboy boots and a tiny fringed skirt that matched her top. She immediately sized up the three men as inspectors from the City of Dallas come to test Crystal's Palace's compliance with the city's non-discrimination ordinance. As she was checking them out Josh thought that from the waist down she looked like one of those novelty lamps molded in the shape of female legs wearing cowboy boots with fringe around the bottom of the shade.

The room was rectangular, slightly longer than wide. The bar was located on the back wall opposite the entrance. The cowboy lamp led them to a semicircular banquette in the corner where the front wall met the lateral wall to the right of the bar. There were stages on each side of the bar and several others located around the room.

As they were being seated the only occupied stage was one on the other side of the room. A young woman—at least at a distance of twenty-five feet, she appeared young—was gyrating to ninety-plus decibels worth of something that sounded to Josh like a steel garbage can full of empty beer bottles rolling down a bare concrete stairwell. The dancer was attired, so as to be minimally compliant with the city ordinance, in pasties on top and a g-string on the bottom. During her routine she kicked up her leg a few times displaying the six-inch pumps that adorned her feet. Josh would have bet that the shoes were not Christian Louboutins.

After a couple of minutes the music ended and the strobe light illuminating the stage went dim. No one applauded. A couple of patrons at a table near the stage did, however, reach up and stuff a couple of dollar bills down the front of the dancer's g-string.

There were a pair of skinhead types seated a couple of tables away from Josh, Louis and Nate. They were wearing black leather vests over plaid western shirts with the sleeves cut off, black jeans and western boots with blunt toes and walking heels. For headgear they wore gimme caps advertising Anheuser-Busch products. The one facing the banquette leaned forward across the table and said something to his companion who turned and looked over his shoulder taking in the fact that neither Josh, nor Nate nor Louis—especially Louis—looked like they belonged in Crystal's Palace. The second skinhead got up from his table and walked over to a man standing next to the cash register at the bar. The man had shoulder-length hair and was wearing a black dress shirt with a silver tie that was loose at his unbuttoned collar.

They were too far away for the conversation to be overheard, but it was evident that the customer was unhappy about something. The confrontation went on for a minute or so and ended when black-shirt took several drink coupons out of his pocket and handed them to the unhappy customer. Skinhead hesitated a moment and then accepted the coupons. He went back to his table and finished his Bud Lite.

Apparently the complimentary coupons were for another night, a night when the two customers would not have to be offended by being forced to witness a black man leering at nearly-naked white women. Such a pastime is one that, in the skinhead culture, is properly reserved for white men only. The two men got up from their table and headed for the door. As they passed the banquette they glared at Louis who smiled pleasantly back at them. The pair, to Josh's relief, elected not to say anything in response. They simply turned their heads and headed out the door.

"Louis, I'm so sorry. If I'd known, I…"

"Don't worry 'bout it, Mr. Josh. I ain't. Not the first time it's happened. Probably won't be the last. I'm jes' glad they kept their mouths shut. They'd said somethin' I suppose I would have had a word or two with them outside."

"With DeMontrond as back-up?"

"No need for that Mr. Josh. Don't need for DeMontron' to be gettin' into no bar fight. Police come, an' it's goodbye DeMontron'. Anyway, day comes when I couldn't whup those two fools, that'd be the day after the day you come to my funeral."

"You're not carrying in here, are you?"

"No, it's in the trunk of the Chrysler 'long with Nate's walker."

The house lights dimmed until the room was nearly in darkness. A male voice came through the sound system, "Gentlemen, for your viewing pleasure, now ascending our center-right stage, please welcome the Princess of Crystal's Palace, 'Princess Tiara.'" A pair of spotlights, one pink and the other a sort of bronze, illuminated the small round stage which was just a few feet from the banquette. While the lights were dimmed a dancer wearing a gold lamé cape and a jeweled tiara had stepped up onto the stage. She smiled and strutted around the stage a couple of times as the sound system began producing a country western standard at a more tolerable decibel level.

To demonstrate that Crystal's Palace also complied with the employment non-discrimination laws, management had assigned an African-American waitress to serve Josh, Louis and Nate. She wore the same black-sequined costume as the hostess. She had straightened hair which she wore shoulder-length. There were blond streaks on each side.

"Gentlemen, welcome to Crystal's Palace." She smiled displaying a set of sparkling white teeth. She leaned slightly forward watching the men as they took in the view of her perfectly-formed breasts. "What can I get you to drink?"

After a moment, Louis answered first, "I think I'll stick with beer. Shiner Bock if you have it."

"Yes, Sir. Coming right up. And you gentlemen?" She looked at Nate and then Josh.

Josh answered next, "What kind of scotch do you have?"

"I'm not sure what the well brand is. We don't get too many scotch drinkers. I think there's a bottle of Johnnie Walker 'Black Label' on the top shelf, but it'll cost you two coupons an' I won't promise you that what's in the bottle is what it says on the label."

"I think I'll go with that. Make it straight-up with a glass of water back."

"And you, Sir?" She turned to Nate.

Nate was absorbed first in the waitress' cleavage and then in 'Princess Tiara' who by now had opened her cape and was moving easily around the stage with her arms extended and her breasts swaying to the music.

Louis touched Nate's arm. "Nate, young lady asked what you want to drink."

"What are you having, Louis?"

"I'm drinking a Shiner Bock."

"I don't drink beer anymore. It bloats my stomach. Josh, what are you drinking?"

"Scotch. Johnnie Walker 'Black Label.' Neat."

"I'll have the same thing, Miss. Only I want mine with water. Scotch and water. And tell the bartender he shouldn't make it too strong."

"Don't need to be worrying about that, Mr. Nate. Watered-down drinks are his specialty. Now I'll need five coupons and I'll be back with your drinks in just a minute. In the meantime, relax and enjoy 'Princess Tiara.' And if you don't mind me saying it," she looked at Louis, "I just loved the way you smiled at those two skinheads. But you all need to be careful when you leave. There's a whole bunch of them comes in here jes' about every night. You might want to take a look around before you go out. And my name's 'Sondra' if you need anything." She gave Louis another smile and flounced off toward the bar. Josh wondered what Sondra's name would be if they didn't need anything.

Princess Tiara was down to her g-string and pasties by this time and Nate was fully into her performance. The performance came to an end with the Princess bowing deeply first to the left side of the room so that her backside was displayed in all its splendor to Josh, Louis and Nate. Then she repeated the bow facing in the direction of the bar. As she was turning to face the banquette Nate got up and started walking toward her.

Louis started to get up and assist Nate. "Nate, you want me to go with..."

Nate steadied himself with one hand on the back of an empty chair at the next table and with the other hand emphatically waved Louis back. " No, no, Louis. I can make it on my own."

And he did. No shuffling, no missteps and no holding on to anything.

Princess Tiara's pasties had tassels hanging from them. Using her hands to get them started she had the tassels twirling in opposite directions: left breast clockwise and right breast counter-clockwise. She kept this up using just the muscles in her chest. Nate reached the stage and took out his wallet. The Princess squatted down on her haunches so that the twirling display was at Nate's eye level. Still in that position she stopped twirling after about half a minute. The tassels were detachable from the essential part of the pasties. She detached the left one and handed it to Nate. Then she stood and thumbed open the front of her g-string so that Nate could insert the bill he was clutching between his thumb and forefinger. After he completed the transfer another patron who had come up to the stage after Nate, inserted his bill and in return received the other tassel.

Nate made it back to the table a moment before Sondra arrived with the drinks. He held up the tassel and shook it back and forth. Louis reached over and plucked the tassel from Nate. "Nice souvenir, Nate."

"Best twenty bucks I ever spent."

"Can I ask what you're going to do with it now that you own it?" Louis handed the tassel back to Nate.

Nate paused a moment as he pondered the question. Finally he lay the tassel on the table. Then he thumped it across the table in Josh's direction and shrugged. "Maybe for another twenty Princess Tiara will let me stick it back on." Sondra placed the drinks on the table and took a ten-dollar tip from Josh.

Josh took another ten out of his wallet and held it between his thumb and forefinger. "Sondra, when does Jasmine come on? We were hoping to see her and we don't have much time."

"'Fraid you gentlemen goin' to be disappointed; Jasmine don't work Fridays. Only Tuesdays, Thursdays and Saturdays. Been that way since about May."

"That's a disappointment." Josh took a sip of his scotch.

"I ain't seen you all in here before. How come you know Jasmine?"

"Well…" Josh paused, "We've heard a lot about her and had to see for ourselves. Have you been here since May, Sondra?" Josh held out the ten. Sondra took the money.

"Since December of last year."

"I guess you like it here?"

"Tips are pretty good. Working here got a whole lot better since they run off the old manager."

"You mean Andy Biggers?"

"Yeah, that's the one. You know him?" Sondra's voice took on an edge.

"Only know of him. And what we know isn't too good."

"Well, you probably don't know half of what he done when he was runnin' the place. Made the girls show their twats to what he called 'special' customers, usually them skinheads, altho' I don't know why they was so special. Made the girls show their twats to him too; said he was checkin' for signs of disease. There's a room back over there," she pointed to an unmarked door next to the bar. "Made the girls go in there and do 'special performances' for his 'special' customers. An' I ain't just talkin' about lap dances. Tried to get me to do it, but I told him I'd go to the cops. I don' need this job that bad."

"What about Jasmine?"

"I 'spect Andy was her fancy man. Anyway, he sure acted like he owned her. Even more so than the other girls. An' she sure acted like he owned her.

"When Andy Biggers got kicked out by the judge, that night he come by in a big stretch limo. Got Jasmine to come inside the club and bring all the other dancers out to the limo. Said, 'Andy wants to have a farewell party; thank all the girls.' They all went out, got in the limo and drove off. Place had to close down for the night. Next night too. I didn't go; wasn't invited.

"Two nights later a couple of the girls come back to work. Said Andy had some meth, a bunch of cocaine and a case of champagne in the limo. They drove around all night gettin' high and goin' to other clubs. Since then, Andy just drops

Jasmine off at work; doesn't come in the place at all. Most nights he drives off. Some nights he just parks and hangs out in the parkin' lot. That is if the manager don' catch him and run him off."

Sondra glanced over her shoulder toward the bar. "You see that dude in the black shirt with the silver tie? The one mean-muggin' you all?"

Josh nodded. "The manager, I take it."

"Well, it's been nice talking' to you gentlemen, but I don't get back to slingin' drinks, he liable to start actin' like he's Andy Biggers. He already not real pleased with you being' here. You all done run off two of his regular customers."

Josh finished his drink and turned to Louis and Nate. "Louis, Nate, have you seen enough?" Both men nodded.

Josh picked up the remaining drink coupon and handed it to Sondra. "Give this to the manager; tell him to have a drink on us." He then took another ten out his wallet and handed it to Sondra as well. "Just a couple more questions."

"Well ask 'em real quick."

"Okay. One: Do you happen to know Jasmine's real name?"

"She and I were kind of friends. At work, I mean. We never went anywhere together; Andy wouldn't allow it. I suppose you know that she *passe blanc*? Her real name is 'Jolene.' We just use first names around here, so I don't know her last name. "

"Second question: Do you know whether Jolene had any regular customers?"

"How come you askin'? She in some kind of trouble?"

"More like Andy's the one in trouble."

"You tellin' the truth?"

"Yes, Sondra, I'm telling you the truth. It's Andy Biggers who's in trouble."

"Only regular customer I know about is this one she calls 'Sy.' Older man; thin gray hair; kind of fat. Come in almost every Tuesday and Thursday, but I ain't seen him this week. Drinks vodka. She does table dances, lap dances. She shows him her twat and he stuffs money in it. When he leaves she goes outside and gives Andy the money. I don't think Andy lets her keep any of it."

"Sondra, thank you. One more thing." Josh handed Sondra another ten. "Do you know whether Sy was here a week ago Thursday?"

"If it was Thursday, yeah, he was here."

"Are you sure, or are you just saying that because it was Thursday he must have been here?"

"No, I'm sure. I was working the front desk that night."

"Is that the only time you worked the front desk?"

"No, I take my turn, two, sometimes three nights a week."

"Then …"

"'Cause when Sy come in he asked me whether anyone had been in askin' about him."

"Had there?"

"No, at least no one asked me."

"You mentioned that Andy Biggers, when he brings Jolene to work sometimes hangs around in the parking lot. Do you know whether Andy just dropped Jolene off that night or did he hang around in the parking lot?"

"Yeah, I 'spect he was hangin'. I saw Jolene run outside right after he left. She must have been out there ten, fifteen minutes."

195

"What kind of car does Andy drive?"

"A big funny-colored Mercedes. Now, that's all. I got to get to work."

Chapter Twenty-Six

Sondra's words of caution were justified. The skinheads had moved their pickup to a handicap parking space next to the entrance. They were leaning against the truck with their thumbs hooked in the front pockets of their jeans. Louis had insisted on leading the way out the door. Josh and Nate were a step behind with Nate holding on to Josh's upper right arm. Louis was less than ten feet away from the men when Josh put his free hand on Louis's shoulder.

"Louis, maybe we'd better go back inside and wait until they get bored and drive off."

"How long you think that'd be, Mr. Josh? An hour? Maybe two? Besides, you want to pay another seventy-five bucks to get back in. I don' remember getttin' my wrist stamped. Do you? How 'bout you, Nate? You think I ought to call Leticia, tell her to hold dinner? You think she might want to know why? Since I can't tell her where I am, what should I tell her? Besides that, if I have to choose between stayin' in there any longer and dealin' with those two gentlemen, I think I'd rather have a little discussion with them about race relations."

"Then let's go back in and get the manager to call the police."

"How long it take for them to get here? You said they all out lookin' for *El Chupacabra*. Anyway, you know how it is when you call the police? One thing leads to another and you never know who gonna end up handcuffed in the back seat of the police car and who get to go home. My experience, the black man usually the one don' get to go home to his wife and a nice dinner.

"You and Nate just hold here for a minute. Take this," Louis handed Josh his cell phone. "Things don' quite go the way I think they will, you jus' push the star and the number nine. Take DeMontron' 'bout two seconds to get from the car to here."

"Louis, don't do…"

As Josh was trying to convince Louis to back down, the skinheads had left their leaning positions and were now standing shoulder to shoulder directly facing Louis. Louis, smiling broadly, started walking toward them. As he closed the distance to the two men Louis raised his arms and held them out at shoulder level.

"Gentlemens, how you all doin'?" When he had closed to just outside arm's length he lunged forward and smashed their heads together with his open palms. The skinheads' knees buckled and they fell face down to the asphalt pavement. Louis took a step to his right and another forward. The skinhead on Louis's right was clutching an unsheathed Ka-Bar Mark 2 fighting knife with a seven-inch blade. Louis kicked the knife toward the rear of the pickup truck. "Don' reckon he be usin' that thing tonight."

The skidding knife just missed DeMontrond's feet. "You okay, Uncle Louis?"

"Yeah, I'm jes' fine, DeMontron'. But these two gentlemen? They could probably use some assistance in gettin' back into their vehicle. You think you could give 'em some help?"

"Yes, Sir, Uncle Louis." DeMontrond stepped between the two bodies and lifted them, one in each hand, by their belts. "Inside or outside, Uncle Louis?"

"Hol' on jes' a sec." Louis lifted each man's head and placed his glasses under their noses. When the lenses fogged up he let their heads drop back down. "They still breathin'. Guess you can just lay them in the cargo bed." Louis wiped off his glasses with a pocket handkerchief.

As DeMontrond was lifting first one man then the other over the side of the pickup, Josh's cell phone rang. "Josh Loeb...Oh, hi, Detective Turner...Alana. You got my message, obviously...Yes, I have the video from the parking lot and building lobby from both the burglary and the abduction...I also have the key-card access logs...The security company gave them to me on CDs, but Alicia said it would be easier if they were on—it's this little black thing you stick in the side of a computer—a...yeah, 'thumb-drive'—that's what she called it. So she put the video and access logs on thumb-drives.

"I'm sorry, Alana. I called you as soon as I could...Yesterday afternoon...Because you didn't tell me that I needed to give the information to your boss, or even who your boss is...Apology accepted...Right now?...I'm in a meeting with Louis, DeMontrond and my forensic accountant...No, we're not at my office...Does it matter where we are? Just tell me where you want to meet and when...Yes, I know where Matt's is...on Skillman...Gosh, from here, in the traffic, around forty-five minutes. That's if you don't mind me bringing my brain trust along. Otherwise, an hour and a half...Let me ask them and I'll call you back in a minute."

While Josh was on the phone with Detective Turner, he and the brain trust had gotten into the Chrysler. DeMontrond had started the engine and was awaiting instructions. "That was Detective Turner on the phone. She's having a fit because I didn't turn over the video from Sy's building. She wants to meet right now. Anyone in the mood for Mexican food?"

"I'm good with that. Wouldn't mind a *cerveza* or two go along with it. Amazing how a little light exercise can work up a thirst. And DeMontron' never did get his Dr. Pepper and pork skins. You okay with that, DeMontron'?"

"Yes, Sir, Uncle Louis. Pickin' those folks off the groun' made me awful hungry."

"Then we be glad to keep you company, Mr. Josh. I jes' need to call Leticia and let her know."

"Nate? Do you need to get home? It's not a problem. Detective Turner will just have to wait a little longer."

"Josh, are you trying to get rid of me again?"

"Nate, I...I was just thinking about Rose..."

"You worry about Elaine and I'll worry about Rose. I haven't had this much fun since Abe Weinstein closed the Colony Club back in the early seventies."

"I thought you said you'd never been to a topless bar?"

"I haven't. The Colony Club was a nightclub. A high-class place. Right across Commerce Street from the Adolphus

Hotel. I even took Rose there a few times. Candy Barr had real class."

"Okay. I'll call Detective Turner back and tell her table for five. Now let's get the hell out of here before the 'gentlemen,' as Louis calls them, wake up and call their friends."

Chapter Twenty-Seven

By the time dinner was finished and they'd driven Nate home, it was close to ten o'clock when Louis and DeMontrond dropped Josh at his home. Josh had left his automatic garage-door opener and his house key in his Jaguar. It took Elaine a few minutes to come to the door. Josh was beginning to think that maybe she wasn't going to let him in. Louis and DeMontrond had driven off as soon as Josh had gotten out of the car. Josh was considering whether to use his cell phone to call them to come back. When the porch light went on and she opened the door Elaine did not have a rolling pin or cast iron frying pan held behind her back. But to Josh, getting bashed over the head would have been preferable to the look she gave him as she let him in. Having no words to add to the look, Elaine turned and went back into the bedroom. Josh made sure the front door was locked and followed her.

Elaine had been watching TV. She was already back in bed when Josh came in, took off his suit jacket and sat down on the couch. Elaine clicked the TV off. Reaching down to slip off his shoes Josh asked, "Do you mind if we watch the news?"

Elaine tossed the remote in his direction. It landed on the couch cushion next to him. Josh pressed the on-button and the screen was filled with the words "breaking news" in fat yellow capital letters against a red background. The regular ten o'clock weeknight anchors were in their places wearing their concerned looks and peering through the camera into their viewers' bedrooms to be sure they were paying attention.

Tonight the female anchor led off. "Big changes in the weather coming in time for Thanksgiving. The Metroplex could be in for our first freezing weather of the season just in time for Thanksgiving. But before we turn things over to our chief meteorologist Dick Jaynes in our weather center, we have breaking news to report. Police are investigating two incidents involving alleged members of the 'Caucasian Council' a group labeled by local and federal officials as a white supremacist gang, notorious for their shaved-heads, tattoos and penchant for violence as well as for the manufacture and distribution of methamphetamine.

"The first incident occurred between six-thirty and seven o'clock this evening at a gentlemen's club on Harry Hines Boulevard. Our reporter Steve Blessing is on the scene to tell us all about it. Steve…"

"Thanks, Marcy. Ladies and gentlemen I'm standing outside Crystal's Palace on Harry Hines Boulevard in Northwest Dallas. Police and EMTs were called to the scene when a patron entering the club discovered two semi-conscious men lying in the back of a pickup truck illegally parked in a handicap spot next to the front door. The patron, who declined to give us his name or to be interviewed on camera, said that the two men were moaning in the back of the truck and that's what attracted his attention. The patron notified the club manager who called 9-1-1.

"The patron said as he walked next to the truck to see who was making the moaning sound, he stumbled over a large military-style knife. Detectives have taken custody of the knife together with a number of Crystal's Palace drink coupons found in the back of the truck next to one of the victims.

"As you can see from the activity behind me, police are still scouring the parking lot for any other weapons or clues as to who might have assaulted the two men. And as you can also see, a wrecker is just now leaving with the pickup truck in tow." The director cut to a wide shot of a wrecker hauling away the pickup truck. Then the camera changed to a tight focus on the Confederate flag in the truck's rear window.

"The club manager also declined to speak with us on-camera. He did tell us, however, that the men are not regular patrons of the club and had not been inside. He said that it is likely the men were assaulted elsewhere and left in front of Crystal's Palace. He says that the drink coupons were from Crystal's Palace, but they could have been planted to make it appear as though the assault was a continuation of some altercation that occurred inside. He mentioned that there are a number of competitors in the area and that one of them might be responsible. That's all from here. Back to you, Marcy."

"Thanks, Steve. Now to Sofia Salado who is standing by at the Parkland Hospital emergency room. Sofia…"

"Good evening, Marcy. It's less than a fifteen-minute ride by ambulance from Crystal's Palace down Harry Hines to the Parkland Hospital emergency room. Neither Parkland officials nor the DPD are releasing much information. However, we've been able to learn that the two men were treated for concussions in the emergency room and then moved to intensive care where they are being closely monitored for any signs of cranial hemorrhaging. The two victims are listed in serious but stable condition. Hospital and police authorities have declined to release the victims' names.

"DPD detectives did tell us that the men had regained consciousness and were lucid enough to be interviewed by DPD detectives. The men voluntarily confirmed that they were members of the Caucasian Council, but they refused to identify their assailant or assailants or to talk further with detectives. Back to you, Marcy."

"We'll be following the story closely as further details emerge. Be sure to tune in to the Channel Ten 'Morning Show' beginning at five a.m. for the latest update. Now to our other breaking story. Tracy…"

"Thanks, Marcy. *El Chupacabra* has apparently claimed another victim. At about the same time police were called to the gentlemen's club on Harry Hines, another mutilated victim was discovered in Northwest Dallas. The body was discovered in a dumpster behind an apartment project on Brockbank Street, just south of Royal Lane.

"The address is less than three miles from the gentlemen's club location. And it may only be a coincidence, but a DPD spokesperson tells Channel Ten that the victim is also a member of the Caucasian Council. The Department spokesperson said the DPD was able to identify the victim because he was well-known to narcotics officers and has an extensive record of arrests and convictions for possession and sale of methamphetamine. The name of the victim, however, was not released pending notification of next of kin.

"The DPD spokesperson declined to speculate as to whether the two incidents, both involving the same group of people, are related. She declined to answer this reporter's question asking whether the homicide might be a copycat killing perpetrated by members of a rival gang. However, she did say that the Department is considering all possibilities. Again, tune in to the Channel Ten 'Morning Show' for the latest updates on both breaking stories.

"Right after the commercial break our chief meteorologist Dick Jaynes will show you what's in store for the Metroplex weather-wise and how it will affect your upcoming Thanksgiving holiday travel plans."

After listening to the weather, Josh turned off the TV. "I hope the weather doesn't mess up Caroline's travel plans."

"I heard the same weather report on the six o'clock news. I called Caroline. She said she'd try to change her flight and come in Tuesday night."

"That's going to be a challenge. Thanksgiving is the busiest travel week of the year. When will she find out if she can?"

"She said she'd call me tomorrow and let me know."

"Do you want to hear about dinner?"

"I don't know, Josh. Do I want to hear about dinner?"

"Elaine, this evening was strictly business. I would much rather have been home eating dinner with you."

"You like reheated chicken and leftover green beans?"

"Not especially. But I do enjoy eating dinner with you. You're much better looking than Louis, DeMontrond, Nate or even Alana...Detective Turner."

"So she's 'Alana' now?"

"Yes, she's 'Alana' now. You remember that Russian saying 'Keep your friends close and your enemies closer?'"

"And she is your enemy because...?"

"Because I'm trying to keep her out of Sy's personal life for Estelle's sake."

"By 'Sy's personal life' you mean his affair?"

"It looks that way."

"So tell about dinner."

"I actually managed to leave Sy pretty much out of the conversation. I gave Alana the security camera video and entry logs from Sy's office building. She brought her laptop so we watched the video."

"Which shows...?"

"That the burglars entering the building Sunday night and that the same two people kidnapping Margie on Monday night."

"God, how awful!"

"As they say on TV, 'Some viewers may find the images disturbing.' I did; we all did. According to the time stamp on the video and the entry log, she was taken right after she left the voicemail message for Alicia around ten o'clock."

"So Margie's kidnapping and murder and Sy's death are connected?"

"Detective Turner is convinced; she just hasn't figured out the connection."

"Is that all you talked about?"

"She told me about her trip to Arkansas."

"What's in Arkansas besides the Clinton Library and the Crystal Bridges museum?"

"Margie's ex-husband, Orville Karl Carver. They tracked him down in Arkansas. Detective Turner's boss insisted that she question him in person, so she had to drive up there yesterday. She just got back this evening. The ex-husband lives in a mobile home...Alana described it as more of a trailer...a beat-up old aluminum AirStream. It's parked on a couple of acres outside of Eureka Springs. Orville—or 'Karl' as he prefers to be called—works, when he's sober, as a fishing guide on the lake up there.

"He lives with a woman. Alana said the woman could be his wife, his sister or both. Anyway, the woman confirmed Karl's story that he got drunk Sunday and spent the whole day Monday sleeping it off. So there's no way he could have had anything to do with Margie's murder. They told Alana that they don't read newspapers or watch the national news, so they'd never even heard of *El Chupacabra* or the killings in Dallas. Alana said Karl seemed genuinely upset to learn what happened to Margie.

"So the whole trip was a waste of a day and a half. But at least Alana's boss is satisfied."

"That was it?"

"By 'it' you mean dinner conversation?"

"I mean is that all you're going to tell me."

"Well, we did have an interesting conversation about 'Honky Tonk Woman.' You remember the song?"

"Yes, Josh, I remember the song. I remember you loved it and I thought it was vulgar. But what in the world does 'Honky Tonk Woman' have to do with a murder investigation?"

"The other night—Monday night, when I identified Margie's body—Alana mentioned that she's a Tina Turner fan. I mentioned it to Louis and Nate during dinner. Turns out Louis is a Tina Turner fan as well. So is Nate. Nate even likes Ike Turner.

"Alana said she liked the original version of 'Honky Tonk Woman' better that any of the covers...Tina Turner's and even Joe Cocker's. Nate disagreed. He hates the Rolling Stones. Says they sound like Spike Jones and the City Slickers on a bad night. Louis agreed with Nate and so did I."

"I'm surprised Nate has even heard of the Rolling Stones. Did Detective Turner know who Spike Jones was?"

"No, but Nate filled her in. Evidently, Nate hasn't been eighty years old all his life. Turns out that when Nate was in college he got hooked on listening to radio stations that catered to black audiences. He's an expert on rhythm and blues and early rock and roll. Can't remember what he had for dinner last night, but he remembers who first recorded what songs and most of the lyrics. He has a huge collection of forty-fives and albums but he had to let his daughter keep it for him because there's no room at *Chai* Manor."

"What about DeMontrond? Did he have an opinion?"

"He had no idea what we were talking about. Anyway, he was busy with his chicken-fried steak with a side order of tamales."

"And now are you going to tell me about Sy's affair?"

Josh took a dollar bill, which was about half of the cash he had left after Crystal's Palace, and handed it to Elaine who dropped on the nightstand.

"What's that for?"

"I just hired you as a special consultant."

"'Special consultant' in what?"

"The female perspective."

"As to why men think with their dicks?"

"I wouldn't put it quite in those terms, but yes; that'll do for a job description."

"So now I'm an official member of Josh's Posse?"

"Welcome aboard, Deputy Elaine. I'll have to teach you the secret handshake and password."

"Okay, I'm ready."

"Can it wait five minutes while I get ready for bed?"

"You mean ready for the couch?"

"Elaine, come on."

"All right, Josh. But you stay on your side."

Buying time to think of how to tell Elaine about Jasmine and Crystal's Palace, Josh took as long as he could with his bedtime ablutions. He finally crawled into bed and Elaine put away her Louise Penny book. Elaine turned her bedside reading lamp so that it was shining directly into Josh's eyes. "Okay, Loeb, spill your guts."

Josh did; almost completely. He told her what Margie Morrison had told him and what he'd learned from his own reading of Sy's file. He told her about the visit to Crystal's Palace. He left out Nate's conclusion that Sy had apparently been cooking the books and he didn't feel it necessary to mention Louis's encounter with the skinheads.

"Josh, what were you thinking? Taking Nate to a topless bar. I'm surprised he didn't have a heart attack. If Rose finds out she'll wring his neck and then yours...providing I don't wring it first."

"Rose won't find out and neither will Leticia. Nate and Louis are both members of 'Josh's Posse' as you call us.

They're covered by my work-product privilege and sworn to secrecy, just as you are."

"I can't believe that Louis, much less Nate, let you talk them into going there."

"Nate had a terrific time. Said it was the most fun he'd had since the Colony Club closed in the nineteen seventies. Louis did too; made some new acquaintances."

"And DeMontrond?"

"He didn't have much fun. Because he's still on parole he couldn't go in; had to wait in the car."

"That was mean."

"He didn't mind; he knew it was for his own good. He's a smart kid and he really means to stay out of trouble from now on. Louis is training him to take over the business when he decides to retire."

"So what happens now?"

"Tomorrow I'm going by the condo to try and square things with management and give Miss Jasmine and her 'fancy man'—as the waitress called him—their eviction notice. Hopefully, now that Sy's not supporting their lifestyle, they'll go without me having to take them to court."

"So you're sure that this Jasmine and...what is his name..."

"Andy Biggers."

"...that they're the tenants?"

"Maybe not, but it would sure be a surprise if they weren't."

"And what if they don't go quietly?"

"Then I'll file a forcible detainer and let the constable's office and the JP court deal with them. Harmon hired me to be the lawyer for HP Investments. I don't see any reason for Estelle to know about it."

"Can't you just have the constable serve the eviction notice?"

"No. The constable doesn't get involved until the forcible detainer—the eviction suit—is filed and I can't file the suit until I give them the eviction notice. Also, I have to make nice with the condo manager so that Harmon doesn't get sued. If that happens, he'll drag me in as executor of Sy's estate and Estelle will find out for sure."

"Can you at least get a constable—even an off-duty one—to go with you?"

"I don't need one; I've got DeMontrond. Louis took him to a big and tall men's shop this afternoon while Nate and I were working at the office. Got him outfitted in a nice blue blazer, a good pair of gray slacks, a white button-down dress shirt and a pair of cap-toe oxfords, size sixteen and a half. First good clothes DeMontrond's ever had."

"What will DeMontrond do?"

"All he needs to do is a little mean mugging and that ought to keep things civilized."

"'Mean mugging?'"

"Giving someone the evil eye. You know, the *kine hora*. Like your grandmother used to do to me when we were dating."

"DeMontrond has supernatural powers? Like a *golem*? Like my grandmother?"

"You can see for yourself tomorrow. I'll invite him in to meet you when he picks me up in the morning." Josh reached over and took Elaine's hand. She started to pull it away, but Josh tightened his grip. "I have to teach you the secret handshake. And I have to move over next to you so that I can whisper the secret password in your ear."

Chapter Twenty-Eight

Attired in his new wardrobe, DeMontrond made a favorable impression on Elaine whom he insisted on calling "Miz Elaine." She persuaded him to try a bagel with cream cheese with a diet Coke since she didn't have any Dr. Pepper. He passed on a slice of lox with the bagel, so Elaine reluctantly got a jar of grape jelly out of the fridge to spread over the cream cheese. At her insistence he tried to give her a demonstration of "mean mugging" but they both started laughing so hard that he finally gave up.

DeMontrond found a place in the visitors' parking area next to the porte-cochere in front of the Olympus Condominium Residences. The lobby was decorated in a nineteen-sixties version of Louis Quinze: burgundy-colored wall paper in a flocked paisley print over white wainscoting; large gilt-framed mirrors; and lithographs of Eighteenth-Century pastoral scenes that screamed: "Reproduction!" The load-bearing interior columns were finished in a Doric style and painted with a chalk-white enamel. The columns were adorned with gold and crystal lighting sconces that matched the enormous chandelier hanging in the lobby center. The seating area was furnished in white, gold-accented Louis Quinze with white brocade upholstery.

There was a concierge desk to their right as they walked in. An elderly man—a smaller, older version of Louis—was seated at the desk. He wore a gray doorman's uniform with "Olympus" embroidered in thick red thread on the left breast pocket. As they approached he stood and gave a small smile. "Morning, gentlemen. May I help you?"

Josh took out one of his cards and handed it over. "Good morning. We'd like to see the manager please."

"May I tell Miz DuMont the nature of your business?"

"I represent HP Investments, the owner of Unit Six-*E*. We're here about the tenants. My client received a letter…"

"Yes, Sir, Mr. Loeb. Let me call Miz DuMont and let her know you gentlemen are here. I'm sure she's most anxious to see you."

The doorman picked up a phone and spoke for a moment. "Miz DuMont said you're welcome to join her in her office." He pointed to a door behind him. "Just through that door, Gentlemen. Then it's the first door on your left."

The door to the manager's office was open. Ms. Dumont was seated behind a Louis Quinze writing table that served as her desk. As they came in she stood and held out her hand. When she stood she barely came to DeMontrond's waist. She was nearly as wide as she was tall. She wore a burgundy knit dress that clung to her body emphasizing her pendulous breasts and the rolls of fat that bulged above her hips and below her bra. She wore a Bedat watch with a mother-of-pearl face and a David Yurman bracelet on her left arm and a ruby ring on her right ring finger. She had apparently given up trying to style her reddish-blond hair. Her pudgy face, comprised of narrow-set porcine eyes, a pug nose and a small cruel-looking mouth, ended in a prominent pointed chin. Josh thought that instead of his coming here, he should have let Harmon Polikoff deal with her as he had intended until Josh talked him out of it. Harmon might have done the surgery right there on her desk.

"Mr. Loeb, I'm Elizabeth DuMont. I'm the general manager of the Olympus Condominium Residences. I'm so happy to meet you."

Josh took the extended hand. "I'm pleased to meet you as well, Ms. DuMont. This is my associate, Mr. Prejean."

She didn't offer her hand. "Mr. Prejean." She nodded to DeMontrond. "Won't you both have a seat so we can get right down to business?" She indicated the two guest chairs arranged in front of her desk.

When they were seated Josh handed her his card. "I'm here on behalf of my client HP Investments, Ms. DuMont. My client is of course aware of the issues you've been having with the tenants in Unit Six-*E*. We're here to see if we can put those issues to rest."

"How do you propose to do that, Mr. Loeb? Although I of course haven't been here that long, I understand that in the entire fifty-year history of the Olympus we've never had this type of problem before. We have a mix of residents, all races, religious preferences, what have you. We have elderly, retired residents; widows and widowers; professionals, doctors and lawyers, bankers; singles and married couples; even a few families with young children.

"It's especially those that are of concern to our board of directors. In fact the board met Thursday night and voted unanimously to have our legal counsel write a letter to your client pointing out the provisions in the condominium by-laws that prohibit conducting a business on condominium property and those which prohibit any nuisance, illegal or other obnoxious activity. The board also authorized our legal counsel to initiate legal action to enforce the by-law provisions if the problem is not taken care of immediately."

"You mentioned 'business' and 'illegal activity.' My client is wholly unaware of any such occurrences. All my client is aware of is that there have been some incidents of loud parties and one instance of an inebriated party-guest relieving himself in an elevator. Do you have proof that the tenants are operating a business or engaging in illegal activity, Ms. DuMont?"

"Mr. Loeb, do I need to call our legal counsel to participate in this meeting? He does live in the building."

"Suit yourself, Ms. DuMont."

"I thought you were here to solve the problem."

"Indeed I am, Ms. DuMont. I'm just trying to get a handle on the scope of the problem. I'm also here to assure you that *a*, my client is wholly unaware of anything beyond what I just told you, and *b*, my client has every intention of complying with his legal obligations, including those imposed by the condominium association by-laws."

"Well, would you agree that operating a...a...house of ill-repute constitutes operating a business and conducting an illegal activity, Mr. Loeb?"

"I certainly would, Ms. DuMont. If that is in fact the case I'm appalled, as my client will be when I inform him. But again I must ask: Do you know this to be true?"

"People coming here—day and night—at all hours. That woman, Miss Pervis, she dresses like...like...a streetwalker. When a single 'guest' comes, always a man, Mr. Biggers comes down and sits in the lobby. In fact Henry, our concierge, told me that he's in the lobby right now. Just sitting there reading a magazine.

"Dozens of empty liquor bottles in the trash along with just as many used condoms. Building maintenance being called because the toilet is stopped up with more used condoms. A couple of times other residents on the sixth floor have mentioned that they smelled what they think is marijuana smoke in the hall between Unit Six-*E* and the elevators. What would you conclude, Mr. Loeb?"

"What you say is very convincing, Ms. DuMont. Even though it's only circumstantial it's enough to persuade me and therefore my client that it's past time for Mr. Biggers and Ms. Pervis to leave. Would you mind inviting Mr. Biggers to join us in your office? In case he makes a scene, I'd prefer to hand him his eviction notice here, in private, rather than in your lobby. Then Mr. Prejean and I will go up to the unit and provide an identical notice to Ms. Pervis."

DuMont picked up her desk-top phone and dialed an internal number. "Henry, is Mr. Biggers still in the lobby?...Good. Would you ask him if he could spare me a few minutes?...Yes, here in my office...No, don't mention anything about Mr. Loeb...Thank you, Henry."

Andy Biggers took his time strolling his way across the lobby to Elizabeth DuMont's office. When Henry called back to say that Biggers was on his way, Josh suggested to Ms. DuMont that she remain seated at her desk and that the office door be closed. Then he and DeMontrond moved to the left side of the room so that Biggers would not see them when he opened the door and first entered the room.

Biggers opened the door and walked into the office without knocking. "You want to see me about something, Elizabeth? What is it this time?" He sat down in one of the guest chairs. "Did I park in the wrong parking space again? I'm so sorry; sometimes I just forget." He flashed a contrite smile at Ms. DuMont.

DeMontrond gently closed the office door. At the sound Biggers turned in his seat becoming aware of DeMontrond and Josh for the first time. The smile froze on Biggers's face. He rose from the chair and turned to face Josh and DeMontrond. Biggers stood about five-foot ten. He had broad shoulders, a thick neck and chest and a slim waist. Josh guessed that Biggers had at some earlier time perhaps done something athletic. He put Biggers's age at early-perhaps mid-forties.

Biggers was dressed in a cream-colored raw silk sport coat over tan gabardine slacks. He wore brown crocodile Gucci loafers. Peeking out from his left sleeve was a genuine-looking gold Rolex with a gold bark bracelet. Under the sport coat he wore a Hawaiian-print shirt with the collar and the top two buttons unbuttoned. Around his neck hanging down onto his bare, hairless chest he wore a "Mr. T" starter set featuring an elaborate ormolu Eastern Orthodox cross with a silver inlay of the traditional three-arm cross in the center. He had a diamond stud in his left ear. He had thick wavy blond hair and a broad, flat face. His irises were almost colorless, showing only the faintest blue-green. His teeth may not have been original equipment.

"What? Who are..."

"I'm Joshua Loeb, Mr. Biggers." Josh handed Biggers a business card which Biggers looked at for a moment and then tossed on DuMont's desk. "And this is my associate, Mr. Prejean. We represent HP Investments, the owner of Unit Six-*E*."

Biggers slammed his open hand on DuMont's desk. The grin was now gone and Biggers turned up his vocal volume. "What do you mean 'owner?'I never hear of this 'Investments'...what you call it? Owner is..."

Josh raised his voice to drown out Biggers, "Sit down, Mr. Biggers. And listen carefully." DeMontrond took a step forward and put on what must have impressed Biggers as a genuine mean-mugging look. Anyway, Biggers sat back down.

Josh reached in his suit jacket and took out a folded document. "Here's a certified copy of the deed to the unit showing ownership in my client, HP Investments. I'm sure that Ms. DuMont will also be glad to confirm that HP Investments owns Unit Six-*E* according to the official records of the condominium association. Right, Ms. DuMont?"

"That's correct, Mr. Loeb. Mr. Biggers, Unit Six-*E* is owned by HP Investments." Ms. DuMont smiled smugly, clearly beginning to enjoy the encounter.

Josh continued, "The gentleman with whom you are used to dealing is no longer involved. For what little business we have left to discuss, you will have to deal with myself and Mr. Prejean." Josh sat down in the other guest chair. DeMontrond remained standing, his back to the office door. "Now that the ownership issue is behind us, I'd like to conclude our other business as quickly as possible and in a civil manner. Is that agreeable, Mr. Biggers?"

"*Da*...yes, is agreeable. What is 'other business' you mention?"

"Do you have a lease, Mr. Biggers?"

"Of course I have lease."

"Then could you please show it to me?"

"Is upstairs. Can't go up now. Jolene...my wife...not well; is sleeping."

"Jasmine...I mean Jolene...is your wife?"

"Of course she is my wife."

"When and where were you and Jolene married?"

"Sometime. I don't remember when."

"Or where?"

"I forget these things. This make Jolene angry with me." Biggers shrugged his shoulders and held his hands palms-up. He tried the smile again, but Josh did not reciprocate.

"Do you even know Jolene's maiden name?"

"I knew it, but I forget. You make me very upset. All these questions."

"Well, let's try another subject: Does your memory allow you to tell me the terms of the lease?"

"Terms? What is 'terms?'"

"For example: How much is the rent?"

"This I don't remember."

"What about the term of the lease? When does it expire?"

"I don't remember this. I know is a long time. Yes, a long time."

"Do you know whether the lease says that you have to abide by the condominium by-laws and occupancy rules?"

Now desperate to find something to agree about, Biggers perked up. "Maybe. Yes, I think so."

"Okay, that's good Mr. Biggers. You remembered something." That brought back the smile to Biggers's face. This time Josh reciprocated.

"Do you know what the condominium by-laws say about running a business on the premises? How about engaging in an illegal activity? Creating a nuisance? Any of those ring a bell?"

"I do not know these things, Mr..." Biggers looked down at Josh's card lying on the desk..."Loeb."

"Well, let me tell you how I see it: One, you don't have a lease; never did have one. Two, you and Jolene are no more married than Mr. Prejean and I. Three, you are operating a whorehouse in Unit Six-*E*. And four, it stops right now." Josh extracted another piece of paper from his jacket pocket. "Mr. Biggers, I'm handing you a formal, written notice on behalf of my client, HP Investments that yours and Jolene's occupancy of Unit Six-*E* in the Olympus Condominium Residences is hereby terminated. On behalf of my client, I am hereby making demand for immediate possession. I have a similar letter for Ms. Pervis. Mr. Prejean and I will accompany you upstairs to personally deliver it to her."

Josh extended the letter toward Biggers who let it drop to the floor. "I have rights; you cannot do this. I have lease."

Josh stood up. "And Mr. Biggers, I have a JP sitting at his desk ready to sign an order for immediate possession. All I need to do is call him." Josh took out his cell phone and put it on the edge of the desk. I also have a pair of constables standing by to serve the order and to remove you by force, if necessary. Do you really want a couple of law enforcement officers poking around in your things? Maybe checking Jolene's lingerie drawer to see if there are any illegal substances?"

Biggers stood also. His face was red and contorted with rage. "This is bullshit! No fast-talking *zhid* lawyer and his gorilla are going to push Andy Biggers around! I'll show you! Biggers launched a looping right toward Josh's head. Josh saw it coming and tilted his head to the left so that Biggers's fist landed in the space where Josh's jaw had been the instant before.

Josh grabbed Biggers's wrist with both his hands and at the same time brought his heel down hard on Bigger's right instep squarely on top of the Gucci brass *D*-rings. Josh used the momentum of the punch to pull Biggers forward. He then folded Biggers's arm behind his back and jerked upward. Biggers grunted in pain and fell to his knees. Using his left hand, Josh slammed Biggers's face into the chair in which Josh had been sitting.

It happened so quickly that Elizabeth DuMont did not have time to react. Her reaction, after half a minute, was to reach for her phone. "This is unacceptable, Mr. Loeb. I'm calling 9-1-1."

"No need for that now, Ms. DuMont. As you can see, we have things under control. Mr. Prejean, would you please take over now?"

DeMontrond stepped next to Josh and took over the hammer-lock duties. He used his left hand to seize a handful of Biggers's hair and pull him to an upright position. "Man got an awful bad attitude, Mr. Josh. You mind if I tune him up just a little?"

"That's not a good idea, DeMontrond. Better leave the 'tuning up' to me. Besides, I think that Mr. Biggers has gotten the hostility out of his system and is ready to cooperate.

"Isn't that right, Mr. Biggers? Are you ready to cooperate?"

"*Yob vas!*"

DeMontrond lifted Biggers off the ground using only Biggers's forearm which was still in the hammerlock position behind his back. To his credit, Bigger didn't scream; he just gritted his teeth and mumbled something in a language Josh did not recognize.

"What's that you said, Mr. Biggers? I didn't quite understand what you said."

"Yes, yes. I said 'yes,' we will go."

"Put him down, DeMontrond. I think Mr. Biggers is ready to cooperate. Get his key to the unit and…"

"Ms. DuMont do you need an access card for the elevator?"

"Yes; it's the same one you use for the garage."

"Get his access card also, DeMontrond."

"How many keys and cards are there, Ms. DuMont?

"Just two of each."

"Okay, we'll pick up the other set when we get upstairs. I'll call a cleaning service, Ms. DuMont. I'll try to get them to come out here this afternoon, but it may be Monday. I assume that you have a service elevator?"

"Yes. Just call and let me know whom you've hired. Tell them to contact me and I'll see that they get to where they're supposed to be."

"Mr. Biggers, do you have any firearms in the unit?"

"No, no gun…" DeMontrond dialed up the pressure on Biggers's arm. "Yes, I have pistol. Is on shelf in closet in bedroom. I'll get it for you."

"That's okay, Mr. Biggers. I expect we'll be able to find it. Now, are we ready to go upstairs?"

"No! Now is not good time! Jolene is in bed."

"I think it'll be a fine time, Mr. Biggers. You'll just have to tell the man who's in there with her that he'll have to go. I assume he paid in advance, so I think in fairness he ought to get a refund."

When they got to the door leading to the lobby Josh led the way with DeMontrond a step behind guiding Biggers lightly by his right arm. Biggers was limping from the damage to his instep. They made it across the lobby and into the elevator without incident. Once in the elevator, Biggers turned to Josh and tried his most ingratiating smile. "Can we talk about this, Mr...Mr. Loeb? You are making big mistake throwing us out. We—Jolene and me—we have money, plenty money. We make a deal. Yes? You people like money, like to make deals. I know this is so."

"What do you mean by 'you people,' Mr. Biggers?"

"You are a *zhid*, aren't you? If I am wrong, I apologize most humbly. I do not intend to insult you."

Fortunately, for Andy Biggers at least, the elevator arrived at the sixth floor and the door opened. An elderly woman holding a King Charles spaniel was standing at the door waiting to enter the elevator. She gave the three men a disgusted look and the dog started yapping at them.

"Excuse us, Ma'am." DeMontrond gripped Bigger's damaged arm and led him out of the elevator.

Unit *E* was two units to the right of the elevator. Josh slowly inserted the key and quietly opened the door. Jolene and her john were engaged on the living room sofa. She wore only a pair of black fishnet hose and a garter belt. The john, who was wearing only a pair of black dress socks rolled down around his ankles, was sitting back and Jolene was astride his groin facing forward. Jolene was energetically pumping up and down as he fondled her breasts. The john was moaning loudly. Jolene had her head down and her long black hair was in her eyes. As Josh opened the door further she looked up and stopped in mid-stroke.

"Oh, shit!" She put her hands on the cushions and lifted herself off the sofa. With one hand she covered her hairless pubic mound and wrapped her other arm around her breasts.

The john opened his eyes. "Baby, what's the matter?" His condom-clad penis was already going flaccid. "Andy, you asshole! What the fuck is going on? Is this some kind of goddam shakedown?" He then noticed Josh and quickly covered his face.

"DeMontrond, you go with Mr. Biggers and retrieve his gun. Ms. Pervis, you sit down in that chair over there." Josh pointed to an armchair situated at right angles to the sofa.

Jolene, tears starting to form, took one of the sofa cushions and used it to cover herself as she did as she was told.

"Judge Waller, I assume those are your clothes?" Josh gestured toward a pile of clothing on a wooden ladder-back chair against the wall opposite the sofa. Judge T. Grayson Waller, judge of one of the Dallas County district courts, his hands still covering his face, nodded.

"May I respectfully suggest to Your Honor that you put them on and leave as quickly as you can. I'm sorry, I don't know what to tell you about the condom."

"Mr. Loeb...Josh...I...I..."

"No explanation is necessary, Your Honor. What you do when you're not on the bench dispensing justice is your business and nobody else's including mine. So far as I'm concerned, you were never here."

Judge Waller began putting on his clothes. Josh could not help but notice that the judge had left the condom on. "Josh, thank you, thank you. Believe me, I owe you one."

"No you don't, Your Honor. Remember, you were never here." The judge had quickly gotten dressed and out the door. Josh shook his head trying to clear away the vision of Judge Waller on the bench naked under his robe except for a pair of black socks rolled down to his ankles and a condom on his limp penis.

Jolene started to get up. Josh stood in front of her blocking her way. "Not yet, Ms. Pervis. You and I have some matters to discuss."

"Mr. Josh, I got the gun." DeMontrond came back in the living room holding Biggers by his damaged arm with one hand and in the other hand holding a medium-size semi-automatic handgun with a five-inch long metal cylinder attached to the business end of the barrel. He handed the weapon to Josh. Josh unscrewed the silencer and ejected the eight-round clip. Then he worked the slide back and ejected the round in the chamber. He then put the weapon in one pocket and the silencer, clip and loose round in the other.

"Thanks DeMontrond. Now would you take Mr. Biggers back in the bedroom and keep a close eye on him while he packs his and Ms. Pervis's belongings?"

"Mr. Loeb, I tell you we can fix this. We can make a deal. We can be partners..."

"Take him out of here, DeMontrond, please. And if he says one more word about making a deal or being partners, I would not object if you were to give him that tune up you mentioned downstairs." DeMontrond clasped Biggers around the back of his neck, turned him around and marched him back into the bedroom.

"You sure that all you want to do is talk, Josh?" Jolene had let the sofa cushion slide to the floor beside the chair. She smiled invitingly and spread her legs slightly. "You see anything you like, Josh? Could I fix you a drink? I bet you drink scotch, don't you? How about I fix you a scotch and we can sit together on the sofa and talk about whatever you want to talk about?" She cupped her hands under her breasts as if holding them out for closer inspection.

Despite his best efforts Josh felt a stirring in his groin area. "Ms. Pervis, I do not want to be partners with Mr. Biggers nor do I want to have sex with you. Please put the cushion back in your lap and stay where you are.

"When did you last see Sy?"

Jolene stuck out her lower lip in a pout. "Thursday a week ago. Tuesdays and Thursdays were his regular nights."

"Then I take it you saw him at Crystal's Palace?"

"Where else would I see him?"

"How about here?"

"Well, maybe a couple of times. But not last week."

"Was he alone?"

"Sy? Yeah, he was always alone. Never had anything to do with the other regular customers. They didn't like him much either."

"How much did he have to drink that night?"

"He never had more than two drinks. They make you pay for two drinks when you come in. Sy didn't like to waste money"

Josh shook his head over the irony in what he just heard. "I suppose the two-drink minimum helps keep out the riff-raff."

"Huh?"

"Never mind."

"Did Andy come in that night?"

"Andy? No, he never comes in. He just drops me off then picks me up when the place closes for the night. I guess you know he used to own the place and that the other owners kicked him out? After that he didn't feel welcome."

"Didn't Sy have something to do with Andy being kicked out?"

"I don't know anything about that, Josh. You'd have to ask Andy." She raised her voice so that she could be heard in the bedroom. "Andy…"

"Jolene, you don't talk anymore to that…" Josh heard a loud smacking sound such as a large open hand would make if struck with force against the side of a person's head. This was followed by a weak grunt, the sound that a person would make if struck forcefully in the gut by a large closed fist. Then the bedroom door closed screening out any further sounds.

Recognizing that Andy didn't have her back, Jolene tried another tactic. "He—Andy—made me do it."

"Do what, Jolene?"

"Come on to Sy. At first, I was just friendly to him. All the girls were. I even gave him a picture…"

"Do you happen to know where that picture is now?"

"No, and what's so important about that stupid picture? You want one? Come by the club tonight and I'll give you one. Even sign it if you want."

"Why did Andy want you to seduce Sy?"

" Because Sy was fixin' to dime him to the judge."

"But Sy did it anyway, didn't he?"

"He told Andy he had to; there was no way he could avoid it."

"Andy got real mad. Told Sy he'd have him taken care of. Sy said if that happened some other accountant would just come in and find the same stuff and Andy probably go to jail for murder as well as stealing.

"Andy told me maybe it was time for us to move on. But I didn't want to. I like Crystal's Palace. I'm friends with some of the girls and the money's good—as much as Andy lets me keep. I begged him and he finally gave in. So Andy made a deal with Sy. Sy turned in his report but he did some stuff so that the income tax man wouldn't come after Andy or me. I don't know what he did. Part of the deal was that I kept seeing Sy. As long as I kept Sy happy he wouldn't tell the judge all he knew.

"Then, after a while, Sy said he loved me and wanted to take me away from Andy and get me out of the life. He got me this place and said it would be mine as soon as he figured out a way to get rid of Andy. He told me that he was going to talk to a lawyer and figure out a way."

"When was that?"

"Last week on Thursday."

"Exactly what did he say?"

"He didn't speak to me. He wrote a note and stuffed it in my g-string along with the hundred dollars he always gave me. Then when I got back to the dressing room I put it in my purse. When Andy picks me up from work he makes me give him all the tip money. I gave him the money, but he could sense I was nervous about something. So he took my purse, emptied it out and found the note "

"You said Andy just dropped you off and never came in?"

"Yes, it's true. He drops me off and leaves. Then he comes back to pick me up when I get off."

"Is that what he did the last time you saw Sy? Or did he hang around in the parking lot? Please don't lie to me. You'll only make it worse for yourself."

"No, he never…"

"Ms. Pervis, I have eyewitnesses who saw him in the parking lot that night. He drives a big Mercedes, doesn't he?"

In tears now, Jolene nodded her head up and down. "For some reason Sy was actin' kind of nervous that night. He even left his car keys on the table. The waitress found them and gave them to me. I ran outside to give them to Sy. I gave him his keys. Then we got in his car and I gave him a quick blow-job, just to put him in a better mood. When Sy left I went to Andy and gave him the money. After that I went back inside and I haven't seen Sy since. He didn't come in this week either night.

I figured maybe he had to work or went on vacation or something."

"You do know he's dead, don't you?"

"Dead? My God, no! I can't believe it! Andy told me that he wouldn't be bothering us anymore, but he didn't say why. When? How?"

"Ms. Pervis, you should ask Andy those questions. Now go get dressed, you and Andy are done here."

Chapter Twenty-Nine

Biggers was unfit for porter duties. The left side of his face and his left ear were red and swollen. His lower lip was split and his right eye was swollen shut. His right arm was useless and he had to walk hunched over in deference to the effects on his lower abdomen of DeMontrond's tune up. Hunched over and limping from Josh's stomping on his instep, Biggers made Josh think of Quasimodo. DeMontrond had found a box of large plastic garbage bags and had filled them with the man's and woman's clothing in the closets and scattered about the bedroom. He made Biggers empty the dirty clothes hamper into one of the bags and carry it with his one functioning arm. They'd allowed Jolene to shower. She'd been unable to locate any clean underwear, so she was dressed commando-style in a pair of skintight jeans and a Dallas Stars replica jersey.

With DeMontrond doing the heavy lifting they went down to the garage in the service elevator. Biggers's car was an old Mercedes S-600 painted a copperish-brown. The exterior and interior were immaculate. Given the color scheme and the vehicle's immense size, it reminded Josh of a picture he had seen of the Russian Soviet-era T-64 main battle tank. All that was missing was a cannon mounted on the roof.

Thinking about the cannon made Josh remember the gun. He carefully wiped down the gun and silencer and gave them to Jolene along with the empty clip. He kept the ammunition.

Biggers turned the ignition key and the Mercedes started immediately and ran quietly. Evidently the mechanical systems were the beneficiaries of the same careful maintenance as the body and cabin. Fortunately, the Mercedes was equipped with an automatic transmission. Biggers said something to Jolene and she put the transmission into reverse. Using his left hand only, Biggers backed out of the parking space. Jolene then moved the transmission lever to the drive position and they started to drive away. As they reached the exit ramp they stopped and rolled down their windows. They stuck their arms out the windows and gave Josh and DeMontrond the one-finger salute. Josh smiled in return, "Drive safely, y'all. And have a nice day!"

Josh then turned to DeMontrond and stuck out his hand. "Good job, DeMontrond." DeMontrond took Josh's hand in a surprisingly soft, very brief grip.

"Sorry, Mr. Josh. Don' mean to be rude, but my hand got a little sore when I slapped old Andy upside th' head. You done a pretty good job on him yourself."

"Your Uncle Louis isn't the only middle-age guy who's been in a bar fight, DeMontrond. Let's just say Andy Biggers wasn't my first rodeo."

"Where we goin' next, Mr. Josh?"

"I need to call Detective Turner. Even if Biggers didn't murder Sy Blonstein, he knows who did and probably put them up to it."

"Mr. Josh, that Jolene, she a fine lookin' woman an' maybe a good one inside. Uncle Louis say she *passe blanc*. She need to get shed of that Biggers; find herself a good man, her own kind. How come she get mixed up with a fool pimp like him in the first place? I bet you right now he makin' her tell him everything she tol' you."

"You're probably right, DeMontrond. I don't understand how a woman can let a man own and abuse her like that. But then I don't pretend to know how women think, my wife and daughter included. But I can pretty well guess what you're thinking, DeMontrond. And you might want to think about it some more, a whole lot more. In the unlikely event she doesn't go to prison, she's had a lot of damage done to her and I'm not sure it can be fixed."

DeMontrond nodded. "I 'spect you right, Mr. Josh. Still and all..." DeMontrond shrugged his shoulders, "...guess it don' matter none anyway. Probably now Biggers gonna get out of town. Go back wherever it is he come from and either take Jolene with him or dump her somewhere along the way.

"How come you didn't call the po-lice?"

"I doubt that Biggers will get very far. While you were loading the last of the bags into the car I was using my phone to take pictures of the car, the license plate, Biggers and Jolene. I held off calling Detective Turner because I'm not yet sure how much I want to tell her. And just calling 9-1-1 would be a waste of time." Josh activated his phone and started to punch in Detective Turner's number.

"Mr. Josh, can I ax you somethin' else?"

"Sure, DeMontrond, ask away."

"Did you really have a judge and some constables waitin' aroun' on a Saturday for you to call?"

"What do you think?"

"What I think is that I wouldn't want to play 'Texas Hold 'Em' with you."

Josh smiled and punched in Detective Turner's number.

She answered on the first ring. *"Detective Turner."*

"Alana, it's Josh. I guess I shouldn't be surprised that you're at the office. Do you ever take a day off?"

"I'm at home. I put my office phone on call-forwarding. I ran a few errands this morning. Now I'm on my computer trying to run down that Ford pickup."

"Can I ask whether you're having any luck?"

"Not so far. Our tech people worked with the video and managed to get me the last and maybe the next-to-last digits of the license plate. Those will make the search go more quickly. But because of that brush-guard wrap-around bumper it's hard to even tell the model-year. So I've got thousands of trucks to look at. It's going to take a while."

Josh glanced at his watch. "Can you take a break and let DeMontrond and me buy you lunch? We've had a busy morning and we've got some new information for you."

"Can't you just give it to me on the phone?"

"I suppose…"

"Oh, what the hell. Meet me at Barbec's on Garland Road. I assume you know where it is. Just call me when you get there. I live about two minutes away. Get a table and I'll be right there."

"Good deal. See you in about…twenty…thirty minutes max."

Chapter Thirty

Barbec's was typically crowded with the Saturday mix of cyclists and joggers taking a respite from their excursions around White Rock Lake, tradespeople on their lunch break, laid-back types who lived nearby and the North Dallas affluent desirous of real food served in filling portions and at fair prices. However the wait was short. They managed to score one of the red vinyl booths along the front wall.

Josh had called Alana and she showed up just as they were being seated. She was wearing close-fitting jeans, cross-trainers and a long gray sweatshirt with "U.S. Army" in stencil-type lettering on the front. As usual she wore no makeup and her hair was pulled back in a ponytail. When she sat down next to him Josh could see a bulge beneath the sweatshirt at the small of her back where her handgun was tucked into the waistband of her jeans.

As the waitress brought their water glasses, handed out menus and took their drink orders, Alana noticed that DeMontrond was massaging his right hand. "What happened to your hand, DeMontrond?"

"Oh, nothin' much Miz Turner. I jes' hit it on somethin' while I was doin' a tune up."

"Hope you didn't damage the vehicle."

"He...I mean...it'll be alright, Ma'am."

"Well you be careful, DeMontrond. I'm sure your Uncle Louis wouldn't be too happy if he had to repair damage to a customer's vehicle when all the customer came in for was a tune up."

"Yes, Ma'am. I'll be extra careful next time."

Conversation stopped while they considered the menu. When the waitress came back with two ice teas and a Dr. Pepper she asked if they were ready to order. This time Josh ordered the chicken-fried steak, DeMontrond ordered the hamburger steak and Alana a Cobb salad. They all ordered the biscuits with sausage gravy for the table.

Josh had gotten his ice tea properly lemoned and sweetened. "I heard on the news last night about the skinheads. Then there were a couple of long articles in the paper this morning. Is there anything new you can talk about?"

"I don't know much more than what you heard on TV and read in the paper. The *El Chupacabra* task force says the deceased one is a genuine *El Chupacabra* killing. But they can't explain the two injured ones in the back of the pickup truck. The gang unit and narcotics people both say the murder must be a copycat killing and there's obviously a gang war about to break out. So they're busy arguing about whose case it is. The two in the hospital have been upgraded to 'fair' condition, but they still won't talk to us."

"Maybe they don't know who attacked them. Maybe they were attacked from behind."

"Oh, they know who it was. They just won't talk to us. Talkin' to cops is against their religion. The doctors at Parkland said that from the x-rays and the external bruising it's pretty certain that they were attacked from the front. So they must have seen who it was. The doctors say that their best guess is that one person approached them from the front and slammed their heads together.

"There were fingerprints on the knife that matched one of the victims. But carrying a knife isn't a crime. You've got to use it or threaten to use it."

"Maybe the headknocker—the assailant—was just defending himself?"

"And maybe you should take up criminal law, Josh. But you said you have something new for me. Now it's your turn."

"Looks like it's all our turns to eat." DeMontrond drank the last of his Dr. Pepper as the waitress brought out their meals and arranged them in their proper order.

"Can I get you folks anything else right now?"

"Could I get a Dr. Pepper refill, Ma'am?"

"You sure can, honey. Bring it right out. How 'bout you all? More ice tea?"

"Yes, please," Josh answered. "And some Tabasco sauce."

"I'll have a tea refill too, please."

"I'll bring out the pitcher, Miss. And I'll bring out your desserts soon as you're done with your lunches. But you have to clean your plates." She looked at Josh. "You sure you won't have some pie? There's only a few slices left."

"No, I think I'll pass. Thanks anyway."

"Well, y'all enjoy."

No one had much to say as they obeyed the waitress' injunction to clean their plates. As promised, the waitress brought out the dessert orders: lemon meringue pie for Alana and chocolate meringue for DeMontrond. Alana took a bite of her pie and used the tip of her tongue to remove a morsel of meringue from the corner of her mouth. "Okay, what have you got for me?"

Josh took out his phone and opened the stored-photo app. "Meet Andy Biggers." He handed the phone to Alana so she could see the picture.

"Okay, 'Hi, Andy Biggers.' Why do I want to meet you?"

"Andy Biggers probably hired the person who murdered Seymour Blonstein and Marjorie Morrison."

"And why would Andy Biggers want to do that?" Alana enlarged the picture and studied it for a moment. "What happened to his face? Why is he hunched over like that?"

"I imagine there are a lot of people that don't much like Mr. Biggers."

"Would that include you and DeMontrond? Do I need to read you both your rights?"

"When I tell you about him, I doubt that you'll like him very much either. Can we just leave it at that?"

"For now. I'm interested in solving two murder cases. I'm not interested in arresting two upright citizens such as yourselves for simple assault, especially if you convince me that Mr. Biggers deserved it."

"Fair enough. Here's the executive summary: Mr. Biggers is the former manager of a gentlemen's club. The owners suspected that he was stealing and brought a lawsuit. Sy Blonstein was hired by the court to investigate the financial records of the club. To say that Mr. Biggers was playing fast and loose with the investors' money is an understatement. On top of that he was skimming and treated the dancers like slaves. He even made them pay him kickbacks. The story's a lot more involved than that, but that's the gist of it. Sy found out enough to get Mr. Biggers kicked out as manager. As a result, Mr. Biggers threatened to have Sy 'taken care of.' It's possible—indeed likely—that he carried out the threat."

"What's the name of this 'gentlemen's club?'"

" 'Crystal's Palace.'"

"Isn't that the club where the two skinheads got clocked in the parking lot last night?"

"From what I read in the paper, that's right."

"I don't believe in coincidences, Josh. Did Mr. Blonstein ever tell you that he was involved with skinheads or that he took Biggers's threat seriously?"

"Well, he never mentioned skinheads but Sy was worried about something. The night he died, Thursday, he was at Crystal's Palace. He wanted to know if anyone had been asking about him."

"Unless you were there with him, how do you know that?"

"I'm sorry; I can't tell you. It's a matter of work-product privilege."

Alana took a long drink of her ice tea. "Josh, I gotta tell you, this work-product privilege thing is getting to be pretty irritating. I thought you said we'd work together. Now, it looks like we're back to square one."

"Alana, how I got the information isn't important. What's important is that Sy was feeling threatened. He thought somebody was out to do him harm, and somehow that someone is ... or was ... connected to Crystal's Palace. If Biggers didn't do it himself, maybe he hired someone, maybe it was the skinheads."

"That's pretty thin. Hiring a contract killer—especially one with enough smarts to at least try to make it look like an accident—costs money. Why would Mr. Biggers pay good money to have someone murdered if the damage had already been done? And that doesn't explain Marjorie Morrison. Why make her murder look like an *El Chupacabra* killing?"

"Maybe she saw something and the hitman was just cleaning up loose ends. The killer decided to do a copycat killing to make the two murders look like just a coincidence; focus your attention away from Sy's murder. Like I suggested the other night, there could be a bunch of *El Chupacabra* wannabes out there."

"I'm not sure I buy that, as interesting as it is. Usually revenge doesn't hold up as a motive unless there's a woman involved. And as far as we know, that's not the case here." Alana paused, leaving the unspoken "Is it?" hanging in the space between her and Josh. Josh said nothing.

"But okay, let's say that what you've told me is enough to make this Andy Biggers a person of interest. Obviously you've met him. Where do I find him so I can ask him some questions?"

"Let me have my phone a second." Alana handed back the phone and Josh brought up the picture of the Mercedes. "This is his automobile." He handed the phone back to Alana.

"Nice ride. What is it?"

"A Mercedes 'S-600.'It's got to be over thirty years old. I also have the license plate." Josh took back the phone and brought up the picture of the license plate, skipping over the photo of Jolene.

"Do you have a picture of where he lives?"

"No, this is the best I can do."

"Well, it's better than nothing. How'd you find out about Crystal's Palace?"

"That's one of the files I mentioned that I was looking at."

"I gather that's one of the files you won't let me have? And by the way, I checked with our department legal advisor and he agrees with what you said. So how come you can give me the information now?"

"I'll do better than that; I'll give you a copy of the file. It's all a matter of public record, so there's no reason to withhold it."

"When can I get it?"

"I'll have Alicia make a copy Monday morning and deliver it to your office."

"Can't you do it before then?"

"It's locked up in my office. If you can live without it, I'd rather not go downtown today. The file's pretty thick so it'll take a good while to copy, especially with me running the copier. By the time we get done, the afternoon will be shot. My wife and I have symphony tickets tonight, so I need to get home. Also, DeMontrond and I have one more errand to run. It may take a while."

"I'll need the photos at least. Let me have your phone so I can send them to myself. I'll call my boss and let him know what you've told me. Maybe I can get him to authorize a BOLO for the vehicle. If we find him I'm going to need something to use as leverage. If I can't charge him with anything all he has to do is say, 'Nice talking to you, Detective Turner, but I'm outta here.'"

"He has a gun. Will that help?"

"So do lots of folks. Remember, packin' is legal in Texas assuming that he has a permit. I take it that the weapon is a handgun?"

"Yes. A semiautomatic with an eight-round clip and it holds one in the chamber."

"Do you happen to know what kind? So I'll know it if I see it."

"It didn't have a manufacturer's name on it, but it did have some Cyrillic lettering on the frame and on the slide."

"Is it medium-size? With walnut insets in the grip?"

"I'm not sure what kind of wood it was. As for the size, yeah, I'd say medium. Not as big as a forty-five or the ones police officers carry; not as small as one of those small-caliber 'purse-size' guns. I'm sorry I didn't take a picture of it."

"From your description it sounds like a Makarov—Soviet standard-issue military and civilian police sidearm. Still in use today, although they've modified it over the years. Early on, if I remember correctly, they had some accidental-discharge issues. Otherwise, it's pretty reliable and accurate up to about fifty feet. Fires a nine-millimeter Parabellum round."

"Oh! Speaking of bullets. I unloaded the gun and kept them. Here…" Josh reached in his pocket and started to take out the bullets.

"Wait until we get outside. We don't need to cause a commotion. Some cowboy sees them and pulls out his own weapon…"

"Sorry."

"But even if he's carrying, that's not going to help me. I don't have probable cause to check him for weapons unless I can arrest him."

"There's one other thing: The gun has a silencer."

"Now that I can use. A reliable informant tells me that Mr. Biggers is in possession of a silencer. I call the ATF. I get them to ask him if he has a federal license for his silencer. Bet you lunch he doesn't. They'll work him over pretty good, but then they'll probably let me have him at least for a while.

"But I'm still going to need the file to ask him about Blonstein and Morrison. So how about this: Suppose we do manage to find him, and ATF lets me have him. If I call you, will you bring me the file?"

"As long as it's not in the middle of the concert, sure. Just call me. If I don't answer, it won't be because I don't enjoy the sound of your voice; it'll be because I'm listening to Beethoven. Just leave a message and as soon as the concert is over, I'll get the file and bring it to your office. You're at the Jack Evans building, aren't you? I'll be downtown at the Meyerson anyway."

"Right."

Alana started to take out her wallet. Josh put his hand on her arm to stop her. "I've got this one. I invited you."

Chapter Thirty-One

"Where to next, Mr. Josh?"

"I'd like to look at the place where Sy died. I doubt there's anything to see, but maybe we can talk to the owner of the property where it happened. Probably the fastest way is to go back to Northwest Highway and across to Midway. Take a right on Midway and go up to Walnut Hill. When we're done there, we'd better call it a day."

"What about tonight, the concert, Mr. Josh?"

"I think I'll handle the driving tonight, DeMontrond. You can use some time off. Give your hand a rest. We'll take my wife's SUV."

"I'm not sure Uncle Louis be too happy about that, Mr. Josh. If you and Miz Elaine don't mind too much, I'd rather drive you."

"Well, we don't want to make your Uncle Louis mad at us. I've seen first-hand what can happen when he gets mad. Do you think he'd knock our heads together?"

"No need us findin' out. What time the concert start?"

"Seven-thirty. Just in case the traffic's heavier than usual, better pick us up at a quarter to seven."

"Don' mind my sayin' so, Mr. Josh, that was real decent of you not to show Detective Turner the picture of Jolene Pervis. I don' think she had anything to do with killin' Mr. Blonstein."

"I agree, DeMontrond; that's why I left her out of the story. While you were helping Mr. Biggers pack, she told me that Biggers made her come on to Sy. I believe her. Like you asked earlier, how can a woman let herself be owned by a sleazy pimp like Andy Biggers? Maybe it's time someone gave her a break. Even if she just goes back to dancing at Crystal's Palace, that's a hell of an improvement over living with that scumbag."

It was not difficult to spot the incident-site. There were tire marks where the Buick had jumped the curb, crossed the lawn and struck the bois d'arc tree which stood about ten feet back from the curb. The tree bark had been stripped off at the point of impact. Other than that, the tree had fared far better in the collision than Sy Blonstein's Buick.

When Josh and DeMontrond drove up the homeowner was in the yard with a plastic garbage bag picking up the last bits of detritus from the collision along with a few early-falling horse apples from the bois d'arc tree. Josh got out of the Chrysler and took out one of his business cards as he approached the homeowner.

The man glanced at Josh's card and then stuffed it in the breast pocket of his plaid flannel shirt. "I was beginnin' to wonder when one of you lawyer fellas was gonna show up." He held out his hand. "I'm Bert Blankenship."

Josh took the proffered hand. "Joshua Loeb, Mr. Blankenship. I guess better late than never."

"I been calling the office phone number for the driver—the fella got himself killed—since Monday. Didn't want to disturb his widow. Couldn't get anybody to answer the phone. Finally, I couldn't wait any longer. Felt kind of bad about it, but I called her on Wednesday and again yesterday. She didn't answer either. But I guess someone got the message and sent you out here."

"That was very thoughtful on your part, Mr. Blankenship, waiting to call the widow, I mean. Anyway, here I am. I assume that you have some information about the incident?"

"Well, maybe. But mainly, I want to know who's gonna pay for the damage to my bois d'arc tree?"

Josh glanced at the tree thinking, "It takes all kinds..." He took out his cell phone. "Is it okay if I take a picture or two?" Before Blankenship could ask why or say no, Josh snapped a couple of quick shots of the tree. "If you'll send me an estimate I'll turn it over to Mr. Blonstein's insurance company. They may want to see a photo of the damage. With a photo and an estimate from a reputable arborist, I'm sure they'll take care of your claim promptly."

"Please see that they do. I'd hate to lose that tree. Better tell your boy to pull up in the driveway. There's no parking on the street. Cop comes by, you'd get a ticket for sure."

The passenger side window of the Chrysler was down. Josh hoped that he and Bert Blankenship were standing far enough away so that DeMontrond did not hear the word "boy." Josh walked over to the car.

"We done already, Mr. Josh?"

"No, looks like we're just getting started. Mr. Blankenship suggests that you pull up in the driveway since there's no curbside parking. He says we'll get a ticket for sure."

"Okay. Do you want me to stay in the car or come with you?"

Josh wondered whether DeMontrond had heard the word "boy" after all. "Stay with the car, DeMontrond. I'll ask Mr. Blankenship to join us. I don't see anything to sit on besides the front steps and I didn't hear an invite to come in the house. Be back in a second."

Bert Blankenship was amenable to Josh's suggestion out of curiosity to see what it would be like to sit in a high-powered lawyer's luxurious chauffeur-driven vehicle. Once Blankenship was seated in the back next to Josh, Josh introduced him to his "associate, Mr. Prejean."

"Were you at home the night it happened, Mr. Blankenship?"

"Sure was. I was in the den watchin' TV. My wife, 'Betty' is her name, was at her bridge club. On bridge nights she usually doesn't get home until just after ten o'clock. Glad she wasn't there to see it. They'd already got the body out of the car and into an ambulance before she got home. Near scared her to death driving up and seeing all those police cars, fire engines, TV news trucks, and what have you. I'd meant to call her on her cell phone, but in the excitement I clean forgot."

"I can imagine what my wife would do. I hope you've managed to get things smoothed over."

"Pretty much."

"I take it you heard the crash?"

"Sure did. Knew right away what it was, too. I put my shoes on, then I went outside to see if I could help."

"I'm sure you've told the story a dozen times, but would you mind telling Mr. Prejean and me what you saw?"

"Actually, besides Betty—that's my wife—I haven't told anyone."

"The police didn't take your statement?"

"All they asked me is whether I'm the one called 9-1-1 and whether I saw the collision happen."

"I told 'em yeah, it was me called 9-1-1, and no I didn't see it happen; just heard it."

"If they'd asked you any more questions about what happened, what would you have told them?"

"You sure the insurance company's going to take care of my bois d'arc tree?"

"Mr. Blankenship, as I understand it, your bois d'arc tree didn't run into Mr. Blonstein's Buick. So, yes, the insurance company will take care of your tree. If for some unknown reason it fails to do so within a reasonable time, the estate will take care of it."

"I haven't had much dealings with lawyers, Mr. Loeb. My daddy got jewed out of some oil and gas property back in the nineteen-fifties. He didn't trust lawyers and I guess it kind of got passed on to me."

Josh clenched his teeth for a good while. Finally he asked, "Mr. Prejean, do we have anything in the car to write on?"

"There's a yellow pad you put in the trunk Friday afternoon. Want me to get it?"

"Yes, please. Mr. Blankenship, as soon as Mr. Prejean gets me something to write on, I'll put in writing what I just promised you. Will that be satisfactory?"

"Well, if you wouldn't mind. I'd feel a lot better about having something in writing."

Josh wrote out what he'd promised and signed it. He tore out the page and held it in his right hand, away from Blankenship who was seated on the left side of the car. "Do we have a deal, Mr. Blankenship? You tell me everything you know about what happened that night. If we have a deal, just say so and I'll hand you the paper."

"That's fair; we have a deal." Blankenship held out his hand as though to shake hands to seal the bargain. Instead of responding in kind, Josh handed him the piece of paper.

"There's not much more to tell. When I got outside the Buick was smashed up against the tree with the hood sprung back. I run up to the driver's side to see if there was anything I could do. There was a truck stopped at the curb just the other side of the tree. I figure he must have been right behind the Buick; probably saw it happen or maybe was even involved. And like I told you, all I did was hear it happen."

"Did you speak with the truck occupant at all?"

"No, I seen that the driver of the Buick was in pretty bad shape. I couldn't tell if he was even alive. Seemed the best thing to do was for me to go back in and call 9-1-1. So that's what I did. It took a few minutes for me to tell the 9-1-1 operator what happened and give the location. She kept asking if she could speak to the driver. I kept telling her no because he's either unconscious or maybe even dead, and anyway, whichever it is, he's stuck in the car and I'm inside my house. She wanted to know whether there were any other vehicles involved. Then she wanted to know whether there were any passengers in the vehicle. She wanted me to go out and look. I said that I would and for her to hold on.

"I did what she asked. When I went back outside the truck was gone. There weren't any passengers in the Buick, so I went back inside and told the 9-1-1 lady. Then I went back outside to wait for the police."

"Did you happen to see what kind of truck it was?"

"Yeah. Like I said before: It was parked right over there, just past the tree going east. It was a big white pickup truck. Didn't see what kind it was. But it had those big tires and stood high off the ground. ."

"Thank you for your time, Mr. Blankenship. I'll contact the insurance company just as soon as you get me the estimate."

"I'll get that to you soon as I can get one of those tree companies out here."

Blankenship got out of the car and Josh got in the front seat shaking his head in disgust. "DeMontrond, what's the world coming to? A man dies in a horrific car crash in his front yard, and all he cares about is his goddamn bois d'arc tree."

"Mr. Josh, can I ax you another question?"

"Sure, DeMontrond, ask away. But don't necessarily expect an intelligent answer from me. Obviously I don't know anything about how the world works anymore. Bois d'arc tree! If I had a chainsaw I'd come back here tonight after the concert and cut the goddamn thing down."

"I could maybe take care of that for you, Mr. Josh. Uncle Louis has a chainsaw that I could borrow."

"Forget it, DeMontrond. Now what's your question?"

"That Mr. Blankenship, he got an attitude problem worse than Andy Biggers. How come you didn't kick his sorry ass out the car when he say his daddy got 'jewed' out of some property?"

"DeMontrond, people like Bert Blankenship have been using the word 'Jew' as a verb even longer than they've been using racist terms to describe people of color. If I'd said or done something, would it have changed his attitude? I don't think so. All that I would have accomplished is to make him understand that his prejudices do sometimes come with a price.

"If I'd done what I wanted to do—which is a lot more than just kick his sorry ass out of the car—I would likely have ended up in the slammer charged with assault and we wouldn't have learned about the white pickup truck. Which reminds me, I need to call Detective Turner and let her know what we found out."

"Mr. Josh, you somethin' else."

"Alana, it's me again. Sorry to bother you. Any luck with tracking down the pickup truck?"

"Still looking. But I did convince my boss to get out a BOLO for Biggers.
If he's still in the Metroplex area, he'll get found. What are you and DeMontrond up to?"

"You may want to get some more people working on identifying the truck. DeMontrond and I just got through interviewing the owner of the property where Sy was killed."

"If I come talk to him, is he going to look like Mr. Biggers?"

"No, he looks just fine, for an old fart who's mean-as-a-snake and a bigot to
go along with it."

"Gee, I'm looking forward to it. I knew some guys like that in the Army; they were called 'colonel' and you had to salute them. What'd the old fart have to say? There's nothing in the incident report."

"He says he wasn't interviewed. They just asked him if he'd made the 9-1-1 call and whether he'd seen the wreck. He said he'd called it in, but he didn't see it. He was in his house watching TV so he only heard the impact."

"But you gave him the 'third degree' and he gave it up. Are there any visible bruises?"

"Alana, believe me; giving him the 'third degree' crossed my mind. But the only thing I gave him was a promise to take care of the expense for an arborist to repair his precious bois d'arc tree. I think he's anxious to preserve it in case lynchings become fashionable again."

"And what did he give you in return?"

"That when he got outside to see what happened, there was a white pickup truck parked at the curb a few feet east of the bois d'arc tree. He says the truck must have been right behind the Blonstein vehicle. Blankenship said that it might have even been involved in the 'accident.' Blankenship went back in his house and called 9-1-1. By the time he got back outside the truck was gone. Oh! And, according to him, the truck had jacked-up suspension and oversize tires. He didn't know the make of the truck."

"What about descriptions of the driver?"

"He didn't get one."

"So now all I have to do is find the truck and if I do, and do a photo-array lineup, he won't be able to pick anyone out."

"Maybe Andy Biggers will be able to help with that. With the death penalty in play, you'll have plenty of leverage."

"Josh, thanks. I need to call this in. I'll let you know when we get Biggers. 'Bye.

Chapter Thirty-Two

With Maestro van Zweden at the podium, the Dallas Symphony Orchestra was in top form. The first part of the program consisted of Bartok's *Dance Suites*, a 1923 composition based on Rumanian folk-dances. This was pushing the envelope a bit as the typical Dallas symphony audience generally prefers not to venture beyond the baroque, classical and romantic periods. The performance was rewarded with polite applause as the late-comers found their seats.

The first half of the program was completed by Haydn's Symphony Number Twenty-Two, the *Philosopher Symphony*. The performance got the typical enthusiastic but truncated standing ovation from the audience, half of whom were anxious to get to the head of the queues at the cocktail stations and the other half anxious to get to the head of the queues at the restrooms.

The second half was devoted to the Beethoven: his *Violin Concerto* followed by the *Seventh Symphony*. The soloist was one of those pubescent female Asian fiddlers whose technical skill was absolutely perfect but who had yet to develop even a kernel of nuance. Predictably, she opted for the conventional Kreisler cadenza. Evidently her scrawny right arm was beginning to flag when she reached the rondo movement. Maestro van Zweden, despite his renown ability to adapt to the soloist's pacing, was beginning to lose her. In a remarkable tour de force of orchestral conducting he was able to keep the right side of the orchestra, the violas, cellos and the double basses, under control so that soloist and orchestra finished pretty much at the same time.

Dallas audiences will give a heart-felt standing ovation at a public hanging. So the young violinist got hers along with a bouquet of white roses handed up from the front row. Maestro van Zweden, a forced smile on his face, returned to the stage for but one curtain-call, although the duration and volume of the applause warranted at least two.

The *Seventh Symphony*, with its heavy emphasis on the horns and kettle drums, was as always a crowd-pleaser. It too earned, in this instance, a well-deserved, prolonged standing ovation.

The parking valet at the Stephan Pyles flagship restaurant on Ross Avenue thought it odd that the well-dressed couple—Josh was wearing a "good" suit and Elaine was wearing her fur coat—would invite their chauffeur to join them for dinner. Swallowing his misgivings and encouraged by a five dollar tip from DeMontrond he magnanimously bestowed the honor of parking the Chrysler in front of the restaurant along with a Bentley, a Ferrari and a Tesla. Josh's Jaguar had never merited such consideration.

As they were seated, DeMontrond took in his surroundings. "Nice place, Mr. Josh. You know, that's the first time I've ever given anyone a tip."

"Obviously it had an effect. Either that or he mistook the Chrysler for a Bentley with a different kind of grille."

"Are you allowed to drink wine, DeMontrond?"

"No ma'am. No alcoholic beverages."

"Then I guess we'd better order by the glass and not get a bottle, Josh. I hope you don't mind, DeMontrond."

"No, ma'am, Miz Elaine. You all go ahead. I'll jus' have me a Dr. Pepper if they got one."

While Josh studied the wine list the bemused waiter retreated to consult with the maitre d' who, after a moment's incredulousness, went off to see whether the unprecedented beverage request could be fulfilled. Eventually a Dr. Pepper was produced from a six-pack that belonged to one of the line cooks. After consulting with Elaine, Josh ordered a vouvray for Elaine and himself.

That night was one of the infrequent occasions when the proprietor himself was at the helm in the kitchen. Thus there were no hiccups in the quality of the food or service such as there had been on recent occasions. This also likely accounted for the willingness to accommodate the Dr. Pepper request.

When the beaming waiter returned with the beverages, he set out the vouvray and ceremoniously poured DeMontrond's Dr. Pepper into a cabernet glass.

During the early years of their marriage while Josh was finishing law school and then struggling to build a law practice, Elaine had taught English in a low-income public middle school. This led her to draw out DeMontrond about his experience in a large public school system.

With no father in the picture, DeMontrond's mother had worked two jobs. Although she had done her best at parenting and DeMontrond's grandmother had helped out as much as she could, raising DeMontrond was pretty much left to DeMontrond. He told Elaine that he actually liked school, especially reading. Algebra was more than he could handle on his own, but because he was a starter on the football team from junior high on, he always managed a passing grade. Elaine asked what books he'd liked. DeMontrond remembered a few of them and Elaine was familiar with them as well.

DeMontrond was totally baffled by the menu choices so he asked Elaine to choose for him. They all settled on the house-special southwestern caesar salad and for main courses ordered from the seasonally-varied appetizer menu. Discussing the books had occupied the table conversation. DeMontrond said that he would follow Elaine's suggestion that he look into enrolling at one of the Dallas County Community colleges.

Chapter Thirty-Three

It was a little after midnight when DeMontrond dropped Josh and Elaine at home. He declined Elaine's offer to spend the night in the guestroom. Josh would have been happy for DeMontrond to stay overnight, but he was hoping to extend what had been, despite the nearly chaotic third movement of the Beethoven, an enjoyable evening. He sensed that Elaine might be inclined to prolong the evening as well. As he helped her out of her fur he nuzzled the back of her neck and she murmured approvingly.

When he started to unzip the back of her dress she stopped him. "Whoa, sailor. Josh, we're not teenagers anymore. Let's play like we're grownups and get ready for bed. Then we'll see what happens. I'll even take a sip or two of your single malt. You go pour and I'll check for phone messages. Maybe Caroline called to let us know whether she was able to change her flight. See you in a minute."

Checking phone messages reminded Josh of his promise to Alana Turner. She had called just after seven o'clock to tell Josh that Biggers was now in custody so she needed the file as soon as possible. Then at nine o'clock she left a voicemail saying not to worry about the file and to call her in the morning. She did not sound happy.

"Good news, bad news, Josh."

"Good first and maybe we can skip the bad."

"Caroline changed her flight. She gets in at eight o'clock Tuesday night. It cost three hundred dollars to change the flight."

"The three hundred dollars? Is that the bad news? If it is I can handle it."

"Unfortunately, that's not the bad news."

"Can't you tell me later? I'll go get our night-cap."

"I wish. We should have kept going when we had the chance. Estelle called, three times."

"Geez, what now?"

"She wants you to call her back no matter what time it is. Somebody broke into her house. She's at her daughter's in Houston. Josh, she's hysterical. I could barely make out what she was saying. You're the only person she can turn to. I think you should call her."

"And what am I supposed to do? I'm not Sherlock Holmes or even the Dallas Police Department. Dammit, Elaine, if Sy Blonstein were still alive, I'd murder him myself. 'The evil that men do lives after them...' That sorry son-of-a-bitch. I assume she left a number?"

Elaine sat down on the bed next to Josh and put her arm around his shoulder, He turned toward her and she kissed him lightly. "Josh, go pour us a scotch. Call Estelle, and I promise to make it up to you in the morning. Afterward, we can have a nice, leisurely brunch and forget about anyone named 'Blonstein' for the rest of the day."

"Sounds like a plan. "I'll hold you to it. Be back in a minute."

Chapter Thirty-Four

"Estelle, it's Josh."

"Thank God. I've been waiting and waiting. Where have you been?"

"Elaine and I went to the symphony. Tonight was one of our season ticket nights."

"Well I hope you enjoyed yourselves. I haven't been having any fun at all. Did Elaine tell you?"

"That someone broke into your house? Yes, she did. I bet someone was watching the house and figured out that you were away. That's been happening a lot lately. It's awful. How'd you find out?"

"My next door neighbors. You know...Alex and Helene Grossberg?"

"Don't they own a travel agency? I don't believe I've ever met them, but I think Elaine used them to arrange that Alaska cruise we took a couple years ago. I didn't know that they are your neighbors."

"They've lived next door for at least ten years. He and Sy play...I mean played...golf...together...sometimes." Estelle started sobbing and gasping for breath. *"Hold...hold...on...for...for a minute. I'm sorry...I...I... need to get a tissue."*

While Estelle was presumably regaining control, Josh took a swallow of scotch and handed the glass to Elaine. "You're right, she is hysterical. She probably needs to get on some kind of medication."

Elaine took a small sip and handed the glass back to Josh. I know I would be. Poor Estelle; she doesn't deserve this. How could someone be that cruel? Thieves are like hyenas; they pick out the most vulnerable ones in the herd to attack."

"Isn't that sort of jumping to conclusions? How do you know that whoever did this knew that Estelle is a recent widow?"

"It's possible, Josh. I suppose that even burglars read the obituaries."

"And it's equally possible that they've been casing the neighborhood and figured out that she was gone. They may have been watching for days. There have been a bunch of burglaries lately. It seems like as soon as the cops get one off the streets another one takes over the territory. They're like franchisees or street-corner panhandlers. Did Estelle stop the newspaper and mail deliveries before she left town? I bet not."

"Sorry, Josh. I'm back."

"Estelle, do you mind if I put you on the speaker? Elaine's right here and she's worried about you."

"Sure, go ahead. I haven't talked to Elaine since Sunday night."

"Estelle, I'm so sorry. We called as soon as we got home. Is there anything I can do?"

"I can't think of anything right now. But just to hear a friendly voice is a comfort."

"While you were away from the phone Josh and I were wondering whether maybe you should see a doctor about getting a prescription for something to help you cope. Maybe Marlene could get her doctor in Houston to see you."

"That's a good idea, Elaine. I've been drinking so much vodka that my grandchildren—not to mention Marlene and Steven—are beginning to wonder whether their 'Nana' is a lush."

"You started to tell me about the burglary. Are you up to finishing?"

"It happened late this afternoon, Josh. Alex told me that he was putting some newspapers and empty bottles in the recycle bin in the alley. He saw a truck drive away from behind our garage. Then he saw that our back gate was open. He looked in the yard and saw that one of the French doors outside our bedroom—you remember, where you and Margie were talking—was open.

"He looked in the bedroom and saw that it was a mess. The dresser drawers were on the floor. The closet doors were open. Clothes scattered all over everywhere. He didn't want to go in, so he went back to his house and called the police. Then he called me. He knew I was out of town. I had asked him to pick up my mail and the newspapers. Sy and I did that for him and Helene lots of times because they travel so much in their business. He had my cell number."

"I take it the police came?"

"Yes. They took a statement from Alex and I spoke with them on the phone."

"Is the house secure?"

"As much as it can be. I called Sharon right away. She went over and took pictures for the insurance. Then she got hold of a handyman that she's used. He came and put up plywood to replace the doors. From what Alex told me they used a crowbar or something to break open the doors. So they'll have to be completely replaced. She also called a locksmith to change the door locks on the front and back doors."

"Could Sharon tell what was taken?"

"Just some costume jewelry. Thank God I took my good jewelry to Sharon before I left for Houston. They also took the TV in the bedroom and the one in the breakfast room. They didn't touch my good china or silver for some reason."

"Maybe they thought they were running out of time. Anything else?"

"The only other thing was they took Sy's computer. You remember, the laptop that was on the desk in Sy's office?"

"Did you record the serial numbers of the TVs? How about descriptions of the jewelry? They'll probably try to pawn what they stole or sell it at flea markets. The police have people that check the pawnshops and flea markets. Maybe something will turn up."

"We had all that, even photographs of the better jewelry. Unfortunately, Sy kept it all on his computer. He had an external hard drive, but he kept it attached to the computer."

"We've been saying 'they' like there was more than one burglar. Do you know that for a fact?"

"Alex said he saw two people drive off in the truck. The truck was going away from him so he didn't get a good look at them. But he's sure there were two of them."

"Did Alex say what kind of truck it was?"

"A...a white Ford. One of those that have the big tires and is high off the ground. It had a row of lights on the roof...you know...like a police car."

"What can I do to help, Estelle?"

"Will you call Harry Wexler? He handles our insurance. Sharon got the policy out of Sy's desk if you need it."

"Sure, I'll do it first thing Monday morning."

"Thanks, Josh. You too, Elaine. It makes me feel a lot better just having friends like you to talk to. Keep me...Oh! Josh, what's happening with the police investigation?"

"They still haven't released the car. The detective, Detective Turner, says the incident report was finally filed but I haven't seen it yet. I'll get a copy on Monday. I've got Nate Mendelovitz working on Sy's files so we can start letting Sy's clients have them. There's only one that's been a pest about it and I'll get rid of her as soon as Nate gets through reviewing the file."

Elaine took the phone out of Josh's hand. "'Bye, Estelle. Remember, call me if you need anything."

"Thanks, Elaine. I'm going to stay here for Thanksgiving. Sharon and Todd decided they'd drive down with their kids. Helping Marlene get everything ready will keep me busy. Hopefully no more catastrophes will happen. 'Bye, Elaine. 'Bye, Josh."

"Do you think I ought to call Detective Turner and tell her about the burglary and the white truck? The truck can't be a coincidence. Whoever broke into Estelle's house also broke into

Sy's office and murdered Margie. They must still be looking for
whatever it is they're looking for. They didn't find it in Sy's
car. They didn't find it in Sy's office. Evidently Margie didn't
know where it is. And now they've ransacked Estelle's home
looking for it."

"Who do you think it is?"

"I'm still voting for the ex-manager. But he drives an
antique Mercedes, not a pickup truck."

"Maybe he hired someone to do it?"

"That was my thought, but Detective Turner doesn't
think so. And I'm almost convinced she's right. Sy did all the
damage he could do months ago. So why seek revenge now?
Hiring hitmen, according to Detective Turner, costs money. Is a
low-life like Biggers going to spend big bucks just because he's
pissed off at Sy? And why now? Apparently Sy was paying the
rent on the condo and paying Jasmine at least two hundred
bucks a week. And let's not leave out the money Biggers was
making off Jasmine turning tricks in the condo and dancing at
Crystal's Palace.

"Besides, the revenge motive doesn't account for either
burglary. Why break into a dead man's office and then his
house? Or for that matter, why kidnap and murder his
assistant?"

"Josh, there is one hypothesis that does fit the facts."

"And that is?"

"Suppose that your assumption is wrong."

"Wouldn't be the first time. Which assumption?"

"That Sy did all the damage he could do months ago."

"So Sy held something back and is...was...blackmailing
Biggers?"

"I would never have figured Sy Blonstein for a blackmailer, but what else fits the facts?"

"That's certainly possible. Jasmine...Jolene...said that Sy had a plan to get rid of Biggers and get her out of the life.

"Maybe he was going to trade whatever he had on Biggers for Jolene's freedom."

"But wouldn't Sy and Biggers have been at a stalemate? If Sy dimes Biggers, then Biggers rolls over on Sy and they both end up as guests at the Club Fed."

"But not if Biggers gets rid of Sy *and* recovers whatever it is that Sy had on him."

"In other words, if Biggers runs the table, he wins. But as much sense as that makes, it doesn't account for the pickup truck."

"True. But what if there are others who were...are...in cahoots with Biggers? Maybe there is someone else—maybe one of the investors—who is at risk if whatever it is that Sy was holding back becomes known. Did you check out the investors? If one of them was involved with Biggers I imagine the others wouldn't be very happy about it. Maybe one of the investors has a white Ford pickup, or hired the hitmen."

"Good thought, Dr. Watson. And here's another one: I'm going to have another wee dram of whisky and then I'm going to sleep. I'll call Alana Turner after brunch. I love you."

"I love you too, Sherlock. Goodnight. Don't stay up all night thinking about *'L'Affaire Blonstein.'* I'm going to want you well-rested in the morning."

Chapter Thirty-Five

Josh did his best. He tried to pick up his place in *Operation Condor* but couldn't get his head into it. He went into the den and poured himself another wee dram of whisky which he consumed along with a couple of brownies he found in the freezer. After a while, he returned to bed and finally fell asleep. But sleep did not wipe the name 'Blonstein' from his brain.

In his nightmare Josh was blindfolded and loaded into the back of a white pickup truck with oversize tires and jacked-up suspension driven by a heavily-tattooed skinhead. The drive seemed to last for hours. It finally ended at a ruined medieval castle perched on top of a craggy mountain. Josh was led into the great hall of the castle. He shivered in the damp chill of the night air. When the skinhead left him he was standing in front of what appeared to be some kind of altar illuminated on each side by *menorah*-like candelabra on tall stands.

There was a claret-colored velvet curtain at the back of the altar. The curtain parted in the middle and an anthropomorphic figure stepped out. He—or it—was wearing a long black cloak with a tall upright collar and was holding a black fan that covered his—or its—face. The figure lowered the fan to reveal the head of a chupacabra. "Welcome, Joshua. Glad you could make it. Please follow me." The voice sounded familiar.

The figure turned and started toward the curtain. Josh mounted the steps of the altar as though pulled forward by some invisible force. The creature held the curtain aside with the fan and with the other hand motioned Josh through. As Josh passed by he noticed that the creature was wearing blue surgical gloves.

The area behind the curtain was fitted out like a surgical suite. There was a surgical gurney, an overhead surgical lamp and next to the gurney an instrument tray laid out with a full complement of instruments. A naked man was strapped to the gurney. His head was turned away from Josh. When Josh reached the side of the gurney the man turned to face him and smiled. It was Sy.

The creature went around to the other side of the gurney, took off the cloak and let it fall to the floor. He—or it—turned around facing away from Josh and removed the chupacabra head. When he turned back around to face Josh the chupacabra had become Harmon Polikoff. Then another figure came out from a dark corner of the room and stood next to Harmon. It was Estelle wearing a nurse's white cap and a tiny white skirt with nothing on in between. She was holding a glass in one hand and a bottle of Stoli in the other.

Harmon picked up a large chef's knife from the instrument tray. "And now, my dear Joshua, we will finally find what it is that you've been looking for." He traced the tip of the knife from Sy's sternum to just below his navel creating a line of bright red blood. Sy continued smiling at Josh as the blood grew to a torrent. Estelle held the empty glass into the fountain of blood until it was nearly full. She took a sip and then offered to Josh, "Here, Josh, would you like some?"

Chapter Thirty-Six

"Josh..." Elaine rolled over next to him. "Would you like some coffee now...or later." Josh opted for later.

It had gotten much colder during the night and there was a prediction of precipitation, possibly sleet, so they decided to have brunch at home. Elaine made an omelet with gruyere cheese and fine herbs. She found a few new potatoes in the vegetable bin in the refrigerator along with a piece of a yellow onion. These she used to make cottage fries. Josh found a half-bottle of champagne festering in the bottom of the temperature-controlled wine vault in the bar. There was a can of frozen orange juice in the freezer—probably left over from when their grandchildren last came to visit—so he made mimosas to go along with the omelets, fries and coffee.

After they'd finished eating and sharing the Sunday New York Times "Week in Review" section, Josh decided he'd best go ahead and call Alana Turner. With that out of the way he could spend the rest of the afternoon watching football—the

Cowboys had the late game that week—and then, if he and
Elaine weren't socked in, he would take her out for some kind
of Asian food.

"Alana, it's Josh. I hope I'm not disturbing you."

*"I'm at home watching the Texans and the Ravens with
one eye and looking at pickup truck registrations with the other.
How was the symphony?"*

"Good. It was nice to have an evening off. You should
try it sometime."

"You know the DPD never rests."

"I take it that you haven't found it?"

*"No, but I'm in the mid two thousands, so I'm getting
there."*

"Why is it never in the first dozen?"

*"That would make the job too easy and you wouldn't
need a highly-skilled, trained detective to do it."*

"While you've been looking for it the truck's been
busy."

"What now?"

"Estelle Blonstein's home was broken into yesterday
afternoon. I gather you haven't gotten the incident report."

"Right again, Counselor. Wanna tell me about it?"

"Estelle's out of town—at her daughter's in Houston.
When she found out that Marjorie Morrison had been murdered
she decided—and in hindsight rightly so—to get away for a
while. She's staying in Houston through Thanksgiving. Her
next door neighbor reported the break in. He was putting some
stuff in the recycle bin in the alley behind their houses when he
saw a white pickup driving away. It matches the description of
the one you're looking for. Unfortunately he didn't get the
license plate number. He knew Estelle is out of town, so he

checked the house and saw that it had been broken into. He called 9-1-1 and then called Estelle.

"Apparently they took some costume jewelry, a couple TVs and a laptop Sy kept at home. They left the silverware and good china."

"And you know all this because...?"

"When we got home last night—around midnight—there were three messages from Estelle on our voicemail. She said it was urgent so I called her back. I decided that I didn't need to bother you since you were probably either tied up with Andy Biggers or off duty. Can I ask how you made out with Biggers?...Sorry, Alana, 'made out' was a poor choice of words."

Alana actually laughed. *"Counselor, 'poor choice of words' may be the understatement of the week.*

"The BOLO got pretty quick results. A patrol car spotted the Mercedes—a car like that does tend to stand out—at a 'No-Tell' motel on Harry Hines. They called for backup and surrounded the building. They knocked on the door. They didn't have a warrant, so they tried knocking a few more times. The lead uniform thought he heard someone moaning inside and decided they needed assistance..."

"The tried-and-true 'exigent circumstances' drill?"

"Right. First thing they teach you in cop school. But in this case it was justified. They got the motel owner—a Mr. Patel—to open the door. Biggers and his girlfriend were both passed out on the bed. There were a couple of empty vodka bottles on the floor and a bottle of Vicodin on the nightstand. Biggers had a prescription for the Vicodin in his name. He had evidently gone to a doc-in-the-box for his recent injuries and they rewarded him with the prescription. He had a soft cast on

one arm and one foot was badly swollen. There was also a really nasty bruise on his abdomen and another on his left cheek. The Vicodin prescription was for thirty pills—a ten day supply. There were less than a dozen left."

"So the officers took Biggers and...and...the girlfriend...into custody?"

"They called for a bus and had them transported to the Parkland ER. Then they called my boss and he called me. That's when I called you the first time to bring the file. I had a fingerprint kit with me so I grabbed a set of his prints as they were wheeling him into one of the rooms where they work on people who don't have bullet holes or major knife wounds or otherwise look like they need surgery.

"While I was waiting for the doctors to get through working on him and on the girlfriend I got out my laptop and accessed VICAP. About five seconds after I entered the name 'Andy Biggers' my screen went blank. About ten seconds after that a big, ugly 'access denied' screen popped up. About an hour or so after that two big, ugly US marshals showed up with a federal writ of habeas corpus and kicked me out. They must keep a supply of pre-signed blank fill-in-the-name writs in a drawer at their office. So as of now the feds own him."

"So you never even got to question him?"

"Nope. But I did run the prints through AFIS. Apparently the Marshal Service forgot to block that one."

"I was told by the officers who responded to Margie's 9-1-1 call about the burglary of Sy's office that it took weeks to get prints run through AFIS."

"It usually does. But I called an old Army buddy. We used to have a fake access ID to use when we needed it. It's still working and supposedly untraceable. He ran the prints for me.

"If anyone ever finds out about it I'll be lucky if I end up back in uniform working the graveyard shift out of the Southeast Substation. That's Pleasant Grove in case you don't know. More likely I'll be wearing an orange jumpsuit and mopping floors at Leavenworth."

"Alana, isn't that pushing the envelope a bit too much? Is this case really worth that much to you?"

"Isn't that for me to decide, Josh? As I told you before, I'm a big girl. Do you want to hear who he is, or not?"

"Let me guess: 'Andy Biggers' isn't his real name. His real name is 'Guido' something and he's in the federal witness-protection program."

"Three for three, Counselor. You win the Kewpie doll. Only his name isn't 'Guido,' although it does end in a vowel."

"Okay, I give up, but only if I get to keep the Kewpie doll. What's Andy's real name?"

"Andrei Borisovich Biegrubinich. B-i-e-g-r-u-b-i-n-i-c-h."

"Damn! I should have recognized the accent. I was sure that English isn't his first language, but I couldn't place it. Is he some kind of defector? Ex-KGB?"

"Josh, don't let your imagination get the best of you. He emigrated from the Russian Federation to the US in nineteen ninety-three. Landed in the Brighton Beach community in Brooklyn. The area is almost all Russian immigrants. Has been for years. He got hooked up with the Russian mob: drugs, prostitution, truck-hijackings, computer crime. He was probably mixed up with them before he left Mother Russia. They're probably the ones who sponsored him to get him into the US.

"In any case, the feds nailed him when they took down a computer phishing operation that was stealing social security numbers. Biegrubinich was the marketing manager. They got him with a sting operation. He thought he'd sold fifteen hundred guaranteed matching names and social security numbers for seventy-five K—dollars, not rubles—to a Nigerian. Turns out the 'Nigerian' was an undercover FBI agent. Biegrubinich was looking at some serious time and probably deportation after that.

"The feds offered witness-protection and he jumped on it. I expect that the threat of deportation worried him a lot more than doing the time. Anyway, by the time the feds had wrung all they could out of him, he'd rolled over on at least a dozen street-level mobsters and two or three more who were higher up the food chain."

"So Biggers...or I suppose I should say"...Josh had written down the Russian's name as Alana had spelled it out..."'Biegrubinich' has a get-out-of-jail-free card signed by the US Attorney General and co-signed by a federal judge. I understood that one of the terms of the witness-protection program is that you have to stay out of trouble. If you screw up they forget they ever knew you."

"Josh, for a guy who doesn't miss much, you sure can be naive at times. To get kicked out of witness protection you pretty much have to go in and take a dump on the Attorney General's desk. I'm not even sure that would do it. The Marshal Service starts cutting the Biegrubiniches of the world loose, right away they head back to their old neighborhoods and as soon as they do they end up dead—conspicuously dead. Like in having their severed heads—with their genitals stuffed in their mouths—delivered by FedEx to their mother's or sister's

apartment on Coney Island Avenue in Brighton Beach. That's not a good marketing strategy for the program. They get some douchebag's cojones in a vise, offer him a deal and he says: 'Yeah, sure, you promise that you'll take care of me just like you took care of the late Andrei Borisovich. Thanks, gospodin officer, but nyet. I want now to call my advocat please.'"

"Alana, for an auto-crimes detective, you sound like you know your way around both the federal witness-protection program as well as the Borough of Brooklyn."

"My first posting after I completed my advanced MOS training was at Fort Hamilton. It's on the Brooklyn side of the Verrazano Bridge and not too far from Brighton Beach. I worked quite a few cases with the NYPD. There are a lot of military retirees at Fort Hamilton. The Ivans thought because the retirees were elderly, they were fair game for everything from muggings to 'pigeon drops' to fairly sophisticated investment scams. So yeah, I got to know Brighton Beach. As they say, 'Nice place to visit, but I wouldn't want to live there.'

"Did you pick up any Russian words?"

"A few. Why""

"Biggers…I mean Biegrubinich…yelled something at me and I was just curious."

"I'll give it a try."

Josh paused for a moment. "It sounded like 'yob vas' or something like that."

Alana laughed. "Yeah, I know that one. It's the verbal equivalent of shooting the finger…only in Russian."

"Kind of what I figured. How'd you get to be an expert on witness protection?"

"This isn't the first time my prom date has stood me up. I worked with the Garland PD on a case nine months ago. We *took down a guy who was wholesaling stolen parts for expensive sports cars: Corvettes, Porsches, Lamborghinis. Asian guy. 'Resettled' here from California. We take him to the Garland slammer; he asks to call his lawyer. Makes a call. Next thing we know two US marshals fly in on a magic carpet and whisk him away. At least we shut him down in our neighborhood."*

"Can I ask you where you got your intelligence on Biegrubinich? It can't have been from his fairy godmothers and I doubt that he has a Facebook page."

"I've still got a couple of friends in the NYPD. I managed to catch one of them at home and he filled me in."

"What about the girlfriend? What happened to her?"

"I hung around the Parkland ER until she woke up. That was after ten o'clock. Complete waste of time. She wouldn't talk to me. I didn't have anything to hold her on so I gave her my card and said, 'Glad you're okay. You ever want to talk about anything feel free to give me a call.' She said thanks and asked to borrow my phone. She called someone named 'Sondra' who said she'd come pick her up after she got off work. I asked her if she wanted me to wait with her but she said no."

"Did you at least get to keep Biegrubinich's gun?"

"Gun? What gun? I was going to charge him with carrying without a license but an ATF guy showed up with the marshals, waved a magic wand and made the Makarov disappear along with the silencer."

"Sorry I wasted so much of your time. I hope you didn't get into any kind of trouble."

"Well I almost got myself in trouble. I was arguing with the marshals trying to get them to at least let me have an hour...even half an hour...with Biegrubinich. One of the

marshals kept calling me 'Little Lady' and we kind of got into a shoving match. Then the three of them—the two marshals and the ATF guy—all grabbed me and handcuffed me to a gurney—with my own handcuffs—and threatened to charge me with obstruction of federal officers in the performance of their duties. They loaded Biggers/Biegrubinich into a wheelchair and got out of Dodge. Parkland Security uncuffed me after they were out the door. I told the Parkland guy that if he ever said anything about it he was a dead man walking."

"So now that Biegrubinich is in the wind so to speak, where do we go from here, partner?"

"I'm going to send it up the food chain. Maybe a deputy chief can reach out to the Dallas County DA. And maybe the DA will get his fat butt in gear and call in a marker from the US Attorney. But in the unlikely event he does, I'm not sure that even the US Attorney has enough weight to get Biegrubinich back. So all we've got left—for now—is finding the truck, which is what I've been trying to do since eleven o'clock last night."

"I've got another idea. Actually, one of my consultants came up with it."

"How many 'consultants' do you have? Is he one of the ones I've met?"

"You haven't met this one yet. But I assure you she's quite capable...in many areas."

"And what has the lady 'consultant' come up with?"

"You didn't buy into the revenge motive and I now agree with you. We both were assuming that by getting Biggers...Biegrubinich...kicked out of Crystal's Palace Sy had done all the damage he could do. What if that isn't the case?

"Maybe Biegrubinich isn't the only person associated with the gentlemen's club who needed Sy Blonstein silenced permanently. There were at least a couple of dozen investors. Maybe one or more of them were in on the scam along with Biegrubinich. What if they were shills who helped Biegrubinich suck in the other investors? What if they got a slice of what he stole from the investors and were getting their taste of the skim from operations and the kickbacks from the dancers? From what you found out about Biegrubinich's background, he evidently likes to run with a pack rather than operating as a lone wolf.

"Another possibility is that Biegrubinich was using the club as a money laundry."

"You're going to have to explain that one to me, Counselor."

"I had to think about it for a while. Even now, I'm not sure it holds up. I'll ask Nate about it in the morning; see what he says. If he thinks it's feasible, then I'll share it with you. If it doesn't work for Nate, there's no point in my wasting your time or making myself look like a fool."

"Counselor, the last thing I'd ever think about you is that you're a fool. Just tell me this: If Nate thinks your idea is credible, what do we do with it?"

"I didn't recognize any of the investors' names, but that doesn't mean anything. I'll ask Alicia to google the names. At least we can find out if any of them have criminal records. We can also check civil suit filings and get some idea of what kind of business problems they may have had. If we can track down any businesses they're involved in we can drill deeper on those.

"Not all of the investors were plaintiffs in the lawsuit. I'd start with the ones who weren't. Alicia's fielded calls from two people asking about Crystal's Palace. I haven't talked to either of them yet. I'll get on it first thing tomorrow."

"I like the idea, Counselor. Run with it. The only thing I don't like about it is that money laundering, tax evasion, securities fraud: Those are all federal crimes. If there is anything, I'm damn sure not going to let the feds hijack my case. Those assholes handcuffed me with my own handcuffs! So let's keep this between us as long as we can."

"Don't worry about that. You know I'm pretty good at keeping my mouth shut. I'll call and leave Alicia a voicemail right now so she can get started first thing. I'll also have her copy the file and send it over by courier. Will you let me know if you find the truck?"

"We'll see, Counselor. 'Need-to-know' is the byword. Good hunting."

Chapter Thirty-Seven

The "sky-is-falling" weather forecast, as usual, proved to be mostly inaccurate. The public school closing-protocol was geared up. The City, State and Toll Road Authority sand trucks were loaded and ready to roll. But the "wintry-mix" stayed well to the north and west. The temperature did, however, drop to an unseasonable low. It was so cold that when DeMontrond dropped Josh and Nate off at Josh's office, as they were entering the building they saw a UPS delivery guy in long trousers. While riding up in the elevator Josh crossed his fingers hoping that Marisol Obregon-Robertson had decided that it was too cold for the short skirts she evidently favored and had decided to hold off on her lawsuit.

No such luck. During the drive in from *Chai* Manor Josh had given Nate instructions to go through the Crystal's Palace files again with an eye toward either a possible money-laundering scheme or any systematic payments to any of the investors. After getting Nate situated Josh got a cup of coffee and reported to Alicia's work station outside his own office. Alicia handed Josh a familiar looking bundle of papers. "I went ahead and accepted service for you. The process server would have just hung around until you showed up and ambushed you in the building lobby. I guess that I should have called you on your cell phone."

"You did the right thing. It doesn't look good for a lawyer to appear to be ducking service. What's Ms. Obregon-Robertson trying to do besides make me mad?"

"I didn't try to read the whole petition, Josh. But you need to read it pretty soon. The judge granted her request for a hearing on a temporary injunction to make you turn over the Tezcatlipoca file and set it for three-thirty this afternoon."

"Alicia, please tell me I'm asleep and I'm having a nightmare. Maybe you're right. Why fight about giving the lady what she has a right to anyway? I'll go tell Nate to hold off on Crystal's Palace and work on Tezcatlipoca instead."

"Josh, hold on a minute. When I suggested doing just that the other day you gave me three good reasons why you shouldn't. Forget about her insulting me; I can live with it. However, she would be wasting her time asking me for money or my vote when she decides what she running for in the next election cycle.

"And I know how you feel about bullies, especially lawyer-bullies. But maybe you ought to be thinking about what Abraham Lincoln said about a lawyer who represents himself."

"And as for the third reason…?"

"I can't rationalize that one away. Why does she need to get her perfectly-manicured little hands on that file so badly?"

"I agree. Let's see what she has to say in her petition."

It took Josh a little more than an hour to read what was in the artfully written petition and to draft a two-page response. Alicia had already set up the case caption in her word processor so it did not take long for her to type Josh's pleading. Josh read over his response and signed it and Alicia filed it electronically with the court. The electronic filing automatically served a copy on Ms. Obregon-Robertson. Josh accessed Lexis from his desktop computer and in a few minutes more pulled up some case citations to support his arguments. He forwarded the citations to Alicia who printed out three copies for Josh to take with him to court: one for the judge, one for the other side and one for himself.

They ordered lunch from one of the take-out sandwich places in the underground warren and ate in Nate's office. Nate was ready to report but Josh insisted that they eat first. When Nate had finished his meatball sub, potato chips and chocolate-chip cookie he began his report.

"Josh, I can't tell yet if any of the investors were in on the scam with Biggers...I mean Biegrubinich. I looked through the Crystal's Palace bank statements for any checks payable to either of the two names you gave me: 'Oakley' and 'Singh.' Nothing. Then I looked for payments of even amounts, five thousand dollars or more, to any of the investors. Still nothing. But I have tell you that I really didn't expect to find anything."

"You mean you don't think much of Elaine's conspiracy theory?"

"I do. Elaine's theory is a reasonable one. The problem is that I don't have enough data. Alicia hasn't had time to do a complete search for business affiliations for even the two names you want to focus on much less all of the investors who didn't join in the lawsuit. Thieves like Biegrubinich may not be geniuses but they're not completely stupid either. If Biegrubinich had a silent partner or partners, he would never have made payments to them directly. He would have made the payments to a fake name, most likely a company of some kind."

"Were there any…"

"I found several that are worth looking into further. Sy had flagged most of them in his work papers."

"So what do we need to do to drill deeper?"

"What I really need besides matching up the names of the investors with their companies—those who have them—is the bank records for the companies that Biegrubinich controlled. If he did in fact have partners, he probably ran the payments through one or more of his own companies. In fact there was a Post-It note showing the questionable payments stuck to the list Sy prepared. The note is to himself to ask the investors' lawyer to subpoena the bank records for Biegrubinich's companies. But I don't see that anyone followed through."

"Anything to my money-laundering idea?"

"There could be. You remember the waitress, Sondra? She said that the skinheads were regular customers, not just the two that…" Nate caught Josh's look toward Alicia who was sitting next to Josh and across the desk from Nate. "…that got their skin heads smacked together the other night.

"I read in the paper that the skinheads are members of a gang…'Caucasian' something…and that they deal in drugs. They could have been paying the drug money to Biegrubinich and he was depositing it along with the legitimate receipts from the club. A place like Crystal's Palace deals in mostly cash. You remember how the hostess fumbled with your American Express platinum card? It's probably the first one she'd ever seen. What *schlemiel* would want 'Crystal's Palace' showing up on his MasterCard bills that his wife looks at every month?

"A bank has to comply with the Treasury Department 'Know-Your-Customer' rules. So if the bank knows that its customer is a business that deals mostly in cash, the bank is not going to look too hard at sizeable cash deposits every day. Biegrubinich would have to keep each of his deposits well under ten thousand dollars to avoid having to file the currency-source forms and to avoid getting flagged for not filing them. If that's a problem, he can use two or more banks. In fact, he probably did: He'd use one account for legitimate receipts and one or two others for the money-laundering. That way he wouldn't have to report the money-laundering receipts on the sales tax quarterly reports that he has to file with the state."

"Then what? How does Biegrubinich get the money back to the skinheads?

"That's when I begin have a problem—the same one. Without the bank records from Biegrubinich's companies I can't trace the money any further. If he was laundering money, it would be easy enough to generate some fake invoices and write checks to fake payees, less his commission, and presto change-o the money's successfully recycled."

"So once the judge shut Biegrubinich down, the money laundry also closed up shop. Maybe the skinheads thought that Sy knew more than he actually did. They knew that Sy went to Crystal's Palace every Tuesday and Thursday night. As soon as Sy's inside and is focused on Jasmine, one of the skinheads slips under Sy's car and diddles with the collision sensor. We know that at least one of them drives a pickup truck. I doubt that he's the only one. Is there anything else you can do without Biegrubinich's bank records?"

"I could sit down with the detective. She could maybe get a subpoena?"

"Too complicated, Nate, for several reasons."

"Well, I'll keep going over what I have. I've just been looking for large, round-number checks to investors. Maybe there are checks to others."

"I'll leave you to it. Before I have to leave for court I want to return the calls from the three people who called me."

"What about Tezcatlipoca? What happens if the judge..."

"Ain't going to happen, Nate. But if it does, I'm sure I can at least buy you a day or two."

Chapter Thirty-Eight

Before he left for the courthouse Josh filled in Alicia and Nate on his phone conversations with the two investors. He had not been able to reach Victor Ortega so he had just left a message. Angus Oakley owned a couple of area automobile dealerships. He had not wanted to be a plaintiff in the lawsuit because if the case made it into the newspaper or got on TV, as a prominent lay leader in his church, he could not afford the publicity. After Biegrubinich had been booted out, Oakley sold his interest to the other investors for pennies on the dollar. As part of the sale he had gotten a confidentiality agreement from the buyers that would prevent disclosure of his former interest.

He had called Josh to find out what was going to be done with Sy's files and whether there was any reason for him to be concerned about disclosure. Josh thought briefly about jerking Angus Oakley's chain. Instead, swallowing his dislike for hypocrites, especially religious ones, Josh told him that he could think of no reason for Sy's Crystal's Palace file to go anywhere but to dead storage and after a few years to the shredder. Angus Oakley audibly let out his breath, said "God bless you" to Josh and hung up.

Doctor Rajitraman Singh owned a chain of chiropractic clinics that specialized in trauma care: automobile accidents and worker's compensation. His concern was approximately the same as Angus Oakley's. The differences were that Dr. Singh had put his interest into a limited liability company and had decided to hang on to it. Instead of being worried about publicity, he was terrified that his wife would find out. Sy had apparently contacted him in the course of his investigation so he wanted to know whether Sy had left a paper trail that would lead back to him.

Josh decided that he should have jerked Angus Oakley's chain after all so he jerked Dr. Singh's instead. He told Dr. Singh that possibly the Dallas County District Attorney or even the US Attorney's office might be investigating Andy Biggers and Crystal's Palace for several reasons: prostitution and tax fraud while Biggers was running the place, just to mention a couple. So yes, it was possible that one or more subpoenas might be issued and Josh would be obliged to turn over the late Mr. Blonstein's files. Josh warned that once those agencies had a name they could be like a dog with a bone. They would keep gnawing on it until there was nothing left. So there was no way to tell where they might go with the investigation. Dr. Singh wanted to know if they could investigate his own business—his clinics. Josh replied that he wasn't Dr. Singh's attorney so he couldn't give him legal advice. But, that said, Josh told him that anything is possible. Josh wished Dr. Singh well with his investment and ended the call.

When Josh got back to his office from the courthouse it was a few minutes after five o'clock. Alicia and Nate were waiting for his report. They settled in Josh's office. Josh warmed his hands around a cup of coffee. He'd not wanted to inconvenience DeMontrond so despite the cold he had walked to the courthouse and back.

Alicia knew from Josh's demeanor that the hearing had gone well. "That was quick. Did she…"

"No, no Louboutins. She wore over-the-calf boots."

"Huh?" Nate asked.

"Just a private joke, Nate. Alicia didn't care for Ms. Obregon-Robertson's choice of footwear when she came to our office the other day."

"Did she at least wear a short skirt?" Alicia took a sip of coffee.

"No, but she did manage to flash her ass anyway."

"I knew I should have gone to law school instead of into accounting."

"I promise you, Nate, I was speaking metaphorically only. Although literally might have been even more interesting."

Alicia muttered something unintelligible in to her coffee cup.

"Just imagine," Josh continued, "your worst battle with the IRS. That's roughly the equivalent of spending an hour in court with Ms. Obregon-Robertson.

"The injunction was denied. Alicia, as you know we made several arguments. But the one that resonated the most with the judge is the one where I said that Ms. Obregon-Robertson couldn't get a temporary injunction because it would grant all the relief that she could get after a full trial. A temporary injunction can only be granted to preserve the status quo. And the status quo is that I've got the file and she doesn't.

"She also had a tough time explaining what 'irreparable harm' her client would sustain if it didn't get the file today. I think that despite my status quo argument the judge might have given her something if she had come up with a plausible argument for irreparable harm. She danced as fast as she could, but the judge wasn't impressed. I got the sense that she didn't want to open the kimono very far, so she couldn't come up with anything."

"What happens now? Do I have time to go through the file?"

"You've got at least three weeks, Nate. I hope that's enough time. I explained to the judge the problems we were having accessing and organizing the files: the burglary, Margie's death, the stolen computers, no password or encryption key, the cost of getting someone in to do the work. Despite all that I promised the judge that by the time my answer to the suit is due we'd probably be able to turn over a copy of the file to the plaintiff.

"When I said 'copy' Ms. Obregon-Robertson nearly got herself held in contempt. She started screaming that she wanted the original file—not a copy—and that I was not to keep even a copy. The bailiff started toward her, Eloy got up and moved between her and the bailiff. The bailiff actually unfastened the strap holding his sidearm in its holster. The judge was banging his gavel. But before things got totally out of hand everybody calmed down. I told the judge that I'd discuss the matter further with Ms. Obregon-Robertson and we'd see what could be worked out. And that was about it. Ms. Obregon-Robertson gave me her thousand-watt smile and we actually shook hands."

"I knew I should have been a lawyer. You guys have all the fun."

"Do you want me to order a transcript?"

"Absolutely. And if you don't have anything else, Nate and I are out of here. I told DeMontrond a quarter to six. I expect he's downstairs waiting."

"Oh, Josh, I almost forgot. You had a couple of strange phone calls and you got a package delivered by courier while you were at the courthouse. It was marked 'personal' so I didn't open it. It's on your desk. Do you want it?"

"That's okay; I'll get it on the way out. Maybe Elaine ordered something online and had it delivered to the office because she's been going to so many meetings lately with 'Project Do Over' and didn't want to miss the delivery. Tell me about the phone calls first."

"They both asked for you. I told them you weren't available and asked if I could take a message. They wouldn't give me their names or phone numbers; they just said 'Crystal's' and hung up."

Josh frowned. "I wonder what that's about? See you tomorrow."

Chapter Thirty-Nine

Josh got in the back seat of the Chrysler and while DeMontrond was stowing Nate's walker in the trunk he started to open the package he had retrieved from his desk. "Louis, do you have a pocket knife I can use to open this thing? It's got so much packing tape on it you'd think there were loose diamonds or something inside."

Louis unfastened his seatbelt so he could dig around in his pocket. He fished out a key ring with a small pen knife dangling on a chain among the keys. He handed it back to Josh. "This is the best I can do, Mr. Josh. It ain't big, but it's sharp enough to do the job. You 'spectin' a shipment of loose diamonds?"

"No, I wasn't expecting anything. It was delivered by courier to my office this afternoon while I was in court. It must be something Elaine ordered and had delivered to my office instead of home."

"Maybe it's a present for you."

"It's not my birthday, or our anniversary…"

"Maybe she just wanted to buy you a present. It say who it's from?"

Josh looked again at the label. "Nope. It's handwritten. No store name, not even a return address. All it says is 'Mr. Joshua Loeb, Lawyer' and my firm's address. And it's marked 'personal.'"

Louis frowned and put his hand on Josh's to stop him from cutting the tape. "I reckon you ain't 'spectin' a bomb either. You sure you want to open it?"

"No, now that you mention it, I don't suppose I am. But who would want to send me a bomb? Ms. Obregon-Robertson got a little testy in court this afternoon when she didn't get her file back, but she got over it. We even shook hands after the hearing."

"I doubt that Mr. Blonstein was 'spectin' what happened to him either, Mr. Josh."

DeMontrond got in the car. "Where to, Mr. Josh? We gonna take Mr. Nate home?"

"Hol' on a sec, DeMontrond. We got us a little issue here. Mr. Josh, he got himself a mysterious package; don' know where it come from. Maybe it's jus' some cookies or somethin', maybe it's somethin' gonna blow up when he opens it."

"Can I take a look, Mr. Josh?"

Josh hesitated and then handed the package to DeMontrond. "Careful, DeMontrond. Your Uncle Louis has got me worried now."

"Maybe we ought to get out of the car…"

"No need for that, Mr. Nate. I ain't gonna try and open it. Jus' feel around the outside a little." As everyone held their breath, DeMontrond took the package and ran his index finger all around it and shook it gently. "Ain't no wires that I can feel, so it's safe to take the wrapping off. Feels like something soft sloshin' around inside. Don't seem really heavy like it would be if it had batteries inside or if it was packed with nails."

"So maybe it's just a little bomb."

"Josh, how big is a 'little bomb?' What about a letter bomb? Doesn't the Secret Service x-ray every envelope that comes to the White House...at an off-site facility?"

"Maybe you're right, Nate. You all stay in the car. I'll walk down the street and take the wrapping off."

"'Fore you go doin' that, Mr. Josh, can I make a suggestion?"

"Sure, DeMontrond, just as long as it doesn't involve anyone but me opening the package."

"Uncle Louis, can we go back to the shop? Get one of those magnets we use for body work? We could run a magnet over it, find out if there's any metal inside. Be pretty hard to make a bomb without using some kind of metal parts."

"Why don't we just call the police bomb squad? They're experts in dealing with things like this."

"I don't think so, Nate. I'd like to leave the cops out of this for now. If it is a bomb, they're going to want to know who'd send me a bomb. If it's not a bomb, then they're going to want to know why I thought it might be. Either way, they're going to be asking a lot of questions that I'm not especially interested in answering just now."

"Josh, you remember what I said a while ago in your office about lawyers having all the fun? Can I take that back?"

"Already forgotten, Nate. Louis, if it's okay with you, I think DeMontrond's got a good idea. If the magnet doesn't tell us anything, we can at least take the wrapping off and then decide what to do next. Don't you have a welder's mask and some fire-retardant coveralls? If it's not too big a bomb, maybe I'll survive."

Prejean Automotive occupied a one-story brick building on Main Street east of downtown. Louis raised one of the overhead doors and DeMontrond drove inside parking in the empty service bay next to the office. While DeMontrond located a magnet Josh placed the package on the concrete floor in an empty bay farthest from the office. Everyone but Josh retreated to the office. Josh ran the magnet over all five exposed sides of the package. He then turned the package on its side and ran the magnet over the bottom. He walked over to the office. "Well, there's no iron. So unless the bomb's made of aluminum or plastic, I guess it's safe. Just to be sure, Louis, is it okay if I put on the welder's helmet and fire-retardant coveralls?"

While Louis was assembling the welder's garb, Josh took the package back out to the far bay. Using a larger pocket knife that Louis had given him he slit the tape and removed the brown paper wrapper. The box itself was made of corrugated cardboard. The lid had an extended flap that folded down inside the front edge of the box. There was a semicircular tab where the lid met the edge of the box so that a finger could be inserted in order to lift the lid.

Josh zipped up the fire-retardant suit and was about to fit the metal mask over his head and face. "I've got an idea, Mr. Josh. Bring the box over to the workbench and let's put it in the vise. Instead of you jus' holdin' it, the vise will hol' it steady. An' instead of you standin' right next to it, try this." Louis went over to a supply closet and came back with an aluminum pole with a spring-loaded claw-like device on the end and a bead chain that opened the claw when pulled. "We use this for gettin' small parts boxes down off the high shelves. Stuff like headlights, oil filters...save havin' to get a ladder an' climbin' up an' down. You stand back, use the claw to open the box."

"I'll give it a try. Thanks, Louis. You go ahead back to the office and all of you duck down below the window."

Josh secured the box in the vise as tightly as he could without crushing the sides. He left about half an inch sticking out above the top of the vise. He eyeball-measured the length of the aluminum pole and manhandled a nearly-full fifty-five gallon drum of used oil close enough to the vise that he could shield at least part of his body behind the drum while he manipulated the claw. He extended the pole and worked the chain a few times to get the feel of it. Then he tried picking up a couple of hand tools that were lying on the workbench.

Inside the helmet and coveralls he could feel himself drenched in perspiration. After a few tries he finally got the claw to pick up a screwdriver from the workbench. He put it back down, released the claw and then used it to pick up a socket-wrench driver. By now the pole felt like it was made of solid iron rather than hollow aluminum. His fingers were so tired they were shaking.

He raised the mask so that he could be heard in the office. "Okay! Fire in the hole!" He lowered the mask and crouched down behind the drum as low as he could and still be able to manipulate the claw. In order to get a good angle on the box tab he had to hold the pole at arm's-length over his head. He managed to get the claw on the top of the box a couple of times but could not get the tip of the claw inside the tab. Now, in addition to his hands shaking, his arms were exhausted.

"Come on, Loeb. You can do this," he mumbled to himself. He stood up behind the drum and guided the pole so that the bottom arm of the open claw was resting on the top edge of the vise. He tightened the chain to open the claw. Then he slowly rotated the pole until the tip of the claw penetrated the opening below the tab of the box. He relaxed the chain so that the upper arm of the claw secured a grip on the tab. Then, ducking a bit lower behind the drum, he rested the pole on the edge of the drum so that he could use the drum as a fulcrum. He pushed down on the end of the pole. With the extra leverage of the fulcrum the top of the box opened, then the box pulled loose from the vise and fell to the floor spilling its contents. Josh let go of the pole and dropped to the floor behind the drum. There was no explosion, just a couple of soft splats. He counted to ten slowly and pulled off the mask. "All clear!"

Josh unzipped the front of the fire-retardant suit and walked toward the workbench. When he got within a couple of feet he looked down at the former contents of the box, sank to his knees and threw up.

Louis was the first out of the office with DeMontrond half a step behind and Nate bringing up the rear. When Louis reached Josh he looked at what was on his shop floor then he too sank to his knees beside Josh and tears began to well up in his eyes. DeMontrond looked for an instant, moaned and then turned away sprawling his upper body across the hood of a car parked in the adjacent service bay. Nate clumped up to the workbench, looked down and passed out where he stood.

Josh was the first to regain a measure of composure. He helped Louis to his feet. They lifted Nate off the floor. DeMontrond opened the door of the car he'd been sprawled on and they got Nate into the passenger seat. Louis felt Nate's carotid pulse as Nate's eyes began to flutter open. "You gonna be alright, Nate. Jus' take a few deep breaths." Louis stepped back to give Nate some breathing room and rested his hands on the top of the open car door. "Jesus, Lord! What kin' of motherfucker do that to another human bein'? They bad as that *El Chupacabra*. Maybe worse."

"I wonder who they belonged to. And why send them to me?"

"I think I know who they belonged to, Mr. Josh. I guess you was busy all day and didn't hear about it."

"About what, Louis?"

"It was on the five o'clock local news. I was finishin' up some insurance forms an' half listenin' to the TV. Late this morning they found the bodies of two homeless men under the Corinth Street viaduct—one white and one black—both of 'em with their private parts cut off. Medical examiner say they alive when it happen and that they bled to death."

Josh forced himself to look at the severed genitals. "How do they know they were homeless?"

"Police showed their pictures around at the Bridge shelter. People there knew them. Even knew their first names, but the police ain't releasin' that information."

"Okay, and now the big question: Why send them to me?"

"Answer might be in here, Mr. Josh." DeMontrond pointed to a folded piece of paper lying on the floor next to the bloody genitals.

"Wait, don't pick it up with your fingers, DeMontrond. You sure don't want your prints on the paper.

"Louis, we can't just leave them lying here." Josh retrieved the claw device. Using it he picked up the genitals and put them back in the box. He put the gloves back on and closed the box and placed it on the workbench.

"DeMontron', go look in the supply closet. There's an old picnic cooler in there. Get whatever ice there is in the refrigerator. We'll put 'em in the cooler with the ice and I'll lock the cooler in the closet in my office 'till we figure out what we gon' do.

After Nate was sufficiently revived they went into Louis's office and stood around his desk. Still wearing the heavy gloves, Josh unfolded the piece of paper.

"Death to jews!
Especialy to nigger-loving jews!
Your first, Jewshua Loeb,
then your nigger friend.
Were going to cut your dicks
and balls off just like thes ones. "

"Well, I guess that answers your question and mine, Louis. While I was in court this afternoon, Alicia took two hang-up phone calls. Both calls, the person just said the word 'Crystal's' and then hung up. I guess they didn't appreciate the lesson you taught their pals. But if they're pissed at you, why send the package to me?"

Nate sat down heavily in Louis's desk chair. "I hope you don't mind, Louis, I'm still a little shaky. To answer your question, Josh, they didn't know who Louis was. If they had gotten the license plate number off the Chrysler, that would have only led them to the owner, not to Louis. It had to be the credit card, Josh. Remember how long she took to process it?"

"You said it was because she'd probably never seen one like mine before."

"That's probably true, but I'd bet that's not the first credit card she's hijacked. They've got all kinds of ways to steal your credit card information at the point of use. Wouldn't be a bad idea for you to call Amex and get a new number. Also check for any unauthorized use. And Louis, you ought to call your customer, just in case."

"Can I ax a question?"

"What are we going to do about the...the package?"

"Yes, Sir, Mr. Josh. Don' seem right jus' leavin' 'em in that ice chest."

"Josh, you need to reunite them with their former owners. It's the only decent thing to do. At least somebody at the morgue can maybe sew them back on. I never have been a believer in an afterlife, but at my age you tend to start wanting to hedge your bets. So I spend more time thinking about it than I ought to. If there is an afterlife I sure don't want to spend mine without my original equipment. And I doubt that the gentlemen to whom these belong would feel any differently."

"Nate, you're right as always. But I'm not quite ready to call the artillery down on my own position. Turning them over to the cops would be just like calling the bomb squad before we opened the box. If we hand it over to the cops I could always plead ignorance, even though they'd know I was lying. I might be able to tough it out with Alana and the DPD, but it's clearly a hate crime. That'll get the feds involved sooner or later. Probably sooner. I don't tell them what I know, they'll charge me with obstruction of justice as fast as they can draw up the indictment. They can't make it stick, but my professional life is over. If you were a member of my firm, or if you were a client, how would you react when you opened the Morning News and saw the front-page headline: 'Prominent local attorney Joshua

Loeb implicated in mutilation hate crime?' What about Elaine, my kids, my grandkids?

If that's not enough, unless I clam up and fade the heat, how do I keep Louis and DeMontrond out of it? Isn't the FBI going to be just a little curious about who the...the...who my...'friend' is? I asked Louis and DeMontrond to take a look at Sy's car, nothing else. Now they're up to their asses in alligators and it's my fault. If I give up their names...Sorry, Nate, I can't do it even though it is the only 'decent' thing to do."

"There's also an old saying, Josh: 'When you find yourself in a hole, the first thing you do is stop digging.' Maybe it's time…"

"Nate, I appreciate your wisdom; and most likely you're right. But I'm not ready to just hand this mess over to the DPD, the FBI or anyone else. Not yet. If you want out, just say so. I'll understand. I realize it's a matter of principle, and not because you're afraid of these *mamsers*. Same goes for you, Louis, and you, DeMontrond."

"What the hell, Josh. If one of the skinheads comes after me, I'll jab him in the balls with my walker. If the cops want to question me, I'll tell 'em it's the Alzheimer's; I can't remember a thing."

"Whatever you wantin' to do, Mr. Josh," Louis glanced at DeMontrond who nodded his assent, "DeMontron' and me, we're in."

"Thank you all, gentlemen. I appreciate it. Here's what I want to do: This was just a warning——more explicit than the hang-up phone calls—but just a warning. I don't think they've got the guts to do any more. If they intended to harm us, why the warning? It would have taken more effort than killing two homeless men, but if they wanted to take us out, it could have been mine and Louis's genitals in that box.

"Once we dig up enough to give Alana a basis for taking official action, I'll turn over the box. I'll say that I stuck it in the trunk of the Chrysler without opening it and just forgot about it. If the cops want to know how Louis got involved, I'll say maybe they followed me to the impound lot and saw him with me.

"Now let's get out of here before our wives put out an APB for us."

Louis stowed the cooler in the closet in his office and joined the others in the car. DeMontrond backed out and Louis closed and locked the overhead door. They headed east on Main toward Peak Street. They got to the intersection just as the traffic light turned red. DeMontrond came to a stop and put the transmission in neutral.

"What you doin', DeMontron'? Ain't you turnin' left here? Better put your blinker on; don' need to get a ticket for failin' to signal."

"Don' know, Uncle Louis. There's a red Dodge pickup, second vehicle behind us. May be followin' us. I saw it parked on the other side of the street a few yards west of the shop when we backed out. Pulled away from the curb and made a u-turn soon's I backed out and started headin' east. I think it might have been waitin' for us; thinkin' maybe we was goin' to go back west on Main, the way we come."

"Guess we better find out, DeMontron'. I don' see no cop cars. Go ahead and run the light. Turn left. Truck do the same thing, then we know for sure."

"You gentlemens got your seat belts fastened? If they's followin' us, I may have to use some of the things I learned 'fore I went to the joint." DeMontrond slipped the transmission in low gear, glanced quickly to the right for oncoming traffic on Peak and whipped the steering wheel hard left. The wide rear tires bit into the concrete burning rubber and the Chrysler turned north onto Peak heading toward Ross Avenue accelerating flat out.

The truck whipped around the car that had been between it and the Chrysler and into the westbound lanes on Main. Barely missing a northbound car on Peak, its customized mufflers roaring, it turned onto Peak and accelerated after the Chrysler.

DeMontrond barely made the yellow light at Gaston and ran the red lights at Bryan and Live Oak. The truck ran the lights at Gaston and Bryan and then had to stop at Live Oak because cars on Live Oak were already in the intersection.

As they came closer to the Ross Avenue intersection DeMontrond had gotten up to eighty miles per hour. The light at Ross turned red for Peak traffic and there were already cars in the intersection going in both directions on Ross. DeMontrond hit the brakes and managed to bring the Chrysler to a stop just as a gasoline tanker truck trundled through the intersection heading east on Ross. Josh had turned around in his seat and was watching for the Dodge through the rear window. "They're still after us. About a block and a half back."

"You sure, Mr. Josh?"

"I'm sure, Louis. Big red pickup."

DeMontrond swung the wheel hard left and red-lined the engine. There was a minivan approaching the intersection in the outside lane heading east on Ross and an SUV heading west in the inside lane on Ross. DeMontrond aimed for the westbound outside lane on Ross and somehow made the turn onto Ross without hitting, or being hit by, either of the two vehicles the drivers of which stood on their brakes and blew their horns.

Seconds later the pickup did a four-wheel power drift through the intersection taking off the bumper and driver's-side headlight of the minivan and then clipping the rear bumper of the SUV. Both the Chrysler and the pickup were now heading west on Ross.

DeMontrond had to slow down a couple of times to weave his way between westbound vehicles on Ross and one time had to cross into the middle left-turn lane to pass a Dart bus. "They're gaining on us! They're just a few car-lengths back," Josh reported. Josh was looking out the rear window using his left hand to shade his eyes from the glare of the truck's headlights. Then the rear window of the Chrysler exploded showering Josh and Nate with shattered glass.

Louis had already taken out his handgun and was turned in his seat looking out the back. "You all best get down on the floor! Some motherfucker standin' up in the back of the truck aimin' a shotgun." Louis fired two rounds, both of which struck the pickup's radiator. Vaporized liquid immediately began spurting out from the punctures. Damn! I was tryin' to shoot out the tires but I can't get a good angle."

"Darn, Uncle Louis, one of the pellets musta clipped me on th' ear." Blood was dripping from DeMontrond's ear and there was a spiderweb pattern where the pellet struck the windshield in front of DeMontrond.

"You okay to drive, DeMontron'?"

"Yeah, Uncle Louis, I'm good."

"Slow down jus' a little bit. Let 'em get a little closer. We had enough of this shit. Soon's I fire, you floor it and get us the hell out of here."

"Okay, Uncle Louis."

"DeMontrond slowed to sixty. Resting his wrists on the back of his seat, Louis fired two more rounds, both of which struck the windshield of the pickup. The driver swerved into the inside lane. DeMontrond hit the brakes and forced the steering wheel to the left as far as it would go. The Chrysler's tires screamed in protest and the ones on the passenger side came at least a foot off the pavement as the gods of physics made known their dislike of DeMontrond's defying their laws. But using all five lanes on Ross, DeMontrond managed to make the u-turn and was now red-lining it east on Ross.

The Dodge, with its higher center of gravity and less skilled driver did not fare as well. The truck attempted the same u-turn, but from the inside westbound lane. It got about ninety degrees through the u-turn, flipped on its side and came to rest next to the curb on the eastbound side of Ross.

"You can slow down now, DeMontron'. They done for the night. Get back to the shop. Better take side streets. Be cops all over the place any minute an' they be lookin' for this car like we was *El Chupacabra* or somethin'. An' I need to get rid of this gun. Bran' new, too. Jus' got it. Been meanin' to try it out. I ain't use to it yet."

Josh and Nate swept the shattered rear window glass off the back seat and retook their seats. "Hadn't we better get DeMontrond to a doctor?" Josh brushed some shards of glass out of his hair. "Looks like I may need a band-aid or two myself." Josh held up his left hand which was bleeding from a small round hole in the outside of his left palm. "Good thing I was shading my eyes, otherwise that pellet might be in my left eye instead of my hand."

"Let's get rid of the car and the gun first, Mr. Josh. We can swap the car for your Jag an' I can get my old gun. I got a doctor friend in South Dallas. He's an old-timer; pretty much retired. But he's as good at takin' care of gunshot wounds as anybody they got in one of those hospital emergency rooms, 'specially when he sober. Best thing is, though, he's downright religious when it comes to patient privacy. He been knowin' how to keep his mouth shut way long before they passed those federal patient-privacy laws a while back."

"Does your doctor friend by any chance drink scotch? My hand is starting to hurt like hell, so I'm gonna need something for the pain."

"I'll see what he can do, Mr. Josh."

Chapter Forty

It was after nine o'clock by the time Louis's doctor friend finished stitching DeMontrond's ear, removing the pellet from Josh's palm and tending to a couple of minor scalp wounds Nate had received from the shattered rear window. It had taken another hour at the all-night Walgreen's at Mockingbird and Matilda to fill the antibiotic prescriptions the doctor had written for them. After taking Nate back to *Chai* Manor, it was close to midnight when Louis and DeMontrond dropped Josh at home.

Josh was hoping that Elaine would be asleep. She wasn't. She had apparently finished the Louise Penny and had started the new Michael Connolly "Harry Bosch" police procedural. She looked up at Josh over the rims of her reading glasses, "Another tedious night at Crystal's Palace?"

"I haven't been anywhere near Crystal's Palace. "I'm going to pour myself a single-malt. It has been a tedious night...and a tedious day...but no Crystal's Palace." In a few minutes Josh returned with three fingers of scotch and a sandwich he'd made from the London broil he'd found in the refrigerator.

"The London broil would have been even better if you'd eaten it when I first took it out of the broiler thinking that you'd be home for dinner. What happened to your hand? And why is there blood on the cuff of your shirt and the cuff of your suit?"

"I...I...it was an accident, Elaine. We were at Louis's shop and I cut myself."

"What were you doing at Louis's shop?"

"We had to drop off a package."

"And that took until almost midnight?"

"I was in court all afternoon with Ms. Obregon-Robertson, and then we worked late on Sy's files."

"Which were so exciting that you forgot to call? Or was it Ms. Obregon-Robertson that made you forget to call."

"I'm sorry, Elaine, I just forgot."

"You haven't done that in a long time, Josh. I was worried. Rose called. She was worried about Nate. You must have had your cell phone off. I tried calling you, but..."

"Sorry again."

"Eat your sandwich and drink your scotch then you can tell me about it. In the meantime, give me your shirt and suit jacket. I'd better put something on them so the stains will come out."

Josh put his sandwich and glass on the coffee table in front of the couch. He got up and handed Elaine his suit jacket and started stripping off his tie and shirt. Elaine noticed the small bulge in the breast pocket of the jacket. She pulled out the prescription bottle. "Who is Dr. Griggs?"

"He's...he's the doctor who bandaged my cut. He gave me a prescription for an antibiotic...just in case."

What did you do? Go to some 'doc-in-the-box?'"

"No, he's a friend of Louis's."

"Josh, let me see your hand."

"It's okay, Elaine. It's nothing."

"Joshua..."

Reluctantly, Josh held out his hand. Elaine carefully peeled back the bandage. "Josh, this doesn't look like a cut; it's a puncture wound. No wonder you need an antibiotic. Josh, what the hell happened to you?" Elaine pressed the bandage back in place.

"Ouch, Elaine. It's sore and hurts like hell."

"It's not as sore as I'm about to get with you. Did someone stab you with an ice pick? There's bruising all around it. Josh, what's going on?" I'm your wife. I have a right to know."

Josh started to pick up his scotch. "Better leave the scotch, Josh. Take some ibuprofen or acetaminophen. Those will work better than the scotch and you won't fall asleep before you tell me what happened to you."

"Okay, you win. Would you mind wrapping up the sandwich and putting it in the fridge? I'll go take my pills. Then I'll tell you about my 'tedious' night."

By the time Elaine got back from the kitchen Josh had taken his medication and had gotten into bed. "I'm sorry, Elaine. You're right; you have a right to know.

"When we were at Crystal's Palace Friday night, as we were leaving, Louis got into an altercation with a couple of skinheads. They apparently took offense at his being there."

"You mean the two that ended up in the hospital with concussions?"

"Yeah. Anyway they must have followed us to Louis's shop."

"How did they know how to find Louis?"

"Best we can figure, they must have gotten my name from my credit card and followed us from my office."

"So they attacked you in Louis's shop? I thought you said Louis always carried his gun?" And where was DeMontrond?" You said he was all the protection you needed."

"They fun didn't start until we left the shop and were heading home. They started chasing us in their truck…"

"Josh! You were involved in that car chase and gun battle on Ross Avenue? The one that was on the ten o'clock news?" My God! Have you lost your mind? Did you get shot? Is that what that puncture wound is?"

"It's only a shotgun pellet, Elaine. DeMontrond caught one too, in his right ear. Took ten stitches to close it. I was lucky."

"How about Nate? Louis?"

"Louis, not a scratch. Nate got a couple of superficial scalp wounds when they shot out the rear window."

"On the news they said that there were bullet holes in the truck."

"That was Louis firing back."

"They said on the news that the black sedan escaped and the police are looking for it. So I assume you didn't call them."

"We talked it over and decided not to risk the potential blowback."

"Blowback? How about nearly getting your heads blown off?"

"Elaine, I got Louis and DeMontrond into this mess. I'm not going to be the one that gets Louis charged with aggravated assault and DeMontrond sent back to prison...just for helping me out."

"So Louis and DeMontrond are now permanent additions to our family? I love Louis as much as you do. And DeMontrond's a really nice young man. But are they going to be a part of our lives from now on?"

"I think the skinheads have had enough of us. We've taken out four or five of them: the two in the parking lot at Crystal's Palace and two or three more tonight. Now that they know we fight back, I doubt that we'll be seeing them again."

"Gee, Josh, that's really comforting."

"Besides slapping the cuffs on Louis, DeMontrond and probably me and Nate, what are the police going to do?"

"I don't know...there must be something."

"There is, and maybe we won't need to put Louis and DeMontrond at risk in order to put the skinheads out of business permanently. Do you want to hear about my 'tedious' day?"

Elaine curled up next to Josh. She reached over and took his wounded hand. She kissed it and then kissed Josh softly on the lips. "Okay, Wyatt Earp, how'd things go at the OK Corral?"

Josh told Elaine about his day in court. Elaine was pleased to hear that he'd won the lawsuit. She asked whether Ms. Obregon-Robertson wore her Christian Louboutins. Not wanting to rekindle the butt-ogling argument, she wisely decided not to ask what else the councilwoman was wearing. Josh went on to describe the brick wall Nate had run into in trying to tie one or more of the investors to Biegrubinich and thus to Sy's murder.

"Isn't there another way...I mean besides trying to get a subpoena for the bank records? Couldn't you or Detective Turner question the other investors?"

"In case you hadn't noticed, Elaine, even though I've admittedly put on a few pounds, I'm not Perry Mason. Do you think that just because I start questioning some yahoo he's gonna break down in tears and come clean? 'Yeah, Mr. Mason...I mean Mr. Loeb...I done it. I was in cahoots with Andy Biggers. But don't you see? I was desperate: My business is circling the drain; I gotta put my aged mother in a nursing home; my little daughter has to have an operation...' Trust me, my love, even if I could get every one of the investors under oath, on the witness stand or in a deposition, those things don't happen in real life. People lie under oath all the time. Some feel like it's their sworn duty to lie.

"It's almost the same thing if Alana...Detective Turner...is doing the asking. Most likely the only thing they'll say to her is 'I want my lawyer.'"

"Well, now I'm sorry I thought of it. But..."

"No 'buts' Elaine. It was...is...a good theory. Don't apologize for thinking of it. Your theory gave me another idea which may be the more likely one."

"What?"

"That Biegrubinich was laundering money for the skinheads."

"So maybe they're after you and not Louis?"

"I'm thinking that's the case. Although evening the score with Louis must be somewhere high on their agenda as well."

"But won't you have the same problem finding the evidence as you do with the investors?"

"True. We've got to get a lead on the bank records. As difficult as that would be with the investors, it'll be ten times harder with the skinheads."

"Josh, there's has to be somebody else. Who did Biegrubinich's tax returns? Wouldn't they have records?"

"You're assuming that Biegrubinich actually filed tax returns. And even if he did, the person who prepared them, if he or she is a CPA, would have to be served with a search warrant or court order. It's the same run around I gave Detective Turner. I guess what goes around comes around...

"Wait...Elaine, you are a genius. There is one person who might be susceptible to being leaned on: Biegrubinich's former lawyer. She's already sensitized to the crime-fraud exception to attorney-client privilege. If I promise not to dime her with the State Bar grievance committee or turn Detective Turner loose on her, maybe I can get something out of her that we can follow through on."

"Josh, that's not like you. I know from the few times when you talk about your cases that you can play hardball. And I know that you enjoy it, especially if you win. But why are you taking this on? Wasn't tonight enough? Didn't you say when Estelle first told you about the airbag not opening that if it turns out that there is a case you'd have to bring in a lawyer who specializes in product-liability and wrongful death cases? Why is this any different? If all our speculation does amount to something and Sy was in fact murdered, isn't finding his killer a job for the police? You've said that Detective Turner seems competent; why not let her run with it? You told me that's what she wants. Let her do her job."

Elaine used the top of the bedsheet to blot away a couple of tears. "If that leads to Estelle finding out, so be it. I...I...feel terrible for her, and maybe we'll lose a friend, but we...you...didn't create this mess. I'd much rather lose a friend than lose you. Let it go, Josh. I want you out of it."

"Elaine, you know me. I don't quit. I want to know who murdered Sy Blonstein and Marjorie Morrison. I don't care that Sy turned out to be such a moron, he didn't deserve the death penalty. And what about Margie? What'd she do to deserve having her living heart ripped out of her chest and eaten by some...some...monster?"

"I do know you, Josh. At least I like to think that I do. So, yes, you're stubborn and I've watched you work your butt off on every case you've ever had. I've listened to you grinding your teeth in your sleep. How many times have I had to pull you out of the funk you get into when things don't go your way? And when things do go your way I've also watched you prance around like Muhammed Ali in the ring when he knocked out Sonny Liston."

"Actually, he didn't knock him out, at least not in the first fight. It was a technical knockout because Liston didn't come out for the seventh round. Do you mean that I actually do the "Ali Shuffle?""

"Josh cut it out. This isn't a Trivial Pursuit contest. I want a straight answer. I also know you well enough to know when you're not telling the whole truth. I promise: No more sports analogies."

"To be honest, I'm not really sure. Certainly part of it is that I don't like to give up on anything. And part of it has to be what I said a minute ago: I really do want justice for Sy and Margie. And for our sakes I damn sure want to put the skinheads out of business. But I also have to admit that part of it has to be ego; I want to be the one who 'cracks the case' so to speak.

"Maybe you need to lay off the paperback mysteries for a while."

"Possibly. But, now that you've made me think about it, I wonder if maybe I'm just bored. Each case I handle is different. But at the same time they're all alike: the same paper war, sometimes even the facts and the clients and the lawyers are almost interchangeable.

"And in addition to being bored, I'm becoming more and more cynical with every case I handle. Just about every lawyer I deal with nowadays will say or do anything to win. You say I grind my teeth at night. You should see me in court.

And judges? Because they're elected, most state court judges care about one thing above all else: getting reelected. A lot of them are not the sharpest knives in the legal system's drawer to begin with. And they know that however they rule they're going to make at least one side mad. So their first instinct is to not rule if there's any way to avoid it. 'Can't you lawyers work this out?' 'Have you been to mediation yet?' Then if they actually do have to rule they rule in favor of the side who they think has the best chance of upholding their ruling on appeal. Who's right rarely factors into their calculus.

"I've been spending a lot of time lately engaging in, to borrow your term, 'memento mori' asking myself whether I've been doing what I've been doing too long and wondering whether I'm serving any useful purpose on this earth. What is it that the Russians say, 'Womb to grave and nothing in between?' When my time comes, what's the rabbi going to say to sum up the life of Joshua Loeb?"

"Even if you're right about the practice of law, do you want to end up being *dead* right? I'm not ready to call for the rabbi and order a tray of doozies, Josh. Not for a long, long time. What am I supposed to tell the rabbi: that you got bored practicing law so you went out and got yourself killed? In effect you committed suicide? If being bored——or even disgusted—— with practicing law is what's driving this maybe you should take up something that's less risky than chasing killers: How about skydiving? Bull riding? Extreme skiing? Photographing great white sharks feeding?"

"Those are hobbies, Elaine. I'm a long way from retirement. I want to do something meaningful."

"And becoming a professional avenging angel or even a private detective is the answer? Josh, it's possible that in addition to having a gang of thugs chasing you, you may actually be hunting for *El Chupacabra*. But that doesn't mean you have to become him. Maybe there's something to be said for not looking too hard into the abyss. Threatening another lawyer with a grievance isn't like you."

"Elaine, I'm not going to cut her heart out and eat it. I'm just going to gently remind her that sometimes 'when you lie down with dogs you get up with fleas.'"

"Josh, we need to talk about this some more. But not tonight. Go to sleep."

Chapter Forty-One

"Josh, wake up." Elaine shook Josh's shoulder. "Detective Turner is on the phone. She needs to speak with you right away."

"Hi, Alana…"

"Sorry to wake you, Josh."

"What's up?"

"My boss wants to meet with you."

"When?"

"Half an hour ago."

"What...what time is it?"

"It's eight-thirty."

"How about ten-thirty? I have to get dressed, pick up Nate and deliver him to my office. It will take at least that long."

"Then I guess ten-thirty. When you come in the main entrance…"

"Whoa, Alana. I didn't ask for this meeting. If your boss wants to meet with me he can come to my office. I'm happy to meet *you* at Whataburger, Matt's, Barbec's and even the morgue. But your boss? That's not in our partnership agreement. If your boss wants to interrogate me he can come to my office. If he wants to do it at your place, tell him to get a warrant."

Alana lowered her voice. *"I told him that's what you'd say. But he made me try anyway. See you at your office at ten-thirty."*

"I'm looking forward to it. Beside just poking my thumb in some arrogant SOB's eye, I think it's better that we meet in my office; Alicia and Nate will both be available if we need to ask them anything."

"I agree. That's what I'll tell him. I think I'll leave out the poke-in-the-eye part. 'Bye."

Alana's boss, whom she introduced as Lieutenant Sam Cloud, had a world-class beer belly. He eased himself into the chair across the conference table from Josh and handed him a business card like the one Alana had given Josh at the impound lot. The lieutenant wore a mustard-colored plaid sport coat over shiny blue slacks. When he sat down he tugged at the knees of his slacks exposing a few inches of pale white flesh above his brown socks and black rubber-soled shoes. The collar and cuffs of his white dress shirt were slightly frayed and his brown tie looked like it had been the victim of more than one mishap with chips and salsa. He did not wear a wedding band, the absence of which probably accounted for his haphazard attire. He still had most of his grey hair above his creased forehead and bushy eyebrows. He had saggy jowls and a flattened, pock-marked nose. His blotchy, reddish complexion marked him as a drinker or sufferer from essential hypertension. Probably both.

Alicia had ordered two carafes of coffee, one regular and one decaf. These were waiting on the console behind the chair at the head of the conference table along with ceramic mugs, a pitcher of ice water and some glasses. Josh took the coffee orders and did the pouring.

"How can we help you, Lt. Cloud?"

Lt. Cloud reached in one of the side pockets of his jacket and took out a miniature voice-activated recording device. "Do you mind if I record our conversation, Mr. Loeb?"

"Actually, I do mind. If you intend to record this meeting, then you need to read Ms. Flores and me our rights. If you need to do that, then you must suspect that one or both of us has committed some crime. And if Ms. Flores or I are suspects, I will insist on having a lawyer for myself and one for Ms. Flores present."

The lieutenant shrugged and put the recording device back in his pocket. "Okay, Mr. Loeb, it's your house so we'll play by your rules."

"I have very little experience in criminal law, Lieutenant, and none whatsoever in investigating complex murder cases. But I can readily understand how vexing these cases must be for you and Detective Turner. From what I read in the newspaper, the *El Chupacabra* investigation is taking away massive amounts of resources from these and other cases and has become a platform for political demagoguery."

"You're right on both counts, Mr. Loeb."

"So let me be clear, Lieutenant: My associates and I want to help you in any way that we can, consistent with our ethical obligations. We do so not only as concerned citizens, but because people we had feelings for were callously murdered. So we have a special interest in the perpetrator or perpetrators being brought to justice."

"I appreciate that, Mr.Loeb. So let's get to it. First, Detective Turner tells me that you have one or possibly two theories about why Mr. Blonstein was killed. Why don't you lay those out for me?"

"Actually, there are two possible motives and two separate suspects or groups of suspects. I'll tell you our thinking in general and if you have any questions I can have my accounting expert join us so he can fill in any blanks."

Over the next hour Josh explained what they had come to call the 'conspiracy theory' and the 'money-laundering theory.' Alana asked if she could take notes on the 'money-laundering theory' since Josh hadn't told her about it before. Josh agreed.

"So what you're telling me, Mr. Loeb, is that we're spinning our wheels in the mud without the bank records?"

"My accounting expert, Nate Mendelovitz, is still plugging away and may yet come up with something. And I've still got at least one more card to play. What about getting your hands on Biegrubinich?"

"No luck. By now he's probably holed up in an apartment in the Watergate stuffing his face with borscht and caviar. My boss's boss contacted the DA and the DA reached out to the US Attorney. We got the usual federal run around. 'Sorry, we'd love to help, but...' The US Attorney actually did say that if we can show them a solid case that Biegrubinich did the Blonstein murder, they'll reconsider. We gave them all we had: the airbag sensor photos, a synopsis of the Crystal's Palace file that you gave Detective Turner, the security camera footage and the homeowner's statement, but that's it. We can't place him under the vehicle, or even at Crystal's Palace when the tampering occurred, if in fact that's where it occurred. We can't connect him to the white pickup. So basically, all we have is a possible motive, and as Detective Turner has told you, even that's pretty thin."

"What about locating the truck?" Josh got up and stepped over to the console. He refilled his coffee and offered refills to the others.

"Still working on it. I'm almost out of Dallas County registrations. If it was registered somewhere else...there are two hundred and fifty-three other counties in Texas beside Dallas...it could take months. Then, if we find it, we'll have to get a warrant to check it for collision damage. By then it could have been repainted so finding the truck may not do us any good either."

"Do you mind telling me what else your accounting expert, Mr..."

"'Mendelovitz,'" Alana supplied.

"Yes, Mr. Mendelovitz. Do you mind telling me what else he's looking at? Our people have been all over the file you gave us and we can't find anything that looks like payments to one of the investors or that smells of laundry soap."

"I can't do that, Lt. Cloud."

"So you do have some other documents?"

"I do, but they're privileged."

"How can they be privileged? Blonstein was an accountant, not a lawyer."

"I explained all this to Detective Turner, Lieutenant. If you want me to, I'll go over it with you as well. However,

Detective Turner tells me that your department legal advisor agreed with me."

"Lana?"

"He's right, Sir. His hands are tied."

"If you ask me, instead of tied, they ought to be in handcuffs."

"Lieutenant Cloud, I don't make the laws; I just obey them. You may not like having to read a suspect his rights, but you do it anyway. At least I assume that you do. My situation's not any different. If I turn what else we have over to you, I could possibly get disbarred. That may not matter to you, but it does to me. What should matter to you—as I explained to Detective Turner—is that any case you make as a result of that material is likely to get thrown out of court.

"If we find something...a third-party document for example...that's not privileged, you'll be notified immediately and you can take it from there. I suggest that you go ahead and file a case against Biegrubinich for embezzlement, fraud or even murder. Have the DA sit on it until I have something for you. With Biegrubinich in the wind, the filing doesn't have to be made public. If and when we do find something, the DA can get out grand jury subpoenas and they'll likely stand up to a motion to quash. Now are we clear? Can we talk about something that hopefully will be more productive?

"Ms. Flores has been wearing out every conceivable online source of information on the other investors. She gave her report to Mr. Mendelovitz just this morning, so I doubt he's had sufficient time to have found any tie-ins to the Crystal's Palace bank records. We can check with him later. Alicia, do you have an extra copy of what you found that we can give to Detective Turner?"

Alicia produced a manila folder that she had been keeping on the chair next to her. She took out a stapled bundle of internet printouts and passed it across the table to Alana.

Alana passed the bundle along to Lieutenant Cloud who took out a pair of reading glasses and began perusing the material. "Josh..." The Lieutenant looked up briefly when Alana used Josh's first name. "... Mr. Loeb, do you think we could subpoena the investors' personal and business bank records to see if there were any payments from Crystal's Palace?"

"Nate hasn't found any payments directly to any of the investors that would constitute probable cause. If there are any large checks, or even better a series of checks over a period of time, that would probably be enough. If Nate finds any checks made out to any of their businesses, that would definitely work. That's why Ms. Flores has been trying to find out what these guys do with their time when they're not sitting around at Crystal's Palace soaking up the ambience.

"Hopefully that will turn up something, but Nate thinks that if Biegrubinich had a secret partner in the scam, he'd most likely have made the payments through one of his moustache companies. The same thing's true if he was laundering money for the Caucasian Council. Those are the bank records we need. I suppose you could just issue subpoenas to every bank in town, but without account numbers they'll take months trying to run down the accounts."

"Which theory do you like best? Maybe you could just concentrate on that one."

"At this point, if I had to pick, I'd go with the money laundering."

"I hope you're right, Mr. Loeb. Between *El Chupacabra* and the skinheads— I suppose you heard about the gun battle on Ross Avenue last night— Dallas is becoming Juarez North. Something needs to be done about them."

"Lt. Cloud, Sun Tzu wrote in *The Art of War* something to the effect that when your enemies are busy destroying each other, the best strategy is to hide and watch. Maybe DPD should take a page from his playbook."

"I doubt that the DPD would be interested in taking advice from some Chinese Communist general."

Out of the corner of his eye Josh could see Alana holding her hand over her mouth. He could barely keep a straight face himself. "Lt. Cloud, Sun Tzu wrote *The Art of War* fifteen hundred years ago. I doubt that there were many communists around then."

"Whatever. In any case, I don't think I'll be passing your advice along. Why don't you tell me why you like the money-laundering scenario?"

"Two reasons: One, based on my telephone conversations with the two investors who called, I think that investing in a 'gentlemen's club' is about the limit of their desire for a walk on the wild side. One of them has already gotten out and the other ... maybe it's just my intuition ... but he didn't strike me as the type. He's scared to death that his wife's going to find out."

"You sure it's his wife, or is it the DEA or us?"

"That's possible, but ..."

"So money laundering is your default setting?"

"Well, there's more than that."

"Such as?"

Josh hesitated for a moment. "Two hang-up calls that Alicia got yesterday afternoon while I was in court. Alicia, tell Lt. Cloud about them."

"There's not much to tell, Lieutenant. They both came in between three-thirty and four o'clock. They each asked for Mr. Loeb, 'Joshua Loeb' they said. I said Mr. Loeb was not available and I asked who was calling and whether I could take a message. Each one said 'Crystal's' and then hung up."

Alana asked, "Could you tell anything from their voices?"

"They were both men, Anglo. They didn't sound old, more like twenty-somethings. The way they said it—drawing out the word—I got the sense that they were warning Mr. Loeb to stay away from Crystal's Palace."

"How did they know you'd been there?"

"I didn't say that I'd been there, Lt. Cloud."

Lieutenant Cloud took off his reading glasses. "Have you, Mr. Loeb? When?"

"I'm sorry, Lieutenant. I'd rather not say."

"How is that privileged, Mr. Loeb?" Lieutenant Cloud folded his large hands on the table and glared at Josh. "And when you're done answering that, why don't you also tell us how you located Biegrubinich and evidently met him in person? Then you can tell us how you knew Blonstein was in Crystal's Palace the night he died. And after that, maybe you can tell us what you know about how Biegrubinich came to be slapped silly, punched in the gut, had his foot stomped on and his elbow dislocated."

"Is Mr. Biegrubinich pressing charges, Lieutenant? If he is, then I'm going to exercise my Fifth Amendment right to remain silent."

"What about your bodyguard? Did he do that to Biegrubinich? He's on parole isn't he? Things could get mighty tough for him. One phone call…"

"Mr. Prejean is protecting me because whoever murdered Seymour Blonstein and Marjorie Morrison is still out there and the DPD has nothing to go on to take this person—or more likely persons—off the streets except what my associates and I have willingly provided to you. If you think you can force me to breach my ethical duties by pushing around a nice, hard-working young man who has toed every mark of his parole, there's a phone right there on the console. Just dial nine for an outside line…"

"Nobody talks to me that way, Mr. Loeb."

"Well, perhaps it's time somebody did, Lieutenant Cloud. I thought we had an understanding and a continuation of the respectful and productive relationship that Detective Turner and I have established. If Mr. Prejean gets as much as a single phone call or visit from the parole people that is not previously scheduled, you can be sure of three things: One, all cooperation from this office will cease; two, any subpoenas will be fought in the courts; and three, you will find yourself a defendant in a federal civil rights lawsuit with the entire resources of this firm against you. You want to pick on somebody? Pick on somebody your own size."

"Look, Mr. Loeb, I'm just trying to do my job. I…"

"I thought your job was to help your detectives close cases, Lieutenant Cloud. If I hadn't pressed Alana…Detective Turner…to allow me to inspect the Blonstein vehicle, and if DeMontrond Prejean hadn't convinced Detective Turner that the collision sensor had been tampered with, you'd still be treating Seymour Blonstein's death as accidental. If I hadn't identified Marjorie Morrison's body and made the connection to Seymour Blonstein, the *El Chupacabra* task force would be standing around massaging their prostates while trying to figure out what connection she had to the drug business and Detective Turner would still be running around in the woods in Northwest Arkansas. If we hadn't tied the white pickup truck to the Blonstein murder and to the Morrison murder, you would have nothing at all with which to work the cases. And if I hadn't given you Biegrubinich, you wouldn't have a single theory to work through.

"That's all true, I suppose, but..."

"No 'buts, ' Lieutenant Cloud. Either you keep the parole office people off DeMontrond Prejean's back and let Detective Turner continue to work the cases, or we're done."

"Your house, your rules, Mr. Loeb. I'll leave you and Detective Turner to it. Thanks for your time."

"Alicia, would you please show Lieutenant Cloud out? And get his parking claim check stamped. Just charge it to me personally."

Chapter Forty-Two

Josh sat back down across from Alana. For a long while she said nothing; she just stared out the window at the dull overcast sky. Josh got up and refilled her coffee cup and his own. "Okay, let me have it. I screwed up pretty badly, didn't I? Maybe the 'massaging-their-prostates' remark was a bit too much. And I agree that I shouldn't have threatened to sue him. But when he threatened to lean on DeMontrond…"

"I didn't know whether to laugh or cry, Josh. Let me tell you a story: When I was in Afghanistan and I'd just made W-1 I got assigned to a forward supply base: a half a dozen trailers filled with ammunition, MREs, electronic gear, and a couple of tankers filled with fuel. I had the guard detail one day. Late afternoon, a guy comes walking up the road. He's dressed like a local: dirty white robe, black vest, a *pakol*—one of those hats that kind of looks like a turban.

"I immediately get suspicious because he's not wearing a bandolier across his chest and he's not carrying a rifle. I'd been taught that no self-respecting Afghan gentleman goes out without his rifle and bandolier; it would be like you going to court in shorts and a T-shirt and without your briefcase. Anyway, I let him get within about sixty yards and I yell 'Halt! Down on your knees! Hands in the air!' I say in in English and in Pashto. The guy keeps walking. I figure: Okay, I'm kind of new here so maybe my Pashto isn't too good. So I yell at him again...in both languages. He takes a few more steps and I fire a three-round burst into the ground right in front of him. Then he starts to run toward me. I say to myself 'I ain't lettin' this guy get near those fuel tankers and munitions trucks.'

"I switch to full automatic and I fire. First time I've fired my weapon except on the firing range. The rounds catch him in the chest and there's this huge explosion. Lucky for me the rounds knock him backward so that most of the blast wave goes up and not directly at me. I'm in full combat body armor so the only thing happens to me is that I get blown back against my Humvee. I did catch a few pieces of shrapnel and I end up with a sore back and rear end. My butt actually made a dent in the door of the Humvee. I get a purple heart out of the deal along with a photo of the side of the Humvee. All that's left of the guy is one of his sandals.

"Alana you don't need to impress me with your courage and cool-headedness. I'm already more than impressed by you."

"That's not why I told you the story, Josh."

"Then…"

"I told you the story because what happened to that guy is exactly what just happened to my career in the DPD: Blam! Nothing left of it but a cheap rubber sandal and me sitting on my butt in a world of hurt."

"Alana, if I may quote that famous philosopher Yogi Berra, 'It ain't over 'till it's over.' My investigation isn't over and your career in the DPD isn't over until you say it is. Do you know who Marisol Obregon-Robertson is?"

"The city councilwoman from West Dallas? The one who's been riding the Department so hard about the *El Chupacabra* cases? Yeah, I know who she is. You should hear what the C-A-P people call her: *'Senorita Boca Grande.'* And that's the polite term. Do you know what *'chingala madre'* means?"

"No, but I'm pretty sure I wouldn't want to ask Alicia to translate it. But do you know that she's also called 'Chair of the City Council Public Safety Committee?' And do you have any idea how much juice that gives her at 1400 South Lamar?"

"So tell me: How much juice does she have? And so what? What's she got to do with anything?"

"I have something *Senorita Boca Grande* wants very badly. I won't give it to her. She even sued me to try and get it and got poured out by the judge at a preliminary hearing. I don't need it or even want it..."

"Then why didn't you just give it to her?"

"Because she insulted Alicia and tried to bully me like your lieutenant did just now."

"And now?"

"And now I've got something to trade with her."

"You mean you're going to give her whatever it is that she wants and in return she tells the brass at 1400 South Lamar that she's my fairy godmother, so don't mess with me?"

"Something like that."

"Thanks, Josh. I mean it. But I gotta pass on that one. The last thing I need is 'PI' stamped in red on the outside of my personnel jacket."

"PI?"

"Political Influence."

"Okay then, let's go to Plan B."

"Which is?"

"You keep hunting for the Ford pickup."

"And?"

"Josh got up and walked over to the window and stared out for a good while. He turned back and leaned half-way across the conference table resting his weight on his fingertips. Give me forty-eight hours. I'll either hand you who murdered Sy Blonstein and Marjorie Morrison or I'll hand over everything I have and let you and Lieutenant Cloud question me to your hearts' content."

"You said you still had another card to play."

"It's something I have to do myself. It involves another individual and some tactics that I'm not especially eager to use. I promise you don't want me to share them with you. If this person has the information, I'll get it. If this person doesn't have it, the person should not be dragged into your investigation."

"Are you going to do something with Biegrubinich's girlfriend. Is that who you're going to see this afternoon and who you want to keep out of it? Is she how you knew that Blonstein was at Crystal's Palace on the night he died and was worried that someone was after him? Josh, I hate it when someone tries to piss in my ear and tell me it's raining. Is that what you're doing?"

"Alana, I can't tell you who; you'll just have to trust me a while longer. Believe me, I'm not that Afghan guy wearing an explosive vest. I have no intention of blowing myself up and you along with me."

"Dammit. I don't know whether to handcuff you or hug you."

"I'll settle for a warm smile and a sincere handshake."

"Okay, you got 'em. But remember: forty-eight hours."

Chapter Forty-Three

Alana declined Josh's invitation to join him, Alicia and Nate for lunch telling Josh that she'd better get back to the office and to her dwindling stack of Ford pickup registrations. As they waited for the elevator she asked if it would be okay for her to relate to Lieutenant Cloud the promise Josh had made to her. Josh asked her to hold off until he was ready to deliver. He explained that knowing about Josh's promise would be unlikely to mollify the lieutenant and was more likely to result in the lieutenant doubling down on his efforts to browbeat the information out of him before he was ready to play show and tell. They argued about it with Alana standing in the elevator and Josh holding the doors open with his body. When the elevator alarm started bleating Alana reluctantly agreed when Josh promised to keep her updated.

A bemused Alicia was waiting for Josh when he got back to his office. "That certainly went well."

"Don't rub it in. I know that I shouldn't have let him get to me that way. It's just that when he threatened DeMontrond…"

"Do you think he'd actually follow through?"

"I don't know. But if he does, he'll find out that I meant what I said. Actually, I'm more worried about Alana."

"What about Detective Turner? For a second I thought she was going to lunge across the table and strangle you or just pull out her gun and shoot you."

"While you were getting rid of Lieutenant Cloud I had to get down on my knees and grovel to keep her from doing just that. She thinks that I just trashed her career in the DPD. Only she put it a lot more colorfully."

"I take it your groveling did some good?"

"For now. But if I don't produce who murdered Sy and Margie in forty-eight hours, things are going to get really complicated for me. It won't be just Alana who ends up in *effluvia profundo*."

"Josh, did you actually promise to solve both cases in the next forty-eight hours? If you'll pardon me for asking, what in the world were you thinking?"

"Right now I'm thinking about lunch. For some odd reason all I've been able to think about for days is a hot pastrami sandwich and a cold can of Dr. Brown's Cel-Ray."

"What is Cel-Ray?"

"A soft drink. It's an acquired taste."

"Where do you go for a pastrami sandwich and a…a Dr. Brown's?"

"Cindi's on North Central is the best, but I think we'd better order out. There's Capriotti's—the pastrami isn't great—but they do have two downtown locations and they deliver."

Josh ordered his sandwich and Dr. Brown's Cel-Ray. Nate also opted for a pastrami sandwich and added a slice of cheesecake. Alicia ordered half a turkey sandwich with Russian dressing and a cup of matzo ball soup.

They adjourned to the kitchen/breakroom to wait for the delivery from Capriotti's. A wall-mounted TV was on, tuned to the mid-day local news. The anchor was giving a wrap-up of a press conference called by the Mayor.

"For you viewers who haven't heard or read by now, open gang warfare has now come to the streets of Old East Dallas. Last night, according to the eye witness and police reports, a running gun battle occurred on Ross Avenue between North Hall and North Peak around eight o'clock last night. Motorists driving east on Ross called 9-1-1 to report that a red pickup truck was apparently chasing a black sedan of unknown make. The sedan had tinted windows, so no one got a clear look at the occupants. "According to one witness the rear window of the sedan was missing and shots were fired out of the missing window at the pickup truck. A witness estimated that the sedan was traveling west on Ross at more than sixty miles-per-hour when it applied its brakes and made a u-turn back to the east. The truck then tried the same maneuver, but the driver was evidently not as skilled. The truck was unable to complete the turn and rolled over.

"One person who was seen riding in the back of the pickup standing up and looking over the cab was thrown out before the roll over. His head struck the curb and he was pronounced dead at the scene. Police found a shotgun lying in the street near the deceased. Officers at the scene said it appeared that the shotgun had been fired recently, but declined to speculate on whether a blast from the weapon had shot out the rear window of the black sedan.

"One passenger inside the pickup was also pronounced dead at the scene apparently from injuries suffered in the rollover. The apparent driver of the pickup also sustained life-threatening injuries and remains unconscious and in critical condition at Baylor Hospital.

"It is unknown whether the occupant or occupants of the sedan sustained any injuries. A first responder at the scene was overheard saying that there appeared to be at least two bullet holes in the windshield of the pickup. A DPD spokesperson declined to confirm or deny that this was true.

"And now to our City Hall reporter Roger Daley who has just left the Mayor's press conference. Roger ..."

"Thank you, Phil. I can tell you that the scene at City Hall was a grim one. At the podium with the Mayor were the Chief of Police, Donald Green, and the chair of the City Council Public Safety Committee, Marisol Obregon-Robertson. Live TV and radio coverage were not permitted; reporters were allowed only written notes.

"The Mayor spoke for barely seven minutes. Neither he nor the Chief or the Councilwoman took questions. The Mayor read a prepared statement. He expressed the City's outrage and disgust at last night's events that you've just described. He appealed to the public for any information that might help the police locate the black sedan.

"He praised the Chief and the DPD for their heroic efforts in keeping the people of Dallas safe. When he said this I could see Ms. Obregon-Robertson rolling her eyes.

"Then the Mayor got to the most newsworthy part of the press conference. He made three announcements: first, he is going to ask the council for approval for the City Manager to take funds from the so-called 'rainy day fund' to provide for a temporary one-third increase in funding for police overtime so that more officers can be on the streets at night when these crimes occur.

"Second, he has called on the Dallas County Sheriff to provide additional detectives and patrol officers to be placed under the command of the DPD. He has sent a copy of his request to the County Commissioners' Court for their approval and assistance with funding.

"Third— — and what may prove to be the most controversial—the mayor has contacted the Governor and the Commander of the Texas Department of Public Safety and requested a company of Texas Rangers to work with the DPD *El Chupacabra* task force. The mayor again expressed full confidence in the DPD. However, he did point out that once *El Chupacabra* is off the streets, the level of violence will certainly decrease.

"That's it from City Hall. Back to you Phil."

"Thanks Roger. Ladies and gentlemen our producer has just informed me that the President of the Dallas Police Association, Senior Corporal Ardis Beckwith, is about to issue a statement. As many of you know, the Dallas Police Association is the largest union-type organization, representing a majority of the uniformed officers. We have a live-broadcast crew and a reporter, Francesca Sotomayor, at the DPA headquarters. Here's Francesca ..."

"Corporal Beckwith is about to speak. Stand by."

"Ladies and gentlemen. Thank you for coming on such short notice. We received a copy of the Mayor's statement less than half an hour before he issued it to the public. The Mayor's statement is an unprecedented and unprovoked attack on the dedicated, hardworking officers who put their lives on the line every shift of every day. If anyone deserves a vote of no-confidence, it is the Mayor, the City Council, the City Manager and the senior management of the police department. What you are seeing is the product of years of under-funding: non-competitive pay and benefits, too few officers on the streets and obsolete equipment.

"What you are seeing is a failure of top management to push for improvements and an eagerness to punish officers when they act to protect themselves and the public.

"What you are seeing is a broken system made worse for political gain.

"Yet despite this, our morale is as good as it can be in these trying times. And despite this slap in the face, we will continue as always to do our duty.

"Thank you. No, no questions at this time."

"Back to you Phil."

"Thanks Francesca. We'll take a short commercial break and then be back with sports."

Alicia walked in with three bags from Capriotti's. "Gentlemen, lunch is served."

After the press conferences Josh filled Nate in on the meeting with Lieutenant Cloud. Nate had about the same reaction as Alicia when Josh came to his self-imposed forty-eight hour deadline. "Josh, so far I've got *bupkis* on the other investors and *bupkis* on the Caucasian Council." Nate glanced at his watch. "Forty-seven hours from now—without the other bank records—I'm still going to have *bupkis*. There's more than enough to send Sy, may he rest in peace, and Biegrubinich to the penitentiary, but that's not what you hired me to do and anyway it's not going to happen to either one of them."

Alicia took a sip of her ice tea. "Can I make a suggestion?"

"Please do." Josh took a bite of the cole slaw that he had ordered with his sandwich. "It's already beginning to look like the check I wrote to Alana on Nate's account is going to bounce big time."

"Why don't you just give Detective Turner the whole Crystal's Palace file including Mr. Blonstein's work papers? Is Andy Biggers going to file a complaint with the state accounting board? Is he going to sue you either as executor of the estate or personally? Andy Biggers doesn't even exist. Is Andrei Biegrubinich going to show up and admit that he conspired with Mr. Blonstein to cheat the IRS just so that he can sue you?"

Josh put down what was left of his sandwich and instead chewed on Alicia's suggestion. "That works in Biegrubinich's case but what about Pervis?"

Nate removed his napkin that he'd tucked in under his shirt collar and used it to blot his lips. "She's a risk, Josh, but not a big one. In order to cause you *tsuris*…grief…" Nate translated for Alicia's benefit, "she'd also have to admit to fraudulently understating her income to the IRS. As you put it last night, she'd be calling the artillery down on her own position. What lawyer is going to advise her to do that in order to sue you to recover zero damages?"

"Last night?"

"Oh, just a conversation Nate and I had on the way home."

Nate continued, "Sy can't be hurt. And you're not licensed by the State Board of Public Accountancy, so they can't touch you. I don't know about the State Bar, Josh. Can they do anything to you for something that you did not as a lawyer but in your capacity as executor?"

"Not unless it's also a crime. I couldn't steal money from the estate. If I did, I'd be disbarred for sure."

"So why not just give it to her?" Nate pushed his cheesecake across the table in Alicia's direction. Here, try some. You'll like it.

"Alicia?"

"Sure, I'll have a bite." Alicia paused for a moment and then laughed. "Sorry, Josh. I thought you were worrying about my waistline. I'm with Nate. Give her the file. What good is it going to do her? They're going to run into the same dead ends as Nate did."

"And what about the fraudulent tax withholding form...the second quarter '941?'"

Alicia finished the last of her sandwich. "They can't prosecute Mr. Blonstein or you, and maybe they can do something with the checks that Biggers—I mean Biegrubinich—wrote to his dummy companies."

"That's a possibility." Josh wadded his sandwich wrapper into a ball and tossed it in the trash. "And it's also possible, indeed likely, that they'll grab Jolene and wring her dry. And what she gives up will no doubt include the episode at the Olympus."

"I figured from what the lieutenant said that the eviction process must have gotten physical at some point."

"Actually, at two points." Josh gave Alicia and Nate the short version of the encounter in the manager's office and

DeMontrond's tune up of Biegrubinich in the condo unit bedroom.

"Josh, you're the lawyer and I'm just your assistant. But I've been at this long enough to have picked up a few things. She wasn't present in the manager's office, so she has no personal knowledge as to what happened. They could question the manager, but I'm sure she'll tell the truth: That it was self-defense. He swung at you first.

"Same thing as to what happened in the condo unit. She didn't actually see DeMontrond do anything, and whatever Biegrubinich told her would be hearsay and inadmissible."

"When I get charged with assault are you going to defend me?"

"Josh, be serious. Do you really think that with no victim and one credible witness who says it was self-defense that they'd prosecute you?"

"I guess not. So okay; I'm not going to the slammer, at least not for assaulting Biegrubinich. And another good thing is that I won't have to go beat up on Biegrubinich's former lawyer. That isn't something I was looking forward to. So where do we go from here?"

Alicia looked at her watch. "I need to make a couple of personal phone calls, then back to work."

Chapter Forty-Four

When Alicia got back, Josh and Nate were in Nate's temporary office. They had gathered up the Crystal's Palace file and put it aside. "Alicia, would you make a copy of the file and courier it over to Detective Turner? She's in Auto Crimes at police headquarters, 1400 South Lamar. I'll call her and let her know it's on its way and tell her that after they've had time to look at it, I'll try to answer any questions they have."

"Do I give her the copy or the original?"

"Give her the copy. I'll tell her we're sending a copy and we'll make the original available if they need it for any reason.

"Nate, if you want, why don't you go ahead and get started on the Tezcatlipoca file?"

"Any thoughts about what I'm looking for?"

"Whatever strikes you as a reason for Ms. Obregon-Robertson to sue me to get it back and to have a meltdown like a two-year-old when I said I'd give her a copy and keep the original."

Josh had Alana's office phone number stored in his phone. He got her voicemail and left a message. He went out to Alicia's work station and retrieved Lieutenant Cloud's card.

"Auto Crimes, Lieutenant Cloud's office."

"This is Joshua Loeb. Lieutenant Cloud was in a meeting in my office this morning. Is he available? I have some information that's pertinent to our meeting."

"I'm sorry, Sir. Lieutenant Cloud is not available. Would you like to leave a message?"

"It's about the Seymour Blonstein and Marjorie Morrison cases that Detective Turner is handling. I already left her a voicemail that I'm sending over some papers that you all are anxious to see. But since Detective Turner's apparently away from her desk and the papers will be there fairly soon, I thought I'd give Lieutenant Cloud as heads-up as well."

"Are you sending the papers to Detective Turner?"

"That's my intention…"

"Well, if they haven't already gone, you'd best send them to Lieutenant Cloud. Detective Turner's no longer assigned to those cases. Lieutenant Cloud is handling them himself at least for now."

"I see. Is Detective Turner in the office? Even though she's off the cases, I'd really like to speak with her."

"I'm sorry, Sir. She's back working her regular cases and she's out in the field just now. Anyway, you really should speak with Lieutenant Cloud if it's about those two cases. If you'll give me your name again and a phone number where Lieutenant Cloud can reach you I'll be happy to pass along the message."

"Thank you. My name is Joshua Loeb, J-o-s-h-u-a L-o-e-b. He has my contact information. I'll be waiting for his call. In the meantime, I'll just hang on to the papers until I speak with him.

"Alicia, don't send…"

"I won't. I heard. What a son-of-a-bitch. He's scared of you, so he's taking out his frustration on Detective Turner. He can make her life miserable and there's probably not a thing in the world she can do about it."

"She may want to reconsider my offer to try and get Ms. Obregon-Robertson in her corner."

"I think she was right to turn that down. By the way, I had a voicemail message from that Victor Ortega. It was pretty long, but it boils down to: If he doesn't get back his *facuturas*—his invoices—today he says he'll have to close his business. Josh, I think he was actually crying. You might want to put the Crystal's Palace file aside for the time being."

"How does Mr. Ortega know we even have them? Did he tell you who his customer is?"

"Three guesses. I'll even give you a hint: She wears Christian Louboutin shoes."

"Why am I not surprised? Let me check with Nate to be sure we have Ortega's invoices. If we do, please call Mr. Ortega back and tell him he can pick up them here at five o'clock. I'll call you from Nate's office and let you know whether we have them. Did he tell you the name of his company?"

"He said 'Victor Ortega Lawn and Landscaping Service.'"

"Okay, I'll call you in a minute."

Nate looked up from the stacks of papers on his desk. "Has Alicia finished copying the file yet? I wasn't quite finished going through the vendor payables. I want to see if the invoices match up with the amounts of the checks and to see whether there are any irregular endorsements."

"Irregular endorsements?"

"Endorsements that don't match the payee of the check."

"That isn't an unheard of occurrence in my experience. Banks never look to see whether they match. If a check is stolen and the endorsement forged, the banks usually just eat the loss. And that only happens if the customer discovers it which they don't most of the time. It's a lot cheaper for the bank to eat an occasional loss than it is for them to examine each check like they're supposed to do."

"You're right, Josh. But what I'm looking for is the same endorsement on checks made out to different payees. If I find a check that's payable to 'ABC Company' and it's endorsed by 'Hymie Schwartz' and then there's another check made out to 'XYZ Company' and it's also endorsed by 'Hymie Schwartz' then 'Hymie Schwartz' has two different companies doing business with Crystal's Palace, something which is highly unlikely. What is more likely is that 'ABC Company' and 'XYZ Company' are just moustaches for 'Hymie Schwartz' who is getting money funneled to him through the Crystal's Palace bank account."

"Did Sy do that kind of analysis?"

"From what I've looked at, I think it might have occurred to him, but I don't see any evidence in his work papers that he followed through. Sy didn't have a big audit practice; mostly he was a tax guy. I don't think he had that much fraud-audit experience. Maybe he didn't know enough to follow through. Maybe he felt he had enough to report to the court, or maybe that's when he started messing around with Jasmine...or

Jolene...whatever her name is. Whatever the reason, I think it needs to be looked at."

"The way you're making excuses for Sy, you're starting to sound like me. In any event the file's not going anywhere for now, so we've got some time. The lieutenant took Alana off the cases so I'm not sending him the file, at least until I speak with Alana. I got Alana to promise not to tell him about my self-imposed forty-eight hour deadline. So at the moment all bets are off."

"Good. I saw him in the hallway as Alicia was walking him out. I was coming back from the men's room. He reminded me of Captain Hank Quinlan without the fedora. I guessed he was a real *mamser*. Looks like I was right. Can I get the file back? I want to get started on the vendor checks."

"Nate, the way you describe this payee-endorsement comparison it sounds like something Alicia...or for that matter even I...could do. I think it's time you started taking the Tezcatlipoca file apart."

"That's what I've been doing for the last half an hour. Do you think maybe I could get some Rolaids or something? The pastrami is giving me heartburn. Or maybe it's just Lieutenant Cloud. Isn't there a c-store downstairs in the tunnel?"

"I'm sure there's a bottle of Rolaids in the medicine cabinet in the lunch room. I'll go get it for you. In the meantime, look for a pile of invoices from Victor Ortega Lawn and Landscape Service. Alicia got another call from him literally begging her to give them back. If we have them I'd like to meet Mr. Ortega and personally return his invoices to him. Maybe he can tell us why Ms. Obregon-Robertson is so hot to get her file away from prying eyes. I'll be back in a minute."

When Josh returned Nate traded him the Ortega invoices for the bottle of Rolaids and a glass of water. "Hold on a minute, Nate. I need to tell Alicia to call Victor Ortega and get him down here.

Josh dialed Alicia's work station. "Alicia, Nate found the invoices. Please call Mr. Ortega and ask him to come pick them up."

As Josh was talking to Alicia, Nate thumbed through the invoices and separated them into two piles. He thumbed through the two piles for a couple of minutes. "Josh, this isn't kosher." Nate pushed the stacks across the table. "Look. The stack on the left is made up of Xerox copies; the ones in the stack on the right are Ortega's carbon copies which I presume came from his file. Look at the copy of the invoice from Ortega's records dated April First."

"Okay, I see one, two, three...six line items. Landscape services for six different properties, all Tezcatlipoca this, Tezcatlipoca that. Total seven hundred ten dollars. What's not kosher about that?"

"Now look at the Xerox copy. Same date, same six line items."

"Okay, but I still don't..."

"Josh, look at the total."

"Damn. Seventy-one thousand dollars. They took the original invoice and added a couple of zeros. The Xerox copies look clean. If you didn't have Ortega's copies you'd never notice that they'd been altered."

"Give them back to me for a second." Nate flipped through the two stacks again. "Each one has been altered. Rough number, it looks like they jacked up the total by some six hundred fifty to six hundred sixty thousand dollars. And that's just last year."

"And that's just one vendor. Are there others?"

"I'll look." Nate rummaged around in the files for a few minutes. "There are a bunch more invoices or what look like copies of invoices that may have been altered by Tezcatlipoca just like Ortega's. You can tell because the amounts are in five figures when they probably should be in three or four at the most. But none of them have vendor copies.

"Here's one bunch from a 'Metroplex Brick and Paving.' It has a Post-It note that says 'Get vendor copies.' Just from the amounts, these look like they were probably altered also."

"Who was the vendor?"

"Metroplex Brick and Paving."

"That's not good news, Nate. I'm certain that's the name of Alicia's husband's business. Let's keep that one to ourselves for now. I don't want to upset Alicia unnecessarily. If Sy didn't follow through so that Leo—he's Alicia's husband—hasn't given Sy his vendor copies, then there's probably nothing to worry about. I'll call Leo myself and ask him. Let me check with Alicia to find out whether she was able to get in touch with Victor Ortega."

Alicia knocked and then came into Nate's office. Nate shoved the Metroplex Brick and Paving invoices under another stack of papers. Alicia gave him a quizzical look but decided to say nothing. "Josh, I called Mr. Ortega's cell phone—that's the number he gave me—and got his voicemail. I looked up the number for his business and called that. No answer. Maybe he was serious about shutting down. Should I keep trying?

"I think I need to pay Mr. Ortega a visit in person. And if you would, I'd like for you to come with me because I'm likely going to need an interpreter."

"Do you want to go in my car?"

"I think we'd better get DeMontrond to do the driving and I'm going to ask Louis to ride shotgun." Josh picked up the Ortega carbon copies and handed them to Alicia. "Make copies of these for us to keep. Can they make color copies in office services?"

"Yes, but it may take a while. It depends on how backed up they are."

"Don't worry about that. I'll call the office services manager and make sure that they process your job as soon as you get there. And in the meantime I'll call Louis and DeMontrond."

"Do you want me…"

"Nate, I'd love for you to come along, but I think it would be a better use of your time if you stayed here and continued doing what you're doing. Alicia will arrange for another assistant to help you with anything you need."

Chapter Forty-Five

Victor Ortega evidently ran his business out of his home, a well-maintained brick bungalow on a residential street off of South Edgefield between West Davis and West Jefferson in Oak Cliff. The neighborhood was undergoing a steady gentrification not unlike the M Streets neighborhood in East Dallas back in the nineteen-eighties. The homes were very much the same as the M Streets: single-family brick and Austin stone bungalows with steeply-pitched roofs and one-car detached garages.

DeMontrond parked Josh's Jaguar at the curb in front of the Ortega house. Josh and Alicia went to the front door and rang the bell. After a minute's worth of no response Josh rang again; still no response. While they were driving from downtown to Oak Cliff Alicia had tried calling both numbers getting the same result as when she'd tried in the office while they were waiting for DeMontrond and Louis. Thinking that possibly the doorbell was broken, Josh knocked on the solid core door.

"Looks like no one's home, Josh. Should we just leave the invoices? I could call and leave a message on his cell phone."

"No, I want to talk to Mr. Ortega. If we just leave the invoices I doubt that he's going to be too interested in talking with me. Just leave him a message that we brought the invoices but no one was home. Tell him that he needs to contact me."

As they were going back down the front steps Alicia tugged at Josh's coat sleeve. "Hold on a second. I saw someone watching us through the window of the house next door. You go back to the car. Let me see if whoever it is will talk to me."

Alicia walked across the driveway between the two houses and Josh returned to the car. When she got to the front steps the door opened and she went inside. After about ten minutes she came out and quickly walked back to the car. When she got back in she looked upset. "Josh, I think we need to get out of here. Mrs. Munoz was reluctant to talk to me. She's afraid that someone would see us talking."

"Okay. DeMontrond, let's head back to the office. Louis, do you have anything at the shop that's going to keep you tied up? I may need you and DeMontrond on short notice.

"Not anything can't wait 'till tomorrow. But I do need to get back and close up the shop. I'd get Bonerack to do it but he has a doctor's appointment this afternoon."

"Bonerack?"

"You know, Sirlester Loomis...tall, real skinny guy. Was a damn good basketball player in his day. Played a couple of seasons with one of those teams that travel with the Harlem Globetrotters and provide the opposing team. His team was called the 'House of David.' Mostly a bunch of Jewish guys from Brooklyn. He had to grow a beard and those long curls like the Orthodox Jews wear. Had to wear one of those little skull caps, but that didn't bother him none. He quit because he couldn't stand the beard; said it itched all the time and 'bout drove him crazy.

"After he left basketball he became a burglar. He was so skinny he could crawl through a space no more than ten, twelve inches wide. Made it easier to get in without setting off the alarm. Got caught by motion sensors a couple of times and ended up doin' a dime in Huntsville. I met him in the joint. He was goin' in and thanks to you I was comin' out. I gave him a job when he got out. Been with me for years. Best transmission man in town."

"Yeah, I've seen him in the shop lots of times. He's worked on my car a time or two. But I didn't know his name was 'Bonerack.'"

"They hung that name on him in the joint and it's kind of stuck with him."

"Alicia, sorry for the digression. What'd Mrs. Munoz have to say?"

"Her name is 'Esmeralda Munoz.' She's a homemaker. Her husband, Sergio, works for the City Parks Department. He's a supervisor. They've been in their house for twelve years or so. The Ortegas bought their house not long after the Munozes bought theirs."

"So they know the Ortegas pretty well? They get along okay?"

"Yeah. The Munoz's youngest, a daughter, goes to school with the Ortegas' oldest. Also a girl. The Ortegas have two other children, one boy and another girl. The Munozes have an older son; he's in the Army. The Ortega's eldest daughter and the Munoz's daughter are good friends. In fact they're such good friends that they're planning to have their *quinceaneras* together."

"Did she say that it's unusual for no one to be home at the Ortegas this time of day? She have any idea when they'll be home?"

"She says they're gone...to Mexico. She told me that they go back every year to spend Christmas with family. A lot of families in the landscaping business do that because there's hardly any work at that time of year. But the Ortegas have never left this early. They wait until the kids get out of school just before Christmas when the break between semesters starts."

"Did she know why they decided to go early?"

"No, Mrs. Ortega wouldn't tell her anything except they had to leave right away. When Mrs. Munoz spoke to her Mrs. Ortega seemed very upset about something but she wouldn't say what."

"It must be something serious. I mean to pull their kids out of school and light out for Mexico…"

"That's what Mrs. Munoz thought. But all she knows is that two men came to the Ortega house around noon. They went into the house and came back out a few minutes later. Mrs. Munoz was in her kitchen which is on the driveway side facing the side of the Ortega's house. So all she saw is the two men drive up, get out and go to the door. When they came back out they got in their truck and drove away.

"About an hour later Victor Ortega drove up in his truck with their kids. He backed his equipment trailer into the garage and locked the garage. About half an hour later the Ortega family came out, threw some suitcases into the back of the truck and drove off."

"Alicia, did Mrs. Munoz get a good look at the truck the two men were in?"

"She says she doesn't know much about cars and trucks. All she knows is that it was a big white pickup."

Chapter Forty-Six

"That's too bad." Nate shook his head at the news that the Ortega family had decamped to Mexico. "But from what I've found while you were gone, Ortega may be just the tip of the iceberg. I also looked through the invoices from Alicia's husband's company. Since I only have the Tezcatlipoca invoice copies to work with I can't be sure of the amount they were jacked up but the total amount of the invoices is north of a million, four. That's a lot of brick repairs and parking lot paving for just three apartment projects."

"So you think they were inflating the apartment operating expenses in order to understate their net income for federal income tax purposes.

"There is no other explanation, Josh. But I think that overstating expenses is only a part—a small part—of the scam."

Alicia stuck her head in the door of Nate's office. "Josh, is it okay if I head out? I need to stop at the dry cleaner and they close at six. I've also got to stop at the grocery and pick up some stuff for dinner. Maybe I'll make some matzo ball soup. If you add a little onion, a dash of chili powder and a dash of cumin it's just like tortilla soup."

"Sure. See you tomorrow. If you do make the soup, save some for me. And I still want to look at the pictures from the Thanksgiving pageant. Also tell Leo 'hi.' Oh, and Alicia can you put my direct line on call forwarding so it rings in the conference room? We're going to be here for a while and Nate's office is too small. We're going to need some room to spread out."

"I think so. Let me get the conference room extension number and I'll figure it out. Then I'm outta here'

"*Oy!* Such a woman: She's smart, she's beautiful and she can cook."

"Nate, forget it. You're retired. Remember?"

"I could reopen my practice. There are enough people just at my minimum security prison to keep me busy. They all want me to do their taxes, and for free. Also, I could probably steal back some of my old clients. In fact I talked to one of them just a while ago. I need to tell you about it."

"Let's get moved to the conference room first."

After they'd moved to the conference room, Josh had gotten coffee for both of them. He handed Nate his cup. "Okay, what's the rest of the scam? Ms. Obregon-Robertson is also smart and beautiful, but I doubt that she can cook...except for cooking the Tezcatlipoca books. What evil scheme is she up to?"

Nate took a sip of his coffee. "Josh, I think you've been barking up the wrong tree. Crystal's Palace is not the only money laundry in town. There's a money laundry located on Ft. Worth Avenue, as well as the one on Harry Hines Boulevard.

After last night, I'd bet my next Social Security check that Biegrubinich was laundering money. Someone will prove it when they make a connection between Biegrubinich and the Caucasian Council. Where there are illegal drugs there is illegal money. And where there's illegal money, there's money laundering. What good does it do to have bales of money if you can't spend it?"

"But you think Ms. Obregon-Robertson has her own little washateria as well?"

"I wouldn't call it 'little,' Josh."

"Obviously you found something more than some diddled invoices"

"A lot more, Josh. Take a look at these rent rolls." Nate handed Josh a thick stack of print-outs.

Josh riffed through the pages for a few minutes and then put the stack aside. "Ms. Obregon-Robertson is wasting her time practicing law. She's got the best-run apartment business I've ever heard of. Vacancy rate averaging less than one percent and no collection losses. I guess if somebody doesn't pay on time she must send Eloy around to inquire as to when they can expect payment. I know I'd pay up if I saw him at my front door.

"And the rents? I had no idea that low and moderate-income apartments went for so much. How do working people afford them? For some of these rents you could probably get a unit in one of those high-rises on Turtle Creek or at least at the Olympus."

"But not at *Chai* Manor, Josh. Trust me on that subject.

"I said a while ago that I called one of my old clients? Do you remember Meyer Ashkenaze?"

"Yeah. I represented him in a lawsuit once. It was a breach of contract case; a lot of bucks on the table.   If I remember rightly, I won it. Some of our real estate lawyers still do transaction work for him occasionally and we've handled a couple of other lawsuits over the years. What was the name of his company?"

"It's 'Kingfish Investments.' He loved the 'Amos 'n' Andy' show."

"It all comes back to me now. That's why he always called me 'Calhoun, Algonquin J. Calhoun.' That was the lawyer character on the show."

"I was Meyer's accountant almost from the time he got started in the apartment business. He's a Holocaust survivor; still has the tattoo on his arm. Came here in about nineteen forty-nine or fifty. Got a job as a fabric cutter for Elfman Neckwear. He could cut any fabric—wool, silk, rayon—you name it. Perfect every time. Never a slub or a single loose thread. He could get more neckties out of a yard of fabric than even Harry Lewis, no matter how *farkakte* the pattern. He was a Michelangelo with a pair of fabric shears instead of a paintbrush.

"And he ran his apartments the same way: no cutting corners, no cheap tricks—not with his lenders, not with his tenants, not with the government."

"I never did know why he hired me for such a big case. I was a young punk..."

"Because I told him to. I said you were good."

"And I worked cheap."

"Well, there was that too."

"I hardly knew you back then, Nate."

"Remember, you handled a divorce for the daughter of one my good clients, Blackie—Baruch—Kalman."

"Yeah, he had the liquor stores. His daughter...Sheila. Pretty girl; a little *zaftig* if I remember. Married some *schmuck* named 'Catchman.' He was a lawyer. She caught him *shtupping* his secretary."

"I thought you did a good job, so I recommended you to Meyer."

"Thanks for the referral. Gee, Meyer must have owned at least five thousand apartment units even back then."

"More like six thousand if memory serves...which it doesn't always do these days, Josh. He started out with a couple of rent houses in Old East Dallas. Quit Elfman and started buying apartments: East Dallas, Mesquite, Garland, Richardson, Carrollton. Now, he has about ten thousand units although his children and grandchildren run the day-to-day operations.

"I did his tax returns and prepared compiled financial statements for his lenders. I also went over the books of every project he was looking at buying. So I think I know a little about the apartment business. But nobody knows more than Meyer."

"He knows Ms. Obregon-Robertson?"

"Doesn't know her personally, but he is familiar with Tezcatlipoca. They tried to buy a couple of his projects two, three years ago. But he's not a seller, so he said 'Thanks, but no thanks.' He did go so far as to check them out at the time. He told me that he drove around and looked at a few of their properties. He said they were nothing special. Some obvious deferred maintenance—repairs that needed to be made—'For Rent' signs at each property, a few junk cars in the parking lots here and there. In other words typical projects operated by an owner operating on a tight budget."

"Well, from these rents rolls it sure looks like she's cleaned up her act. No wonder she's so hot to inflate her expenses."

"If all you look at is the rent rolls you would get that impression. But I asked Meyer about the rents and he said 'No way.' His units are a lot nicer—better maintained. He's only getting four seventy-five to six-fifty a month and happy to get it. But nine hundred to seventeen hundred a month, with no vacancy or collection loss? Meyer says it's not possible. He said that if she's getting those kinds of rents he's going to fire his family and hire her to manage his properties."

"I hope you told him that's probably not such a good idea."

"I told him I'm working as a consultant to a lawyer and he needed to keep our conversation confidential. He promised he would, but I doubt that his promise will last past dinner time."

"So you think she's keeping two sets of books? One for the IRS showing the inflated rents and expenses and a secret one showing the real numbers?"

"There's no doubt in my mind and there probably wasn't much doubt in Sy's mind either."

"Sy obviously had suspicions that the expenses were overstated. Do you think he was also suspicious of the rental income?"

"I think he was getting there and that's why they murdered him. There's a copy of an email in the file from Sy to someone named 'Josephina' at Tezcatlipoca. He's asking if she could send him copies of the notes and mortgages on the properties. He said he needed to verify the interest rates and payment terms.

"Sy was hired to do tax returns for the partnerships. The engagement letters are in the file. Ordinarily when you are just doing a tax return engagement you are entitled to rely on the materials the client gives you. It's not like an audit where you have to satisfy yourself that what the client is giving you is free from material errors, either accidental errors or fraud. The only exception is that if you have good reason to suspect fraud, then you can't do the return. So Sy must have suspected something."

"Any idea why he asked for the mortgage documents?"

"Same reason I would have: to verify the debt service. I suspect he was concerned and was probably thinking about firing the client. If I couldn't get comfortable, that's what I would have done. The monthly debt service payments are eating up almost all the cash. She was wire-transferring over a million eight a month—twenty million a year—all to the same mortgage-holder: Banco Inmobiliaria de Piedras Negras. I had Margaret—that's the young lady Alicia got to help me while you were gone—do a google search. It's a private bank in Piedras Negras, Mexico. That's right on the border across the Rio Grande from Eagle Pass. Margaret also looked that up for me."

"I think I get it, Nate. I was wondering why she'd report inflated rents to the IRS. Usually it's exactly the opposite. If you're going to cheat the government, you want to understate the rents and overstate the expenses. But she's got to show the money coming in from somewhere to fund the monthly debt service payments. She's got massive amounts of cash coming from somewhere so she accounts for it by overstating the rental income. Then she's shipping the money to the bank in Mexico in the form of mortgage payments. What doesn't go to Mexico, she keeps. She uses the inflated expenses to hide it. A near-perfect money laundering scheme. The only flaw was she picked the wrong guy to do the tax returns.

"Did you find anything else?"

"There was another stack of invoices...from an HVAC contractor...but I haven't done an analysis yet. Heating and air conditioning work is expensive to begin with, so I may need to call the contractor to get verification."

"So you can end up like Sy?"

"You're right. Maybe I won't call them after all."

"Anything else?"

"There are a few single invoices that may also be falsified. Look at this one." Nate handed Josh a piece of paper.

"Twenty-four thousand dollars to install a truck bumper? I think you could buy a new truck for twenty-four *K*. Let me call Louis. He'll probably know. At least he won't murder me for asking."

Josh fished his cell phone out of his pocket and pressed Louis's number on the speed dial. "Louis, it's Josh."

"You need us back? Hold on a second. I'm talking to Leticia." Louis put Josh on hold for a minute. *"Okay, I'm back. You need us to come get you?"*

"No, not yet. I just have a question. How much does a truck bumper cost? Parts and labor."

"Just a standard bumper, or a special one? What kind of truck?"

Josh paused and looked at the invoice. "A deluxe brushguard for... It says a 'Ford F-250' 'Super Duty.'"

"That's an aftermarket product, Mr. Josh. Installed, it can run anywhere from one thousand to four thousand dollars."

"This is a 'Warn 63600.' Ever heard of it?"

"Sure. It's a mid-range product. Runs about twenty-eight hundred to three thousand installed."

"But not twenty-four...Damn! Louis, I think we may have just found the owner of the white pickup. Let me call you back." Josh ended the call and set his phone on the table.

"Nate, I think you have just nailed Ms. Obregon-Robertson for Sy's and Marjorie's murders. The invoice has the license plate number—'E2Y-6106'—and says that the owner is 'E. Truxillo.' I'd bet *my* next Social Security check that '*E*' stands for 'Eloy,' Ms. Obregon-Robertson's bodyguard. He probably gave them his name because it was easier than trying to spell 'Tezcatlipoca.' And I bet you the check after the next one that I know exactly where that truck is right now. I need to call Alana."

Josh tried Alana's office number and got her voicemail. "Dammit, she's still out and I don't want to call Lt. Cloud. He hasn't bothered to return my call from when we finished lunch. Josh tapped his phone with his index finger trying to think of what to do. In his random tapping he hit the "Text" icon. "Wait, maybe it's here." I hardly ever send text messages. "Got it! When I gave her my phone last Saturday with the pictures of Biegrubinich and his car to send to herself she must have attached them to a text message and sent them that way. He pressed the number box. Alana answered on the second ring.

"Josh, I'm busy now. And how'd you get my cell number anyway?"

"Alana, please, just give me one minute. I got your number from when you sent the pictures from my phone to yours last Saturday."

"Okay, Josh, one minute. I've been working my bait-car all afternoon, without my crew. Lt. Cloud reassigned them when I started working the Blonstein and Morrison cases. Anyway, I finally landed a couple of fish. I'm at Zang and Colorado in Oak Cliff. I can't get a paddy wagon to haul them off, also probably thanks to Lt. Cloud, or maybe I should say thanks to you. So I've got to take them in myself. I'll have to take them to Lew Sterrett and get them booked in."

"Alana, I beat my forty-eight hour deadline by a day and a half. I found the truck...I think...and I know who murdered Sy Blonstein and Marjorie Morrison."

"You think you found the ...Hold still asshole! You want to see what it feels like to get Tased? Here...take this leg chain and put it on your right ankle. Take the other end and chain it to your partner's left ankle. And if it's not locked when I check it out, out comes the Taser. ZAP!

"Sorry, one of my new friends here was starting to get a little unruly. You said that you 'think' you found the truck?"

"Do you remember the license plate number?"

"Do I remember the license plate number? What have I been thinking about for the last few days? I remember the last digit, it's six. And the next-to-last is either an eight or a zero. If I had the whole plate we wouldn't be having this conversation.

"Just a minute. Good, now if you gentlemen would kindly get into the back seat of my vehicle...Yes, that's right. Watch your head."

"The next-to-last digit is a zero. The entire plate number is E2Y-6106."

"And the proud owner is?"

"Tezcatlipoca, LLC."

"Say that again. No wait. I'll pull it up on my computer. Hold on a minute. E-2-Y-6-1-0-6. Here it is. 'Tez...cat...li...poca.' No wonder I didn't find it. It's registered in Maverick County. That's down on the Mexican border."

"That figures. I assume Eagle Pass is the county seat?"

"Yeah. That's what it says. Who or what is Tez...cat...li...poca?

"It's a partnership. They're in the apartment business...and in the money-laundering business. It's run by your almost fairy godmother."

"The city councilwoman?"

"That's the one."

"And you're about to tell me that she murdered Blonstein and Morrison and made the Morrison murder look like another El Chupacabra *killing?"*

"I..."

"Josh, I already told you that I hate it when someone tries to jerk me around. First it's Biegrubinich that's laundering money; now it's Ms. what's-her-name. Are you maybe just a little obsessed with money-laundering?"

"Alana, this time I've got the proof."

"Proof that she murdered two people?"

"Either she did it herself or had it done."

"Can you put her behind the wheel of the truck when it ran Blonstein off the road and into a bois d'arc tree?"

"Well, no, but..."

"Got a witness that can put her under Blonstein's Buick tampering with the collision sensor?"

"No, but I..."

"Got her fingerprints on the knife that gutted Morrison?"

"No, but…"

"But what, Josh?"

"I do have proof of the money laundering and that her company owns the truck."

"As far as I'm concerned you can turn the money-laundering evidence over to the feds. As for the truck, how do you know it's the same truck that ran Blonstein off the road?"

"Or that was used in the burglary of the Blonstein office and the kidnapping of Marjorie Morrison? I've got pictures of those, Alana."

"Josh, I'll tell you what. Give me an address. If the truck's parked where I can look at it without a warrant, I'll take a look. I can't let my boss know unless I find something. If I do, I'll see if I can talk him into meeting with you...at our office...and you can show him what you have."

"Fair enough." Josh gave her the address of Obregon-Robertson's law office on Ft. Worth Avenue.

"Okay. That's only about a mile or so from Lew Sterrett, straight west on Commerce. After I get these two clowns booked in and retrieve my own car I'll head over and take a look. I gotta go. I'll let you know...maybe. And Josh, please delete my cell number."

"Alana…" Josh put his phone down.

"Let me guess: Detective Turner thinks you're the like little boy who cried 'Wolf!' too often. Too many money laundries for her to take you seriously."

"That's about it. She's got to book a couple of car thieves into the jail. She said that when she's done, she'll go take a look at the truck."

"What are we going to do?"

"Follow the money trail as much as we can. Where do you think the money's coming from? I bet that all of her tenants are illegals. She does practice immigration law—or at least advertises that she does. Maybe she provides them with false documents or something. What if she threatens to turn her tenants in to ICE unless they pay her every month? I wouldn't put either one past her.

"Tomorrow, I'm going to ask Alicia to call some of the Tezcatlipoca apartment projects and pretend that she's looking for an apartment. She can ask how much they rent for and whether they have any vacancies."

"So that Alicia can end up like Sy?"

"Okay, bad idea."

"Just like it was when I was going to call the HVAC contractor, Josh. Anyway, it would be a waste of time. We can run those numbers ourselves and that still won't tell us where the money's coming from. There's no way that the people who live in those apartments can pay that kind of money every month. They have to eat, make car payments—what have you. And I expect that a lot of them send money back home every month on top of their living expenses."

"So where is the money coming from?"

"Remember what I said a while ago? About Biegrubinich?"

"Where there's illegal drugs there's illegal money. And where there's illegal money there's money laundering. The money's no good unless you can spend it and you can't spend it unless you launder it first. Is that about right?"

"That's right, Josh. Now run the paradigm backwards. It's like a palindrome; it reads the same either way."

"So if there's money laundering, there's got to be illegally-obtained money. And where there's illegally-obtained money, there's got to be illegal drugs. That's crazy Nate. The woman's one of the loudest voices in the city calling for cracking down on drug dealers. She's been riding the police department relentlessly. Did I tell you what the DPD calls her?"

"Josh, what did Sherlock Holmes say about what's left when you throw out all the solutions that don't work?"

"The solution that's left, no matter how improbable, is the correct one."

"Close enough. I'll bet you my next *ten* Social Security checks that Ms. Obregon-Robertson is laundering drug money."

"Nate, I...Wait a second let me get the phone. It's probably Elaine wondering where the hell I am." Josh picked up the conference room phone. "Hi, Honey."

"Josh. It's Leo, Leo Flores."

"Hi, Leo. Sorry, I thought you were my wife calling. Funny you should call. I was going to call you tomorrow to ask you about a customer of yours."

"Josh, is Alicia there? She always calls me when she's going to be this late. I've been calling her direct line and her cell phone. She's not answering either one. I'm getting sent to voicemail. I'm sorry to bother you, but I thought maybe she's in your office with you and didn't hear her phone. She keeps her purse at her desk, so if she doesn't hear her office line, she wouldn't hear her cell phone either."

"Leo, she's not here. She left a few minutes after five. She said she had to stop at the cleaner's and the grocery store. Maybe she got stuck in traffic or had a flat tire and her cell phone's out of juice."

"She has a charger in her car."

"Then maybe her car battery died. Do you know which grocery she shops at? Maybe you should drive over there and take a look. She's probably stuck in the parking lot."

"I guess it's worth a try. If she's not there I'm calling the police."

"Don't worry, Leo. I'm sure Alicia's fine. I'm about to leave the office. Give me a call when you get her home. She has my cell number. Remind her to save me some soup."

"Okay. Thanks, Josh. We'll give you a call."

"Nate, Alicia's gone missing."

"Josh, don't get paranoid. It's probably just like you said: a dead car battery."

"I hope you're right, Nate. I'll go ahead and call DeMontrond. It's already," Josh looked at his watch, "five after seven. I'll give Elaine a call to let her know we're on the way. What about Rose?"

"I already called her and said to go ahead and have dinner."

"What about you? I'm sure Elaine would love to have you join us. Then I can drive you home in Elaine's SUV after we eat." Josh picked up his cell and called Louis. "Louis, we're ready any time."

Josh dialed his home and got the voicemail. "Nate, I gotta give you a raincheck. I forgot that Elaine's got some kind of meeting tonight. Maybe we can stop on the…

"Great! I bet that's Leo calling to tell me that Alicia's home." Josh picked up the conference room phone. "Leo, is everything…"

"Leo isn't here, Sr. Loeb. This is a friend of Senora Flores. Hold on a moment; she would like to speak with you."

Josh heard a ripping sound like duct tape being removed. *"Josh, Josh...they grabbed me in the grocery parking lot and..."*

"Bastante, Senora *Flores.*" Josh heard a few more muffled sounds then the male voice continued, *"You no doubt recognize the voice of* Senora *Flores,* Sr. *Loeb?"*

"Let her go! I know who you are and where you are and I'm calling the police immediately."

"And we'll be long gone with Senora *Flores before they can get here. You are an intelligent man,* Sr. *Loeb, a distinguished* abogado. *Perhaps you should listen before you act in haste."*

"Okay, you have my attention, *Sr.* Truxillo. I assume that you are *Sr.* Truxillo?"

"My name does not matter, Sr. *Loeb. What does matter is what happens to* Sra. *Flores, and that depends entirely on you."*

"Alicia has done nothing to you. If you hurt her..."

"What you say, Sr. *Loeb,* es la verdad—*the truth.* Sra. *Flores has done nothing. The responsibility for her current predicament is entirely yours. If it were not for your arrogance she would now be at home safe in the arms of her loving husband and children. Thus it is you and only you that can relieve her of the consequences of your foolish behavior."*

"Okay, what do you want?"

"Only the Tezcatlipoca file, Sr. *Loeb. The original documents, including Victor Ortega's copies of his* facturas."

"How do I know that you'll release her unharmed?"

"You are not in a position to bargain, Sr. *Loeb. You will simply have to trust us. Once we have the file, you need not be concerned for* Sra. *Flores's well-being, or for that matter your own well-being or that of* Sra. *Loeb."*

"How do you know I won't go to the police?"

"Listen, Sr. *Loeb."* There was a pause of a few seconds and then a horrific scream. *"I'm sure you heard,* Sr. *Loeb. If you call in the police, now or later, you will hear that scream again and again, first from* Sra. *Flores, then from* Sra. *Loeb and finally from yourself. You have one hour and you must come alone. You said you know where we are?"*

"I assume on Ft. Worth Avenue."

"One hour, Sr. *Loeb."* The line went dead.

"They've got Alicia, Nate. They're threatening to murder her, Elaine and then me if I don't give them the Tezcatlipoca file."

"So call 9-1-1, or better yet call Detective Turner back. She'll know what to do."

"I can't. He said if I call the cops they'll clear out before the cops can do anything. And then, after they murder Alicia they'll hunt Elaine and me down."

"The police, they'll protect you until they're caught."

"And what if they don't catch them right away? Are we supposed to live the rest of our lives looking over our shoulders? Go into federal witness protection? How do I practice law? Do I take a US marshal with me when I go to court?

"And what about Alicia? How do I live with her blood on my hands? I already have the blood of those two homeless men on my hands. How am I supposed to live with that? I can't do that to Alicia, Nate."

"Then give them the file, Josh."

"Do you really think that all they want is the file? They've got to be thinking that I know at least as much as Sy knew. In their minds why else would I have been playing hide 'n' seek with the file? They've got to shut me and Alicia up permanently. Look at what they did to Sy and to Marjorie Morrison. They murdered Sy because they thought he knew too much. Then they murdered Marjorie either because she couldn't tell them where the file was or because they thought she knew too much. Likely it was both. Truxillo doesn't know how right he is. I am an arrogant asshole. I should have listened to Elaine; she told me to get out and leave it to the police. But no, I had something to prove to myself, Elaine and the rest of the world: That I'm the smartest guy in the room ... any room. That's why I made the idiotic promise to Alana to solve both cases in forty-eight hours. What's the word ... oh yeah, 'hubris.' And my hubris is about to get three more people murdered.

"Godammit, Nate! What the hell am I supposed to do?" The only thing I know how to do is to use the legal system. Should I get a restraining order? How much good would that do? The legal system isn't designed to deal with people like these. They have no respect for human life, much less for the law. They make money...gobs of money...not just exploiting human misery, but creating it. Human lives mean nothing to them. They murder children every day, for profit, and think nothing of it. Somebody gets in their way...Sy, Marjorie, Alicia...me...they murder them, us, and go on about their business."

Josh picked up the rent roll and threw it across the room. "If Sy weren't dead already I'd kill him myself with my bare hands! Why didn't he just fire the client as soon as he suspected something? I'll tell you why: Because he was so besotted with that damn girl he was thinking with his *putz* instead of his brain..."

"And what are you thinking with, Josh? Sit down a minute. There's got to be another way."

Josh sat down and put his head in his hands. After a minute he looked up and stared at his reflection in the conference room windows. After another minute he spoke. "Nate, there is another way." Josh picked up his cell phone and punched Louis's speed-dial number. "Louis, are you packin'? Good. You're gonna need it. I'll fill you in when you get here. Tell DeMontrond to put the pedal to the metal. We're running out of time. Okay, see you in five downstairs."

The next call was to Jason Bragg. "Jason, Josh Loeb. You offered to help if I need you?...Thanks. The people that murdered Sy Blonstein and Marjorie Morrison have kidnapped my assistant Alicia Flores...Yeah, I'm sure. They called me with their ransom demand...Yeah, I know where they're holding her...No, no cops. Cops get anywhere near and they'll clear out and then kill Alicia...Trust me, it's a long story and we've less than an hour...I'll give you the address in a second. Do you by chance have your M-16 handy?...Well get it down, we're going to need all the firepower you've got.

"Okay, here's the address." Josh gave Bragg the address on Ft. Worth Avenue. I need to get going...I'll be in a black Jaguar XJ6 with two other men...Got it: a GMC Denali with a camo paint job. I remember seeing it in your parking lot. Let's talk again in ten minutes. I'll call you...Good idea, Jason. I'll look at Google Maps too so we can coordinate. Thanks. See you ASAP."

"So you're going there with your own army and get Alicia out? What are you, Seal Team Six? You'd better pick up the file."

"Leave it there. I'm not taking the file, just an empty briefcase. You're staying here with the file. If I don't call you by nine…"Josh looked at his watch, "…say nine twenty, call 9-1-1 and call Alana. Here's the address where we'll be. And Nate, if I don't call, tell Elaine that I love her."

Chapter Forty-Seven

By the time DeMontrond had made it through the triple underpass and stopped at the light at Riverfront Josh had gotten Jason Bragg on his cell phone. With the speaker on he briefed Bragg as well as Louis and DeMontrond on the situation.

Bragg reported that he was heading south on Stemmons Freeway and had just passed the Inwood Road exit. He said that he'd put an illegal red plastic temporary cover over the light bar on the roof of his SUV and so long as he didn't pass any police vehicles he'd be there at the same time they arrived. He promised to turn the light off when he exited I-30 at Sylvan just west of the Stemmons/I-30 intersection.

Louis had opened the Google Maps feature on his cell phone and had pulled up the location of the office building. He described it to Bragg verbally so that Bragg could concentrate on driving.

They met in the parking lot of the bank at the corner of Ft. Worth Avenue and Sylvan across the street from the

Belmont Hotel. They had fourteen minutes left. After looking at Google Maps on their cell phones they decided that Louis and DeMontrond would go with Bragg in his SUV. He would park on the street that ran along the west side of the hotel and slip back down the street on foot. There was an abandoned factory fronting on Ft. Worth Avenue across from Obregon-Robertson's office. Bragg was wearing body armor. He had brought heavy-duty bolt cutters along with his rifle. They would cut the chain link fence on the east side of the factory property and take up positions at the front facing the office on the other side of Ft. Worth Avenue. Josh would drive his Jaguar. He would exit the bank parking lot on Sylvan, turn left onto Ft. Worth Avenue and pull up in front of the office building. Bragg would provide cover with his M-16 which Josh noted was now fitted with a silencer and night-vision scope. As soon as Josh was inside the building, Bragg, Louis and DeMontrond would follow right behind him. Bragg instructed Josh to hit the deck as soon as he heard them coming. Josh admitted that he didn't know how many were inside or how they were armed. He said that he'd only talked on the phone with Truxillo, but he assumed that Obregon-Robertson was there too and that there might be others.

They decided to stay in contact by cell phone. When Josh got to the door he was to put his phone in his pocket but leave it on. DeMontrond showed Josh how to connect both Bragg's and Louis's phones to his so they would have three-way contact. Bragg told Josh to wait three minutes to give them time to get into position. They synchronized their watches then shook hands. Bragg, Louis and DeMontrond drove off. Josh got into the Jaguar and pulled over to the Sylvan exit. There were five minutes left.

After two minutes, fifty seconds Josh put the Jaguar in gear and eased out on to Sylvan. The light was red for Sylvan traffic. Josh saw it turn yellow for Ft. Worth Avenue traffic and put on his turn blinker. An instant before the light turned green a red Nissan 350Z made it through the intersection heading west. There were two minutes left.

As Josh made the turn on to Ft. Worth Avenue he saw the red Z slow and put on its left turn blinker. The Z pull up in the short driveway of the office building and stopped in front of a tall chain-link fence protecting the parking lot adjacent to the west side of the office building. A white Ford pickup was parked inside the fence parallel to the street. The rear of the truck was about six feet away from the west side of the building.

Josh, took his foot off the accelerator so that the Jaguar was barely moving forward. He watch as Alana Turner got out of the Z with a flashlight in her left hand. She pressed the remote lock button and slipped her keys in her jacket pocket. She walked toward the rear of the truck so that she was close to the corner of the building. She turned on the flashlight and pointed it at the license plate.

"Josh, are you seeing what we're seeing," Bragg asked.

"It's Alana Turner. I tried calling her on the way here but she didn't pick up. She may have still been at the jail. What should I do? We're out of time. I'll have to get rid of her somehow."

"Maybe you won't. Don't stop, keep going and make a u-turn first chance you have and come back slowly. It looks like someone's going to beat you to her. Don't stop. I'll let you know what's happening."

After Josh had passed the office building Bragg reported that when Alana had turned on her flashlight two men who had been concealed in the tall shrubbery at the corner of the building grabbed her arms and pinned them to her sides. One of them put his hand over her mouth and between them they frog-marched her into the building.

"They took her in the building, Mr. Josh. So it looks like altogether there's at least three, probably four of them, we got to deal with."

"Plus one more hostage to worry about," Bragg added. "How do you want to play it?"

"Let's stick with the plan. They'll be busy with Alana for a few minutes. At the least they're going to want to find out what she's doing there."

" 'Less they be the kind of folks that shoots first and ask questions later."

"Let's hope not, Louis. The two out front were obviously waiting for me. That means they'll have to come back out and wait for me to show up. That'll leave only one or two inside to deal with both Alicia and Turner. Handling Alana may be harder than they think. Okay, I'm turned back around, I'm about fifty yards west of the parking lot."

"Hold your position until I tell you that the guards have come back out and gotten back in their position. Then park next to Detective Turner's vehicle. On my signal exit your vehicle with your briefcase and start toward the door. Then it's game on. Okay?"

"Good. I'm holding where I am. Let me know."

"Mr. Bragg, do you happen to have an extra gun I could borrow? I feel kind of naked."

"DeMontron' you don't need to be carryin'. Mr. Bragg, let DeMontron' use your bolt cutter. Might come in handy in a close space."

"Loeb, they're back outside. It looks like they're taking up positions on each side of the door. Each one's carrying what are probably AK-47s with sound suppressors."

"That's not good, Major. What if they start shooting as soon as I drive up?"

"Then roll across the console and get on the passenger side floor. But don't worry about them shooting. The second you drive up I'm going to take them out. Actually, I like this set up a lot better. To be honest, I was a little squeamish about waiting until they'd gotten hold of you and were escorting you into the building."

"Are you worried about hitting me?"

"No, at this range there's no chance of that happening. I was squeamish about shooting them in the back. I've killed lots of men, Loeb, but I've never shot one in the back."

"Okay, then, here I go."

Josh put the car in drive and started forward. When he came to Alana's Z he put on his right turn blinker and eased the Jaguar into the space next to the Z. The two men at the door had been holding their rifles at port-arms. They started to move the weapons to firing position. As Josh opened the car door he heard two distinct pops. Both men crumpled where they stood and slid noiselessly to the ground. The only sound was their rifles striking the concrete entryway. Josh approached the two bodies. Both bodies had small red holes in the chests of their white guayaberas. No blood was emerging from the wounds so Josh assumed that their hearts had been stopped instantly. Josh bent down to pick up the AK-47s and waited for the others to cross the street and join him.

Bragg and the Prejeans had to wait for a couple of westbound cars and one eastbound car to pass before they could cross Ft. Worth Avenue. Bragg did not look at the bodies. The Prejeans looked only for a moment. Bragg looked at the corners of the building. "I was afraid of that."

"What?" Josh shouldered one of the rifles and held the other pointing at the ground.

Bragg pointed to the roof overhang. "Security camera."

"Then they probably know we're here."

"Don' expect they got time to watch much TV, Mr. Josh. But jus' in case, maybe you ought to give DeMontron' one of those guns. DeMontron', you take that bolt cutter to cut the camera wire. Then use it to cut the lock on the gate. Go 'round back. Anybody try to come out the back way an' you don' know 'em, shoot 'em. Got that?"

"Yes, Sir, Uncle Louis. Can I ax a question though? Mr. Bragg, how's this thing work?"

Bragg showed DeMontrond the safety and the on/off positions. He then set the fire control on single-shot. DeMontrond headed toward the gate. Josh had watched the lesson. He set his rifle on single-shot and released the safety. "Gentlemen, shall we?"

The interior was configured somewhat like Bragg's office. There was a reception area and a door leading to a corridor with private offices on both sides. The corridor was dark. The light from the street did not penetrate that far. With his night-vision scope Bragg led the way with Louis behind him and Josh bringing up the rear. He left the briefcase on the receptionist's desk. After about forty feet the corridor ended at a wooden door.

Bragg motioned to Louis and Josh to stand to the left. Using his rifle as a pointer he indicated that on his signal Louis should try the door handle. He pressed a finger to his lips indicating that Louis should be as quiet as possible. He raised one finger pointing first to himself and then to the left indicating that he would go in first and clear the left side of the room. He pointed next to Josh indicating that he should clear the right side. Finally, he pointed to Louis indicating that he should clear the center. Louis and Josh both nodded that they understood. Josh pointed to the doorframe; there were no hinges visible, indicating that the door opened away from them. Louis and Bragg nodded.

Holding his rifle in his right hand, Bragg held up three fingers of his left. Again the other men nodded. Three fingers, two fingers, one finger. Louis tried the handle. The door was unlocked. The door had a pneumatic closer on the other side so Louis had to throw his entire weight into the effort to force the door all the way back. As he did the three men piled through the opening.

The room was some kind of warehouse made of corrugated metal. The walls and ceiling were lined with a thick layer of insulation. The only illumination was provided by candles mounted atop tall wrought-iron candelabra. The room was hot and smelled of burning candle wax and human sweat. A sound system was blaring a wordless melody produced by a tom-tom interspersed and a recorder.

In the center of the room Alicia was spread-eagled flat on her back chained by her hands and feet to a raised concrete monolith with her feet facing toward the door. She was naked except for a tiny skirt made of interlocking layers of hammered gold and silver metal. On the altar all around Alicia there were dark brown splotches. Alicia was whimpering softly, perhaps praying.

Truxillo was standing at the far end of the concrete altar behind Alicia's head. He too was bare-chested. His lower body was covered by an elaborate loin cloth made of dark-green velvet. There were wide gold chains wrapped around his waist at the top of the cloth garment. His right wrist was encased in a gold cuff that reached almost to his elbow. Long gold cylinders hung from large-diameter gold earrings that pierced his ear lobes. On his head he wore a heavy gold tiara with feathers sticking out of the top. His right arm was raised above his head. In his left hand he carried a short gold scepter adorned with more feathers. His face, chest, arms and lower legs were covered with tattoos in the form of leopard spots. He appeared to be in a trance-like state.

Obregon-Robertson was also in a trance. She was standing on the right side of the altar next to Alicia's bare chest, her face turned slightly toward Truxillo as though waiting for his command. She was wearing a chupacabra headdress and the same type of skirt as Alicia. She wore a multi-strand necklace made of highly-polished obsidian that reflected the candlelight into sparkling pinpoints. Her upper body glistened with perspiration. A rivulet of sweat ran down between her bare breasts and splashed onto the altar merging there with steady streams of droplets from her nipples. Her arms were raised over her head. Her hands held a large knife.

Truxillo dropped his left arm as the signal for Obregon-Robertson to begin the ritual slaughter. Just as she started the knife in a downward thrust aimed at Alicia's heart, Louis fired his handgun. The first round caught Obregon-Robertson in her left side just below her armpit. The second round caught her left breast and tore it away from her body splattering blood and breast tissue over Alicia and the altar. The knife fell from her hands and clattered on the concrete floor. She slumped to the floor coming to rest with her head on the altar next to Alicia's arm. Her lifeless eyes and the red glass eyes of the Chupacabra stared straight at Josh.

Truxillo stared for an instant and then started to reach for a handgun stashed in his gold belt. Louis emptied his weapon into Truxillo's chest. Truxillo stood there for a few seconds, reached his arms toward Obregon-Robertson and then fell forward just missing Alicia's head.

In the less than ten seconds that this had taken, Josh stood paralyzed with his rifle pointing in no particular direction. Bragg, in keeping with his military training, had skirted the left corner of the altar and was moving along the left wall toward a pile of canvas on the floor. As soon as Louis fired the first two rounds the pile started moving. Bragg cautiously approached the now writhing pile and with the barrel of his rifle lifted one edge. As he did the pile stopped moving. Bragg dropped the edge and looked quickly back over his shoulder. He motioned to Josh to approach the pile from the back side.

Josh went around the other side of the pile and with Bragg pointing his weapon at the pile cautiously began peeling back the edge. Alana was handcuffed with her hands behind her back. Her ankles were wrapped in duct tape as were her eyes and mouth. "Alana, it's me, Josh. Louis and Jason Bragg are with me. DeMontrond is outside. It's okay, you're safe now. So is Alicia. Obregon-Robertson and Eloy Truxillo are dead."

"Josh, go ahead and get that tape off her mouth before she suffocates. I'll go out the back door and tell DeMontrond to stand down." Bragg looked over at Louis. "Louis, you okay?"

"I guess so." Louis had taken off his jacket and used it to cover Alicia's nearly-naked body. "Make sure he brings the bolt cutter in with him. Gonna need it to get Miz Flores loose from these shackles."

"Roger that." Bragg headed toward the back of the building to find the door.

Josh had removed the duct tape from Alana's mouth. "Hold on a second, Alana, and I'll get the tape off your eyes. I'd better go slow so I don't pull out your eyebrows and eyelashes."

"Don't worry about my damn eyelashes, *Mister* Loeb. Just find my cell phone. I need to call this in. Do you realize who these people are? You've just taken down *El Chupacabra!*"

Josh thought for a few seconds before answering. "Alana, maybe you ought to wait a minute or two before you call this in. This could get really complicated if we don't handle it right. Now don't move your head." Josh began to slowly peel away the tape from Alana's eyes. When he had removed the last of the tape Alana sat up and blinked for a few seconds letting her eyes adjust to the light. Josh showed her the sticky side of the tape. "Look, not too bad. Only a few lashes missing."

"Yeah, you're right, Mr. Loeb. Things could get a little complicated, especially for you and your posse. You used me as a goddamn decoy! Keep 'em busy while you and your...your posse sneak up on them. Thanks a lot, *partner!*"

"Alana, hold on a second. Take a deep breath. If I was in your position, I'd be pissed off too. But it's not true. I didn't know they had taken Alicia until right after I talked to you. Nate and I were getting ready to go home and wait for you to check out the truck, just like we discussed. Right after you and I spoke I got two calls: one from Alicia's husband wondering where she was, and right after that Truxillo called. He said they had Alicia and demanded that I bring them the Tezcatlipoca file. Said they'd kill Alicia, my wife and me if I didn't deliver the file here. They gave me one hour. "

"Why didn't you call 9-1-1? We do have personnel trained to handle hostage situations."

"They said that if I called the police they'd take Alicia and clear out before your people could do anything. They'd kill Alicia and then hunt down Elaine and me and murder us. I couldn't take that chance, not with Alicia's and Elaine's lives. I got Alicia into this, so I figured I'd have to get her out of it. Fortunately I had Major Bragg and the Prejeans to do the heavy lifting."

"Why didn't you at least call me?"

"I did. Check your cell phone voicemail. You must have had your phone off while you were at the jail. I left you a couple of message warning you not to go near here. I was running out of time and couldn't keep trying to reach you."

"Okay, I believe you, Josh. You're a goddamn hero. Now find my car key. My handcuff key is on the ring with it. And find my cell phone so I can call my boss. And maybe, while you're looking, if you happen to see my service weapon bring it too."

As Josh and Alana were making peace Jason had found DeMontrond who was just then applying the bolt cutters to the last of Alicia's shackles. When he'd cut the last one he helped her to her feet. She wrapped Louis's coat around herself and DeMontrond helped her down off the sacrificial altar. She pointed to her clothing which was piled on a wooden crate standing against the right-hand wall. She took a couple of steps and started to fall. DeMontrond caught her and picked her up cradling her in his forearms. Louis picked up her clothes. "You safe now, Miz Alicia. Can't none of them hurt you no more. DeMontron', you bring her this way. We take her to one of the offices so she can get dressed in private."

"I...I...need to call my...husband. He's probably worried to death by now."

"You go ahead and get dressed, Alicia. I call Leo. He called me right before we came here."

"Alana, let me call Alicia's husband real quick. Then I need to call Nate and stop him before he calls 9-1-1." Josh fished out his cell phone and found Leo's number in his "Contacts" list. "Leo, it's Josh. Alicia's safe...Yes, she's fine. I'm here with her and so are the police...It's a long story, Leo. Alicia just went to the ladies room. She'll be back in a minute and she'll give you a call...Yes, she's fine. Not a scratch...I don't have time to tell you the whole thing. Some very nasty people took her. Something to do with a case we're working on. But I got her back. She's shaken up, but no physical harm...Rest easy, Leo, she'll call you in a minute or two, I've got another call I need to make.

"She's safe, Nate. We're all safe...No I can't say the same for Ms. Obregon-Robertson or *Sr*. Truxillo. Do *not* call 9-1-1. Alana's here. She's all the police presence we need...probably more than we need. It'll be at least a half an hour before we can get back there to bail you out. Do you want to call a cab?...You can just leave the file where it is. Ms. Obregon-Robertson won't be needing it any longer...It's okay to call Rose. See you in half an hour."

Josh found Alana's purse with her wallet, cell phone and keys still in it. She told Josh how to open the handcuffs. After they were off she lay on her back with her feet on his knee as he unwrapped the duct tape. Louis had removed her Sig Sauer p226 from Truxillo's body and returned it to her.

After making sure the back door was locked, Bragg had located the security camera monitor. It was not hooked up to any recording equipment. Then he dragged the two bodies inside the reception area and took up sentry duty in case they had not accounted for all of the *El Chupacabras*.

Alicia had gotten dressed and had wiped off the blood and breast tissue. She refused to go back into the warehouse. Josh had secured her promise not to tell Leo any of the details, just that she was okay and would be home as soon as she was through giving a statement to the police. DeMontrond had found a kitchen with a table, chairs and a refrigerator containing bottled water and Dr. Peppers. Louis joined Josh and Alana in the warehouse.

Alana, drinking from a bottle of water that Louis had brought her, walked around the altar stopping to inspect the corpses. "Nice shooting, Mr. Prejean."

"I'm glad I keep in practice, Detective Turner."

"Josh, it looks like you kept your promise…"

"And don't forget to mention the lagniappe: Not only did I give you who murdered Sy and Marjorie, I also led you to *El Chupacabra*. I always like to do something a little extra for my clients; keeps 'em coming back."

"Then why shouldn't I call it in right now? You'd better have a damn good reason. "

"How are you going to explain what you're doing here? You were taken off the Blonstein and Morrison cases and you've never been assigned to the *El Chupacabra* cases. How are you going to explain four bullet-riddled bodies and the fact that you haven't fired your gun."

"Four?"

"These two plus the two who grabbed you out front when you first got here. Jason Bragg took them out from across the street. That's how we were able to get in without being heard."

"I'll just tell the truth…"

"That you were playing the female version of Jack Reacher? Decided to go into a dangerous situation, without backup, in connection with a case you're not even supposed to be working? Alana, forget about back in uniform and working the graveyard shift out of the Southeast substation. That vindictive son-of-a-bitch Cloud will get you kicked out on your butt."

"But…"

"Alana, that's only half the problem, if that. You think ATF's going to be real happy about Jason possessing and using a silenced fully-automatic rifle? And that's only the feds. You don't think the DA will file murder charges against Jason? Or Louis? Is the DA going to pass up a chance to go on TV and denounce vigilantism, whether it's *El Chupacabra* or a bunch of crazy old men and a kid just out of the joint running around with guns? You think DeMontrond won't get sent back to the joint just for being here? And how about old Josh? You think I'm gonna skate?"

"Okay, dammit, I guess I'll have to dance with who brung me. What do we do, Counselor?"

"Give us ten minutes to clear out. Then call it in."

"What do I say about the two extra corpses?"

"Don' you be worrin' 'bout those gentlemens, Miz Turner. We'll just have them come with us. I'll take care of them later."

"How?"

"You don' want to know that, Ma'am. I'm sorry it won't be a proper Christian burial, but I'll see that someone says some words over them...not that the words will do 'em much good."

"What happens when the officer-involved-shooting team asks to see my weapon and wonders why it hasn't been fired? Or asks why there's no GSR on my shooting hand?"

"I've been thinking about those questions since I pulled that canvas off of you. Louis, do you mind lending Detective Turner your gun for a while...maybe a couple of weeks?"

"What you thinkin', Mr. Josh?"

"Alana, shake hands with Louis so that any gunshot residue on his hand rubs off on yours. Louis's gun is your backup weapon. They took your service weapon but were too dumb to search you for your backup."

"Josh, that's a US Army-issue 1911-model Colt forty-five. That's way too big for a backup."

"How hard are they going to look at your story, Alana? You just took down *El Chupacabra* single-handedly. As much as the brass at 1400 will hate it, having you break the case will be a lot better than explaining why a bunch of civilians broke the case after the entire police department has been running around for weeks imitating the Keystone Cops.

"As for the gun, tell them it's a souvenir from your Army days. You keep it for sentimental reasons. Tell 'em you keep it in the glove box of your car and that you stuck it in the waistband of your slacks at the small of your back."

"Why the hell not? I guess it's worth a try. But how do I explain what I'm doing here?"

"That one's easy. After you finished booking your car thieves in at Lew Sterrett and picked up your car you decided to get something to eat. You heard that barbecue place next door to the Belmont Hotel, 'Smoke,' is really good and decided to give it a try. You were looking for a parking place when you spotted a white Ford pickup. You stopped to check it out. You approached the building and heard a woman screaming. Remember 'exigent circumstances,' policing one-oh-one? You didn't have time to dig out your cell phone to call for backup, so you drew your service weapon and went through the open door shouting 'Police!' all the while.

"As soon as you entered the building a man dressed in some kind of native costume assaulted you and seized your weapon. He marched you at gunpoint into the warehouse. He made you stand at the foot of this concrete block. A woman was chained to the block. Still keeping your own gun pointed at you he went to the head of the concrete block. You could tell what was about to happen so you pulled out your backup and started shooting. You were certain that your life and the life of the civilian were in imminent danger."

"What about Alicia?"

"I'll talk to her. She'll corroborate your story. I suppose that means she'll have to hang around for a while longer, but I think she'll be up to it."

"How's she going to explain what she's doing here about to get her heart ripped out and eaten?"

"She'll tell the truth. They grabbed her as a hostage to trade for their file. The DPD and the feds won't be very happy with me but I'll fade the heat. I'll say that Nate and I went home and didn't know anything about it until we saw it on the news tomorrow morning. By the time the feds get through taking the money laundry apart, they'll probably love me."

"I don't know, Josh. This isn't me. I can't take credit for what you and your friends did. They're going to make me out a hero, and I'm not. I just got my ass in a sling and you got me out of it. "

"You don't have to make yourself out to be a hero. If others want to do that, all you have to say is the truth: that you're a cop and you were just doing your job. Say it and then shut up. Do you think that when they pin medals on people they're doing it to honor the person? Don't be naive. They're doing it for themselves. They just want a piece of the glory.

"Alana, don't sell yourself short. You would have solved this case on your own and probably a lot sooner if I hadn't kept getting in your way."

"Okay, I guess. It's crazy enough that they may just buy into it. If not, well..." She gave both men a hug. "Get going. Ten minutes, that's all. I don't want the bodies getting cold."

Chapter Forty-Eight

It was two days after Christmas and Alana's last day on the job with the Dallas Police Department. After she had said her goodbyes and accepted the insincere good wishes from her coworkers she met Josh for a drink in the bar at Joule. They had not met in person since Thanksgiving. When Josh had learned that she had no family and no plans he and Nate had hounded her until she had accepted the invitation to celebrate the holiday at the Loebs.

Elaine was gracious, although a little distant. But Adam and Suzanne's kids, Daniel and Sophie, both in their early teens, more than made up for it. Sophie in particular was enchanted with the notion that a woman could carry a weapon and, as she put it, "boss men around." The Cowboy game was an exciting one and everyone managed to stay away from the subject of *El Chupacabra* except when Alana, responding to Sophie's persistent questioning, reiterated her by-now familiar mantra, "I was just doing my job."

This evening Alana was wearing a navy-blue suit with the skirt an inch or two above her knees. Instead of her usual Oxford button-down, she wore a silk blouse with a bit of ruffle. Instead of her usual ankle boots she was wearing heels that matched her suit. Her hair had been cut and styled professionally and she had put on a bit of lipstick. Josh thought she looked great and told her so as he accepted and reciprocated a peck on the cheek.

Josh was drinking his usual scotch. Alana ordered a Manhattan. "Thank God that's over."

"I thought you handled the initial press conference very well. Adding that the entire department deserves the credit was a nice touch. I assume that the Department was glad to keep the TV and print media off your back."

"Actually the PIO wanted me to go on some of the national news shows. Good for recruiting, she said. They made me talk to the producers when they called. But it didn't take a whole lot of acting skill for me to convince them that I was the world's dullest interview and that they'd lose their audience after about thirty seconds. I also had requests from the New York Times, The Wall Street Journal, *Playboy* and *Cosmopolitan.* The only one I hated to turn down was *Vanity Fair.* They wanted me to pose for a celebrity cover."

"You turned that down?"

"We're still talking. They want to do an article to go with the photos. I said I wouldn't talk about that night beyond what I've said already. They're thinking that maybe a good writer could come up with something based on my military experience and my job as a patrol officer and detective with DPD. If they come up with a proposal, I'll have to clear it with my new bosses—the City Manager and the City Council."

"Even without you the media seems to be keeping busy with the story."

"Yeah, the PIO thinks she's died and gone to heaven. First confirming that Obregon-Robertson was *El Chupacabra* by matching her DNA to donor samples recovered from the hearts and matching the bite marks on the victims' hearts with an impression of her teeth was good for a few days. There are some experts that think bite mark matching is 'junk science' but nobody could quibble about the DNA matches. Then matching the DNA from all seventeen victims—including Morrison and the Christian Council gangbanger in the dumpster—to DNA samples taken from the altar…"

"Not to mention your and Alicia's eyewitness testimony."

"True, but we needed the forensics to be sure that this wasn't a copycat case."

"I didn't much care for CNN camping out in front of the ex-husband's home. He'll have a tough enough time explaining to his daughter that her mother was the most horrific serial murderer in US history."

"I wouldn't worry about it too much. From what I've seen the bubble people are well-able to look after their own.

"Are you ever going to tell me the truth about the package?"

"I did, more or less. I put it in the trunk of my car and forgot about it. With everything that happened on Tuesday and spending most of the day Wednesday talking to the DPD and FBI, I didn't think about it all that day. It wasn't until Thursday when I was on my way to my office that I remembered it. It's a good thing I didn't open it at home.

"As soon as I opened it I called you, but you were tied up so I just called Crimes Against Persons."

"Maybe so, but why'd they send you the package? Obviously it was intended for you and Louis. What'd you do to piss them off?"

"I don't know, Alana. Maybe poking around in their business? You'd have to ask them."

"Whatever it was, the Caucasian Council is finished. I couldn't believe those assholes were dumb enough to store the threat letter in a file in their computer. Now the feds have every one of them, including the ones that were in the hospital, charged with hate crimes and conspiracy. Sooner or later one of them will roll over on whoever did the homeless-men murders and that'll get at least a couple of them the needle."

"Couldn't happen to a nicer bunch of guys."

"Are the feds through with you and Nate yet?"

"For now, and I hope forever."

"From what I hear—which by the time it filters down to me isn't much—they're having more fun with the documents and records they seized from her offices than a junior high football team stuck in the locker room overnight with a stack of *Hustler* magazines. They think that she was killing off dealers who balked at using her money laundering service. Apparently she was recruiting customers for one of the Mexican cartels. Offering full service: Buy your inventory from us and let us launder your profits."

"That's the way the big multinational companies like to work: fully integrated operation, keep the profits at every level, from raw material to retail consumer. Freeze out the competition."

"Did you ever get the Blonstein briefcase and computers back?"

"Finally. Truxillo must have taken the briefcase when he ran Sy off the road and into the bois d'arc tree." Josh decided not to mention that the photo of Sy with the dancers was in the briefcase when it was returned. "Some good did come from the feds grabbing the computers. Their hackers managed to get past the password and encryption problems so Nate's been busy winding up Sy's practice. Most of the clients have already gotten their files back."

"How's Alicia doing?"

"I talk to her every day. She's been seeing a psychologist three times a week. She says she's coping pretty well."

"Is she going to come back to work?"

"She says she wants to. At first her husband Leo was dead set against it, but she says she'll handle Leo. She'll probably wait until her kids are back in school. I said that's fine. Whenever she's ready. My work is kind of slow this time of year anyway—everybody I deal with is either on a ski slope or beach—so I'm getting by with a temp."

"I heard the other day that the US State Department and the Mexican attorney general are now duking it out over who gets to keep the money in the Mexican bank account."

"Like heirs fighting over an estate. I suppose that money does tend to bring out the worst in governments as well as people."

"Let 'em fight forever as far as I'm concerned. I'm glad I'm out of it."

"How are you going to feel about being back in uniform?"

"With four gold stars on the collar? I think I can live with it."

"So now instead of a little fish in a big pond, you're a big fish—the biggest fish—in a small pond."

"It's not such a small pond, Josh. Killeen's got over a hundred and twenty-five thousand people and it's right at the front gate of Fort Hood. I'll have over two hundred sixty sworn officers and another hundred civilian employees working for me. And I'll be working closely with the Fort Hood MP unit. In fact the commander, a light colonel, asked me to the officers' New Year's Eve ball."

"I thought you didn't go out with guys that carried handcuffs."

"It's New Year's Eve, Josh. Do you know how long it's been since I've had a date on New Year's Eve? Besides, it'll help promote inter-agency cooperation."

"When do you leave?"

"The movers are coming tomorrow. I could have rented a U-Haul; DeMontrond offered to help. But the City Manager insisted: 'Nothing but the best for our new chief of police.' It would have been rude to turn him down."

Josh finished his drink. "Another round?"

Alana thought about it for a moment. "Sure. Why not? But just one. I don't think it would be a good idea for Killeen's soon-to-be new police chief to get busted for DWI."

Josh caught the waiter's eye and raised his hand making circling motion with his index finger. When the waiter nodded, Josh lowered his hand back onto the small cocktail table closer to Alana's side than his. Alana looked at Josh's hand for a second then placed hers on top of it. She smiled and looked at Josh reading his thoughts. He returned her smile and tried to read her thoughts. They sat that way, saying nothing, for several minutes until the waiter brought the drinks. The waiter, sensing their intimacy, wordlessly set the drinks down and backed away.

After another minute they both laughed nervously and Josh slipped his hand out from under Alana's. Alana didn't try to stop him. "Alana, I…"

"Josh, shut up." She leaned down, picked up her purse and set it on the table. "Want to guess what's in here?"

"Your gun?"

"Nope, locked in the trunk of my car."

"Half a dozen 'Jack Reacher' books?"

"I'm still too traumatized by that god-awful movie."

"Okay, I give up."

"Birth control, a tube of K-Y, a portable CD player with a Tina Turner CD already loaded, and just in case you like fantasy foreplay, a pair of tiny lace panties and a couple sets of handcuffs. When you invited me to have a drink in a ritzy hotel bar I wanted to be prepared."

"Alana, that's not what I had in mind at all…at least not consciously. I just…"

"You don't need to explain and you damn sure don't need to apologize. When I was lying under that tarp thinking that I was about to die, that made me think about all the things I've missed out on in life. And one of those things is making love to a man that I really care about. When I heard you say, 'Alana, it's me, Josh…'"

"You sure had me fooled. I thought you were more than a little unhappy at me. When you called me 'Mr. Loeb' and asked me to find your gun, I thought maybe you were going to use it on me."

"That was for the benefit of Jason Bragg and Louis. What I really wanted to do…"

Josh picked up his scotch and held it up, "Here's looking at you, kid."

Alana picked up her Manhattan and touched it to Josh's glass. "We'll always have…"

"Ft. Worth Avenue? I think I'd like Paris better."

This time Alana reached her hand across the table and Josh held it. They sat silently a while longer. Finally, Alana looked at her watch. "Josh, I better get going. I still have some packing to do."

"Then I might as well head out too. Elaine and I are meeting Louis and Leticia for a late dinner. Louis has a full house at his shop and has to work late. We'll all see you at your swearing in ceremony. Nate and Rose are coming with Elaine and me. Louis, Leticia and DeMontrond are driving down in their own car. Leticia is finally warming up to Jolene, so she'll be there too." Josh signaled for the check and stood as Alana got up. She stepped to his side of the table and kissed him lightly on the lips. As she headed toward the door Josh called after her, "Remember, if you ever need a consulting detective you know how to find me."

As Josh passed through the hotel lobby on the way out, he shrugged his shoulders and tossed the plastic room-access card on the registration desk. That night, he did not dream about Leah Raphael, Estelle Blonstein or pastrami sandwiches.

EPILOGUE

Estelle had stayed on in Houston until almost Christmas. With the kids about to get out of school and underfoot, Marlene had finally had all that a dutiful daughter should be required to handle so she called Sharon. She begged, pleaded, cajoled and threatened. Finally Sharon and Todd drove down on a Saturday and brought Estelle back to Dallas the following day. As soon as their minivan was out of sight Marlene was on her computer looking for last-minute deals on Caribbean cruises for her and Steven.

The first business day after New Year's Estelle was sitting on the couch in Josh's office sipping coffee as Josh gave her the wrap-up of his investigation. Estelle was not happy.

"So you're telling me that I can't sue General Motors or the Buick dealer?"

"Estelle, you can sue; you just can't win. Yes, Sy was murdered but it wasn't by GM or the dealer. There's no doubt at this point that the collision sensor was disconnected. Louis Prejean and his nephew say so. So does the DPD expert. There's no doubt that it was done deliberately — by Marisol Obregon-Robertson and Eloy Truxillo, or someone working for them— to permanently silence Sy and to recover the Tezcatlipoca file."

"Well, couldn't GM have made the...the sensor tamper-proof? Couldn't we sue on that basis?"

"That's a fair question. I thought about it and did some research on my own. I even consulted a product-liability expert and he confirmed my conclusion."

"Which is?"

"That we'd have to prove that this happened a significant number of times and GM knew it had. Then we'd have to prove that there is a cost-effective way to prevent that kind of tampering and that GM knew it. Estelle, no competent product-liability lawyer is going to touch this case. I'm sorry, Estelle. If you want to get another opinion, please do so."

Estelle put down her coffee cup. "Can I sue that *El Chupacabra* woman? Since she is responsible for Sy's death, can't I sue her?"

"You could sue her estate. Because no one actually saw her or Truxillo tamper with the sensor, it would be a circumstantial-evidence case. You'd probably get a jury verdict and there's a fair chance that it would stand up on appeal. But what assets are there that you would seize to satisfy the judgment?"

"What about all the money she was sending to Mexico?"

"Right now, as I understand it, the U.S. government and the Mexican government are fighting over who gets to keep it. That fight will likely go on for decades. In any case, in order to establish a claim to that money, you'd have to show that it belongs to you, not just that you're a judgment creditor."

"So what about the apartments?"

"The feds have already begun civil forfeiture action to seize the apartments. Since you don't have an ownership claim or a lien on the properties, there's nothing we can do at this point."

"That's not fair."

"Estelle, even if you don't have a viable lawsuit, at least you have the comfort of knowing that Sy was principally responsible for bringing down a drug empire and taking two horrible murderers off the streets. Sy was, in his quiet way, a real hero. You should always remember that and take pride in it."

"Well at least is wasn't his *nafkeh* that got him killed."

"His what?"

"His *nafkeh,* Josh, his whore. "

"I know what a *nafkeh* is, Estelle."

"And you mean that you didn't know he was keeping a whore, that dancer from the gentlemen's club?"

"Estelle, I…"

"Josh, I knew something was going on. All of a sudden he's working late every Tuesday and Thursday. Then he has the surgery. After he recovered from the surgery I followed him a couple of times; saw where he went. I hired a detective back in September. He went there. I have the reports if you want to see them."

"Why didn't you tell me, Estelle?"

"I didn't think you needed to know. I thought if it was disclosed that Sy was having an affair and I knew about it, it would hurt the lawsuit against GM. It would have reduced the damages."

"Estelle, I…"

"*Zug nicht*, Josh, say nothing. You're my attorney. What I just told you is privileged. Are we clear on that…Josh?"

"Yes, Estelle, we're clear."

After Estelle left, Josh spent a long time staring. He stared at his fading, yellowing law license framed on the wall behind his desk. He stared at the photographs of Elaine and of Caroline and Adam at various stages of their lives. He stared at the family photograph taken at Daniel's *bar mitzvah* and of Sophie, then still in braces, holding up a three-pound trout she'd caught on a fishing trip to Arkansas. He stared at the stack of appellate briefs and appellate record on his desk impatiently awaiting his attention.

Finally, he took off his suit jacket, loosened his tie and started reading the briefs.

A couple of weeks after the unveiling of Sy's headstone Estelle invited Elaine out to lunch. For the sake of nostalgia they decided on the Zodiac Room in the Neiman's downtown store. Estelle, Elaine reported to Josh, had decided to put her profile on J-Date, the online dating service for Jewish singles. "Just to test the waters," so Estelle had said. Elaine had encouraged her to give it a try "just to see what happens."

The cohort of suitable men for a woman Estelle's age, even for a financially well-off woman such as Estelle, is fairly small. Over the next several months, figuratively speaking, Estelle kissed just about every frog in the pond before she found her prince. The prince asked Josh to be his best man. Josh had nearly bitten through his tongue and started to forcefully decline. But when Estelle asked Elaine to be her matron of honor and she accepted, he shut up and dug his tux out of the off-season clothes closet.

Standing at the corner of the *chuppah,* the traditional wedding-ceremony canopy, awaiting the entrance of the bride, Josh glanced at the *ketubah,* the Jewish ritual prenuptial agreement. After Josh and Elaine had signed as witnesses the *ketubah* had been placed in a tasteful vermeil frame which now stood on an easel to the rabbi's right. The content of the *ketubah* had been fought over by rabbinical legal experts since biblical times. Nonetheless, Josh thought the prenuptial agreement that the family-law and tax-law experts in his firm had drafted and which had been haggled over with equal skill and ardor by the groom's cadre of lawyers, was as deserving as the *ketubah* of a place of honor under the *chuppa.* He had the satisfaction at least of knowing that the total legal fees nearly exceeded the cost of the wedding.

Setting aside his musings he watched with his heart pounding as Elaine walked up the aisle to the violinist's rendition of the *Minuet in G* by Christian Petzold from the *1725 Anna Magdalena Bach Notebook.* Elaine was wearing an emerald-green evening gown. But as Josh saw her, she was in her bridal gown walking toward him on the arm of her father as Josh had stood in the same spot, under the same *chuppa,* nearly fifty years ago.

It was time. The violinist began an arrangement of the third movement of the Borodin *String Quartet Number 2,* an uninspired choice in Josh's opinion. The guests stood as Estelle, in an ivory floor-length gown, began her march down the aisle between her daughters. Estelle was smiling demurely, Marlene and Sharon were grinning ear-to-ear. Josh patted his pocket again checking to be sure that he had remembered the wedding band. He and Elaine stood smiling at one another as the bride mounted the steps to the *bemah.* Marlene and Sharon took their seats with their families, the guests retook their seats and the rabbi began.

The rabbi got swiftly to the point and the ceremony was over in less than ten minutes. Josh had produced the wedding band at the appropriate time and now produced the velvet bag containing a glass—actually a light bulb—and placed it next to the groom's heel. The groom stomped on the bag—as a symbol of good luck—marking the end of the ceremony in keeping with Jewish tradition. The bride and groom kissed and the rabbi announced, "Ladies and Gentlemen, I give you Dr. and Mrs. Harmon Polikoff."

For the recessional, the violinist began an up-tempo arrangement of the title song from *Fiddler on the Roof.* As Elaine and Josh, arm and arm, followed the bride and groom up the aisle Elaine whispered in Josh's ear, "I wonder what Harmon said when he popped the question?"

Josh smiled. "I'll tell you when we get home."

Author's Note

"Pride of authorship" is at best a fleeting emotion. Indeed asking others to critique your manuscript can, at least in this author's case, be a humbling experience. Nevertheless, I am truly indebted to Dorothy Jane Kassanoff, B.A., M.L.A., M.A., Charles Bradley Fischman, B.A., M.A. and Marsha S. Fischman, B.J. for their blunt and ultimately valuable "suggestions." Once again I especially thank my BFF and colleague, Melanie J. Illig, for her editorial comments and for mastering the complex process of conforming the manuscript to Amazon's requirements and making the upload happen. I must also mention my new cover-designer, Rick Schroeppel of Elm Street Design Studio, and commend him for his excellent work.

If you like this book, I'm happy to share the credit with them. If you didn't like it, blame me. Also blame me for any lapses in verisimilitude, holes in the plot or other crimes against the genre. "Like" or "dislike," please let me know.